Praise for

THE ARK TRILOGY

"Fox weaves elements of religion and philosophy into a winning combination of action, romance, and science fiction centering whales in space . . . Fox's whale space opera is both action-packed and thought-provoking."
—*Publishers Weekly, Starred Review*

"Ruth Fox's *Under the Heavens* updates the tale of Noah's ark, transforming it to feature whales in space and a mission gone awry."
—*Foreword Reviews, a Foreword Book of the Day*

"A slow-building science-fiction thriller that deserves a sequel."
—*Kirkus Reviews*

NEW
EDEN

NEW EDEN

THE ARK TRILOGY

RUTH FOX

CamCat
Books

CamCat Publishing, LLC
Ft. Collins, Colorado 80524
camcatpublishing.com

Hardcover ISBN 9780744309706
Paperback ISBN 9780744309720
Large-Print Paperback ISBN 9780744309744
eBook ISBN 9780744309751
Audiobook ISBN 9780744309768

Library of Congress Control Number: 2023930903

Book and cover design by Maryann Appel

5   3   1   2   4

For Rydyr, Quinn, and Whitley

CHAPTER

1

The darkness of space filled with the sudden, menacing presence of a comet. A brilliant trail of fire drifted behind it, transforming it into a small, fierce needle headed directly for their shuttle. Somewhere to her left, an alarm began to blare. Kim gripped the armrests of her chair. "Adonai . . ."

"I think I've got it." He tapped at the holo controls hovering above the shuttle's main console, quickly drawing a kanji against his palm before his hands moved, impossibly fast, back to the steering controls. The shuttle lifted its nose. The comet was still some distance—5.7 miles away. 5.6, 5.5—but Kim wasn't sure their current speed would be enough to move them out of its trajectory.

"Adonai! We need more—"

The last word stuck in her throat as the small shuttle made a sudden turn. The inertial dampeners compensated, but on a ship this small, that compensation was limited. Kim felt herself being pushed into her copilot's chair. The thrust was enough to shoot them straight out of the path of the comet—but it was also enough for Kim to feel like her brain was being squished through a sieve. Gray spots danced at the edges of her vision, and she breathed deeply, knowing her body needed oxygen.

"I apologize, Kim," the droid said as the shuttle evened out.

"It's okay. This is only our fourth time out, Adonai. But I need you to anticipate a bit more. If an object is on your scanners, the computer will do some of the work for you—but it can't do everything."

"I understand."

Kim breathed a sigh, trying to bring her heart rate back down to an acceptable level and reminding herself that the comet had only been a hologram concocted by the shuttle's systems and nothing about the simulation had actually put them in any danger. Taking Adonai out on these runs in the shuttle had taken some convincing—Lieutenant Grand wasn't exactly Kim's biggest fan—and after the first one, where he'd almost accelerated them straight into *Seiiki's* starboard hull, it had been tricky to get him to agree to more sessions. If Kim wasn't so sure that Adonai needed these sessions, she would have abandoned the idea altogether. If it was just that Adonai *enjoyed* learning to pilot, she could have passed the idea off as frivolous and not something she needed to add to her already bulging workload. But it was more than that. These sessions gave him—she was coming to understand—a meaningful place on the ship. The ability to perform a function that was vital to the success of the Ark Project.

"Transfer controls back to me, please."

"Transferring now," Adonai said. He looked out at the cool blackness of space. They could see nothing from here. *Seiiki* and the two Earth United scoutships that were now accompanying her on the mission were behind them. There was no nearby solar system or nebula to break the monotony of the endless field of stars, just distant impressions of gaseous formations in the far distance and so much space between. They were traveling at a fraction of the speed of light—one of the half-day slowdowns that was scheduled—giving them time to run a ship-wide system's check. They'd need to dock soon so that *Seiiki* and her companions could return to hyper speed and resume the journey to New Eden.

"*Daedalus* to Shuttle Two. I need you to return to *Seiiki* to take a communication from Lieutenant Grand. Sorry to interrupt your flight time, Adonai."

The interruption was Airman Cabes's voice coming through the comms. Kim sighed.

"Acknowledged," she replied. "Shuttle Two out." Turning back to Adonai, she shrugged an apology, then turned the shuttle 180 degrees to bring *Seiiki* back into view. The ship was a curious mix of military bulkiness and sleek cruise liner that Kim found oddly appealing. The scoutships that were hovering off her port bow were another matter. Painted bright white with their call signs emblazoned in red, they were stark and functional without adornment. Kim averted her gaze from the reminder that the Ark Project was no longer wholly under the control of Near Horizon. The adjustment had been a rocky one for her, but at least they had outfitted *Seiiki* with a few extra perks, courtesy of Earth United, including the shuttle they now piloted. One of the cargo bays had been converted into a docking bay. Kim swung the shuttle around and brought it in through the doors, landing with a thump as the huge airlock doors closed behind them. She powered down and sat up from her chair, picking up her toolbelt from the storage locker at the rear of the shuttle and buckling it on as she followed Adonai out of the shuttle and into the familiar hallways of *Seiiki*.

"Do you think we'll have time for more lessons before we arrive?" Adonai asked her.

"I hope so," Kim told him. "I can't guarantee it. Things are going to get pretty busy soon. We're getting closer to the Eschol System. But I'll definitely try."

"Maybe when we get to Eschol—after we've landed and put the whales into the water—I could fly between the planets."

Kim had to smile at the childlike eagerness. "I'm not sure, Adonai. It's a pretty dense system. There are twelve planets orbiting the sun, and most of them are close to one another. There's also the Hebron Belt—a belt of asteroids that orbits between New Eden and the next planet out. Piloting might be tricky, and that's before you take into account the possibility of Eschol Thirteen."

"I've read about Eschol Thirteen," Adonai said. His words always came more quickly when he was excited. "It's a . . . a gravitational anomaly? One that hasn't been imaged by any telescopes or radars. But Kim, why can't anyone see it?"

Kim smiled. She had raised the theory of Eschol Thirteen during their training and had won major points from their tutor by doing so. Ever since she'd first heard about it, the theory had fascinated her. "It's something that used to happen all the time in Earth-based astronomy. You couldn't always get a visual on what was causing the unusual orbit of a planet or star, so you'd have to make assumptions based on what you *could* observe. It basically never happens these days since we have much better telemetry or can use computer extrapolation or can send out probes to discover what's causing it. In the case of Eschol Thirteen . . . well, no one really knows if it's a planet or not."

"It seems like there are lots of things that humans aren't sure about, but you are able to believe the theories you develop anyway." He was quiet for a moment. "Kim, what is Heaven?"

Kim looked back at Adonai, tilting her head. "That's an interesting question. Maybe you should ask the computer to help you search on the net?"

"I did. I would like to hear your answer."

They rounded a curving corner of the rampway. "I guess Heaven has a different meaning for a lot of people, but most of them agree that it's a place you go when you die where good actions you've taken during your life can be . . . rewarded."

"Where is it?"

"I guess it's the 'highest place.' Kind of . . . beyond the clouds?"

"In space?"

Kim laughed. "Not really." An autobot scurried past, beeping softly. "It's not an actual place in this world. Think of it as an alternate dimension."

"Do you believe in Heaven?"

Kim thought about that for a moment. "I think I do. I'd *like* to."

"But you're not sure?"

"Maybe I don't want to be sure," she admitted. "Remember what I said about it being a reward for the good things you've done? I've done a lot of bad things in my life, Adonai."

"But you would still go to Heaven," Adonai replied with certainty. "Because you are a good person, Kim."

"I like that you think that," she replied with a laugh.

Kim left Adonai in the Aquarium, where he liked to spend time sitting on the catwalks and watching the whales. Even if he couldn't talk to them, being surrounded by the watery world seemed to bring him a lot of peace.

She took the maglift to Deck One, and when the door opened, she found Wren sitting tilted back in one of the chairs on the outer consoles, feet up on the console while a lush green field scrolled under him. His hands were encased in haptic gloves, and his eyes were covered with a set of goggles. They were translucent, but even though Kim could see his eyes, he didn't notice her. Flashing data patterns rotated and scrolled, dilating his pupils as his eyes absorbed what they were seeing.

"Wren," she said.

Wren's fingers jerked and twitched. "Crap," he mumbled. "Ray, get the one on the left flank. Hurry up about it, too. He's been on my tail for six minutes, and I'm out in the open here."

"Wren," Kim repeated louder.

"Are you kidding me?" Wren growled. "I'm not falling for that. I'm coming for you." His hands lifted as he pulled imaginary triggers. Kim might have rolled her eyes if she weren't so jealous of his ability to fire a gun in any kind of productive manner—even if the environment was only virtual.

Instead, she picked up a memory card that was lying on the central comm desk and threw it at him.

"Wren!"

The card clacked against his goggles. "Ah!" he shouted as he scrambled upright, ripping the shades from his face. "What the heck?"

"What, too haptic for you?" Kim said with a laugh. She swung herself into the chair behind the comms console. "I've got to check in. Don't want you getting in trouble again."

Wren gave a rueful wince. "I don't see why they've got a problem with it. It's not like I'm on duty. This isn't even a military ship."

Kim shrugged. "This is why," she reminded him glibly, "you didn't make it in the Ark Project."

Wren sighed. "I didn't make it in the Ark Project because some little Aussie chick kicked my arse."

Kim grinned from ear to ear as she kicked her own boots up onto the edge of the console.

Wren brushed his hands along her shoulders as he passed her on the way out. "Don't let them keep you too long, okay? I'm making dinner tonight. Just us." His voice was soft, gentle. Kim felt a thrill deep in her stomach.

Deck One was hers alone, save for a maintenance bot that was beeping sporadically, one of its arms extending into an open panel in the bulkhead, welding a new circuit in place. She drew the kanji for *speak*, and the comm system booted up in a string of Japo-English script.

"Kim." A holographic image of Lieutenant Ben Grand's head appeared above the console. He looked harried, and his quick response made Kim uneasy. Had something gone wrong? "Are you alone?"

Kim's eyebrows drew together. "Yes. Why?"

"Lock down, please," Grand continued.

Puzzled, Kim sketched the kanji for *secret* in the air. The Manta Protocol, ironically enough, was a leftover piece of code written by the traitor Zane. An analysis had found the code even stronger than the ones currently used by the military, so Grand had had it modified so it couldn't be co-opted by the Crusaders and installed the new version in *Seiiki*'s computer as well as the scoutships'.

"Right." Grand looked over his shoulder. There was no one visible in the background, and Kim could see blurred shapes of a desk and chair and what could be a bunk bed. Was he in his private quarters? "I want to keep this out of both Mr. Keene's and Ms. Raymond's earshot, okay? We've been noticing some oddities with *Seiiki*'s systems. Nothing alarming," he added when he saw her face. "And nothing that threatens your safety. Or that of the whales. However, there seems to be a slowdown of your computer's responses and overall processing abilities."

"This sounds like a conversation you should be having with Wren," Kim said, frowning.

"At the moment, I'd rather it was kept between you and I," Grand replied. "And to make it clear, Admiral Mbewe has conveyed that you're under orders not to mention it outside of this room."

Kim felt her heart sink. "I don't like that at all, Lieutenant. And I'm not military. You can't order me to do anything."

"For the safety of this mission, Kim, I can. Yesterday, Near Horizon signed a contract with Morosini. Earth United now has control over the mission to New Eden." He held up a hand as Kim opened her mouth to protest. "*Daedalus* and *Minotaur* are here to protect *Seiiki* from the Crusaders and make sure she reaches New Eden unharmed. That's all I'm interested in. We now have reason to believe that the Crusaders might be planning something, and in that respect, you're the only one we can trust."

"You suspect *Wren*? He helped me disarm those explosives!"

"As I said, until we know what's going on, we need this under wraps, and that includes Wren, Yoshi, and Adonai. The increase in data output can't be correlated to any of the ship's systems or normal functions, but we're also limited as to what we can access from the scoutships. I'd be willing to dock but that would require all three ships dropping out of hyper, and at this point, we can't lose that much time and fuel. We'll need you to run a few diagnostics to see if you can work out what's going on."

"Right. Fine." She paused. "Do you think it's the work of Zane? Private Getty? Whatever his name really is."

"He had no direct access to *Seiiki*'s computer following the incident at Edgeward. Security was increased ten-fold during her time in the docks. Quantum technology is new to us, and these computers tend to run a little . . . oddly at times. It may be nothing—a quirk of the computer's minor functions—but a slowdown generally means—"

"—the available memory is being allocated elsewhere. I know that much."

"Good. I'm sending across a few files containing instructions on how to run the diagnostics. You'll need to access the computer's core for this."

"All without letting anyone know. Sure. It's Wren's favorite place on this ship—he'd eat and sleep there if he could—but that's just fine. Leave it to me."

"I appreciate it, Kim, sarcasm and all." He gave her a brief smile.

Kim sat back in her chair. She didn't just *not like* this. She *hated* this. The idea of not telling Wren filled her with a horrible feeling. They were learning to trust one another. Their conversations had begun to deepen. She'd opened up more to him than she had to anyone else in her life—even Constantin, her old mentor. The vulnerability terrified her, but at the same time, it made her feel safe. Nothing she'd told Wren yet had sent him running for the escape pods. But . . . if he found out he'd been suspected of being a spy and she had known and kept it from him?

Kim met Grand's holographic eyes. There was one final question she really needed an answer to.

"Why are you so sure you can trust me?"

"Like I said, we need someone on board who's aware of the situation. And you're the best candidate. You've got experience with . . ."

"Lying?"

"Confidentiality," Grand corrected her. "We know you're capable of doing the mission and keeping up appearances simultaneously. We need you to keep it up. People are shaken after the near miss on Edgeward. The Crusaders have accomplished that much, even if their actual mission was a failure. There's a lot of vitriol out there. Not just against the Crusaders, either. The

Adherants are pushing their own message about how humans shouldn't be using space travel using the Edgeward incident as an example. Even Earth United is on edge; a scientist working on a military project has gone AWOL. The best way to keep the media away from the fear-mongering they do so well is to give them something else to focus on. Namely . . . you. And the whales."

Kim lifted her chin and met the lieutenant's holographic eyes with an even stare. "Of course I can do it."

Grand gave her a brisk nod before he cut the connection.

Kim took a moment to swing past her quarters and wash her face and hands —both of which felt grimy after a day of work and weapons training with Yoshi—then headed to the combined galley and mess hall where Wren was waiting.

He was in the middle of frying some egg-replacement with dried bacon strips. The smell made Kim salivate—and so, she had to admit, did the sight of him working over the hot pan, brow furrowed in concentration. His shoulder-length black hair brushed the collar of his jumpsuit, and she could glimpse the lean muscles beneath the blue fabric. God, he was gorgeous.

The past few weeks had done nothing to make her feel less attracted to him. In fact, their time spent on *Seiiki* so far had made her realize how much they actually had in common outside of physical attraction. She wasn't huge on net gaming, but he'd convinced her, on a few occasions, to leave her endless list of tasks and join him. Spending time alongside him in the virtual world was actually a lot of fun; they'd stormed a medieval castle together, swum in the lakes of Mars, and climbed one of the highest mountains on Orion Six. It was oddly relaxing to take time away from everyday tasks.

But even though these things were fun, she much preferred the time they'd spent watching holo-movies. The movie was irrelevant. Just being with him, sitting near him, was something special. It was new, this feeling of being completely at ease while having someone else in her physical space. She hadn't expected to like it so much, but it had quickly become an addiction.

"Hey," Wren said, breaking into her reverie. "Sorry, it's not a gourmet meal like Adonai would prepare, but I bribed him to stay out of the kitchen for a while so we could have some time to ourselves. I hope you don't mind."

"I don't mind," she replied, sitting down at the table so she could watch him. He noticed her doing so and smiled mischievously.

Wren pulled two dishes from the auto-washer and flipped an even amount of the yellow-and-pink mess onto each. It should have looked unappetizing, but Wren had managed to crisp the edges to a golden brown, and Kim's expectations for food had never been particularly high before Adonai had started cooking.

"Remember the restaurant in Chicago?"

She smiled as she took the plate he handed to her. "Of course."

"You threw a wine glass at those media drones that followed us inside. And called that reporter a—"

"I remember," Kim said, cutting him off and ducking her head, embarrassed.

Wren sat down. "I think I fell in love with you that night."

Kim felt a twist in her stomach. She *did* remember that night. Every second of it. She'd drunk enough rosé to be tipsy and had taken a bathroom break, during which she'd snuck through a back door onto a landing where she'd updated Zane on her progress. And then she'd kissed him as traffic buzzed six hundred and fifty feet below and the sky turned from pale pink to lavender. She'd returned to her friends giddy and elated, not just with her success in the program but with the knowledge that she was fighting for the greatest cause she'd ever known.

"You . . . fell in love with me?"

Wren's smile was small, dimpling one scruffy-bearded cheek but not the other. She'd come to be able to read him so well by now that she knew he was self-conscious. "Is it too soon to be talking like this?"

"Not if it's the truth." Kim weighed up her answer. Could she return the sentiment? She wasn't sure. She'd thought she'd been in love before, and it had ended in disaster. Was she uncertain because she was afraid of falling in love again?

"You don't have to say anything," Wren said with a smile.

"I want to," Kim replied honestly.

"I know," Wren replied, reaching across the table to take her hand. "Take your time."

CHAPTER

2

S o, everyone, I just want you to know that twenty-five days in, I'm getting well and truly sick of Yoshi kicking my butt in training! And Wren—well, I don't even want to go there. All that gaming he does must count for something in the real world.

So, I'm sorry I haven't been keeping you updated every day. But don't worry, I've still been taking good care of the whales. Yesterday, Barak told me he's been thinking about having his own children on New Eden.

I asked him whether he wants a boy or a girl, but he told me in no uncertain terms that "whales don't think that way." In the wild, a male wouldn't have that much connection with his offspring. I'd be interested to see how much the human DNA changes that though.

Anyway, thanks for listening! I promise I'll keep you updated more regularly from now on.

Believe me, I wouldn't be doing any of this if it weren't for all my fans back planet-side.

Love you! Kim out!

Kim terminated the recording. She didn't hate these videos as much as she used to, even though the bubbly "Hannah" personality still exhausted her. Everyone watching was now aware that Hannah Monksman's name and privileged past had been a lie—but everything else about Hannah's personality had to remain in the videos, or she'd risk losing her fans. She was very aware that throughout her training her loyal following had helped shine a light on her in the minds of Near Horizon's board members—whoever they chose needed to be likeable, and though Abdiel had come close second in terms of popularity, both Wren and Yoshi had failed fairly miserably at promoting themselves. Her fans had helped make sure she was still on this mission after the Edgeward incident. She owed them—but the continuing charade wore on her.

She scrolled through a few comments. Most of them were about the whales, but a few were for her alone.

You'll be sorry when this is over.

God will judge you.

Servant of the devil!

She swallowed as she scrolled past them. Adherants, most likely, trying to get under her skin. Unlike the Crusaders, Adherants truly believed that humans should not have ever left Earth. The Crusaders followed the doctrine that tampering with human bodies—with *any* life-form, or environment, or planet—was abhorrent, but they had nothing against technological advancement as long as it was careful, considered, and didn't mess with existing ecosystems or natural evolution.

The Adherants, on the other hand, strictly refused to accept that humanity had any future in space and that God had intended their extinction during the Endless Wars. That meant that this period of history, for them, shouldn't exist; and though they were a lot tamer in their expression of their beliefs than the Crusaders—they didn't tend to blow up buildings or starships, for example—they were a larger group with ties to some pretty highly-placed politicians and significant funding coming in from various interplanetary interests.

Kim ignored the comments. For now, she had a day's work to get through, starting with speaking to Yoshi. She had been avoiding this, knowing it wasn't going to go well.

The hexagonal door led into a wide-open area with five unevenly-sized branching arms surrounding it. Three of these bays held duraglass tanks reinforced with steel. Inside them were the dark shapes of whales: Fifteen, Hosea, and Adonai.

Kim avoided looking at Adonai's tank. The largest of them all, at eighty feet, it dominated the space, but Kim couldn't stand seeing his unmoving form suspended in the ice. It gave her chills.

A holo of a bowhead whale rotated slowly in the air above the floor. Yoshi was standing underneath it, reaching up to draw a kanji over its right fin. The fin swelled in size, then a golden grid sketched itself over the form. "Watashi ga kitai shi ta mono de wa ari mase nichi," she muttered. *It's not what I expected.* Another fin appeared, ghosting over the first. Yoshi tilted her head to one side.

"Yoshi," Kim said.

Yoshi gave a startled squeak. The holo fritzed as her hand jerked through it.

"Some of the whales have been raising concerns." At Yoshi's blank expression, she elaborated. "They don't like having the dead aboard. It's against their beliefs."

"Whales aren't religious," Yoshi told her matter-of-factly. "And none of them see the inside of this room. How can it make any difference to them?"

"They're not religious, but they're not stupid either." Kim felt her fists clenching and forced herself to relax. "They've tried to talk to you about it, and you've ignored them."

"I'm doing important work," Yoshi said. Her gaze was already being drawn back to the holo, unable to look away from her work for more than a few moments. "The whole goal of this is to help the whales."

"Maybe, but in doing so, you're causing them a lot of distress. It'd make a difference if *you* explained what you're doing."

Yoshi sighed. "I don't have time, and they don't want to hear it anyway."

The anger burst out of Kim. "This isn't how this works, you know."

Yoshi's gaze snapped back to her once more. "What?"

"The Link. I get that you don't want to do any video logs or social media stuff, but the Link was given to you so you could help and guide the whales." Unconsciously, Kim touched her head, where the golden filaments made slightly-raised ridges over her skull. Developed by Arden Tech, the company Near Horizon had contracted, they were most known for their work on military projects and planetary colonization. "Remember, the whole point of the Link is that they go crazy if they're left alone in their minds during a space voyage."

"And I agreed to the Link," Yoshi replied calmly. In a seemingly unconscious gesture, she ran a hand over her now-bald head, brushing the golden filaments with her fingertips. "But they have *you* to talk to. They prefer you anyway—the whales, and the fans."

A rush of pride washed through Kim, but she tamped it down. Was Yoshi trying to stoke her ego to make her leave faster? "I know your work is important to the future generations of whales," Kim said at last. "But we can't ignore their concerns."

"I'm the Caretaker, remember?" There was a hint of anger in Yoshi's voice as she circled the holo whale, her face distorting slightly behind the curved, shimmering gray body. "Look, we're not competing against one another anymore. Training is over. Let's focus on the whales, not on petty rivalry."

"You were the petty one!" Kim felt her temper erupt before she could rein it in. Yoshi always seemed to do this—act like she was calm and collected while everyone else was being wildly unreasonable. "Abdiel, Wren, and I played fair. But *you* didn't—and Abdiel didn't deserve what you did to him."

"Abdiel?" Yoshi's face registered a moment of surprise before quickly shuttering. "He wasn't suitable, Kim. Even though you were friends, surely you could see that?"

"He didn't deserve to be publicly humiliated!"

Yoshi shrugged and turned away. "I don't have anything more to say to you."

Kim stared, speechless. Yoshi continued her work, walking around the edges of the holo, tapping and adjusting the holo controls, refusing to look at Kim. Finally, Kim could do nothing except turn for the door.

Seiiki was a big ship. Kim could go a full day without seeing anyone if she wanted to, and right now, she really didn't want to speak to anyone. Wren was spending the afternoon with Adonai recalibrating the Aquarium junction stations, so Kim buried herself in the computer core, running scan after scan. All came up negative.

She commed Lieutenant Grand as soon as she'd arrived back at her quarters.

"I'm still going to send over some data packets," he told her. "We'll run those to make sure, but right now, I think we might be looking at a mistake in the analyses. It's good news."

Kim signed off and fell into bed.

"Kim? I need you up here."

Wren's voice coming through the comm system pulled Kim from sleep roughly. Her face was still buried in her pillow, and she felt a cold patch of drool under her chin. Pulling herself up, she realized the ship was still in its nighttime cycle with the lights dim and the air blowing cool from the vents.

"What is it?" she called out groggily.

"We've arrived."

Kim felt a jolt of energy burst through her. She sat upright, fumbling for her jumpsuit on the floor. "We're not due for another thirteen days!"

"I was halfway through the last level of *Planet Apocalypse* when the computer went haywire. Ray's never going to forgive me for bailing on that mission." Wren paused. "We're out of hyper. I'm hailing Grand now."

Kim wasted no time getting up to Deck One, jumping in the maglift instead of walking up the rampways as she preferred to do. Wren was waiting for her when she arrived, standing inside the ring of central consoles. A holo of Lieutenant Grand ghosted over him at chest height.

". . . kept from you," Grand was saying.

Wren sounded angry. "Why would that even be necessary?"

Kim strode over to stand beside him, crossing her arms and glaring defiantly at their current common enemy.

"The exact location of the Eschol System was never released publicly."

"But you didn't think to warn us," Wren challenged him heatedly.

Grand shrugged. "*Seiiki*'s been programmed to do what she needs to. The scoutships will be staying in orbit for another month before our relief arrives. You're not going to be without protection."

Kim made a wry face. "You think we're going to need it?"

Grand gave her a tight smile. "Look, for now, just sit back and enjoy yourselves while you can. Grand out."

Kim glared at the spot Grand had been for a moment longer, still hardly able to believe what he'd told them. She had never known exactly how long the journey from Edgeward to Eschol would take, but the numerous times she'd asked for details, she'd been given an exact estimate from the computer or from Admiral Mbewe or from Grand himself. Now that was blown out of the water.

"We're not prepared for this," Wren said.

Kim took a deep breath. "Well, we'd better *get* prepared. Quickly."

CHAPTER
3

Kim hadn't left Deck One since she'd heard the news. Apart from recording a few videos for her followers, which were light on the details thanks to a directive from Grand, she was glued to the chair behind the central console. From here, she had the best view of the holo display on the forward wall which relayed images from the cameras on the front of the ship in a three-dimensional array.

Eschol. They were drawing closer and closer by the minute.

Kim had seen other planets before. Her dad had taken her off-world a few times as a kid. She'd been to Earth's moon, to Luna, and to Mars. And she'd been to Ganymede for *Seiiki*'s send-off, of course. But those had all been part of Sol, her home system. *This* system was truly alien.

A blinding white light came from the central star. This star was bigger than Sol, but colder, shifting more to the blue spectrum than red. Its glare angled in from the upper right corner, the brilliance of the white orb having been filtered to a safe level by the cameras. In the center, she could see several spinning rocks of the Hebron Belt arching through the air in slow motion, and beyond it, the three visible planets were tiny dots—Eschol One, Four, and Seven. But it was the middle distance that enraptured her.

There was Eschol Ten. New Eden.

It was a ball of the most brilliant sapphire blue she could have imagined. Striated over its surface were delicate white clouds. Peeking through them were small patches of emerald green. She'd studied everything there was to know about New Eden while she was training. She'd barely slept, letting the facts seep into her very soul.

But actually *seeing* it was something else entirely. New Eden meant a lot to humanity. It had been discovered back in 2061, seventeen years ago, by a scientist working for the last remaining SETI outpost. The Search for Extraterrestrial Intelligence was winding down, the last vestiges of funding drying up as it became undeniably apparent that there was no sign of life in the universe other than that on Earth. The information of its existence wasn't made public until a year later when Antonia Morosini first appeared on all the major media outlets. *"This is a gift from God,"* she had said. *"This is what will unite us."* And it had . . . to an extent. With Morosini's push for peace, the wars broke apart. It wasn't long before the scrabbling race for territories and footholds in space had turned into a collaborative search for other planets like New Eden.

A new world. No human had ever lived here before. Apart from the Near Horizon scouting mission—a month-long expedition that had taken painful care not to impact the environment detrimentally—no human had ever been here before. The planet was completely empty of human life, and, from the reports of the scouting party, even wildlife was scant.

The Link buzzed with the whales' eagerness.

How soon? How soon can we go?

"Soon," she promised.

Seiiki would begin its landing protocol in a few hours. After the first scouting mission to New Eden had returned with their reports, most of the investigations of climate, soil quality, and air purity had been conducted by an automated drone launched early on in the discovery of New Eden.

Called, unimaginatively, "the post," the rudimentary computer on board had also acted as a guide to send the drones that were currently seeding the oceans with krill. Once *Seiiki* was in range, the computers would be able to communicate directly instead of via data packets transmitted over distance, and it would act as a beacon, leading them to their landing site. But every system on the ship needed to be running at peak efficiency. Kim wasn't taking any chances.

"You're still here?" Wren asked from behind her.

"Hmm," Kim replied as she felt his hand drop to her shoulder, gently massaging her taut muscles. His hands felt good. She relaxed against the chair.

"You feel like watching a holo-movie tonight?" he asked. "I found some popcorn in the stores."

"Actual popcorn?" Kim couldn't keep the yearning out of her voice. The last time she'd had real popcorn was at a cinema. She'd gone with Seamus and Elf for Seamus's fifteenth birthday, and they'd ordered every salty, buttery, and sugary treat from the snack counter. The holo-movie was a pretty crap action movie, but the experience of sitting in a cinema with strangers while watching the bad guys try to take out the good guy had felt profoundly old-world and charming.

"It's a pretty big bag, too. How much do you think you can eat?"

"Popcorn isn't a food," she stated. "It's basically salted air. I'm pretty sure I could eat a whole bag."

He laughed. "You want to bet on that?"

Kim shrugged. "Loser has to eat that jar of Andromedan-spiced olives I found the other day."

Wren fake gagged. "Ew. Well, since you're going to lose, I'll take that bet."

After Wren had left to attend to the last of his duties for the day, Kim tore herself from the bridge and headed down to the Aquarium. She didn't have any tasks down there today, but every now and then she liked to go there alone just to be with the whales.

She walked along the catwalks that tunneled through the spaces between the Aquarium's walls. The hum of aeration and cleaning machinery, as well as the gentle buzz of the forcefields and the gentle but persistent noise of water, meant that this was not a quiet space. Still, there was a definite sense of peace that came over her as she entered this space.

Hello, Kim, said Jedidah, swimming alongside her. *It is nice to see you.*

Kim smiled, leaning against the railing. "I'm sorry I've been so busy. I haven't spent much time down here. But at least you've had Adonai."

Adonai is good company, but we can't talk to him.

Kim felt a twinge of guilt. The second half of the mission was always going to mean she spent less time with the whales as she prepared *Seiiki* for arrival at Eschol, but the fact that there were now four other people on board should have meant she had more time for them, not less. The real reason she'd been holding back was that she also knew that she needed to put some distance between her and the whales in preparation for their landing. Once they were in the ocean, physical contact with humans would only happen during the breeding process or if a whale needed medical attention. It would be a rough adjustment if she didn't start initiating the process now.

She was starting to wonder if she had been adhering to these guidelines more strictly than she needed to—for *her* benefit, not for the whales.

"I know," she said. "I'm sorry. But soon you'll be on New Eden with a whole ocean to explore. You won't miss me."

We will miss you, Jedidah said. *But you will still be there, on the planet. Nearby. We can still talk.*

"Until your Link is removed, we'll be able to communicate," she assured him. Still, she could feel his anxiety echoing through her internal grid.

What if I don't want it removed? I don't want to be lonely.

Kim sighed. "I don't either, Jedidah. But things are going to be different when we land. You can't stay Linked to me forever—you need to have your own life."

He swam away from her at last, his nervous energy partly assuaged. Kim swung her legs over the edge of the catwalk and sat a little longer, watching the whales swim past and soaking in the gentle, watery environment as she had so many times over the past few months.

She had a feeling that this would be the last time she'd be able to do this, and she intended to enjoy every minute.

The computer chimed as Kim was drifting slowly awake the following morning.

"Kim, we're ready to start our descent. I'm informing the other Caretakers right now."

"Already?" Kim blinked, pulling herself up. God, it'd be nice to sleep through the night without any interruptions. "Can't it wait until morning?"

"I waited until the last possible moment to wake you. I'm aware you don't like to have your sleep interrupted."

She sighed. "Sorry. I need coffee."

Kim was still rubbing her eyes when she emerged on Deck One. Yoshi, however, looked crisp in a deep purple jumpsuit, hair tied back in a messy bun that was somehow nowhere near messy at all. And Wren—well, he looked like Wren. Scruffy, unshaven, long hair brushing the shoulders of the loose gray t-shirt he wore to bed. Kim found herself eyeing his pectorals, easily visible underneath, and wrenched her gaze away before anyone could see her staring.

"How far out are we?" Kim asked.

Wren, who was sitting at the navigation console, lifted a hand to indicate their position in a complicated holo-grid floating before his face. "We've already begun our descent. The scoutships are following us in."

The holo display showed a view of New Eden alone against a backdrop of black space. Stars were visible only at the upper edge, way above their heads, while the hazy blue corona of atmosphere arced across the middle ground. They were traveling fast—well, fast in terms of the universe. Fast enough to see the planet moving under them, even if it was at the pace of a snail. This close, Kim could also see a weather system just below them, the puffy clouds drawing together in a whirlpool effect.

"Holy *crap*," Wren muttered.

Kim found herself gripping the back of the central comms chair where she stood. Seeing an entire planet below her like this was dizzying. She hadn't watched Ganymede recede—and in any case, she'd left from Utopia Station which was in a high orbit. And the flight from Earth to Ganymede had been so rushed, she hadn't even taken the time to look. She doubted it would have had this kind of impact.

This was a new planet, and they were going to land on it. If anything went wrong, if the slightest calculation was off, if the computer messed up a measurement or angle . . . there were no control towers nearby, no one to intervene with a helpful warning. The scoutships were in the same boat, so they didn't feel like much of a safety net.

"Our trajectory will take us into an elliptical orbit of New Eden," the computer explained. The holo over the nav console changed, a yellow line appearing. It whirled around, making three overlapping egg shapes around the tennis-ball-sized dot that represented New Eden, then changing to a sharp arc that descended to the surface, landing just above the equator. "The elliptical orbit will help slow our speed. The third orbit will take us through the Hebron Belt, and this will allow *Seiiki* to gather valuable data about the possible thirteenth planet in this system."

"You mean, you still haven't detected anything on scanners?" Kim asked.

"Nothing has been detected," the computer said.

A noise from the doorway alerted them to Adonai's presence. He was looking hesitantly into the bridge.

"Excuse me, Kim, Wren, Yoshi," he said. "I was wondering if I am allowed to be here. The computer told me that we are approaching the planet."

"Of course," Kim said, sitting back up. "We should have thought to comm you. I'm sorry, Adonai."

"I could have asked the computer to show me a holo on the lower decks, but I would rather be up here with you. This feels . . . special."

And it did feel special. Kim could hardly take her gaze away from the screen. Everything she'd felt since she first knew they were approaching Eschol was magnified. Here it was—New Eden. The home of the whales. Her Link was alive with chatter from the whales, but she managed to tune it out. She glanced at Yoshi, who had taken a seat at the side of the bridge. Her expression was unreadable. Was she excited or nervous? Kim couldn't tell. Wren, on the other hand, was pacing back and forth, checking readouts on the consoles. He was a pretty good pilot himself, and Kim wondered if he was nervous about the computer having full control over their landing.

She settled back in her chair, her mind churning through what this meant for humanity.

The Ravaging Years had been long and brutal. Humanity was only just starting to colonize Mars and Neptune when climate change caused seven years of catastrophic storms, wiping out a lot of agricultural land. Supply ships stopped going to the colonies. Shops were looted and entire neighborhoods were burned to the ground, both on Earth and Mars. A space station in orbit around Jupiter was abandoned and commandeered by a rebel faction, the scientists forced out of an airlock in the name of freedom. People had started to form gangs big enough to take over entire provinces and states on all colonies. Then they went to war with one another. The Red State Wars.

Those states formed alliances, becoming the Triad. The Mars colonies joined with Neptune and Jupiter, fighting for independence. And the outlying systems that held only a few ships and space stations were stranded, their trade routes cut off. Meanwhile, Earth battled against supporters for both parties, fighting wars on their own ground that mirrored those in human-colonized space.

Kim had been born during the Triad War. She had seen Antonia Morosini give her first speech, had watched humans laying down their weapons . . . but somehow, she couldn't believe that the war was over. Because for her, she was still fighting. Fragments of the Red State gangs still roamed the streets, and people were still poor. There were still food shortages, areas that had been bombed and left, rats running riot, and disease everywhere. So after her father died, Kim had done what she could. She'd joined one of the gangs. Became a shiv.

And then she'd become a Caretaker. It seemed to her that this new planet would be what actually ended the wars that were still being fought. The promise of this untouched beauty, this planet that was ready to support new life, was hard for anyone to ignore. Why were people still living in poverty when *this* was possible? A brand new planet, ready to support the dying whales. Perhaps other species as well. And if there was *one* other habitable planet other than Earth, surely there would be more.

A tiny shudder ran through the ship. Kim found herself gripping the arms of the chair. Adonai stumbled before his servos caught up and balanced his heavy metal body. Yoshi let out a small shriek. When Kim's gaze swung toward her, she was already composed, her pale face turned toward the forward display.

"How long is entry going to take?"

"From now until we land will be nineteen hours and forty-seven minutes, seven seconds and point-two milliseconds. This time will vary according to weather conditions and unexpected atmospheric friction."

"So, not getting any more sleep, then," Kim said, but for once, she didn't mind.

CHAPTER
4

H i! Kim here! Guess what? We're here at New Eden!

I'm so sorry I couldn't tell you. I really, really wanted to, but there are security procedures to follow, and even now, you're not going to see this until after we land. I feel bad about that, but I promise, I'm going to send you some amazing footage.

The whales think this is the best thing ever. Matthew told me he can't wait to swim in the real oceans. As you probably know, he was born in a zoo in Sacramento. He's never been in the proper ocean as most of the whales have.

I'll have more updates on the individual whales under their headings. You can track their respiration and eating habits. I've even left a short message from each of them to you. Read them, and I'll tell them your replies!

And apart from that, I just wanted to say thanks for all your support. Now that we're here in Eschol, I want to let you know that you all played a part in the journey. You kept me sane, kept me grounded, and most of all, you supported me when I needed it the most. It's because of you that I'm still here on this mission and that I get to witness the whales in their new world. I love you all.

Seiiki's solar sails had unfurled from her sides, their finlike flanges turning the ship's elongated body into something resembling the whales it carried. They were no longer running purely on Xenol, and as they approached the system's sun, the solar sails would take over propulsion.

Weapons training took up most of the afternoon, and Kim emerged from it just as bruised and sore as she had every other time. Yoshi won two rounds. Kim won one but got hit five times. Every single one stung like blazes, and not just because of the pain. Yoshi didn't stick around to chat afterward. Not that Kim minded. She took her wounded pride to the kitchen, finding Adonai there mixing something in a bowl.

"Custard," he explained to her. "It's a dessert."

Kim remembered custard, faintly, from her childhood. Her dad had made it sometimes.

"Sounds great. Actually, anything would sound good right now. Video logs always seem to make me hungry."

"I would like to do a video log," Adonai said. "I would like to tell people about our journey, too."

Kim looked up in surprise but shook her head slowly. "That's probably not a good idea."

"Why not? Would people not like to listen to me?"

Kim gave a small laugh. "Believe me, they'd love it. But you managed to stay on *Seiiki* because no one could question your presence here after what you did to save Edgeward. But you're still . . . you."

"And humans would like to study me?"

"Right now, you're under the protection of the mission. But afterward . . ." She shook her head. "Even I don't know. The Ark Project isn't mine anymore."

Adonai stirred his bowl. Was he disappointed? She couldn't tell.

"The custard will need to set," he told her at last. "Do you want me to let you know when it's ready?"

"Okay," she said. "Thank you, Adonai."

She attended to her chores, checking the levels and health of phytoplankton on Deck Eight. She was just finishing up when the computer chimed.

"Kim, there is a blocked drainpipe in Fishery Tank Two."

"The maintenance droid for that area can get it. I'm spent."

"The maintenance droid is the problem. It's become lodged in the pipe. I could send another in to retrieve it, but the report from the lodged droid is confusing."

Kim sighed, wiping her hands on her gray jumpsuit pants, and headed for the Fisheries. They were on Deck Seven and accessible via a narrow corridor.

This entire deck smelled like fish—the tang of their poop mixed with salt water and that particular scent only fish-flesh can ever give off. Kim tapped the door open to reveal large pools of illuminated water interconnected throughout a warehouse-sized space. Catwalks were suspended over them, allowing access for maintenance work.

Kim strode over to Tank Two and looked down. The herring looked healthy, and the gauges on the side of the tank indicated that temperature was fine. She crouched and peered through the railing, hanging on as she looked into the depths. "Where's the blockage, Computer?"

"Port drainage pipe," it replied immediately. "The droid is twenty-three point six feet inside."

Twenty-three feet. Great. With a sigh, Kim returned to the entryway, retrieving one of the water suits and face masks from the decontamination closet. The water suits were a little like EV suits but less flexible.

These feel like wearing a full-body-sized gumboot, Kim thought as she pulled the stiff plastic up to her neck. The mask fit over her face, a clear plate giving her an unimpeded view while the breathing tubes wriggled their way into her nose and mouth. She popped in the earplugs, too. Underwater pressure could take its toll on unprotected ears—particularly if there was a sudden change in course. With *Seiiki* now in orbit, it was a precaution she was happy to take.

Strapping her toolbelt back on over the top, she made her way back to the catwalk, then slid her legs through the railing and dropped with a splash. The fish did a quick double-take then darted in the opposite direction.

Letting herself sink to the bottom, she turned on her shoulder lamp. It swiveled to point in the direction she was heading, spearing the murky darkness. The fish tanks had a lining of natural algae, which helped keep the water healthy and oxygenated, but it was unpleasantly slimy and tended to break apart when the water was disturbed, muddying the tanks.

She could see the outlet pipe just ahead. It was a little wider than her shoulders, deliberately designed so that a Caretaker could gain access if needed. Kim pushed her head in, then kicked her way along the metal.

"There you are," she muttered. The droid was indeed lodged. Maintenance droids came in a few different sizes and shapes. This one had six limbs, each equipped with pincer-like claws useful for cleaning clogs of silt and algae from the pipes. It would normally hold its body in half, putting two claws on top, four on the bottom, ready to inch its way along a pipe. Somehow the top half of the body had unfolded and the bottom claws had attempted to continue onward. The pipe was scored deeply where the top claws had dug in, propelled from behind.

It was a tough job wriggling alongside the droid, but she did it. Once she was in there, her length pressed against the jagged metal body, she realized she hadn't left enough room to reach her toolbelt. With a sigh, she wriggled back out.

Ten minutes later, she was swearing her head off as she tried to undo a stubborn bolt for the fourteenth time. She was just about to give up and leave the stupid droid there when a trembling overtook her.

At first she thought it was a flush. The tanks were regularly flushed, water pumped through from one unit to another so that the water didn't become stagnant. The wall of the pipe, straight against her back, vibrated wildly, and she let out a gasp as the droid bleeped, startled. One of its claws jerked upward, pinning Kim's knee against the side of the pipe. Maintenance droids had scanners that kept them from touching humans, but it didn't pull back.

The pain escalated quickly as her shinbone dug into the droid's metal leg. She rotated her knee, trying to wrench it out but felt skin and muscle tearing.

"Computer!" she shouted. "Computer, shut down maintenance droid—" She couldn't see the number engraved on its shoulder from this angle. "The droid I'm working on!"

There was no response.

"Computer? Computer!" She frantically sketched the kanji for *talk* in the water. "Computer, what the hell's going on?"

"Kim, are you there?" It wasn't the computer's voice; it was Wren's.

"Crap, crap, *crap!* I'm pinned by a damn droid! What's going on?"

"I'm not sure. The computer's throwing up weird readings—"

"Get it to shut down this stupid droid before it rips my leg off!"

"I'm working on it," Wren replied grimly. Kim counted heartbeats in her head. She could feel her pulse in her leg, throbs of pain wracking her entire body. A dark cloud drifted across her flashlight beam. Blood. *Oh God, please make it stop, make it stop . . .* and then the droid was pulling away. Kim kicked with her good leg, thinking about nothing but heading in the opposite direction.

She plunged straight into a cloud of her own blood. It drifted over her facemask, but she used her hands to guide her back to the lip of the pipe.

"Kim, are you all right?" Wren demanded once more.

"Shut down Tank Two! Computer, Computer, *shut down* Tank Two!"

No response. "Wren! The water's contaminated. We can't let it flush through to the other tanks!"

Kim? Kim, I can hear you.

Are you hurt?

Something's happening. Kim? Kim?

Kim blocked out the panicked whales.

Wren's voice held an edge of panic. "I'm shutting it down. What's going on? I can't get anything from the computer. Are you okay?"

"Yes, I'm goddamn fine!" she snapped. "Tank Two's contaminated, but I'm just bloody fantastic!"

The herrings watched her from the opposite side of the tank, swimming back and forth agitatedly. Kim reached for the surface and broke it, pulling off her mask and scrambling onto the catwalk. The trail of her blood swirled through the water. Gasping for air, gasping against the pain, she pounded a gloved fist against the metal.

Kim? Please, what is happening?

We felt the water moving so strangely.

Willing herself to breathe, to calm down, she tried to project a sense of wellbeing toward the whales. "Everything's okay. I promise."

She was still there, dripping water and swearing under her breath, when Wren came.

"Damn, Kim," he called, clattering along the catwalk. "You need to get to the infirmary."

Kim stared dolefully at the water. "An entire batch of herring," she said mournfully.

"It was an accident," Wren comforted her, putting a hand on her shoulder to help her up. She shook him off and did it herself, hopping and wincing when she put her weight on her injured leg. "What were you doing down here, anyway?"

"Stuck maintenance droid. You were busy. Yoshi was . . . being Yoshi. The computer should have told you."

"Kim, the computer's down."

Kim stopped moving. "It can't be *down.*"

Wren turned to look at her. "Yes, it can. I had to go into the systems manually and override the droid's programming using one of the auxiliary computers. Nothing else was working."

Kim tuned her ears to the sounds of the ship for a moment. The slight creakings and clankings of machinery and the ship itself all sounded normal. So did the slight hiss of air. The gravity also felt unchanged. "The environmentals are still on."

"Ship systems are all still functioning. The Aquarium's fine. We're still on course. But we can't communicate with the computer core directly." He shook his head. "I was in the middle of a conversation with Grand when we hit a rough patch. The computer threw up anomalous readings, and I sent them through to Grand before the comms cut out."

"We've got no external comms?" Kim felt a tinge of unease.

"Like I said, we're still on course," Wren told her, but he didn't sound too comforted by this himself. "The scoutships have probably realized something's up by now, but they can't dock with us while we're in descent, and it'd take some time for them to divert any manual controls of *Seiiki* to their systems. Even then, they'll be limited—scoutships aren't equipped with quantum computers, so I'm not sure what they can do to help. Internal comms work if I patch through manually. I know it sounds bad, but we've still got everything we need."

"The computer's what we need!" Kim exclaimed.

"Let's get you to the infirmary," Wren said firmly. "By the time we get you fixed up I'm sure it'll be back online."

A few minutes with the med bot was all that was needed to heal the damage. Kim peeled off the rubber suit gratefully and shoved it into a recycling hatch.

"You should probably rest," Wren told her.

She pushed past him. "You know me well enough by now to know I'm not going to do that, right?"

"Yeah, I guess I do," Wren replied with a small laugh. He followed her as she took the maglift to Deck One.

"Where's Yoshi?" Kim asked.

"On her way up. She didn't want to leave her lab, but I told her we all needed to be in one place."

Kim drew a kanji in the air. There was no answering chime from the computer. She drew another.

"Computer, where is Adonai?"

No answer.

Deck One looked different, and Kim only then realized that the overhead lights were dimmed. It hadn't been noticeable in other parts of the ship, which were mostly dark. The forward holo display seemed much brighter. The blue marble of New Eden was now directly underneath them —in the past four hours, they'd completed one ellipse of the planet. They were heading straight for the Hebron Belt. As Kim watched, several rocks spiraled into nonexistence on either side of the room. Their inward edges were lit by bright white light, and the halo of the central star emanated from the conical nose of the room.

"We're in the Hebron Belt," Kim stated.

"We've been in its outer reaches for roughly an hour. We should be passing through it for another hour and forty-five minutes on this circuit," Wren explained.

"I don't like this," Yoshi said, staring at the spiraling asteroids with wide-eyed wariness. She was seated to the side of the bridge, her white lab coat rumpling around her waist. "Ta sugiru, kin sugiru." *Too many, too close.*

Kim moved to the comms console and brought up footage from the kitchen. Sure enough, Adonai was in there, though he was sitting at the table, his metal fingers tapping on the tabletop. She patched her voice through. "Adonai!"

He looked up, turning his head as if to see her. "Kim? I've been trying to speak to the computer. It's not responding to me."

"It's not responding to anyone," Kim said. "Come up to Deck One."

Cutting the comm, she turned to the others. "Wren? Are you looking into the CPU analysis now?"

"Yep," Wren called. He was sitting at one of the consoles at the left side of the deck, flicking his hands through complicated kanji. Holo displays hovered, code scrolling and pausing in glowing white digits. "There was a major surge in processing power just before it dropped offline."

"What does that mean?" Kim asked.

"Something . . ." he paused, fingers hovering over a section of code. "A large packet of data was downloaded into the core milliseconds before the shutdown."

"Did it overload or something?"

"No," Wren said. "The CPU of a *Hako*-class starship is meant to be able to handle massive amounts of data. Don't forget, this is an Arden Tech Quantacore—the same model computer as a G-class military vessel." He lifted his hands away from the code. "This, whatever it was, was only a few million gig. Not anywhere near enough to knock the computer offline."

"Can you find what this data was?" Yoshi asked.

"I'm looking now," Wren's hands began to dance once more. "Whatever it was, it . . . buried itself. I can't tell what its purpose was or what it's doing now."

"*Tawagoto,*" Yoshi hissed.

"Yeah. There's no sign of where it went."

"Is there any way to trace where it came from?" Kim's heart was racing. *Zane.* Of course, it could have been any agent of the Crusaders, but Zane wrote code like it was second nature. "It could have piggy-backed on the scoutship's transmissions. The computer shut down during a comm with Grand, didn't it?"

"I'm looking into it now," Wren said, tapping a few commands into the console. Something bleeped, and his gaze snapped up. "What the heck? It didn't come from *Daedalus* or *Minotaur.* It didn't come from Edgeward, either." He licked his lips and turned to face both her and Yoshi. Kim had never seen him look so pale.

"The direction of the signal—it came from the belt. Twelve hundred miles off our port bow. *Something out there* is transmitting to us."

CHAPTER

5

"How can it be coming from out here?" Yoshi demanded, as if Wren could be making this up. "There are no ships. No one, apart from us."

"No one *that we know of*," Kim added.

"That's ridiculous. Who else would be out here? And why would they shut down our computer?" Yoshi crossed her arms, sitting upright and glaring at Kim, as if this whole thing was her fault.

"Look." Kim blew a breath into her cheeks. What she was about to do was risky, but she'd known from the start that keeping this a secret was a bad idea. "A few days ago, Lieutenant Grand had me look at the computer. He was worried about the large amount of background processing the computer was handling. I ran a scan. It didn't detect anything, but his suspicion was that someone might have access to *Seiiki*'s computer."

"Sabotage?" Wren's forehead wrinkled. "Why didn't he get me to look..." His eyebrows rose as realization dawned. "Damn. He suspected us?"

"If it's any consolation, no, I don't think he did. But that doesn't mean someone wasn't trying to hijack the computer."

Wren shook his head. "If I'd known about that, I might have been more prepared. It's entirely possible that whatever anomalies were being detected in *Seiiki*'s computer are related to this data packet."

"How?" Kim demanded.

"Older computers are easier to manipulate. They work within a set frame of parameters. The same isn't the case with a quantum computer—it's constantly evolving due to its own discoveries. You can't make actual changes to the quantum computer. So when you need a new system added to *Seiiki*—like, say, a new air filter for the enviro controls—you install the software and programming on the auxiliary computers that it's linked to. The quantum computer then uses that data to update itself. If someone wanted to screw with *Seiiki*'s systems, that's what they'd do—hack the aux computers first."

"But the excess data usage was in the core itself."

"Right. Which suggests to me that the saboteurs probably laid some stepping stones in the aux computers. The core then updated itself, ran through the processes that were installed, and once that was complete, returned to normal operations, until this data packet arrived. It used the stepping stones to move straight into the core and carry out its purpose."

"Which was to knock the core offline?" Kim asked. "Are they just hoping we'll crash into the asteroids?"

"Like I said, the core is still functioning. It's still regulating contact between the aux computers and running us along our course for New Eden. It's just not taking commands—"

The lights went out.

Yoshi's gasp was loud in Kim's ears. Almost as loud as her own. The sudden darkness was all-encompassing. Even the forward holo display had blinked out, and it left her feeling like she was drifting, weightless, in space. The clear glass dome overhead, giving them a view of the stars, gave off a dim glow, but that was all. The familiar hum of the engines—so all-pervasive, she usually didn't even notice it—abruptly cut out.

"Crap," Wren said, his voice sounding hollow and distant.

Kim's only thought was for the whales. Diving into the Link, she searched for presences of the whales.

"Are you there? Are you all right? Can you breathe? Are the forcefields intact?"

Kim! Kim!

Kim—

I am fine. But it is dark.

What happened to the lights?

"Kim, what's going on?"

Twin pinpricks of gold light appeared in the direction of the doorway. Adonai had finally reached them. "The maglift stopped with its doors half open. I had to lever them apart to get through."

"The entire ship just shut down," Wren called, his voice strained. "We're not under impulse."

"We're drifting?" Yoshi's voice was pitched high with worry. "But we're in the middle of the belt!"

"Yeah, it's not ideal," Wren said. In the silence, Kim could hear the fabric of his jumpsuit rustling as his hand moved over the keys on the console. "Nothing's responding on the keypads."

"Are we drawing enough solar power to switch over completely?"

"We're drawing a lot. It should be enough for propulsion, but we can't thrust while the engines are offline. We could shunt that power into an engine restart, but that'd use up a good chunk of our reserve. It'd take another half hour before we could move anywhere."

Kim didn't need to be an expert on navigation to know that a ship that could travel forward but not steer—or check its speed—was in grave danger. They needed the engines, or they'd be sucked down the nearest gravity well.

Wren's voice sounded from her right. "I'm going to have to start us manually."

"I'm coming with you," Kim said. She stood, bracing herself against the console.

"It's too dangerous." Yoshi's voice sounded plaintive.

Kim could hear Wren's booted feet on the metal floor. There was a click of a cupboard opening, and then a piercing beam of light stabbed through the room. He'd found a flashlight and clipped it to the collar of his jumpsuit.

"Here." He tossed one to Kim, who caught it and clipped it to her own collar.

"Adonai, stay here with Yoshi," she said. Not giving him a chance to respond, she raced after Wren as he headed for the door.

"Wait—" Yoshi called.

Kim ignored her. She definitely wasn't going to let Wren do this on his own.

"Stay with Adonai," she shouted over her shoulder as she swung past the hexagonal door and into the small hallway beyond. The doorway to the maglift was, as Adonai said, stuck halfway open. She could see dints in the metal doors where he'd used his hands to force them open. The elevator car hadn't stopped level with the floor of Deck One. It hung five feet below them.

"We'll have to use the access hatches," she told Wren.

"Great," he replied grimly.

Kim knew the access hatches well enough—she'd had to use them only two months ago during the incident with Hosea. She crouched to lever the panel open as Wren moved impatiently behind her. The hallway seemed to be tilting more and more under her feet with every passing second. Were the inertial dampeners going offline? She swung the panel open and stuck her head into the narrow shaft beyond. The light of her flashlight played over the narrow metal walls. She swung one leg onto the ladder rungs leading down the closest wall. With the low gravity, she was able to allow her body to glide while holding onto the ladder with just her hands. Wren maneuvered himself into position above her and began his own descent.

A dull, clanging sound reached Kim's ears. Could that have been something hitting the hull? She knew sound traveled more clearly on a ship that wasn't under thrust.

"Did something crash into us?" she called up to Wren.

"I'm surprised *more* things haven't hit us," he replied grimly. "We're sur-rounded by asteroids."

"The shields are up, though. At least, I hope they still are." The rungs sped up as she propelled herself down the next section. She caught herself, stopping the motion suddenly. "Whoa. Maybe not. Dampeners are definite-ly malfunctioning."

"You're telling me," Wren's voice wavered from above. "I nearly kicked you in the head. Sorry."

Without the familiar hum of the engines, everything was eerily silent. Kim's stomach roiled as the ladder seemed to pitch under her. She felt as if she was horizontal for a moment before the thing righted itself. "Holy crap," she muttered.

The engines were on Deck Fifteen. Kim normally would have used the rampways to reach them, but there was no way in Hell they were leaving the access tunnels to risk being flung around like rag dolls. Grimly, they kept climbing, aware that with every passing second, they were falling further and further into danger. Several more clangs shuddered through the ship.

How many were they not hearing? Kim winced every time, as if the rocks were hitting her instead of *Seiiki*.

She reached a hatch with the stenciled words *Deck Fifteen, Aft, Junction Nine*. She shouldered it open and slipped into the darkened corridor. A con-trol junction sat nearby, its lights and displays dead. And the engines, the incredibly powerful engines, were silent.

Was it her imagination or was the air down here stuffier than usual?

"Come on," she said.

Wren matched her hurried stride as they rounded a corner, then ducked through a door into the long engine bay. Here the turbine protruded in a half circle from the floor, running at an angle down through the ship to emerge from its rear where the thrusters burned. The space was completely dark, the turbine still. The fuel pipes were silent. The red and black warning signs glittered in the light of their flashlights and the smell of hot grease and elec-tricity was thick in the air.

"The control panels are all dead, even the backups," Wren said breathlessly, twisting on the flashlight on his collar to light the walls. Indeed, every control panel in sight was dead. A sheen of sweat coated his brow. Her own hair felt damp, and she could feel patches developing under her arms. "I'm going to have to go inside."

Kim balked at him. "Inside? In my training, they said—"

"I know what they said," he replied somberly. "I studied those vids too. Both Yoshi and I got a crash course before we were allowed to step back on *Seiiki*. But we don't have time to program a maintenance droid without the computer to help us."

"I can do it," Kim said, ashamed to hear a quaver in her voice.

"Don't be stupid. We both know I'm better for this job."

Kim tried for a glare and failed. He was right. She'd spent a lot of time working with *Seiiki*, and she was probably just as good at mechanics as Wren was, but she had the Link. Wren didn't.

Wren turned and scaled the steep steps that led him down to the narrow space on the floor next to the corrugated turbine casing. Kim followed as he scanned the casing, looking for the access hatch. There it was, marked in bright yellow, with an ominous black radiation signature painted boldly upon it. Wren, his dark skin looking a washed-out gray, pulled the handle, turned it, and let the hatch drop open. A breath of hotter air washed out.

"Is it cool enough to go in?" Kim asked.

During flight, the engine chambers would reach temperatures above 5000 degrees Fahrenheit. The maintenance tunnels were "chilled" using specialized coolant to a barely-tolerable 110 degrees, but it was recommended to wait twenty hours after shutdown before entering.

If Kim's reckoning was correct, they'd only been shut down for half an hour.

"I'll keep away from the edges," Wren replied. "Things go wrong with G-class engines all the time. The *Godspeed* once had to have its engines serviced in-flight. They sent an airman in to do it—a replacement valve in the combustion chamber. He was hailed as a hero."

"They sent an airman in?" Kim was appalled. "A *rookie*?"

"Well, at least we're not military, right?" Wren gave a wry grin with far too much humor behind it for Kim's liking. "We get the option of deciding who risks their lives to save the ship."

"Wren . . ." For a moment, she almost told him not to go. *Stay. We'll figure this out some other way. I don't want . . . to risk losing you.* But she knew—as he did—that they had no choice. "Be careful."

"I'd kiss you, but I don't think we have time," he replied. "So, I guess I'd better make it back out alive."

"You better," she echoed, feeling numb.

With a final glance back at her, Wren pushed himself into the small space inside.

Kim watched him wriggle through the tiny tunnel until he was out of view. She shone her flashlight into the gap, seeing the intricate inner workings of part of the hyper drive through a gap in the wall of the tunnel. It looked like a bundled bunch of steel rods of varying thickness, netted through with pipes and wires of all colors. She knew most of the functions of each section; she was now looking at the compressor, where the Xenol reaction was converted into power. Enough power to push *Seiiki* through space at speeds that would have been unthinkable only three decades earlier.

Kim shivered. What if the engines started back up without warning, just the way they'd stopped? Kim leaned back against the casing, trying to breathe. She couldn't fathom losing Wren. Not so soon after they had found one another.

Constantin had promised her the world. She'd be Queen of the Shivs. They would run an empire of stolen goods and trafficked stims, earn easy money. But the trade-off was risking hard-core prison time or a life of being on the run. Then had come Zane and his promises. After five years on New Eden, she'd be free to be with him. He had painted a picture much more sedate but one that appealed nonetheless. A cottage in the mountains on Earth, a real home, and enough food and water, solar panels for electricity, hot baths, and . . . *him.* Yes, there'd be other tasks, but she'd be safe. The

Crusaders would make sure of it. Besides, she'd be fighting on the right side, on God's side.

Neither of those promises had been real. There had been mitigating circumstances that no one had thought to inform her of. Constantin had sold her to the Crusaders. The Crusaders had tried to sell her life for their own ends. But Wren, Wren was different. He reminded her of her life before, the one she'd almost forgotten about, where she had been a small girl with a dad and a house in Melbourne's suburbs, when she had been valued. When she had a real place in the universe without anything being expected from her in return.

Minutes had passed, but it felt like hours. The darkness pressed in. Echoing thumps came from various locations, making her jump every time.

There was another clank, this time coming from her left. In the direction Wren had gone. God, what she wouldn't give for a working comm right now!

She pushed her head through the hatch. "Wren!" she called. "Wren!"

No answer.

Kim paced back and forth past the opening. She stopped. Started again. How many minutes now? Close to an hour? She thought it was likely. A skittering sound made her jump; she pictured the cluster of asteroids that must have made it, hitting, then spinning off in various directions.

Kim. You are distressed.

It was Naomi, a Gray's Beaked Whale. "Just a little."

I wish I could help. I feel very useless.

"You're not useless. Not at all. You can help. Just . . . talk to me."

I can do that. A pause. *I'm wondering what will happen when we get to New Eden.*

Kim felt her mind snatching at the distraction. "Well, we're heading to one of the continents, one of the largest. It's located just above the equator, and it's covered with light jungle. Big trees," she explained. "Bigger than most trees on Earth. And lush, green undergrowth. Like coral and seaweed, but growing on land."

It sounds nice.

"Well, obviously, you won't be living on the land with us," Kim said. "We'll be touching down near a bay. The original scouting mission to New Eden named it Half-Moon Bay because of its shape. That's where we'll set the base up. We'll be running checks on water temperature and ocean life to make sure nothing's been missed by the scouting missions or the probe analyses. We'll need to launch satellites that will be able to monitor the oceans and will help with contacting Earth. Then you—all the whales—will be transferred into the bay."

How long?

"It's hard to say. We have to make sure everything's perfect." Kim smiled. "I know you're eager, but we want to make sure you're safe."

You take such good care of us, Kim.

Kim tapped her fingers against the casing behind her. "I could have done better," she muttered. Another clang came from overhead. Lifting her gaze to the distant ceiling, she traced the metal girders with her eyes.

A sudden sound startled Kim. A soft, low, dull throb, coming from deep under the deck plates. A minute passed, and then there was a noise from inside the turbine casing.

"Wren?"

He slithered out, breathing hard, his jumpsuit smeared with oil and his hair sticking up wildly. "I think I got it," he gasped as his torchlight danced over the walls.

"You're sure?" Kim asked, lifting an eyebrow. Then, at his hurt look, said, "Sorry. Unfair question. Put it down to stress."

Wren huffed lightly. Behind him, the tunnel began to glow with soft light, steadily growing brighter.

Something clunked, and Kim saw the internal workings begin to move. Rods spun, pistons pounded. Something gurgled through the pipes—hopefully something that was supposed to be gurgling.

She closed the hatch.

"We should get back to the—" Wren began to say, but suddenly, *Seiiki* bucked.

The lower gravitational pull launched them up in the air for a half-second, falling in a tumbled heap when they came down.

"Damn!" Kim wasn't sure if she'd said the word or if Wren had. The deck swayed underneath her. The throbbing of the engines increased, but there was an oddly-pitched whine to it. The lights flickered back on overhead, blinding them, then dimmed and brightened intermittently. Kim slid across the deck, her chin stinging where she'd come down on Wren's shoulder, stopping herself before she ploughed into the bulkhead.

The Link exploded.

Kim! KIM! What's happening? Kim! KIM! Kimkimkimkim . . .

Dragging herself to her knees, she clutched her head in her hands. She was vaguely aware of Wren crouching over her, but everything seemed distant.

"Whales," she croaked out.

Kimkimkim! I'm scared. The lights are back, but there's something happening . . .

"WHALES!" The shout ripped from her like a laser bullet from a gun. "Stop, please stop! You're hurting me!"

The voices didn't stop, but they receded to a more tolerable murmur.

Kim found Wren pressed against her, his arms wrapped about her shoulders. "Kim, are you okay? Kim?"

The comm startled them both as Adonai's voice came from somewhere above.

"Kim, Wren, are you there?"

"Yes," Wren called. "We're here."

"The communication systems are back online. However, Yoshi is . . . not well."

"What's wrong with her?" Wren asked.

"I think it was the whales. Her Link began to glow very brightly, and she dropped to the floor, groaning. I've asked for a medbot. The computer is listening to me, but it's still not answering."

"Computer," Wren said. "Medbot to Deck One?"

There was a soft chime but no reply.

"I'm fine," Yoshi's voice came over the comm. It was slightly slurred, but she sounded lucid. "But there's something wrong with the ship. Now that the readouts are back up, there's . . . some kind of gravitational eddy."

"I'm coming," Wren said. He looked down at Kim. "I'm going to leave you here, get a medbot—"

Kim pushed herself to her feet. "Don't be stupid. You know you need me up there."

The ship bucked again. The whine was increasing in volume, a tinny, whining edge to it.

"That doesn't sound good," Kim said through gritted teeth as she headed for the ladder at a run, Wren close on her heels.

"We're fighting a gravitational pull," Yoshi said over the comm.

"That makes sense."

The engine whine grew louder. "That would make sense if we were somewhere other than an asteroid belt!" Yoshi gasped. The speakers tracked their movement, and her voice hovered in the corridor as Kim and Wren headed for the maglift. "There's nothing out here!"

"Yes, there is," Kim said with certainty. "It's got to be Eschol Thirteen."

"Eschol Thirteen? *There's nothing on the sensors!*" Yoshi sounded annoyed. "Nothing! I'm not talking about something hidden by other bodies, not talking about line-of-sight problems or even the possibility of interference. The asteroids are showing a scatter pattern that *might* be an orbit path, but there is nothing out there!"

The maglift doors opened with a swish, and Kim shouldered inside with Wren. "And yet, something with enough gravity to grip a ship the size of *Seiiki* is pulling us in."

"I'm going to rein in the throttle—"

Yoshi's voice was cut off as a loud *bang* echoed through the ship. A second later, Kim's ears popped, and the maglift doors stopped midway. A thunderous *whooshing* sound filled the air. Kim felt her feet being pulled out from under her as the air from the car was sucked out violently. She grabbed the frame of the maglift door and clung on before it took her with it. Beyond, the corridor filled with a raging whirlwind of dust and bits of debris, all of it heading down the corridor under the impetus of a powerful, unending blast of air. Ahead, she glimpsed the Aquarium through a hexagonal door. The green glow of the forcefields illuminated the passage. At least they were still functioning—as evidenced by the fact that there was no water flooding the corridor.

She hung on to the frame, struggling to breathe. Beside her, Wren was doing the same. His long, dark hair streamed past his face like a black banner. "Hull breach!" he yelled.

"What gave it away?" Kim yelled back, but her words were lost in the rush of wind. A hull breach was the most dangerous situation on any starship. The vacuum of space was greedy for air, and the mass exodus of *Seiiki*'s oxygen could cause the tear to widen. Forcefields should be working to reinforce and then seal the tear, but clearly they weren't doing the job fast enough—if they were functioning at all.

Wren motioned with one free hand toward the corridor. "Need to . . . get to . . . access . . . hatches. Can't . . . hang on."

Kim nodded. It was a sensible suggestion. The maglift was going nowhere, and they couldn't hold on against the blasting wind for too long, but the access tunnels would at least give them shelter enough to keep from being bounced off the walls and would allow them to get back to Deck One.

She could see the access hatch to the left, only a few feet away, but getting to it was going to involve some tricky maneuvering since the powerful force of air exiting the ship at a massive rate was trying to haul them down the corridor and smash them into the first available bulkhead. Wren stretched his left hand toward her, indicating that she should take it. Kim shook her head. "You first!" she screamed, sucking in another painful breath. "If you miss the hatch, I can't catch you!" The hull breach was turning the corridor into a wind tunnel, and as soon as they let go, they'd be at the mercy of the racing air. They'd have to allow themselves to be carried by the blasting wind along the corridor to the access hatch. Wren was too heavy for her to catch if he miscalculated his fall—but he'd be able to hold on to her much more easily. He nodded, seeming to understand, and let go.

The wind sucked him feetfirst down the corridor. It looked like he was going to sail straight past it. He stretched his arms out as far as he could. Kim could see the naked fear in his eyes. He was heading straight for the open door at the end of the corridor. If he went through, he'd slam straight into the walls of the Aquarium. At this speed, even if he didn't hit a glass section, a forcefield would sense him as a threat to its integrity. It would arrest his motion with enough force to break bones.

The ship gave a sudden lurch, bucking sideways. It seemed it was timed perfectly. Wren hurtled toward the left wall instead, and, with arms outstretched, the fingers of his left hand wrapped around the strut to the right of the access hatch. A shallow ledge but enough to give him purchase.

With visibly straining muscles, he pulled himself out of the way and reached for the handle of the hatch. It flew open with a bang that probably broke at least one hinge, but Wren didn't pause. He kicked his legs into the space, then adjusted his grip. He looked across at her—*up* at her. The rushing gusts of air had altered her perception of direction, seeming to place him underneath her.

Kim gasped. Her chest felt heavy, and her vision was graying at the edges. She didn't allow herself time to think. She let go, allowed herself to hurtle into the corridor in freefall. She reached for the hatch, arms straining. She could barely see.

Suddenly, a strong grip wrapped around her wrist, jerking her entire body tight. She felt a tiny object—a screw, probably—ping off her left eyebrow. Wren levered her over the edge, and she collapsed against him where he clung to the top of the ladder.

They hung there, breathing hard. The pull was still strong but there was less danger here. They were being pressed against the wall of the tunnel, not thrown along the length of the ship.

"That was . . ." Wren gasped at last.

"Incredible!" Kim finished. She giggled. They were still shouting over the roar, but it didn't matter. She was pressed against his chest, and she could feel his muscles tense beneath his loose gray shirt. This shouldn't feel this good—but oh, it did. It lit her nerves on fire to have him so close.

"Kim—"

"Wren—" she replied, giggling again. He laughed too, which only made it funnier. There was something she was going to say, but it was gone now, lost in the laughter. She couldn't seem to stop. What was wrong with her?

Oh crap.

"Hypoxia," she managed to gasp. Even the word sounded funny, the alarm that should have accompanied it missing entirely. "Wren, we can't . . . can't stay here . . ."

"I know," he said.

"We have to move." Saying the words out loud seemed to help, seemed to give her something to focus on. She could feel the effects of hypoxia strongly now, her brain shrouded in fog, her thoughts wandering off on tangents. She felt another urge to laugh and quelled it. "We need to get back to Deck One."

"We can't go up," Wren said, pointing. "There's too much drag."

He was right. Even thinking about it made Kim's arms ache with the strain. The breach, wherever it was, was sucking air out of the ship. They had limited strength, and what strength they had was being eked away by the hypoxia.

"There's no air down here . . . Can't stay."

Wren pointed. "Escape pods."

Kim gaped at him. Another stupid giggle hovered in her throat. She choked it down. "We can't! The ship . . . The whales . . ."

"No good to them dead. You heard Yoshi. She's . . . got piloting controls. Kim, listen to me for once . . . no stubbornness."

Kim, Kim, Kim, Kim! Are you all right? We haven't heard from you. Kim, please, be all right.

Kim raised a hand to her head. The Link sounded so strong, the voices so loud. She just wanted to lie down . . . just wanted to rest . . .

Be all right.

She made herself move. It was close to impossible. Wren was already well ahead of her. The gust of wind, unending, tried to suck her upward, but she pushed against it with all her strength. Was it getting stronger? Or was she getting weaker?

"It's below me!" Wren called. He'd stopped moving and was tugging at the hatch with one hand, the other arm looped through the rungs. "Just hang on!"

At every second, Kim felt like she would let go. The wind wanted to pluck her up like a daisy in a hurricane, lift her back up the tunnel, slam her into the walls, but she gritted her teeth and clenched her hands. One second more. One more.

And then there was a loud *popping* sound, and Wren gave a cry of exultation. He'd done it. Kim watched him twist his body through the opening, but the hatch was now just a vague shape covered in speckled black dots.

With the last of her strength, she gripped the hatch and pulled herself inside.

They could at least stand upright on this deck, but it was so cold. The vacuum was leeching in, grabbing at her bare skin like fingers of ice. She could see barely anything against the blizzard crossing her vision, just a small tunnel of grayed out bulkheads and doorways. Wren manhandled her to the left, then to the right.

Her vision was assaulted by bright yellow signs emblazoned with the universal "escape" symbol of a stick figure running through an open door. She stumbled upon a set of steps. And there, ahead of her, five escape pods sat in an arc against the walls.

Wren hit a control to open the rear door of the closest. He shoved Kim inside first, then dragged himself in. With another slap he closed the door.

Kim breathed in like she'd never breathed before. Warm, soft air without the hard edges of the vacuum made her feel like she was wrapped in a cloud.

The escape pod was small. There would have been just enough room for four people inside. But it was still cramped with just the two of them.

There were minimal functions to an escape pod. It had two thrusters and enough fuel to last twenty hours at full burn. The controls were rudimentary—piloting, nav, and scanners. These were all on the holographic heads-up display, just under the forward window, which was a curving sheet of duraglass that made it feel like you were sitting in a bubble.

Wren maneuvered into the pilot's seat, tapping controls to life. "What the hell happened? Even if you're right and that's Eschol Thirteen out there, *Seiiki*'s hull should have been able to withstand the gravitational pull of a planet!"

"Agreed," Kim said grimly. "Unless this has something to do with the computer."

Wren's eyebrows lifted. "You think this was sabotage?"

"If you were going to incapacitate the mission, what better way than to ensure *Seiiki* loses computer access on entry to Eschol? An unknown system? And it happens to occur right as we reach the asteroid belt?"

Wren shook his head. "Maybe . . . but we need to have this discussion later." He tapped the controls. "Computer? Deck One, do you read? Yoshi?"

"I am here, Wren," Adonai's voice replied. "Is Kim there? Is she all right?"

"She's fine. We're in an escape pod. Does Yoshi still have piloting controls?"

"Yes. Yoshi says the ship is still being pulled backward. *Seiiki* has lost navigational con—"

Adonai's voice cut off as there was another frightening lurch. The pod bucked against its clamps, and Kim grabbed at the wall to stop herself falling yet again.

"Crap," Kim said. "Adonai, she's got to cut the engines!"

"She has," he told her. "The engines are online but not firing. She says—"

Yoshi's voice broke in momentarily. "I'm going with the current now! I'm reading stress fractures in the hull from Decks Ten downward!"

Kim looked at Wren. He looked back at her, face distraught. "The whales," Kim said hoarsely.

"The forcefields are holding," Yoshi replied. "The fractures on the hull won't penetrate the tank walls. Even if the decks are torn away, the Aquarium will be intact. But Kim, the engine nacelles are going to be torn loose at any moment. I need to get us out into open space. Can you launch the escape pod and use it to guide *Seiiki* out of the belt?"

Kim glanced at Wren. "Can we?"

He shook his head.

"No. Escape pods can transmit their location, but it's rudimentary. It would help, but with a ship the size of *Seiiki*, inside a dense asteroid field, it's not going to be exact enough. Can you get *Daedalus* or *Minotaur* on comms?"

"No," Yoshi replied. "They're not looped in to *Seiiki*'s systems like our shuttles are, and I think that's the issue."

Adonai's voice came back on. "I can pilot one of our shuttles."

"No." The word was out of Kim's mouth before he'd even finished the sentence.

"I need to do what I can to help the whales. I can get to the shuttle. I don't need oxygen, remember?"

"No!" Kim's voice was despairing. "You can't risk yourself like this. Adonai, you stay on Deck One, do you read?"

There was no reply.

"Shit!" Kim slammed the wall next to her. "He's not ready!"

"None of us are ready for this, Kim!" Wren told her firmly. "Give him some credit. Give *yourself* some credit for everything you've taught him."

Traitorous tears were forming at the corners of her eyes. She sank into the chair next to Wren, pulling up the navigation controls. "We need to get out of here."

Wren nodded.

"I was hoping we wouldn't have to jettison, but the fractures on the lower decks are too large. The computer's prioritizing the Aquarium at the expense of the hull. We've got to launch."

"*Seiiki* can't pilot without engines."

"There'll be two forward thrusters," Wren reminded her. "Theoretically, she can still pilot, until the fuel's been used up. We can relay coordinates and get her into an entry pattern."

"Kim?" Yoshi's voice sounded very far away. "*Seiiki's* just lost . . ."

The rest of the sentence was cut off as the ship veritably rang like a gong struck with a mallet. The pod tipped up on its side, and Kim grabbed the control panel in front of her before shrugging her shoulders into the harness. Wren was doing the same. She wasted no more time hitting the green button in the center of the console. Ahead of them, a pod-sized hatch opened in the bulkhead, revealing a long chute that would drop them into space. The pod gave a cheerful beep before rocketing out into the blackness.

CHAPTER
6

The escape pod wasn't made like a ship. It was just a sphere of metal with thrusters, meaning it piloted like a tennis ball. The enviro's were terrible; the inertia of their launch shook them in their seats, and as Wren brought the thrusters online, the shuttle slowed with a sickening swoop. Ahead of them, the asteroid belt spread out, sleek, gray rocks studding space like pebbles on a beach, spinning slowly in a graceful but chaotic dance. In some areas, the density of the rocks was tighter than in others, small pockets of asteroids packed together in clumps, colliding silently.

Wren spun the pod around. They were about 1000 feet from *Seiiki*, still within the bounds of the asteroid belt but sitting at its outer limits. The rocks were not as dense, but they were still a menacing presence, far too close for a huge ship like *Seiiki*.

It was a scene from a nightmare. Pieces of ship were drifting away in slabs the size of buildings. The entire bottom of the ship was coming apart. Kim could see the umbilical of the engine turbine running through it, still connected to the upper decks, but it was in the process of snapping in two as if gripped by the hands of a giant. A piece of steel plating—jagged where it had ripped free of its rivets—drifted lazily past their starboard. Wren pulled the control wheel, guiding them around it, but other smaller pieces of debris littered their view; pieces of equipment, a chair, a handrail.

"Is that a mech droid?" Wren asked, pointing to a floating egg-shaped device. Kim could see the droid folded inside in crisp detail.

"Damn," she hissed. "We've probably lost them all. There were tons of equipment on the lower decks—stuff for setting up the base, monitoring equipment—and, oh God. Yoshi's lab."

She didn't have time to think. The large piece of the lab was behind her, and now she could see the scattered trail of detritus in front of the pod. Combined with the asteroids, it created a minefield of lethal obstacles. Wren jinked left, then up, skirting a corkscrewing girder. The pod responded like an old man with a bad hip. Kim ducked as they narrowly missed having it skewer straight through the pod's window.

"Do we even have shields on this thing?"

Wren laughed without humor, recognizing the rhetorical question. They both knew they had shields but not much of them. They'd survive entry but not a head-on collision.

"Look at that," Wren said, pointing through the cockpit window. But Kim was already seeing it too. The flotsam and jetsam from the ship—it was forming a *pattern*. Throughout the asteroid field, it was already scattered over a radius of several hundred miles, and it was moving much too quickly for drifting space junk. Filtering through the asteroids, it reached a particular spot in the asteroid belt, about a mile from the pod's port side, where, like a clearing in a forest, there was a gap in the asteroids.

The debris was organizing itself into an inward-spiraling arm. No . . . *arms*. She could see at least three inward-most points; its own private Milky Way.

"What's it doing?"

"I think," Wren said grimly, "this has something to do with our gravitational anomaly."

He was right. The debris was definitely arranging itself *around* something and being pulled into place at a speed of hundreds of miles per second. Some of it was already only distant dots. But . . . *there was still nothing there.* A few asteroids drifted by without a care in the world. In the midst of them was nothing but a hollow space, nothing but stars visible beyond. But wait—just at the very periphery of it, Kim could see a slight distortion in the stars, like a heat shimmer—without the shimmer. It curved in a perfect arc, just the way the stars did at the very edge of Earth's atmosphere.

"How big is that empty area?" Wren asked.

Kim frowned as she tapped at the nav controls. "It looks to be about one thousand, four hundred miles in diameter at its largest point. It's roughly the size of Pluto." She paused. "It's Eschol Thirteen."

"Kim, it's not a planet. There's nothing there."

Kim leaned forward, tapping the controls, trying to find the scanners. She flicked them to life and ran a scan of the area they were facing. Gravitational pull of 0.69g at its strongest point. The holographic number hovered in the air, allowing Wren to see it too.

"That's too much gravity for any asteroid," he said.

"It's a little less gravity than Luna," Kim confirmed. "And New Eden's two moons are too small to exert that much gravitational energy at once. Still want to tell me it's not Eschol Thirteen?"

Wren replied. "We've got to get in contact with *Seiiki*."

Kim glanced up through the window. *Seiiki* was there, in the upper left corner. She checked the comms systems. "The pod's designed to hail them automatically. They haven't responded. I'm scanning for Adonai's shuttle."

The readings came back to her. Nothing. No sign that a shuttle had made it off *Seiiki* at all. "I can't see anything, Wren."

"There's *Daedalus*," Wren said, pointing. "And there's *Minotaur*. They're right alongside *Seiiki*. Maybe we can hail one of them?"

Kim nodded and set the comm to hail *Daedalus* first. There was a faint clicking sound, then a screech that made her clap her hands over her ears. "Sorry," Kim said, slapping the comms off.

"I don't like this," Wren muttered. He sounded . . . scared. Lost. Kim felt a stab of panic returning but tamped it down. Someone had to stay levelheaded. But something about this whole situation felt . . . off. Kim was used to the darkness of space—looking out at the stars felt, at most times, comforting. *It's just the unfamiliar configuration of stars,* she told herself. *Only a few other humans have seen this part of space before.* Whatever the cause of this unease was, Wren seemed to be sensing it too. "Does it feel . . . strange to you?"

Kim nodded. The hairs on the back of her neck were standing on end, and something seemed to be telling her *you don't want to be here.* "I'm going to head back to *Seiiki.* We'll try docking on Deck Seven."

"Sounds good to me."

Kim pulled back on the control wheel, and the pod responded sluggishly.

"*Seiiki's* under minimal thrust, and the scoutships are keeping close to her," Wren reported. "But she's drifting. I think she's still on course. Yoshi must be using the forward thrusters. Adonai must be relaying her coordinates."

"Then why can't we see the shuttle?"

Their silence was tense. Neither of them felt the urge or need to speak, only to watch as *Seiiki* filled the window. Below and to the right, New Eden was visible, just a wedge-shaped segment. They were closer than Kim had thought, but even as Kim watched, the view seemed to drift to the left.

"Wren? You still piloting there?"

"Something's dragging us off course," he replied, pulling up on the steering control. The nose of the pod lifted, then slowly, inexorably, dropped once more.

Kim scrolled through the controls, tapping the holographic icon that represented the external scanners. "It's . . . getting *stronger*?" Her voice lifted with the question. "That *can't* be right!" She shut the display down, then pulled it back up. The same readings stared back at her, the numbers moving steadily upward. *0.72g. 0.91g. 1.3g.* She sat back, bewildered. "We're fighting gravity of 1.3g!"

"But we're heading away from the . . . whatever it is!" Wren exclaimed.

"I know! I'm checking the readings." Kim shook her head. "It's pulling us backward." She let out a frustrated noise; the pod's scanners were ridiculously primitive.

"A tractor?" Wren asked. "Who'd have that kind of technology out here?"

"It's working like a tractor beam, but it's not one," Kim replied. "For one thing, can you see any light?" She pointed through the curved window where the only light came from reflections bouncing off the asteroids whirling slowly past and the fragments shed from *Seiiki* high overhead. A traditional tractor beam relied on using a ray of light locking on to the object it was aimed at. This tractor, on the other hand, seemed to be using some kind of gravitational energy, which would explain the elevated readings. "It's definitely affecting our engines, though."

Wren's jaw was set firm. He struggled to push the control wheel back into position to keep them on course. The pod engines whined at the punishment, and the pod began to veer downward.

Seiiki slipped from view.

Kim tapped the holo controls on the HUD, checking *Seiiki*'s current location. The results made her stomach clench in fear and horror. "She's leaving us behind!" Kim broke her promise not to access the comms and slapped the controls again. This time, there was no shriek—there was nothing. No signal at all. "I can't get comms," she said hollowly.

"Can you talk to the whales?" Wren asked. "They can relay information to Yoshi!"

The realization struck her like a hammer blow. She hadn't heard the whales in several minutes. Quickly, she reached into the depths of the Link, only to find nothing there. No data. Her internal grid was empty . . . and silent. The vast space was horrifying without the whales to inhabit it—Kim drew herself back.

"I can't hear them." The reality of this settled in, and Kim felt an edge of true despair. "I should be able to. Quantum signals don't decay over distance. Something's blocking my Link."

Wren swallowed audibly.

Kim scrolled through the controls. Their Xenol supplies were being burned rapidly from Wren's attempts to break free from the gravity source. Engine temperature was on the hot side. "If we keep fighting this, we're going to be dead in the water."

"I'm going to cut the engines," Wren replied. It was what Kim hoped he would say, but it felt like defeat to hit the controls, shutting down their thrust. Sudden, chilling silence came over them.

"What's going on?" Kim whispered, finally feeling true fear. They were out here in a pathetic little soap bubble of a ship, completely alone. She'd give anything to hear the voice of even one of her whales right now.

The pod came to a stop, bobbed gently up and down while the tendril of gravity caressed them, then began to pull backward toward the blank space once more. They picked up speed slowly, but noticeably, until they were traveling about ten miles per second. The asteroid belt loomed, gray rocks like teeth ready to snap their pod to pieces.

Wren turned to her. "Kim, I—"

There was no chance for further conversation. The pod jerked roughly upward, then sideways, and they were pushed back in their chairs, the breath torn from their lungs. Alarms blared, but they seemed distant. Kim could feel the building pressure in her eyeballs, and she squeezed her eyes shut, knowing it wouldn't help. She'd heard of military pilots having theirs explode during uncontrolled reentry. She blinked them open with an effort. If she was going to die, she wanted to see it coming.

Their speed was so fast now, the stars became streaks on the black canvas. The pod wasn't designed to handle that kind of speed. Kim could feel the chair shaking underneath her, vibrations passing into her legs and arms as a sudden spray of brilliant white sparks erupted to her left. Part of her control panel had short-circuited, filling the air with the smell of burnt wiring.

And then . . .

Nothing but blackness.

CHAPTER

7

"Kim, Kim! Wake up!" Someone was shaking her. Wren. It was Wren, and she was sitting upright, strapped into the pod. She shook her head, trying to clear it, but that only made her feel dizzy. "Damn it, Kim," Wren said. "I thought you were dead."

"What?" Kim managed. Her throat tickled. The air in the pod was cold, a vent blowing chilly air directly in her face. "What happened?"

"You passed out," Wren said. "You were out for over a minute. You went cold."

The med systems must have been activated—that would explain the cold air being blown into her face. "Did we break free?"

"I passed out too for a few seconds. The tractor beam—if that's what it was—cut out suddenly, and the nav console short-circuited. The pod drift-ed until I managed to restart the engines. Now I'm trying to get us out of here before anything else horrible happens."

Kim ran a hand over her eyes. They felt gritty and swollen, as if she'd been asleep for hours. She looked out through the window. New Eden was below them. She tapped the controls, bringing up the rear camera and rear scanners. The nav panel was fritzing unhappily—a few sections of the holographic display dark and useless—but she had enough information to be able to tell that they were several hundred miles from the Hebron Belt.

"Where's *Seiiki*?"

Wren's posture was rigid. "I can't find her. The scanners are crap on this thing, but I should be getting some readings. And I'm not getting anything—not even from the post."

"What about Adonai's shuttle?" Kim asked.

"Nothing."

Kim tapped at the navigation controls. The damaged section of the console made soft whining noises but gave her a few grudging bits of feedback from the scanners. "They should be out here, continuing on their course, right?"

"Right." Wren sounded grim. "Maybe something went wrong. Maybe they can't get a response from the post either."

A ship the size of *Seiiki* would leave traces if it was destroyed. Lots of them. She ran the scanners again. "No traces of refined metals. No space junk out here beyond the asteroid belt." Kim shook her head. "I can't read *Daedalus* or *Minotaur*. Or the shuttle. I don't get it. We weren't out of range for more than . . ." She trailed off as she pulled up a chronometer. "Wait a minute. This timecode . . . Something in the belt must have interfered. It's off."

She tapped the holo controls to bring up another chronometer, hoping it would give her a different answer. It didn't.

"Off?"

"By this measurement, we were in the belt for four point seven hours. But we weren't. Right?" Kim bit the inside of her cheek. "Unless we were both out longer than you thought."

"I wasn't." Wren didn't look as sure as he sounded. "I couldn't have been out for that long. It's not possible. We were passing an asteroid shaped like a peanut. I remember seeing it when I woke, only a few miles closer."

"A peanut-shaped asteroid is hardly a scientific measurement," she told him.

Wren shook his head. "You went through training. Fainting means a drop of oxygenated blood to the brain. The pod's med systems would've pumped in more oxygen, waking me up before two minutes had passed. And if those systems failed, we'd both be dead right now."

"Then where's *Seiiki*?" Kim demanded. "Where'd they go in the seven minutes we were in the asteroid belt?"

Wren's face took on the suspicious look of someone who'd just realized something. "Pull up the long-range scanners."

Kim obediently tapped the controls, bringing up a holographic visual of everything within range of the pod's scanners. The console protested weakly but threw up a blue grid of horizontal and vertical lines. A moment passed as the visual zoomed out, the red dot within it that represented their pod becoming smaller until there was a blip of yellow light in the center. It was flanked by two blue dots.

"That's why we couldn't find them. They're in close orbit of New Eden," she said, her voice betraying the bewilderment she felt in her gut. "How did they travel that far in seven minutes?"

The answer came to them both at the same time, and neither needed to voice it. *Seiiki* was at least four point seven hours from New Eden. Somehow, they had lost time.

"The controls might be wrong," she ventured at last. "The nav panel shorted. I'm not sure which systems are damaged."

"Right," Wren said, unconvinced. Kim didn't blame him; she wasn't convinced either.

Kim felt her mind reaching out instinctively for the voices of the whales. She missed the Link with an ache.

"I'm going to try comms again," she said. This time, the equipment powered up without the previous screech. "Escape pod 3 to *Seiiki*, *Daedalus*, or *Minotaur*. This is Kim. Please respond." The channel clicked open. Kim braced herself for a shriek, but a voice came through. "Escape pod 3, this is

Airman Mallory. We read you." There was a pause. "We lost your signal five hours ago. We've been holding orbit scanning for you."

"We're glad you're intact, too. Have you got any readings on Adonai's shuttle?"

"Nothing as of yet. But we only just picked up your pod, so I'm not ruling out the possibility of his survival."

Kim closed her eyes for a moment. *Adonai.* She *couldn't* have lost him. She needed to believe he was alive. There could be no other possibility.

"You can confirm you lost our signal for close to five hours?" She looked sideways at Wren, an eyebrow raised. Wren looked back at her, his eyebrows drawn together in a frown.

"Confirmed." Another pause, before a familiar voice took over.

"Kim, this is Lieutenant Grand. We'll need a full report from you regarding your activities and a dump of your data, but that can wait. Now that we know you're alive and well, we're preparing for entry. The post is nonoperational. You're going to need to prep yourselves to follow us down."

"I don't even know how to start doing that," Kim admitted. "We were expecting to follow the self-guiding system on *Seiiki*, which was supposed to respond to the signal from the post."

"I can do it," Wren told him. "This thing has all the altitude control of a slice of pizza, but I can get us down."

"We'll talk you through it," Grand said firmly. "I'm going to have a series of coordinates sent to the pod's nav computer. You'll be tracing our footsteps exactly, about forty minutes behind us. That way we can tell you won't hit anything unexpected. It'll be like walking in our footprints in the snow."

"I live in Melbourne!" Kim growled. "We don't even get snow!"

Grand laughed. "Come on, Kim. Where's that wild girl I met back on Ganymede? Wren, check the lockers. If you've got any liquor over there, get it into your copilot immediately."

Wren groaned. "Yeah, that sounds like a *great* idea."

Kim made a face at him.

"All right, I'm getting the nav data now," Wren said. "I'm plugging it into the computer. It looks fairly straightforward, but I'm not loving the fact that there's no auto on this pod."

"Yeah, unfortunately *Hako*-class pods are manual-only. But you've just pulled one through an asteroid belt, so I'm gonna say you'll be fine."

Kim wished she shared his optimism. Instead, she flicked the nav data on to the HUD and watched as their projected course scrolled out over the window. Wren adjusted his grip on the control wheel and increased their speed, slowly at first, then picking up speed as he got the hang of it. The guiding line turned green as he hit the right coordinates, and New Eden began to grow closer.

Her tension didn't ease, though. God, it had been a long day.

New Eden grew from a segment to a slightly-curved plane topped by a hazy mist of blue atmosphere. The Eschol sun peeked over its rim as they came in, soon drawing up overhead. She and Wren spoke occasionally, relaying data from the nav unit, but they were both focused on keeping the pod exactly on course.

The surface began to scroll underneath them. "We're eighteen miles above sea level," Wren informed her. "Exactly on course for the equatorial continent. We've got another nine minutes before touch down."

"*Shuttlepod 3*." Petty Officer Durand's voice came over the comm, wavering slightly with urgency. "We're experiencing difficulty. Stand by."

Wren glanced at Kim. "That's not good." Leaning forward, he hit the comm. "*Daedalus?* What's going on?"

Silence answered them, and a long minute stretched into two long minutes. Finally, the voice replied. "*Shuttlepod 3*, this is an alert. *Minotaur* is down."

Kim felt cold pins and needles rush down her arms. "What happened? Where's *Seiiki?*"

"I—I can't talk." Though the soldier's voice didn't betray any flustered emotions, Kim could sense the fear behind it. "I'm—there's—just stay on course, okay?" The comm snapped off. Kim looked at Wren and saw her own emotions mirrored in his expression.

"Nothing we can do," he told her. "We've gotta land this ship."

Below them, the arctic landmass appeared, and they fell into silence, each of them lost in their own worrying thoughts. Kim reached out to the whales but heard nothing in response. She even tried Linking to Yoshi, but again, she felt nothing.

"Earth once had something like that," Wren said, sitting forward to look through the window.

"It's beautiful," Kim replied. Despite her worries, it was impossible not to appreciate the sight. Other planets in other systems had been colonized but only after extensive terraforming. New Eden had a breathable atmosphere and arable soil. It was almost too good to be true. The stacked layers of ice were striated with bruised purples and blues. Cliffs were visible, dropping off sharply into deep crevasses, some of them, the scanners told her, miles deep. Bobbing icebergs clustered near these frozen beaches.

And then, they were back over the ocean. The water varied in color the further north they went, changing from choppy dark black to warmer-looking blues and greens. The vibrance of it in contrast with the white caps of waves made Kim's eyes hurt.

"Oh, they're going to *love* this," she whispered.

"The whales," Wren said—not a question, a statement.

"The whales," Kim replied. "I hope they're all right."

"I'm sure th—"

And suddenly, they were back. They tore through the Link like eager children at an ice cream van, scrabbling first at the edges of her internal matrix and then filling the vast empty space, ballooning outward into the familiar shapes she recognized. Forty whales, all of them healthy and well, though more than a little frightened.

Kim, Kim, Kim! We were so worried. Where have you been? Yoshi said you were fine, but we didn't know for sure. Kim, Kim, Kim, we're going to see the ocean.

"Hey," Kim said, then, when they didn't listen, she repeated more loudly, "Hey! We're trying to land here! I need to concentrate!"

But they weren't listening. It was too overwhelming for them, and after all, it was her job as Caretaker to listen and advise. The cacophony grew. Kim couldn't help it; her concentration was shredded.

She was aware of Wren leaning toward her, concern in his eyes. His lips were moving, but she couldn't hear him.

Where are you, are you almost here? I want to talk to you. Kim—

"Wren, I'm going to—"

Kim, Kim! Something's wrong with the Aq—

CHAPTER

8

The landing was a jolt. Kim came back to herself, finding the stillness disconcerting—her mind was still traveling through the air. At least the voices of the whales had dropped to a manageable level. She pushed herself up from the metal floor and found Wren crouched over her.

"Are you okay?"

"Ugh. No." She put a hand to her aching head, her fingers brushing the slightly-raised filaments of the Link as she pushed herself to her feet. The window showed that they were sitting on a patch of grass, a few rocks poking up past the nose of the pod.

Large green fronds protruded between them, each one the size of an umbrella. It was dark, but only because of the shade from many gigantic trees. She could only see the bases of their huge trunks. She swayed unsteadily before grabbing the wall.

Kim? Are you there?

It was Samuel. She could hear other whale emotions in the background, but they were subdued, muffled. "I'm here."

We were so worried. I have told the others to keep their feelings to themselves as much as possible. Kim, something terrible has happened.

Kim tried to concentrate on what Samuel was saying, but her head was pounding. "It's fine," she told him. "Everything's fine."

Kim—

"Whoa," Wren said, reaching for her and interrupting the internal conversation. "Careful."

She shook her head, trying to clear it. Samuel's anxiety receded to the back of her mind as she struggled to focus. "Where's *Seiiki*? Where are *we*?"

"I'm . . . not exactly sure yet. The pod hit some turbulence. I put us down as gently as I could, but we're not at the designated landing site. I got the scoutships on the comm briefly. Everyone's fine, but *Minotaur* is wrecked."

For a moment, they looked at one another. Exhausted and worried, Wren's eyes were circled with black, his hair lank and his forehead covered with a sheen of sweat.

"Shall we do it?" Wren said, motioning toward the hatch at the rear of the pod.

"I guess we have to sooner or later." She tried to keep the nervousness out of her voice—with little success.

"Come on. Don't tell me you're not excited."

"I'd have been excited if we'd landed on *Seiiki* with the whales safe. And with Adonai standing on the bridge alongside us. And knowing that the scoutships were safe. This," she waved a hand at the forest beyond the window, "this I'm not so sure about."

"At least we're together," Wren said, giving her a smile that warmed her from the inside. He stepped closer, wrapping an arm around her back and pressing his body to hers. She felt her breath hitch as he pulled her close, his hands circling her firmly. "That was the most frightening thing that's ever happened to me. I thought I'd lost you."

He was holding her so tightly she could barely breathe, but God, it felt good. "Yeah, let's never do that again."

They parted, reluctantly, sharing shy grins.

The adrenaline spike of having survived had hit them both, but that didn't make Kim's feelings any less real. Over the past few hours—had it really been hours since the first alarm had gone off on *Seiiki*?—she could have lost Wren five times over. Becoming aware of just how much he meant to her was startling.

It's not over yet, a small voice inside her head reminded her.

Taking a deep breath, she hit the control to open the hatch.

Warm, damp air hit her like a wall, bringing with it foreign jungle scents and sounds. She dropped through the hatch to the ground below, her boots sinking in the soft loamy mud.

Kim stopped moving. She'd only taken a few steps, but already she was feeling fatigued. Gravity. New Eden had 0.94 g, almost as much as Earth. Kim had been living in much less than that for almost six months.

Wren jogged to her side. He was carrying a portable scanner—he must have gotten it from one of the lockers on the pod. He also had a canvas satchel at his waist, bulging with what was most likely provisions. Kim hadn't even thought about taking any equipment with them, let alone food. All she could think about was the whales.

"Which way?" she asked him.

He pointed wordlessly. "*Seiiki's* in this direction. About a ten hour walk."

The going was not easy. The fronded plants were like bird's nest ferns on steroids. Their bladed leaves curled up higher than Kim's and Wren's heads. The ground was covered with various types of lichen and fungi, ranging from pale green to purple in color and slick with moisture that threatened to make them slip. Woven between were tree roots like pale brown pythons, some so high they had to be climbed over like fallen logs.

Everything, *everything,* was so *green.* Kim had never seen so many shades of one color and never so vibrant. There were parks in Melbourne, but those were patched, brownish grass and a few tiny petunias; pale and sickly in comparison to this display of natural abundance.

"Was this what we had?" Kim muttered to herself at one point.

Wren understood her awe.

"Probably. Granted, the flora on Earth wasn't this big at any point when humans inhabited the Earth, but yes. We had this, and we willingly destroyed it."

"That's . . ." Kim didn't even know how to finish that sentence. Horrible? Heartbreaking?

"It'll get better. Look at what we've done with terraforming on the Colonies—we can repair the damage. Have some hope."

Kim nodded slowly. She was about to say more when she spied something through the trees ahead, and the words were forgotten. "What's that?"

Wren followed her pointed finger and frowned. "I don't think that's one of our ships." He tapped the screen of his scanner, and a holographic diagram sprang up. In the top left corner was a medieval-style shield design, a cross running over it in red: the Earth United logo.

Her shoulders relaxed. "It's the post," Wren confirmed.

They emerged from the trees into the small clearing beyond. Kim should have felt comfort to see a piece of human technology in this alien place, but the appearance of the conical drone against the gray trunks of the trees was jarring.

And something else made her blood freeze.

"What happened to it?" she asked.

Wren had no answer. Together, they approached the base of the drone. It was roughly thirty feet in diameter, its sides rising about the same in height. It had come to rest slightly unevenly on the ground, or perhaps the soil under it had shifted under its weight. The large thrusters—its method of steering—were hidden from view, buried under the loam and undergrowth. The white and red paint on the curved plates was scarred slightly from entry to the atmosphere—that was only to be expected. Some kind of black lichen was growing thickly on the metal in places. The drone had been deployed by the scouting mission four years ago, and Kim would have been surprised, given what she now knew about the humid climate, not to find some kind of floral growth on it. What was *not* usual was the gaping hole in the side of the drone.

The panel hadn't been removed gently. There were several jagged scrapes on the surrounding plating, baring the shiny metal under the flaked paint. Some were so deep, they'd bent the metal inward. Around the lip of the missing plate was more worn paint, and a trail of wiring lay exposed to the elements like a lolling tongue. Some of it seemed to have been cut neatly, but other sections looked stretched and frayed, as if someone had tried to tear it with their bare hands.

"Wow," Wren managed. "No wonder we didn't have a signal to follow."

"When did this happen?"

Wren shook his head. "No idea. But look." He indicated the wires coiling on the ground. Some of them had vanished beneath a thick blue coating of moss. "I don't know how fast this stuff grows, but . . ."

Kim transferred her gaze to the side of the craft. Some of the gouges near the destroyed panel were also covered with lichen, and thick streaks of rust showed through. Inside the dark interior, she could see the fronds of a fern that had decided to make its home in there. There was really no way of telling how long the panel had been open, but Kim suspected at least a month. But it might have been longer. Had anyone at Near Horizon noticed that the signal was out?

"I think the more important question is *who* did this," she said, her voice quiet.

Wren's brow wrinkled. "No one's been on New Eden since the scouting mission."

"You think even Earth United can keep tabs on the whole system? They didn't even have a military presence out here until this very moment! EU kept the coordinates secret, but what if it leaked somehow? A small ship could easily navigate its way out here from Edgeward if they filed paperwork saying they were going to Orion Station or Naphtali."

Wren's forehead wrinkled. "Do you think this is the same person—or people—who sabotaged our computer?"

"Maybe. But who would want to do this?" Anger had begun to simmer in the space behind her ribs, a slow-growing fire.

"There are plenty of people who want the Ark Project to fail," Wren reminded her. "The Adherants, for one—"

"You think *Adherants* are on New Eden?" Kim struggled to believe that. Adherants stuck strictly to their doctrine that humans were never meant to indulge in space travel.

The fact that alien life was never mentioned in the Bible was a sticking point for them, and they interpreted that to mean that humans should not be living on other planets, either. During her training in Chicago, they'd been camped outside the Near Horizon headquarters day and night with their placards condemning her, Yoshi, Wren, and Abdiel—and Near Horizon itself—for daring to interfere in God's plan by glorifying space travel.

Wren shrugged his shoulders. "It's not impossible."

Kim thought it kind of was, but then so was the post failing and dumping them miles from their landing site.

"It's also not impossible that it's the Crusaders."

Even though Kim had known it was coming, the statement felt like a punch to the gut. "No. I guess it's not."

"If Zane fled Edgeward just before our docking, he could have arrived here two or three weeks ahead of us. No one needs to register a flight plan to get to New Eden."

Kim looked at the drone, at the ragged, hacked wiring. "I don't think it was Zane."

"You don't know that."

He was right. Zane might be anywhere at this point. He might not even know what the Crusaders were planning. "He would have had to leave Edgeward in a hurry. We didn't give him a lot of time to plan for a deep-space journey. But it's not just that; he's good with tech. Like you." She grimaced as she saw Wren flinch. "So why would he need to do this? He'd remove the panel, go in and cut the wiring needed. Or even just reprogram the computer to bounce the post's signal around. It would only be a matter of hours for him. This . . ."

Wren waved a hand dismissively. "Maybe you don't know him as well as you think you do. Or maybe it wasn't him. Maybe it was another operative."

Kim was still dubious. The Crusaders trained their operatives extensively. No one would be sent out here without knowing exactly what they were doing. "Grigorian would have had to send them out before *Seiiki* left Sol. It takes a year and two months to reach New Eden."

"Maybe this was his backup plan," Wren suggested.

Kim shook her head. "I don't think so. You don't know Grigorian. He's ... driven. The Artifact gives him messages, and he acts on them. So he would have had to have known the attempt to blow up *Seiiki* would fail ... "

"Not necessarily. Kim, you can't really still believe he talks to God through that thing."

"Of course not," she said but hesitated. "But he believes he does, and that's just as powerful, isn't it?" She wasn't sure she fully believed this explanation either, but it was better than the alternative: believing that God had intended the whales to die, along with her and everyone on Edgeward. "Anyway, there are other groups of Anti-Unificationists that might have been thinking along the same lines. Stop humans landing here by sabotaging the Ark Project. They almost succeeded, too."

Wren shook his head. "We need to move on. Lieutenant Grand's going to need to know about this, and the sooner the better."

They retraced their steps into the forest, and Wren took the lead once more, but the image of the vandalized drone remained fresh in Kim's mind for long hours afterward. The Crusaders ... *here*. The thought frightened her, and she wasn't easily scared.

She had told herself that she was expendable to them simply because she hadn't mattered as much as she thought she did. To Zane, to Grigorian, maybe even to Constantin. But what if that wasn't true?

What if the instructions of the Artifact had been broader than the ones Grigorian had relayed to her? What if he had some other plan to kill the whales?

"Are you okay, Kim?" Wren asked.

She gave him a wavery smile. "Fine."

She tried to push it from her mind. She needed her energy and her focus on getting them to *Seiiki*. The whales needed her, and traversing this forest required concentration.

The noises were the most unnerving thing. There was a constant creaking as branches rubbed together high overhead. Every now and then a massive branch would fall in the distance, coming down with a roaring crash, but mostly it was smaller things that fell—twigs with leaves the size of dinner-plates still attached, bits of bark the size of a car door that could probably do some damage if they came down at the wrong angle. Most of Wren's attention was on his handheld scanner as he surveyed the area directly ahead of their path, monitoring the movements overhead. Twice, he saved them from being skewered or crushed.

Numerous insects buzzed through the air. While none of them seemed to have a taste for human blood—how could they, having evolved in a habitat devoid of them?—they were curious. Little things the size of gnats, bright blue in color, landed on their faces and crawled into their noses and ears. Kim was careful with them to start with, but her patience soon wore thin, and she slapped them into greasy smears on her palms.

Kim, are you coming? When will you be here? the whales asked impatiently. *Yoshi won't talk to us now. She says we're annoying her and she's got too much work to do.*

Kim sighed. She was so tired, and they'd been walking for hours. Soon, they'd have to sleep. She sagged down onto one of the curving roots, nestling into a nook. It was rough through her jumpsuit, and slightly damp, but she didn't care. The heat was becoming intolerable. She felt like she couldn't get enough air into her lungs. Her hair was plastered to her head, and her legs and back ached. "Wren's scanner says we're about twenty hours away from you," she said. "I'm sorry I can't get there sooner."

Where is Adonai?

Kim wiped sweat from her forehead. She had to be honest; she knew the whales would pick up on it if she wasn't. "I don't know. But I think he'll find us again." A useless platitude, added for her own sake as much as for the whales, but helping neither.

Will he crash in his shuttle the way the other small ships did? This came from Jedidah, before Levi jumped in, shushing him.

He will not crash. He is Adonai. He is strong and capable.

Wren settled down beside her. His jumpsuit was now coated in dark patches of sweat. There were smudges of dirt on his hands and knees from slipping on the slick fungus underfoot and some small rips where tree roots had snagged him. He looked at her questioningly.

"Why did *Minotaur* crash?" she asked the whales.

One of the small ships went past the landing site, Levi said, true regret in his voice. *It came down in the water. They rescued the humans. There were some injuries, but they are all being treated.*

"The other scoutship is fine?"

It landed beside Seiiki. *But we are not where we're supposed to be, Yoshi tells us. We are far away from the ocean.*

She relayed this to Wren and watched his face turn pale. They sat in silence until the sky darkened enough that they accepted they wouldn't be going any farther that day.

It was too hot to get into the sleeping bags. Wren tried, tying up the drawstring in an attempt to keep the blue gnats out, but the evening air didn't cool as the sun went down. The gnats remained as numerous as ever. Kim used the sleeping bag as a mattress, curled up as best she could in the elbow-shaped nook of the root, put her arms over her head and tried to sleep. Her exhausted body found it, plunging her into deep, dreamless nothing for several hours.

It was fully night when she woke, ripped out of unconsciousness by a sound she couldn't identify. She sat bolt upright, her hand instinctively going out to Wren's shoulder. He jumped, muttered a sleepy "what," then, taking in her alert pose, sat up alongside her. The forest was dark but not as dark as she'd expected. Two moons circled New Eden, and they were both in the sky, penetrating the canopy with a mixture of silver light from the larger moon, and reddish-orange shades from the smaller. The temperature had dropped but only marginally. She looked at Wren. He was fumbling with his handheld scanner.

It came again a few moments later. A lonely, long, desperate wailing. It sounded like the wolves in holo-movies. And yet there was a soft gurgling end to it, something that didn't sound like any animal Kim was familiar with.

She looked at Wren. "New Eden isn't supposed to have any wildlife."

Wren pointed the scanner, tapped a few keys, then said, "There aren't any heat signatures around here. It's either outside the scanner's range or it's underground."

"It didn't sound like it was coming from underground," Kim said worriedly. "And the scanner's range is, what, six hundred miles?"

"Five hundred, roughly," Wren replied. He fumbled in the satchel and came up with a small, cream-colored pistol, which he casually tilted to the side to check the digital readout. "But yeah. There's nothing showing up apart from the crash site."

Kim stared at him. "Where did you get that?"

"It was in the pod," Wren said defensively. "I thought we might need it. Turns out, I was right."

Kim felt a shiver run down her spine. "Good thinking." This was one thing she was happy for Wren to take charge on. Guns were not her thing, a fact made blatantly clear during her recent training. She wriggled back on her sleeping bag, trying to find a comfortable position. A light touch alarmed her at first until she realized it was Wren's arm. It was too hot to lie close, but she laced her fingers through his and they lay on their backs, staring up at the alien night sky.

They heard two more long, low howls that night, but they seemed far more distant, less threatening. Neither of them slept easily. The day-night cycle on New Eden was approximate to twenty-six Earth hours. Though with two moons orbiting, on any night when they were both in the sky, darkness was incomplete for at least half the night. Kim hadn't thought it would take too much adjustment; she was proven wrong.

Morning came suddenly, forcing its way between Kim's eyelids with a deep purple murk that resolved slowly into proper day as they packed their supplies and ate a hurried breakfast of ration bars that tasted like sawdust.

Kim, are you coming today? How far away are you? Why is it taking so long? Humans are so slow to move around.

She's doing her best! She'd be here if she could. She's only out there because she saved us!

It brought a smile to Kim's face to hear them badger her. Whatever had happened, this at least was familiar and welcome.

"I'm coming," she assured them. "Just a few more hours. I can't wait to see you. I've missed you all."

Still, it was a long morning of hiking and a longer afternoon. They reached the landing site as the sun was starting to dip toward the horizon. The forest gave them the first clue. One of the giant trees had been cracked in half, its top separated entirely and resting in the forked branch of its neighbor which had also partially collapsed under the added weight. Both trees groaned incessantly, as if protesting their injuries.

Beyond this was a massive furrow in the ground. Dirt was piled up on both side of a massive trench, which had uprooted several more trees. Ferns had been tossed aside like rags and were wilting, turning a shriveled brown. The gouge was the width of *Seiiki*—almost two thousand feet. And it was deep. The air was laden with fumes.

"Holy crap," Wren said. "That's *not* good."

Kim increased her pace. *The whales are fine. That's what matters,* she told herself. Still, there was a lump in her throat as they traced the trail of destruction. Finally, climbing over a displaced pile of soft, loamy earth, Kim saw it.

Seiiki.

She took a step back, almost bumping into Wren, who was close behind her. It was like being punched in the stomach. *Seiiki,* that massive, indestructible ship she'd first seen at the Ganymede Dockyards and thought it to be the most beautiful and elegant ship in existence, whom she'd lived inside for almost a year, who had taken her across the known universe, was lying there in pieces like a broken toy.

Her hull was crumpled along the sides. She'd come down hard enough to bend steel that was as thick in places as her arm was long. The shields had protected her nose, but clearly nearly all power had gone into keeping the forward section of the ship intact. The rest was mincemeat. Duraglass windows were cracked. The left fin, the one closest to them, was torn free and lay a few hundred feet back along the furrow. The solar sails were shredded, their arms crumpled, the golden polymer flapping in the breeze. The top of the hull showed signs of charring. And the rear section and the lower decks . . . were completely exposed.

The forcefields had held, though. They propped the ship forward now, pushing its nose into the ground. Bubbles of green light shimmered in the hazy light of day, and within them, Kim could see the whales swimming. Or . . . not swimming. *Hovering.*

Every one of the remaining forty whales was now clustered at the very rear end, peering out through the forcefield. Bright sun lit their fins and heads.

It was the first time some of them had felt it.

Kim inhaled. She could feel them basking in the warmth, the delicious, unprecedented sensation of simply having a sun. Tears came to her eyes, unbidden but not unwelcome.

Kim! Kim, you're here! Look at this!

Is this what you meant about the sun? You told us it was life itself.

How can we not have known this?

My children are going to swim in the sun, just like this!

"Kim." Wren had his hand on her shoulder. It wasn't the first time he'd said her name, but she'd been so swept up by the Link, she couldn't be sure how long she'd stood there like a mindless idiot. "Are you okay?"

"Fine," Kim managed. She gestured toward the whales. "Let's go."

"They came in hard," Wren said grimly as they skidded their way down the slope. "God. Whoever sabotaged the post, they must have gotten what they wanted. It's a miracle the whales survived this."

"*Daedalus* is over there," Kim said, pointing. The scoutship was just ahead of *Seiiki*'s prow, at the top of the furrow created by *Seiiki*'s hard landing. It was lying at an angle, as if it had bounced and come to rest just moments before *Seiiki* came down, pushing it out of the way. It was now peeking just over the edge of the ridge. The other, however, was nowhere to be seen. If it had gone down in the water, it would be a few miles from this inland area.

Lieutenant Grand appeared at the top of the ridge. Kim had never thought she'd see him look relieved to put eyes on her, but he was clearly pleased as he came down the slope, skidding a little. His Earth United uniform, always so crisp, was torn across the chest, showing a white singlet smudged with dirt. He had dirt on his hands and cheeks, as well. His blond hair, normally so pale he looked bald, was matted with dried mud too.

"Kim. Wren. You made it down safely?"

"In a manner of speaking," Wren replied.

"Have you heard from Adonai?" Kim asked.

Lieutenant Grand shook his head. "Yoshi told me what he did, but he vanished from our scanners moments after launching. We've been monitoring comms, but most of our equipment is fried."

Kim's heart plummeted. "We need to get a ship up there to search for him."

"Hang on a minute, Kim. We need to debrief before we make any plans."

"Screw plans!" Kim yelled, the words bursting from her violently. "If he's lost, we need to find him! Every second we stand here is wasted!"

"Kim," Grand said. The word was firm, sharp-edged, and loud enough to make her take notice. She had spent most of her life despising Earth United. Like the police and sec-guards, she mistrusted their authority and avoided them like the plague. Lieutenant Grand in particular had been a shining example of arrogance and sneering contempt back on Ganymede. Tasked with the personal security of Kim and Yoshi during the final days before the selection ceremony, he had, several times, reminded her how much he disagreed with such a "young, untried civilian" commanding a large vessel across the galaxy. But in this moment, for the first time, she saw him as a man similar to her dad. Someone dedicated to his job, one he truly believed in. "*Daedalus's* engines are down. No one's going anywhere until they're repaired."

The words hung in the air between them. "What happened?" she asked.

He sighed. "We saw *Seiiki's* computer go offline. We tried hailing you immediately, but there was no response. We weren't getting any response from the post, either. We put ourselves in front of *Seiiki*, hoping we'd be able to guide you in, but the gravitational anomaly hit us, and we had to reroute power from every other system to the engines to break free. By the time we saw the escape pod shooting out, we were pretty sure we were all cactus; that was when we saw the shuttle leave *Seiiki*. It was straining to put itself between *Seiiki* and us. But the anomaly must have been too strong." He paused. "We didn't know, at that point, who was piloting, Kim. I thought it might have been you."

Kim nodded slowly. "What happened to the shuttle?"

"We were able to track your escape pod and the shuttle into the asteroid belt, but then our scanners fritzed. We lost both of you until we regained our comms almost five hours later. I have to say, lasting that long in an asteroid field in one of those pods is quite a feat."

Those numbers again. Kim could feel Wren coming up behind her, and she smiled at Grand. "You can thank Wren's piloting for that." Behind her back, Kim's fingers moved, and she hoped Wren was watching her draw the kanji for *secret*. She hoped he understood.

"Just a few little tricks I picked up while trying to get one of my dad's horses to cooperate," Wren said wryly. "Basically, don't expect too much— and hang on like your life depends on it." He was speaking to the lieutenant, but his gaze slid sideways to meet Kim's, raising his eyebrows questioningly. She shook her head—she'd explain it later.

"You touched down here. That's all that matters."

It was very far away from all that mattered, but Kim didn't tell him that. "The post has been sabotaged," she informed him. "That's why it wasn't responding."

Lieutenant Grand lifted a curled index finger to his bottom lip. "That's disturbing to hear. I was going to send out a team to investigate, but I haven't had the officers to spare. I'm also a little concerned about letting any of my people into the forest. Did you come across . . . anything unusual on your way?"

Kim swallowed. "We did hear something last night."

Grand shifted his boot in the churned mud, leaving a streaky indentation behind. "That concurs with our experience, too. I would have sent people out to bring you in, but under the circumstances . . ."

"Don't worry. I don't mind that we didn't have any military babysitters," Kim told him.

"Well, this wasn't exactly our mission plan, either," Grand reminded her. "We were supposed to spend three weeks in orbit until a permanent guard arrived." A muscle in his jaw twitched. "I need to get back to the team and see how the repairs are going. Kim, I'm sorry about Adonai. I know he means a lot to you. I promise we'll do what we can—but we also have to accept some truths. Adonai won't last more than a day without recharging."

She knew what he was saying; that Adonai might already be dead. If his batteries drained while he was piloting, he could have drifted and hit an asteroid. Or one of the moons. Or even the gravitational anomaly that she was trying very hard not to think of as Eschol Thirteen.

"Adonai is alive," she said firmly.

Grand said nothing.

"I'm going to take a look at *Seiiki*," Kim said. "I need to know what we're facing. How we're . . . going to fix this mess."

Grand nodded and looked down at his wrist, where a sleek military-issue device was strapped. "You've probably got another two or three hours before sundown. It would be best if you both made it up to the camp before then." He pointed over his shoulder in the direction of the trees.

"Shouldn't we be staying in the ship?" Kim asked, puzzled.

"Not a good idea," Grand said briskly. "There are still fires smoldering aboard. They're contained," he added when he saw Kim's look of panic. "And the forcefields will protect the whales. I expect they'll be out by tomorrow at the latest. But it's still unsafe. There could be leakages we don't know about, malfunctions we're not aware of, especially without the computer being online. I can't allow you to stay aboard while everyone else is in camp. It's safer not to have to split sentries over two locations."

Kim nodded. What he said made sense, but she didn't like it. Leaving the whales unprotected while she was camped even just a few dozen yards away left her feeling uneasy. Especially after hearing that creature last night.

"Captain Shannon's down there," Grand continued. "He'll help you enter and exit. And Chief Simons is in with Yoshi."

"I can get in on my own," Kim said, annoyed.

Grand lifted an eyebrow. "Kim, I understand that you're a civilian. We've had this debate before. But I can tell you that from this moment until the minute I leave this planet, you will need to follow my orders. That goes for Wren and Yoshi, too. EU was entrusted with the safety of this mission, and that includes your personal safety. So you will obey my orders and those of my officers. Is that clear?"

Kim pursed her lips. She was not happy about this, but then, she wasn't happy about anything that had happened since they arrived at Eschol. "Yes. It's clear."

Grand evaluated her skeptically, as if he didn't quite credit her sudden acquiescence. She didn't blame him—she was, after all, an accomplished liar, and he knew that. He turned and vanished over the lip of the furrow, leaving her with Wren.

"Why didn't you tell him about us blacking out?" Wren asked. "About the missing time?"

"Because I don't need to give him another reason not to look for Adonai," she replied, a note of bitterness making her words harsher than intended. "If he thinks there's more danger out there than just a gravitational anomaly, he could abandon Adonai altogether. We can't mention it."

Wren nodded slowly. "Until he sends a ship up there and it gets caught in the same field? What if they're caught in the anomaly as well?"

"No ship is going up there without me," Kim said firmly. "And I'll tell them when they need to know. *After* they're on their way to find Adonai."

Wren did not look happy about this arrangement.

"I have to go and check on *Seiiki*," she told him.

"Yeah, I'm going to need to see what's left of the computer." He winced. "I have a feeling I'm not going to like it."

Together, they headed down the slope toward *Seiiki*. All along the furrow were the remnants of spot fires where pieces of the ship had torn off and caught alight, now nothing but ashes and a few dull embers. The tang of smoke in the air was heavy.

Captain Shannon was African American, tall, and broad. He wore a bandanna on his shaven head that was almost definitely against regulations. Kim didn't think he'd have gotten away with it under Admiral Mbewe's command, but since she'd first met him on their departure from Edgeward, he never seemed to be without it. He was standing near one of *Seiiki*'s airlocks that was half-buried in ochre-colored mud. The massive door was marked with a large number "9," meaning it led to Deck Nine. The angle it was on was created by Deck Ten and the forcefields pushing the ship forward. Shannon had a rifle in his arms—a powerful-looking AF-50 that Kim had seen used by EU soldiers at the military barracks where she and the other candidates had trained for a month.

"There really a need for that?" Kim asked as she approached, pointing toward the massive gun.

Shannon looked at her with something similar to distaste. So, not a fan of the Ark Project, she gathered. Or maybe just not a fan of *her*.

"This is an unknown planet," he reminded her crisply. "So yes, there's a need to protect ourselves."

Kim raised her eyebrows and edged past him into the ship. "Do you think the . . . whatever they are . . . are going to try and break into the ship?"

Shannon shook his head. "I have my orders."

Kim didn't like his orders. Having an armed guard on the door meant EU was in control of who came in and out of *Seiiki*.

"Where's Yoshi?"

"Deck Four," he replied. "Store room nine. Tell her we're due back at camp in two hours max."

Kim nodded, glad to leave the sullen man behind her. Entering the ship, however, felt . . . disorienting. She had to fight to keep upright, the slanted decking under her boots threatening to send her sliding into a bulkhead. The odd angles twisted the familiar passages into a maze.

"I'm going to head up to Deck Three," Wren told her. "I want to see what's going on with the computer."

She nodded, barely hearing him.

Seiiki.

Her beautiful ship. She had loved this place, had known it as home.

The lights were on in most corridors, at least. She made her way to Deck Three up the rampways, some sections of which were now so steep, she had to use her hands to climb them. Jagged holes in the hull let in natural light which caught on the swirling currents of dust stirred up by the crash landing, making them look like waterfalls. By the time she reached Deck One, she was in even more desperate need of a shower, but there was nothing she could do about it. Yoshi would have to put up with her stench.

Deck Three was where her, Wren's, and Yoshi's quarters were located. The open door to her quarters gave her a view of the space that had seemed so big and empty during her flight; so impersonal. For some reason, it looked smaller now. There was a crack in the wall where two sections of bulkhead had separated slightly. Her gravity blanket was crumpled on the floor near the door to the bathroom. Her tablet was a shattered mess of glass and wiring.

This room would never be hers again. There was a gaping sadness to that thought, spreading outward now that she had allowed it in: *Seiiki* would never lift off from New Eden, never return to Sol, never ferry more of Earth's endangered creatures to a new home. Kim found an almost physical ache. The months she had spent as Caretaker on *Seiiki* were the best of her life, and now they were at an end in a more final and ultimate way than she had imagined.

Store room four was at the end of the L-shaped corridor. It contained a large amount of smaller but more intricate equipment—portable scanners, a few small, independent computers packaged in clear plastic boxes, monitoring equipment.

Yoshi didn't turn when Kim entered but said, "This droid is malfunctioning."

The droid in question picked up a case of coiled wiring and hovered it over to a large pallet already laden with stacked boxes.

"You've managed to get the computer online?"

Yoshi shook her head. "Just the auxiliaries, and only two of them. Most of the droids aren't working, either. And this one only just barely!"

"Wren's going up there now," she told Yoshi. She noticed, as she drew closer to her, that the white lab coat Yoshi was always wearing was now stained with dust and something that looked like a smear of blood. "*Seiiki* isn't in good shape."

"You could say that," Yoshi muttered, turning to lift the lid on a small crate. "I did my best, but a ship like this can't be piloted by an individual without computer assis—"

"I'm not blaming you," Kim cut her off.

Yoshi glanced over her shoulder, eyes narrowed.

"I'm not! You got *Seiiki* down without any casualties. That's all any of us wanted, right?"

"We lost the dead whales," Yoshi replied, turning back to the crate and digging listlessly inside. "And my lab."

"Your research will all be on the computers, and we'll be rebuilding a lab on the base, right? Assuming we have enough left to do that."

"It's not just that." Yoshi sighed, her shoulders rising and falling visibly. "I feel like I've let them down."

"Who?"

"The whales. My family. Everyone who worked to get me where I am today."

"Your family would be proud of you, wouldn't they?" Kim asked.

Yoshi looked away. "My mother worked very hard to bring me to the attention of the selection committee for the Ark Project. She was pleased when I took over from you, but she still hated that I wasn't Caretaker to start with. I am . . . I try hard to please her."

Kim wrinkled her nose. "Is that all you're worried about?"

"Of course not," Yoshi said with a snort. "The whales deserved to arrive on New Eden, at least. That was part of my bargain with Near Horizon; that I be allowed to bring them so that they could be laid to rest here. At the bottom of the ocean. Where they belonged."

Unexpectedly, Kim's heart lurched. Yoshi's words resonated through the Link with enough conviction that Kim knew she was telling the truth—and the fact that Yoshi had allowed that much emotion to flow through the Link was significant in itself.

"The whales believe their afterlife continues as their bodies break down. In a vacuum, they may not decompose for thousands of years," Kim told her.

"They might hit a comet. Get pulled into a sun." Yoshi's gaze was distant, her words intended to give comfort, not to hurt. But the moment passed, and Kim could feel the other girl pulling herself back through the Link, shutting down their shared thoughts and emotions until she was nothing but a human-shaped presence in the grid. Back to her business-like self, Yoshi returned her attention to the box.

"We've come down two thousand three hundred and seventy-two feet from our expected landing site. It's going to create major problems. I've sent comms to Earth and Edgeward, and they're working on some solutions for us, but it's going to take time, and new equipment they send out will take as long to reach us again as we did getting here. In the meantime, we're running on backup power because we lost almost all our fuel."

Kim shuddered. "That's bad."

"It's worse," Yoshi replied grimly. "We have two tractors left on Deck Seven. And there are five spare tanks on Deck Two that were to be used for my research center once the base was built. Three are cracked, but two aren't. If we can get enough tech droids up and running to weld them to the tractors, we can haul some of the whales into the bay using those. But the capacity of the tractors is one hundred ten thousand and two hundred pounds. We'll be using about two hundred pounds for the tanks, which leaves one hundred and ten thousand pounds for whale haulage. We've got the sperm whale, Levi, and the southern right whale Berenice, both of whom are heavier than that. And the other southern whale Anihoam who's bordering on it also."

"We'll have to rig something up," Kim said. Her mind stubbornly refused to believe there wasn't a solution to this. The whales could survive out of the water for a few hours, but whales bodies were designed to be supported in an ocean. On land, their own weight could crush them, particularly the bigger whales. "We'll have to transport them in water, and that's a nightmare I don't even know how to start thinking about, but somehow, we'll make it work."

"The supplies for building the base," Yoshi went on. "Many of them were damaged also. We lost a lot of the tech droids too. Four of them were working on a power coupling issue on Deck Three, and they're the only ones that survived. This really is the worst case scenario."

Kim swallowed. "We can do this, Yoshi."

Yoshi shrugged. "We still don't know what that anomaly was. But we do know *something* happened. Quantacore computers don't crash. And the issues arising just as we arrived in the system, ready to complete the most complex maneuver of the whole mission?"

Kim's blood turned to ice in her veins as she realized Yoshi was right about that, at least. "It's a hell of a coincidence, yeah. Wren thinks that it might be Adherants."

"Adherants?" Yoshi snorted. "You think *Adherants* flew in ships out to Eschol and messed around with our technology?"

"Adherants aren't cavemen," Kim reminded her. "They know how to fly ships. They just choose not to."

"Because the Bible doesn't ever mention life on other planets. Planets and stars are just there to give us ominous signs and help us count time." Yoshi rolled her eyes. "They sound like cavemen to me."

"Let's get this equipment prepped and ready to go," Kim said firmly. "We've got a base to build."

"Tengoku wa watashitachi o tasukemasu," Yoshi replied. *Heaven help us.*

CHAPTER
9

The sun was going down. Kim didn't feel like going back to the camp. She'd spent the past day directing maintenance droids, dealing with Yoshi's demands that things be loaded in certain ways to avoid damaging some delicate piece of equipment, and she really wanted nothing more than to not talk to anyone right now.

Grand had let EU know what had happened, but they'd decided to keep it from public knowledge, instead sticking with the story that while *Seiiki* made it's landing, there would be no contact. The story wouldn't hold up for long, and he knew it. People would be clamoring for Kim's next update soon. Repairs on *Daedalus* were ahead of schedule, but that still put her three or four days away from being spaceworthy.

It was no surprise that the camp was full of tension. EU soldiers were trained to deal with situations like this, but they were still human, and the presence of civilians—who were much less capable of concealing their emotions—was probably taking its toll. Grand would tell her off for going off on her own. Right now, she didn't care. She stalked away from the camp, heading around the top of the furrow, and stamped through the dense undergrowth until she could see ocean ahead.

She'd seen it from this distance the previous day, while guiding one of the tractors up the slope. But she hadn't gone any closer. All of a sudden, it was the only thing she wanted to do.

The rainforest tried to hold her back. There were vines strung between the trees, thick and ropey and often mistaken for snakes when glimpsed from the corner of her eye. There were plenty of ferns and something like bracken. There were small purple flowers and patches of moss and more fungus, too. For a place without sentient life, this planet was definitely not lacking in plant growth. To her right, an area a few hundred-feet wide had been leveled by the droids, and some of the metal plating and stanchions for the curved roof of the main center were stacked neatly to one side. All the droids were now back on *Seiiki*, recharging overnight, but their industriousness was readily apparent in the amount of work that had been accomplished in so short a period of time.

Up ahead, the land dropped away abruptly. A steep cliff of gray-white rock led down to Half-Moon Bay—named by the original scouting party; Kim had to agree that the moniker was deserved. The crescent-shaped inlet did indeed look like a waning moon, hedged on both sides by steep mountainous cliffs.

At this time in the evening, the water was calm, with gentle waves rippling across it, blown by the heavy but slow wind. The blueness of it swallowed her. Above, the sky was even more intense. There was a violet tinge to the atmosphere of New Eden, caused by concentrations of certain gases, but the difference was negligible to a girl who'd grown up with endless gray horizons. The few clouds hovering were puffy, little marshmallowy things, a different shape to any Kim had ever seen on Earth—or anywhere else. One of New Eden's tiny moons hovered at the edge of the horizon—a lemon-yellow ball named, also by the scouting party, Catseye. Its partner, Kako, was hidden somewhere behind the distant slopes of barely-visible mountains to the east, which was also the direction in which the wreckage of *Minotaur* lay.

It was the sound that really got her. The *shhh-shhh-shhhh* of water lapping the shore. Hearing it up close for the first time was like hearing music on a perfectly-tuned instrument. Oh, she'd been to St. Kilda beach, and she'd spent a lot of time casing Docklands where she and Zane had eventually attacked a stem-cell laboratory. And her dad had taken her to Geelong on little excursions to see the recovering shoreline. Terraforming bots rolled along the sand there, buzzing quietly as they sifted ancient rubbish and microplastics from the water and sand and, in some extreme cases, carved new hollows for shellfish and rockpools for crustaceans into the cliff faces. But those beaches were nothing compared to this. There was no other sound to interfere—no traffic, no voices, no distant thump and grind of dock machinery nor the incessant hum of speedboats or droids.

To the right, the cliff evened out, dropping down to the level of the crisp white sand. To the left, the cliff steepened, and the rainforest encroached upon it, circling the rest of the bay. Kim reached the edge and sat on the tufty grass, not caring that the damp soil soaked into her jumpsuit.

Adonai. She tilted her face to the sky, as if searching the deepening blue expanse would give her some clue. There wasn't a moment she hadn't thought about him in the past thirty hours. The worry had been subsumed by the endless stream of tasks that needed her attention—and the need to keep Adonai's absence from the whales—but now she let it rise, unable to keep it suppressed any longer.

Kim. You are sad.

Berenice.

Kim, where is Adonai?

Kim hung her head in her hands. "I don't know where he is. He's . . . lost."

Then I am sad, too, she replied. *We knew something was wrong.*

"I'm sorry," Kim said. "I should have spoken to you about it, but . . ."

But it is painful for you. Adonai was your friend.

"He was your friend, too," she protested.

Not as much as he was yours. We love him as we love all whales, but he loved you more than any of us.

Kim swallowed, but she couldn't contain the tears that came to her eyes. "I just . . ." A sob choked her words. "Just want him to be safe. I wanted all of you to be safe."

Berenice paused, giving her a moment. *None of us blame you for the loss of Fifteen or Adonai. That was Hosea's doing.*

"I know their presence on board was unsettling to you, but I don't think you wanted them removed like that, either," Kim replied. "I'm sorry."

In a way. Their physical presence is no longer bothering me, but . . . there is a sense of . . . something I can't explain. Something not finished.

"I think that's grief," Kim said, wiping her eyes.

Grief. That is a strange word. Did whales feel this, before the addition of human DNA?

Kim shook her head. She didn't honestly know. "I'm sure Yoshi will figure it out. Or Dr. Jin, back at the Yokohama Institute."

I would rather they didn't.

"Why is that?"

Because when we have our Links removed, we will not feel it anymore.

"You . . . want to feel like this?"

I want to remember Adonai. And Fifteen. And Hosea, before she . . . I do not want to forget, and this feeling reminds me. But if I am going to lose it, I would rather not know before it happens.

Kim nodded slowly.

Ahead of her, the sun dipped low over the ocean, turning the clouds pink and the sky apricot. The water became a sea of molten gold, and it was the most beautiful thing Kim had ever seen.

As Kim headed back toward the forest, clouds gathered with startling quickness.

Kim, there is a new song in the air, Claudia called to her. *It is edged sharp. I can hear the sound of anger.*

"It's just a storm," Kim said, but just as she'd gotten the words out, a re-sounding clap of thunder ripped through the air. It was so loud, the trees trembled. Kim almost lost her footing as she clapped her hands over her ears. It faded to a low grumble, but then came a gust of wind so hard it almost threw her to the ground.

She scrabbled back to her feet and bent low, trying to keep her balance as leaves and small branches whipped past her, slamming into the foliage.

Just a storm? This felt like a tornado.

Kim, are you all right? This storm is different. In the ocean, on Earth, we could feel the pulling of the ocean currents. But this is bigger.

Kim shook her head. "I've never seen . . . anything like this." She could barely hear herself. The sky was so dark now it looked as if it were nighttime and she could barely see anything.

She was too far away from camp. If she kept going, she could end up lost and wandering for days in the forest. She edged into the shelter of the nearest trunk. Ferns bowed and lifted in the wind, and just as she reached the massive, sheltering tree, the rain came.

It was like no rain Kim had ever experienced. Weather patterns on Earth had been unpredictable for decades, but this was something else. The drops of rain were the size of her hand, and they plummeted down with the force of bullets. One caught Kim on the shoulder as she ducked under the cover of a fern, and it felt like a punch. She fell against the slick trunk of the tree, cry-ing out, but her voice was lost. All she could hear was water. It ran down the trunks like waterfalls, soaking the ground. She huddled down and counted her breaths. It was the only way to mark the time.

She saw a light.

At first she thought it was a trick of her mind. The wild wind whipping the trees back and forth, as if being beaten in some gigantic mixing bowl, made it difficult to make out particular shapes. But even after she blinked several times, it was still there, about thirty feet from her . . . and moving.

She held still. Was this an EU officer coming to find her? She didn't think so. The pattern of movement seemed very deliberate, as if whoever was there was following a predetermined path. Kim's hackles rose; her instincts were telling her something was wrong. The light seemed to move to the left, then swerved back toward her. She pressed herself lower to the ground as rain cascaded off her hair and trickled down her collarbone.

The light vanished.

Kim peered into the gloom, trying to see a figure—or some explanation. But all she could see was rain-drenched foliage.

It must have been another half hour before the storm finally began to let up, and when it finally did, it did so with the same suddenness with which it had arrived. The water stopped running and started dripping. Thunder roared, but it was a distant sound now. The clouds drew back, letting through the light of the two moons.

Fungi had caught the water in waiting cups, funneling it into small pools. She had to avoid these; some of them were deep enough to swim in. But already, the night was warming once more, drying out her sodden clothes and boots and lifting the moisture from the ground.

Kim, something's . . . wrong.

"What?" Kim asked. The strange light was already fading from her mind. There had to be a reasonable explanation, she told herself. The dampness of the air was making her chilly despite the fact that it was turning muggy, and her jumpsuit clung uncomfortably. All she wanted was to get back to the camp and dry off. She wanted to climb into bed with a cup of cocoa—or whatever could be found amongst the military rations and the food scavenged from *Seiiki's* galley. It had been a long day.

The water . . . the currents are strange.

Kim sighed tiredly and turned her path toward the furrow. Grand was already there, along with Yoshi. They were standing at the rear of the ship, flashlights shining into the night and the green glow of the forcefields bathing them in strange hues. They were looking at a dark scar across the face of one of the forcefields, where it met with the bent and dented metal of the hull. It was a gaping mouth in an otherwise smooth surface, and from it dribbled a steady stream of water. Overlapping forcefields had come online behind it, making a flower-shaped pattern of green light, but they were clearly out of alignment and were doing nothing to stem the flow.

"Oh, *no*," Kim breathed.

Grand's face looked as stormy as the sky had moments earlier. "Where have you been? Why didn't you take a comm-band with you?"

"I didn't think I'd need one. I was only going for a walk," Kim protested.

"From now on, you check with any of us before you do something so stupid," he barked. With his left hand, he pulled something from the pocket of his trousers and shoved it into her hands. It was a sleek black wristband, identical to the ones she'd seen him and his officers wearing.

"For God's sake," Kim muttered, shoving it into her own pocket. "Shouldn't we be focusing on fixing this?" She pointed to the broken forcefield and turned her back on Grand.

Yoshi held up a handheld scanner. "The tanks hold a lot of water," she said. "1,900,000,000,000 kiloliters, in fact. At this rate, that would take months to drain, but—"

"Kim."

Kim, who was still goggling over Yoshi's ability to translate a number like that into syllables, turned to see Wren making his way along the side of the ship toward them, Captain Shannon just behind him. He looked disheveled, his forehead slick with sweat. "I've just finished looking into the power reserves. The systems are struggling to maintain the Aquarium forcefields as it is. The rupture's putting more strain on them. Honestly, if we're lucky, we'll get seven days before they shut down entirely."

"*Damn*," Kim said.

Beyond the forcefield, the whales clustered, swimming loops in distress.

Kim felt like a zombie. She went through the motions of helping Yoshi. She took orders from EU soldiers and let them trail behind her. She tried not to think about the problems besetting them.

Another storm came through the night after the first one, but it was less fierce. Still, everyone huddled down in the large, dome-shaped temporary shelter they'd pinched from *Seiiki's* supplies which acted as sleeping quarters, and inside *Daedalus*, sharing worried glances. Kim kept in constant contact with the whales, calming them. When it finally passed, she was exhausted but forced herself to head down to the forcefield. Running a few scans helped her understand that the leak was coming from the portion of the forcefield that was pressing against the ground, which made sense. That part of the forcefield was bearing the brunt of *Seiiki's* weight, and the glass portions of the tank that had fractured had needed to be replaced with forcefields, further draining the ship's power resources. The water was not spilling out in a torrent as it would have above-ground but instead was seeping into the dirt at a slow but inexorable rate.

Kind of a good news/bad news situation, Kim thought grimly.

Later that night, on her return to the camp, Kim found that someone had built a campfire. She headed straight past the portable seats arrayed around it and into the shelter instead of taking a bowl of the soup Airman Cabes was dishing out.

Wren was sitting on his bed when she entered. The bunks were set up in orderly rows, and by chance or design, Grand had assigned them beds almost at opposite ends of the shelter. Not that any kind of intimacy was possible in the dormitory-like environment, but still. Kim missed cuddling up to him, even for a few minutes.

"I heard you arguing with Yoshi earlier."

Kim sighed. It hadn't been an argument, not really, just a disagreement over whether a case of food stores was damaged enough to void its nutrition.

"You need to put this feud behind you, Kim. It's not good for you."

"She posted photos of Abdiel, Wren."

"I know. I saw the same photos you did."

Kim hadn't forgotten that. Wren had been at the next table in the Near Horizon cafeteria that morning when Melanie, her assistant, had sat down opposite her and showed her the unflattering photos of Abdiel passed out on a couch, arm dangling to the floor and mouth wide. A bottle of stims had been scattered on the floor beside him. The next image had been a short video, this time showing Abdiel in a dance club, eyes closed as he swayed drunkenly, clearly out of it. Another photo of him in a corner booth with a young woman, his mouth covering hers, his hand down the front of her dress.

Abdiel had been removed from the program that afternoon. Kim hadn't even been able to say goodbye.

"It was dirty," Kim said. "She knew he could win on public opinion—"

"People liked Abdiel, but he never would have won, Kim. Those photos exposed him, and maybe it was unfair, but he was a party boy. He would never have suited the solitude of *Seiiki*."

She turned her face aside, hating that Wren was right about this. But it didn't alleviate her anger toward Yoshi.

"You need more sleep," he remarked.

"So do you," she replied, too weary to put much conviction behind the jibe. "How's the computer looking?"

Wren sighed. "The computer's communication abilities have been overwritten."

"Can't you just reinstall those systems?"

Wren shook his head. "It's not that easy." He held up his hands, one containing a spanner, a few feet apart. "Imagine if I had this much space on a hard drive. Someone installs a new program. It takes up this much space." He moved his hands inward by about a third. "You've got this much space left. If I don't remove that program, you'll never get back this used space." He waved the spanner through the air to indicate the area he'd originally spanned with his hands. "If I do a reinstall, we'll lose a significant portion of the computer's processing capabilities. And the other program will still be there, running in the background."

"Damn," Kim said softly.

"That's a simplified version," Wren told her grimly. "It's not a single chunk of programming. This is a Quantacore, after all. The data's actually in pieces—millions of them. I'm checking the circuits manually to see if there is any physical damage. It might be possible to remove several circuits and allow the remaining drive space to expand. A lot of the ship no longer needs to function, and it might help to move that processing power and battery reserves over to the forcefields. We might be able to stop the leak, if nothing else."

"That's great!" She grinned, then sobered. "But we still might not have a computer."

Wren nodded.

"Near Horizon can get us one, but it'll take time to arrive—time we don't have. And anyway, I don't want to think about that." Wren sighed. "I miss you," he told her. She felt herself blushing and checking over her shoulder to make sure no one else had entered the shelter. The semitransparent walls showed no imminent interruptions, and Kim was suddenly aware that the dim light, coming from a single halogen lantern hanging from the ceiling, was mildly romantic.

"I miss you, too," she replied as she stood from her bunk and made her way over to his. Slowly, hesitantly, she sank down beside him, breathing a sigh as the newly-familiar planes of his body matched up with the places on hers in just the right way. He wrapped an arm over her shoulder and pulled her close.

"This will be over," Wren whispered into the top of her head, breath tickling the bare skin there. "Not right now, but it will be over eventually. And we'll have time."

She smiled at that thought, but when he used a finger to lift her chin, she found that his face was serious. His eyes were filled with a mixture of compassion, hunger, and something she was coming to know as love. She didn't wait another moment, leaning toward him, ready to touch his lips with hers—

Something in her pocket beeped loudly.

"What the heck?" Wren asked, both puzzled and annoyed by the interruption.

"Kim? Kim, can you hear me? Kim?"

Wrenching herself from Wren's grip, Kim fumbled for the comm-band Lieutenant Grand had given her. "*Adonai?*"

Wren struggled upright, his eyes wide. "Adonai?"

"I am here. I am not sure exactly where here is, but I have landed the shuttle. There are lots of trees on this planet, Kim."

Kim's heart was pounding so hard in her chest that she felt like it was shaking her whole body with each beat. Adonai was here, he was back, he was on New Eden, and he was alive.

She tapped the comm-band, and a small holo of Adonai's face appeared, hovering above it like a miniature ghost.

"Just stay where you are, Adonai. We're coming, okay?"

"Okay, Kim. But I have to tell you, there are some strange noises out here. They are making me nervous."

"Stay inside the shuttle," Kim told him. "Just in case." She muted the comm-band and turned to Wren. "How the hell are we going to find him?"

"Your comm-band should have basic scanning functions. Let me have a look."

Kim handed it over to him and sat, fingers tapping her knee, as Wren scrolled through the options, finally bringing up a rudimentary search-and-find program. "It's not going to give us an aerial view, but it'll guide us in the right direction. Kind of like a game of hot and cold."

That was fine by Kim who was already headed toward the shelter door, barging through it, and almost colliding with the tall EU officer entering from the other side.

"Kim." It was Sergeant Renshaw, a robust man who looked like he was about to burst out of his uniform. "What on Earth are you doing?"

"I need a shower," she replied quickly. Too quickly. Renshaw glanced suspiciously behind her, his gaze landing on Wren, and his eyes turned steely.

"We're conserving water," Wren replied blandly.

The Sergeant looked like he didn't know whether to laugh or shake his head in disgust. "Carry on," he said, stepping aside.

Kim couldn't help bursting into giggles as they rounded the shelter, ducking behind *Daedalus* which sat only thirty feet away from the rim of the trees. Wren grinned sheepishly. "Sorry. It was the first thing that came to mind."

"It worked," Kim replied.

"Maybe we could try it out sometime?"

Kim only shook her head. Damn, the idea was intriguing. Enticing, even. But now was not the time for those thoughts. Adonai needed them.

The forest closed around them, cloaking them with shadows. The night was damp, and the light coming from the two moons currently in the sky was a dichotomy of silver and golden rays, most of it bouncing off the tree trunks but never quite reaching the ground.

Wren reached back to take hold of Kim's hand. "Don't want to lose you out here," he said.

"I can look after myself," she replied automatically. "But thanks. This place is like a—"

Wren stopped still as a muffled howl rose in the distance. Kim, taking too long to find her balance, crashed into his back, almost knocking him over.

"Sorry."

"Shh," he replied. They stood there a moment longer before he whispered, "Maybe we should go back. Tell Grand to get his team out here."

"He'll want to wait until morning. We can't leave Adonai out there all night."

"Kim, you don't know that. He might send someone out immediately."

Kim shook her head. Wren was right, but she couldn't take the chance. Grand might also decide Adonai wasn't worth the risk of venturing out at night, and once Grand knew about Adonai, she'd be deliberately disobeying him if she ventured out here against his wishes. That might be all he needed to ship her off back to Earth.

In any case, she wasn't going to waste time arguing about this. She pushed past Wren and plunged onward through the ferns and thick undergrowth.

Moving quietly was impossible, but then, the forest was full of noises. The constantly cracking tree branches and creaking of wood-on-wood provided good cover. She told herself she wasn't afraid of whatever was making those howls. Eerie though they were, if they were anything to be worried about, they would have encountered them by now.

Except she knew that wasn't true.

"You can go back if you like," she told Wren.

"And leave you out here alone? Hardly." He reached into the hip pocket of his jumpsuit and pulled out the white pistol. "Besides, I can't exactly leave this with you. You're a crap shot."

Amazing, Kim thought musingly, how the presence of that gun made her feel both safer and less safe all at once.

"I don't really mix well with guns," she admitted as they slithered down a slope, wet leaf mold skidding under their boots.

"I can tell." He was looking at her sideways as they straightened up and continued to walk, passing between some tightly-knit trunks that forced them to walk single file.

"I know what you're thinking," Kim replied archly. "'You were fine to blow up occupied buildings while you were with the Crusaders, Kim.' Right?"

"Not exactly. More that it seems like something that might have been useful on the streets."

"You don't carry guns on the streets. That's a surefire way of getting killed—if not by a rival gang, who want the gun for themselves, by the cops who find it on you, or by a sec-droid or even one of those neighborhood safety drones the rich areas have. You carry a knife if you want to be sensible."

"A shiv," he supplied.

"You're learning," she deadpanned. "And if you want to know the truth, I carried the Tritominite charges and set them up. I was never in charge of detonating them. That was Zane's job."

She could see the stiffening of his shoulders in the pale, watery moonlight. For just a fraction of a second, and then he relaxed again. "Did you know there were people in the building?"

Kim looked away. "No. Not that it makes it any better, but no. I wasn't told. But then again, I never asked. It was set for 2 a.m.; I just assumed that was why." She paused. "It doesn't make me any less responsible. And you know my file. You know I've killed other people."

"I assume you had a reason," Wren said carefully. "They were all gang members. You needed to defend yourself."

She tried not to look at him, afraid of what she might see. Fear? Horror? Disgust? No matter what he said, Wren Keene couldn't possibly understand what it meant when she fought for her life against some stim-fueled hulk who thought Constantin had ripped him off. How it felt to slip her thin knife into someone else's flesh. The revulsion she felt when sticky blood coated her hands or spattered onto her cheek. Finally, though, she turned to check. His expression was thoughtful, sorrowful. There was no trace of alarm or shock in his features.

After another moment, he spoke again. "Is that why you don't like guns?"

Kim smiled sadly into the night, knowing he couldn't see her. "No. That would be because that's what my daddy used to . . . well, you know."

Wren didn't laugh. Instead, he stopped still. Kim crashed into his back, slamming her nose into his shoulder. She forced down the instinctive protest of pain, knowing something was wrong. A heartbeat later, Wren turned, lifting a finger to his lips. Kim nodded quickly—she could hear it now.

Crunch. Crunch, crunch. Crunch, crunch. The sound of leaf mold under footsteps, only much softer.

Wren lifted the comm-band and spun the holographic display, scanning the surrounding area. *Nothing.* Trees, fungus, ferns. No life signs at all. It couldn't be Adonai, could it? He had no thermal signature . . . but the noises sounded nothing like a tech droid walking through the forest. They were softer, more numerous than a single figure would make . . . and coming closer.

Kim lifted her hand, drawing the kanji for *hide* as quickly as she could, hoping Wren saw it. He nodded, pointing to the side, and when Kim glanced to her left, she saw what he meant. A tree branch, newly fallen—it still had greenery on its massive twigs—was leaning up against one of the massive trunks, giving easy access to the lowest branch.

Wren snapped the comm-band around his wrist and tucked the pistol back into his pocket. He braced his hands against the fallen branch and began to climb, slowly but steadily. Kim itched for him to go faster. Out of the two, she was the better climber, that was for sure, but if she went first, she'd be leaving him behind. Her street survival instincts were still strong enough to tell her that if whatever it was sighted Wren, it would also know her location in a matter of moments. She needed him off the ground first.

The branch's size was what was saving them. Anything smaller would have slid to one side or the other, but this thing was the size of Kim's bunk on *Seiiki*. The bark was rough enough to give their boots traction and provide decent handholds. Still, Kim could feel it sagging a little under their weight. *Hold,* she told it. *Please.*

Ahead of her, Wren, taller by about six inches, had reached the trunk of the tree. Ungracefully, he steadied himself against the rounded surface and moved one foot and then the other to the other branch, swinging his body after it in a maneuver that Kim could have told him was unnecessarily complicated.

She followed him on her hands and feet, crouched low to the branch, gauging the distance she'd need to cover to reach the next branch as she went. At the apex of the fallen branch, she sprang, catching hold of the other branch at its junction with the trunk and swinging her legs over easily.

Wren looked back at her. There was no time for words; they edged together, bracing their backs against the trunk. From behind, Wren's arm came around Kim, and he pulled her in close. It would have been comforting if she couldn't feel his heart racing, the tension in his posture.

They peered into the darkness. There was nothing there, just trees moving in the wind. And then . . . there . . .

Crouched low in the shadows, a shape moved smoothly, in the way only a predator can. The body was doglike, with an elongated torso and a long, whip-like tail trailing behind. But the strangest thing was that it didn't seem to reflect any light from its body. None at all. And Kim knew that was impossible—even without the moon overhead, the beast should be outlined by dim illumination. But the thing was a cutout of blackness, a creature-shaped hole in the backdrop of the forest.

"What is that?" Wren muttered in her ear.

"It shouldn't be here," Kim replied, the words just a breath. Canine-like though the creature looked, it didn't seem to have any noticeable ears, but she wasn't taking any chances. The creature moved onward, stopping for a moment to sniff the air. Kim's heart clenched, but it continued onward without seeming to notice anything. A moment later, a second creature emerged, following close on the first one's tail. And then another. In another three seconds, the forest below was full of the creatures, more than Kim could count. They moved almost silently, a pack of shadows reflecting no light from the two moons above, blanking out the ferns and trees around them with their sinuous silhouettes.

The herd flowed like a river after heavy rain. It lasted two or three minutes before they thinned and the last of them trailed into the trees. Still, Kim clung to Wren for a long moment before finally moving.

"Holy crap," Wren breathed.

Kim stretched her arms, aware of how tightly knotted the muscles were. "Agreed. Where did they go?"

Wren looked in the direction the creatures had headed, then glanced back down at the comm-band. "I can't see any signs of them, but they're headed in the direction Adonai's signal's coming from. I hope we don't run into them again."

They scrambled back down the branch. Kim felt acutely cautious about being back on the ground. She had no idea if those creatures could climb, but so far, there was no evidence that they could. She had to assume there would be safety in the trees if they needed it again; otherwise, she would have to return to the camp, tail between her legs, and accept whatever punishment Lieutenant Grand doled out while Adonai waited, alone, until morning. She wasn't going to let that happen.

It seemed Wren had accepted there was no turning back, either. "This way," he said. "We're actually not that far off."

They resumed their trek, moving much more slowly and quietly. Ten minutes passed, and they saw nothing more of the creatures—heard none of their howls either—but as they rounded the bend of what might have been an old creek bed, Kim's eyes caught on something glimmering through the trees. It wasn't a shuttle; the color was wrong, and the edge of it was too straight where the doubled moonlight cut a right angle against the backdrop of more trees.

"Is that a—" Wren said in a whisper.

"It's a building," Kim said. She couldn't help but be drawn toward it, emerging into a clearing. Or what had once been a clearing, evidently. Trees were edging inward and ferns taking firm hold of this open space, but she could identify several large hummocks that she knew must be overgrown toppled masonry. Other structures remained standing, but they carried the barest hint of what they once were—a tall column, its top and sides worn away, the slight impression of detailed crenellations still visible on the side that was facing her; a set of wide steps leading to nothing; a broken and tumbled archway, lying in pieces just a few feet to her right. What she had seen through the trees was the corner of a building of some kind, jagged walls extending no more than a few inches in either direction.

"What the heck?" Wren replied. "This wasn't in the reports."

"No," Kim replied. "It definitely wasn't."

She stepped closer, examining the fallen archway. All the buildings seemed to be made of the same whitish-gray stone, and this was no rough camp—the smooth surfaces and crisp edges belied careful workmanship.

"For a planet that was supposed to be devoid of wildlife and never supported sentient life, this place is a disappointment," Wren said. He lifted the comm-band and tapped the holo display. It took Kim a moment to realize he was filming the ruins with a sweeping scan. She was about to tell him they didn't have time for this when she saw it. Just on the other side of the clearing, facing into the trees, was the shuttle.

Her way forward was blocked by fallen stone blocks—some as big as the shuttle itself—and she found herself having to lift each foot and place it down gently or she'd risk twisting an ankle on shards of cracked stone hidden under the blue moss and ferns.

"Adonai?" she called as she came closer. The shuttle seemed to be intact; there was no sign of charring, and the hull was a perfect curve of steel. She tapped on the side of it, then cursed to herself.

Stupid. You want to lead those beasts back to you and Wren?

And another horrific thought: *Perhaps they've already been here and found Adonai . . .*

No, she told herself. Adonai was a tech droid. He was more than a match for an animal, even an alien one. Adonai was fine. So why wasn't he answering?

"Adonai?" she called again, reaching the shuttle's door. It was closed and sealed. She kept going, rounding the small ship until she reached the cockpit windows. Peering in through the three layers of duraglass, she couldn't see anything much but the reflection of the moons above and the clawing shadows of the trees. And then, Adonai's face appeared.

He looked at her, his golden eyes glowing fiercely, and he might have been speaking—Kim wouldn't have heard him if he was—but she motioned toward the shuttle's door. Adonai nodded and moved in that direction. There was a hiss, and then Kim was through the gap and hugging him with all the strength she had, heedless of the hard edges of his metal body poking painfully into places on hers.

"Adonai. Thank God."

"I am very, very happy to see you, Kim," Adonai replied. His hands came to rest gently on her back. He smelled strongly of oil and hot circuitry, but Kim didn't care. She never wanted to be parted from him again.

"What happened? Where have you been? We've been so worried—I've been so worried—and Adonai! You landed a ship all on your own!"

"There was a lot of programming in the shuttle's computer. I only had to access it. Kim, there is something more. Something very important I must tell you about."

"It doesn't matter right now. We need to get you back to camp." She glanced over her shoulder at Wren, who had finished filming and was standing behind her. "Lieutenant Grand will want to talk to you."

"Kim," Adonai said. "As I said, this is very important, and I need to tell you immediately."

She shook her head. "It can wait, Adonai. You'll need recharging."

"Actually, I do not. My systems seem to be running at peak efficiency, and my batteries have half their charge remaining."

"How's that possible?" Kim asked. "And while we're at it, how did you manage to get me on my comm-band? How did you even know I *had* one?"

"I scanned the area for life signs. The shuttle gave me your location and also specified that some members of the team were wearing comm devices. I simply asked the shuttle's computer to contact yours. Kim, this isn't important. I have to tell you . . ."

She huffed impatiently, ready to tell him once more that they needed to go and *now*. But Adonai spoke, and his words threw her into silence.

"Kim, I have found Heaven."

CHAPTER
10

Adonai was welcomed into camp like a hero returning from battle.

Most of the officers had had little or no direct contact with Adonai during their journey to New Eden. During his stay on Edgeward, he was kept carefully out of the public eye. Kim had been strict about this, and with Erica Wu's help, she'd been able to limit the media's access—and the access of intrigued EU Officers or curious civilians visiting the station—under the guise that he was now an integral part of the Ark Project. *Daywatch* had been relentless in their pursuit of an exclusive interview, but Kim had advised him not to participate. It had helped that Adonai was wary of such attention. He probably remembered her conversation with him, back when she'd first found out about him, about what would happen if his transition from whale to droid was discovered. It hardly mattered now; his whale body was gone, lost amongst the stars.

She had told him this as they walked back to the camp, speaking in low voices and with constant glances over their shoulders, her and Wren jumping at every creak and crash from the trees. Adonai had seemed strangely unaffected by the news, and Kim felt that he was dangerously close to not caring.

"This is my body now," he had told her, simply. "Even if it was possible for me to go back, I wouldn't want to."

There was a time and a place for this argument, but it was not there, in the forest, where they had just seen those frightening creatures. In any case, Adonai had been determined to talk about his "discovery" and nothing else. She had listened. And the ball of worry that had knotted in her stomach since discovering the leak in the Aquarium had doubled in size.

And while Adonai had been greeted fondly, Kim, on the other hand, received no such adulations.

Lieutenant Grand had called her aside, taking her up the ramp and into *Daedalus*'s interior. *Daedalus,* unlike previous models of scoutships, was relatively spacious inside, equipped with the latest tech and more comfortable than most military ships she'd seen. A narrow staircase led them into a lounge and dining area, circular and studded with chairs that somehow managed to border the line between utilitarian and pleasant to sit in.

"Sit down," he ordered her, pointing to a booth in one corner.

Kim took the seat but didn't relax into it. She knew what was coming, and it wasn't good.

"Shannon alerted me to the comm-band link, Kim. I accessed it and saw the creatures. And you put yourself right in their path."

Kim couldn't meet his eyes. "I'm sorry. But it was Adonai, and I . . ."

"I would have sent a task force out immediately."

"I didn't know that."

"Kim, what you did was incredibly dangerous, and frankly, I'm worried. If it was possible to abort the mission at this point, I'd be doing it. As it is, Kim, I think we need to complete the mission and leave the planet. All of us. And that includes you."

She had known this was coming, had felt it building for five days now since they'd crashed on New Eden. Still, hearing the words sent a cold shock of horror and dread running down her spine.

"We can't," she managed to say, hoarsely. "We don't know anything about those creatures. They might be harmless."

"Did they look harmless to you?"

Kim couldn't reply, remembering the way she had huddled on that branch, the sense that if those things saw her, she was nothing but meat.

"They don't seem to be detectable by scanners, Kim. That means we have no defense against them. They're aliens—do you get that? The first creature we've ever discovered on another planet. Earth United wants another team out here to study them, but that's not going to happen until we find out who sabotaged *Seiiki* and the post. A tactical team is on the way for that very reason. We're not equipped for a situation like this. Once *Daedalus* is repaired and the whales are in the ocean, I'm under orders to maintain orbit until the team from Edgeward arrives."

"*Daedalus* won't fit the crew from both scoutships—plus Adonai, Wren, Yoshi, and I."

"That's why it's fortunate Adonai returned with the shuttle. I'm not saying it's going to be pleasant, Kim, but a month of boredom is a small price to pay for our safety."

"*No.*" The word tore her throat like a razor blade. "I'm not going. If those creatures are a threat, we'd be leaving the whales at their mercy. Not to mention that the whales need constant care."

"It's not up for negotiation, Kim."

Kim leveled her gaze at him. "If you were watching the feed, then you would have heard Adonai."

"Yes," he replied. "And I think it would be a good thing for Adonai to return to Edgeward. We have some of the best engineers—"

"You think he's malfunctioning?"

"I think Adonai has a very good imagination. And I know he loves the stories you tell him, Kim. Look. He was lost for five days. It's possible he dreamed up some elaborate ruse to fill the time. It's not uncommon even for EU officers to experience these kinds of psychological phenomena during times of extreme isolation and stress."

"But he's not an EU officer. He's not even a whale."

Grand shrugged. "He also mentioned that he didn't need to charge himself. Which is extremely unlikely. It's possible he rigged up something on board that allowed him to charge his cells, but that would have been risky. He might have shorted a few circuits and damaged his neural cortex."

"Or maybe he found Eschol Thirteen."

Grand rubbed a hand across his forehead. "And mistook it for Heaven? Kim, *Daedalus* passed the Hebron Belt on our approach, too. There is no planet out there."

"But there is *something*," Kim insisted. "It knocked us all off course. And it tried to tractor Wren and I in. When we broke free, it caught Adonai's shuttle instead."

"And transported him to . . . what did he call it? A field of golden grass?"

Kim thought back over Adonai's words.

Kim, it was beautiful. There was so much grass, and it was soft and thick, like the grass of the plains on Earth. It went on and on . . .

"And he saw . . ."

"Angels." As Kim said the words, she felt her shoulders sink in resignation. Speaking to Adonai, she had been first skeptical and then disbelieving.

Are you sure? she had asked him.

They flew, Kim. High overhead. They were like birds with wings spread, feathers of all different colors. They looked like humans, but not quite. I tried to follow them, and I was calling out . . . and then, I blacked out. That's when I found myself back in my shuttle.

Now, speaking about it to Lieutenant Grand, she could hear how crazy it really sounded.

"So his shuttle never docked or landed. He was simply in his shuttle and then he wasn't. And there were angels there. Kim, I don't really need to tell you that none of this happened."

"No," she replied quietly. "You don't. But Adonai thinks it did, and that's important to me." She spread her fingertips on the table. "And there is something out there in the belt. Maybe it's not what Adonai thinks it is, but it's important, too; if this is going to be the whales' home, then we need to know more about it."

Grand shook his head. "We've got another two days to repair the shuttle. I'll allow five days to get the whales into the ocean and construct as much of the base as possible. Perhaps Wren can even get the computer to automate some of the systems the whales will need. But we're leaving this planet, Kim. That's not up for negotiation."

Kim stood abruptly. "I understand," she replied tersely. "I'd like to get some sleep now, if that's okay."

The lieutenant waved a hand, clearly exhausted himself. Kim left *Daedalus* and headed back to the domed shelter, sliding inside and finding Adonai sitting upright on Wren's bunk.

Wren was kneeling beside him, a panel from Adonai's chest lying on the crumpled sheet next to his left knee, a small screwdriver in his hand. The rest of the bunks were occupied by sleeping figures, but the dim light from Wren's torch illuminated the area around them in a cone. Kim knelt on the plas-tec floor nearby.

"He's fine," Wren told her in a whisper. "Like he said, his battery cells are half-full."

"There's no damage to his circuitry?"

"No sign of it," Wren responded. "He's in perfect health."

"Thank you, Wren," Adonai replied warmly. "Kim, have you been talking to Lieutenant Grand? Is he going to send a team to investigate what I saw?"

Kim shook her head. "It's not likely, Adonai," she replied quietly. "He . . . doesn't believe it."

"Why not?" Adonai sounded surprised, his LED eyes blinking on and off rapidly as his processors responded to the information.

"Adonai," she told him, resting a hand on his metal knee. "I'm not leaving. That much I can tell you. But what you saw up there . . . I don't think it was Heaven."

"Was it Eschol Thirteen?" Adonai asked.

"That's what I suspect."

Wren shook his head as he set the metal panel on Adonai's chest, leaning forward as he fitted the screws back in place. "There's no planet out there, Kim." He paused. "I remember you talking about it during our training. The tutor said she was hoping someone would bring it up. Why are you so sure it's a planet?"

Kim tapped her fingers against her thigh. "Because everyone else isn't!" She shrugged, even though Wren wasn't looking at her. "Isn't it kind of cool that there's *something* about the universe that we don't know? It's . . . kind of a mystery, and I like that."

Wren turned sideways fractionally, just enough to look at her before returning to his task. She could tell he didn't believe her, and she didn't blame him. It wasn't the whole truth.

On joining the Crusaders, she'd had to complete a few small missions. A midnight meeting with a mole working inside a government lab had been one of them. The man had passed her a tiny memory chip which Kim had then taken to a back alley behind a theatre. Zane should have been the one meeting her; instead, a tall man with very dark eyes had stepped out of the shadows.

Wilhelm Grigorian.

She knew him from the newscasts, of course. He was notorious. In person, he looked older, but no less intimidating. And as she'd handed the chip over, he said, "You are doing God's work, Kim Teng."

She had been shivering from more than the cold when she answered. "I hope so."

His eyes had searched hers, and he had smiled a small smile. "Do you know what's on this chip?"

Kim shook her head slowly.

"Everything the Australian government thinks they know about a possible thirteenth planet in the Eschol System. It's hardly a secret that they don't want too much of that knowledge—or lack of it—floating around. Have you heard of the Ark Project?"

Kim nodded. "Everyone has."

"Even though they're aware that they don't know everything about that system, this is being touted as humanity's chance to redeem itself for the damage it's done. They're sending people out there regardless." He looked sad at this. "Eschol Thirteen is a test."

Confused, Kim looked down at her hands. "I—I don't understand."

"Do you believe in God, Kim? Even though you can't see Him or hear Him? Even though bad things still happen to those He is supposed to love?"

She hesitated, and that made his smile widen.

"That is where faith comes in. Belief in something, regardless of all the challenges or contrasting ideas. Unshakable, firm belief, despite the opposing forces. My next task for you, Kim, is to read about Eschol Thirteen. Read everything, and then tell me it isn't there, that this data," he held up the chip, "is meaningless. That we should ignore what we don't know simply because we don't have a frame of reference for it."

Reveling in the awe that Grigorian had chosen to speak to her, Kim had gone home and immediately pulled up everything she could on the net about Eschol Thirteen. She'd waded through both sides of the argument, but she couldn't shake the thought that Grigorian was right. This was about looking past the data—or the absence of it. There was *something else* in the Eschol System, whether people wanted to acknowledge it or not.

Of course, everything else Grigorian had told her had been a lie. Why cling so tightly to this one idea?

She knew the answer: She had been wrong about everything. The faith that Grigorian had told her was so vital turned out to be her weakness, and he had used it against her. But the research she'd done on Eschol Thirteen had nothing to do with Grigorian. She had looked at the information and made her decision.

And there it was, the pure, simple fact that she didn't want to be wrong about this, too.

But she couldn't tell Wren any of this. She knew what he'd think—that she was buying more of Grigorian's bullshit. And it wasn't that. "It's *something,* right?" she said.

Wren fitted the last screw into place. "It's invisible, not detectable by scanners, and it tried to kill us. So, okay, it's *something.*"

"What else can't be detected by scanners?" Kim asked.

"You're talking about the creatures," Wren said.

"And the ruins we found. I don't know what the link between those three things is, but there is one, right?"

When Wren didn't reply, she prompted him.

"Okay. How about this? Adonai's batteries didn't deplete the way they should have over five days. Does that sound familiar?"

"Are you talking about our missing five hours?"

Kim tilted her head to one side. "There's *something* out there. And if EU won't work with us, then we'll have to work it out for ourselves."

"Kim Teng," Wren said slowly, his voice barely a whisper. "Are you suggesting a mutiny?"

Kim leaned in close to him and grinned. "Only if I can count on you."

Wren looked around at the sleeping EU officers. None of them had stirred, but Kim couldn't be sure none of them had been listening in. What did it matter? They knew who she was and what she stood for, and if any of them thought she'd abandon New Eden, they didn't know how hard she could fight when she needed to.

Wren turned back to face her, his expression serious. "Of course you can, Kim."

CHAPTER
11

Lieutenant Grand called Kim into *Daedalus* later that afternoon. He had spent some time talking to Wren about their sighting of the swarm of beasts, and now he wanted her viewpoint.

She gave him the rundown of what they'd seen, trying hard not to dwell on the sensation of dread and horror that had accompanied the experience. She had a feeling Grand wouldn't be too sympathetic to her "feelings," but when she finished, he paused, his mouth pulled into a thin line.

"This affected you deeply, didn't it?"

Kim said nothing.

"I can tell. The way you speak about them doesn't have any of the usual Kim Teng bravado attached to it."

"I'm worried about the whales," she admitted. "What if those things can swim?"

"It's a possibility. But safe to say that they're mostly land-based creatures, based on the description. At least, according to Yoshi."

"That doesn't make me like them any better," Kim said. She paused. "You still want to leave, don't you?"

"The presence of those creatures on top of everything else has me very worried. It's obvious that we didn't have a clear picture of what was happening in this system before we arrived, and very obvious now that we don't have a handle on it. I want to keep my people safe."

Kim remained in her seat, stubbornly leaning back and silently challenging him to remove her by force, if needed. "What about whatever we found up in the belt?"

Grand sighed. "How did I know you'd bring that up again? I've spoken to Adonai. It's not under our jurisdiction, Kim."

"The fact is, there's something out there. We should at least be trying to work out what it is."

"That 'something,' might I remind you, knocked you unconscious for close to five hours. It sounds like some kind of trap if you ask me, and if that's the case, we're lucky you, Wren, and Adonai are here to tell the tale."

"You think it was mercenaries, or the Adherants, or the Crusaders?" she asked. "They could have easily blown us out of the sky—why bother trying to tractor us in and then knock us out cold?"

"If I had the answers to that, this would be a different situation entirely. Kim, you're dismissed."

Reluctantly, Kim stood and left the shuttle.

She found Wren on his way into the shuttle for a shower. Taking one look at her glowering face, he hooked her neck with his arm and pulled her around the corner. On the far side of the shuttle, there was no one around to see them, and he gave her a secretive smile before bending to kiss her gently.

"I've missed this," he said in a whisper. "I miss having space to be alone with you."

A surge of desire ran through her, and she reversed their positions, pushing him back against the shuttle and kissing him, far less gently. Her hands took on a life of their own as they tangled in his messy curls and reached under his shirt for the flat planes of his chest. She pulled back but only because she needed to breathe.

He ran a hand down the side of his face, the backs of his fingernails gently scraping her skin and setting her nerves on fire.

"Wren . . ."

"You don't have to tell me," he said hoarsely. "I know you want to wait, and now we kind of don't have a choice."

"That wasn't what I was going to say," she chided him. "I want this. I want all of it. When EU leaves, when we have time and space . . . I'm ready, Wren."

He kissed her again and she could feel the edges of his lips pulling up in a grin.

Another day passed, and Kim woke once more in her bunk. The shelter was crowded, made to house four people each. With ten EU officers and three Caretakers, snoring was an issue. So was getting up to pee and having to edge around other camp beds. There were smells. Some of them were bad; given there had been limited shower time since the crash and several days' worth of hard work. Some weren't bad; just the smells of strangers living in the same space—unfamiliar aftershave, deodorant, food. Clothes and dirt. The latex composite of the shelter.

Kim missed *Seiiki* so badly it hurt, but under Lieutenant Grand's order, no one was allowed to sleep on board. Kim supposed this was sensible, given the amount of electrical failures and the computer's state, as well as the sudden violent storms—and there was also the howling in the nighttime. Everyone had heard it by now, and it had unnerved even Chief Simons, who Kim thought of as the hardiest of the EU soldiers.

And yet scans of the surrounding area had detected—and continued to detect—no life signs other than their own. Kim couldn't think of any reason why the creatures hadn't been spotted or shown up on scanners. Unlike the possible human intruders who would have access to technology capable of blocking them, the creatures Kim had seen were most likely incapable of such things.

Lieutenant Grand had authorized scouting parties, but so far, none of them had found anything interesting, and he had yet to send anyone farther out than a three-mile radius from the campsite.

"The worst thing we can do is put ourselves in potential danger," he had said. "So far, whatever these things are, they've left our camp alone, and we're much more defendable with our people localized in this area. And if there are more mercenaries out there, I'd rather they came to us than ambush our scant personnel in an unfamiliar forest. I'm not splitting up."

Kim dragged herself into *Daedalus*. Their shower cubicle was at the rear of the ship, down a set of steep steps, and to the right. It was tiny. The water recycler was working overtime, so there was not much water trickling from the shower head. What was there was lukewarm. At least the chill on her skin woke her a little more.

Daedalus was, by now, repaired to the point of being potentially space-worthy. The ship was stocked with everything but water and was ready for takeoff as soon as their mission was complete. As she stepped out of the shower, Kim vowed, as she did every morning, that she wouldn't be on this ship when it took off.

It did, however, raise the possibility that they could investigate the anomaly in the Hebron Belt, and while Kim was sure that any kind of suggestion would bring a response of "Are you kidding me?" from Lieutenant Grand, it was a good opportunity for Yoshi to launch the satellites, and Kim wondered if she might be able to wrangle herself onto the mission.

During the mornings of the past three days, Kim had been working with Yoshi while Wren continued to work on the computer. This morning, at least, he had Adonai to assist him, and Kim walked down the slope of the furrow alongside them before splitting off to make her way toward the store rooms where Yoshi was waiting.

Kim and Yoshi were shadowed at all times by Sergeant Renshaw and Petty Officer Durand, a small brunette woman from France whose voice was probably the loudest Kim had ever heard. They were helpful with lifting and did what they were told, but Kim knew they weren't particularly interested. For them, this was supposed to be an escort mission. Once they arrived at New Eden, they'd have spent a few weeks orbiting in relative comfort before their relief came. Instead, they were being swarmed by the tiny blue midges, hot, sweaty, and working with a prickly Yoshi Raymond and a much more silent and conspicuously brooding Kim Teng than they'd been led to expect by her exuberant holocasts. Kim had overheard them talking about all this. Well, she'd overheard Amelie Durand, anyway. Renshaw had mainly grunted in agreement.

Together, Kim and Yoshi had made an assessment of the fisheries. The herrings that had been contaminated with Kim's blood couldn't be released into the ocean or fed to the whales—the effects of very diluted human blood were probably negligible, but both Kim and Yoshi were in agreement that the addition of this unverified anomaly into an already delicately balanced ecosystem could invalidate the precisely-calculated predictive simulations. They'd wanted to flush the tank, which would at least allow the contaminated fish's offspring to be viable food sources for the whales, but with so much water being lost from the Aquarium, the pair had decided they couldn't risk it.

"As much as I hate to say it," Kim said, "they might have to be euthanized."

Yoshi had shrugged. "We've still got two other tanks full."

Kim didn't even try to explain her hesitation. Yoshi would never understand.

The equipment in most of the store rooms had been sorted out. Anything broken had been moved out of the way, and the useful stuff had been catalogued and categorized, ready to be moved out when it was needed—including the satellites, which were packaged in steel and set to one side. The tractors were sitting at the base of the ship, near the forcefields, being modified by the tech droids. Two of Yoshi's tanks had been welded to their trailers, ready to receive their cargo.

Moving the whales out one by one was going to use up a lot of their fuel reserves. Xenol was made easily by converting hydrogen—a relatively portable process—but it took time, and the original plan hadn't called for the need to tractor each of the whales to the bay. Not to mention there was a significant risk to the whales over the mile-long journey. Kim avoided looking at the tractors. They appeared flimsy and makeshift, far too ridiculous for a job like this.

We are happy to do it, said Berenice when Kim opened up to her about the situation. *It is worth it to risk dying for such a thing.*

But Kim wasn't sure all the whales would feel the same.

Then there was the issue of the leaking forcefield. Already they'd lost thousands of gallons of water. The lowest point of the furrow was becoming swampy and sucked at your boots. A few puddles were forming. Kim knew it wouldn't be long before the ground around the rear of the ship became unpassable. How would they get the whales out then?

She occupied herself with working, trying to keep her mind off everything. She sorted through a crate of plas-tec-wrapped leads, then ordered a maintenance bot to take them down to Wren. They looked like something he could use. The maintenance bot beeped happily and began to trundle off, only to falter in the doorway, turn, come back, and beep confusedly.

"For Wren," Kim repeated, pointing it in the right direction once more. It spun on the spot. Kim sighed and took the crate from it. "I'll take it myself."

"They're getting worse," Yoshi observed. She was sorting through the rolls of canvas, marking down the size and thickness on her tablet. She'd spent the past day working out a plan for their improvised base, and an inventory of building materials would help determine what could be built and how.

"You think?" Kim said sharply. Yesterday, a tech droid had stopped functioning altogether. Four reboots hadn't been able to get it back up and running. She sighed. "Sorry. Too many problems, not enough solutions."

Yoshi said nothing, returning to her task. Kim left the room feeling like a bitch. She'd been trying to make a real effort to be kinder to Yoshi, remembering Wren's words. Today, clearly, was going to be a rougher day in a series of rough days.

The box was heavy, but Kim forced herself to carry it, using the ramps to reach Deck Three. Getting used to the gravity on New Eden was going to be an essential task. She was going to be here for five years, so the sooner that happened, the better.

The twin security hatches were propped open using various tools. Wren—or whoever his EU shadow was today—had obviously thought it was worth the risk. Kim made a mental note to double check that the doors were shut before returning to camp that night. The last thing they wanted was saboteurs getting past the sentries and accessing the core.

Kim ducked through the first hatch, letting it swing shut and clank against the wrench that was wedged into the corner, and then the second, finding Chief Simons leaning against the curved wall of the chamber inside. Simons was a gangly man who reminded Kim a little of her father. He was British, not Taiwanese, but he had the same build—not muscular, more wiry, but strong—and was only a little taller. He had close-shaven black hair, and his mouth quirked up at the corner even when he wasn't actively trying to smile.

"You want me to take that?" Simons asked, gesturing with the butt of his rifle to the crate in Kim's hands.

"No, I'm fine," she puffed.

He raised an eyebrow and let her pass.

The five auxiliary computers were spaced around the room, suspended in wire mesh casings. Their holo monitors glowed brightly scrolling code, but Kim's eyes were drawn immediately to the center of the room. The core hung there, a silver dodecahedron about the size of Kim's arm span, suspended within a forcefield. A soft blue glow illuminated the room as the core spun slowly as if nothing had changed, but it *felt* different. Knowing that the computer was not a sentient being was very different to accepting it, especially when it had been her guide and, dare she think it, *friend* for over a year.

Wren was halfway down the curved floor of the room, perched atop a ladder as he accessed the fourth auxiliary computer's innards. A metal cover hung open before him, spilling wiring like the innards of some beast. Wren had his hands enmeshed in them, a frown on his face, as he used a wire stripper to pull green plas-tec off a copper wire.

Kim dumped the box, drawing his attention. "Oh, hey," he said distractedly.

"Where's Adonai?"

"Deck Four. I've got him looking over one of the junction points, seeing if he can bring it back to life." He paused. "I want him to start doing stuff on his own. He's actually pretty good with the system. I think he picked up a few things when he was transferring himself through the Link and into that tech droid."

"He's clever," Kim said. "He could work on quantum technology someday."

"You sound like a proud parent. But you're right. He could work with Arden Tech."

Kim nodded, feeling a flicker of pride, then guilt as she remembered how Adonai had expressed just such a desire to her many months ago, and she'd shut him down. "I got these. Wires and crap. Don't know if you can use them."

"Are there any insucables?"

"How should I know?" Kim made a face. "They're silvery. Plastic-covered."

"Awesome." Wren twisted the green wire with an already-stripped red one. His face held an expectant look. After a moment, nothing had happened, and he visibly deflated.

"No progress?" she asked, her disappointment mirroring Wren's.

Wren slid down the ladder, landing just a few feet from her. "Plenty of progress, just no results. And results are what we're after if we want the damn thing to speak to us."

"You still think you can fix it?"

"I thought I could. But whatever happened up there . . . I don't even know. The data packet's still in here, roaming around. The really weird thing is, it's not designed to shut the computer down. It's not designed to wreck the interface."

"How can you tell?"

"I can see it. Quantum computers don't use binary. They work on supposition—the 1s and 0s are essentially both a 1 and a 0 simultaneously. But these data banks," he gestured to the auxiliary computers surrounding the Quantacore, "are all binary, and nothing in them has been affected. That's why the ship's most basic functions are still operating. I can use the other computers to get a readout on what's going on in the Quantacore. But *because* they're not quantum, I can't get direct access to what's in there."

"So you can't weed it out?"

"Everything I try, it just boots me straight back out." He sounded so weary. Kim could tell this problem had been obsessing him just as much as the safety of the whales had her. "Honestly, if I do fix this, it'll be through blind luck. Nothing more."

Kim wanted to step toward him. To nestle up against his chest and wrap her arms around him. But Simons was here, and even if he wasn't watching them directly, the intrusion was noticeable. She was beginning to feel like she should have taken more advantage of the time they could have spent alone on *Seiiki*.

The mess of wires Wren had been working on rained sparks down on the floor. They bounced around their boots, taking a few moments to die before more showered down. A buzzing noise reached Kim's ears, and an alarm sounded in time with Wren's curses. "Damn, damn, damn!" He raced back to the ladder, but the fire suppression system was evidently still functioning. A nozzle descended from the ceiling and directed a spray of foam onto the hanging innards of the computer. The sparking stopped, but there was another noise—like a soft *whump*—and the entire computer went dark.

"That's not good?" Simons called from the doorway.

"Nope," Wren said, staring at the charred mess of wires. "That's not good at all."

"I would concur with that assessment," came a cool voice.

Kim's heart leapt. She turned her gaze toward the core, as though it were a person and this was its body. A stupid reaction for a device that was, essentially, an entire ship. "Computer!"

"Yes, Kim. I am here."

Kim couldn't contain her relief.

"You're telling me burning out those circuits brought the computer back online?"

Wren, shaking his head in incredulity, couldn't seem to form an answer.

"The circuits in question govern my core language units. I am now using backups in the auxiliary systems," the computer explained without preamble. "The bypass has restored my vocal functions by rerouting them from the quantum processors. I'm happy to be able to converse once more."

"I bet you are," Kim scoffed, but there was a deliriously happy edge to her voice.

"I say that not only so that I can share witticisms with you once more, Kim. During my time offline, several of my functions had been continuing as normal. One of those was the monitoring of the oceanic drones sent out to New Eden ahead of our mission."

Kim felt a stirring of dread. "What's happened?"

"It appears the seeding process has been subverted. As you know, several species of Earth-native fish, plankton, and krill were introduced into these oceans to prepare them for habitation by the whales. We were anticipating to have 5.4 billion tons of krill built up in the arctic regions in order to support the appetites of the whales and to develop a healthy ecosystem for the continuation of krill growth. This seems to have failed catastrophically. My communication with the drones is showing an estimate of krill amounts to be about two thousand tons."

Wren's brow furrowed. "But that can't be right. Someone would have noticed, right?"

"I have a backlog of data from the drones," the computer said. "I have been analyzing what I can whilst you've been repairing me. There have been several extreme weather events, but storms, however severe, tend to be localized in terms of effects on life-forms. The effects seem to be widespread."

"What about ocean temperatures?" Kim asked, grasping at straws. Her mind was reeling with this terrible occurrence, and she was fighting to keep herself from panicking. She didn't want the whales sensing that over the Link.

"There are fluctuations. Again, they don't directly correspond to the deaths. I assure you, I'm going through all possibilities: solar flares, radiation levels, undetected predators—"

Kim froze at the mention of *predators*. She glanced at Wren, who looked back at her. They both knew what the other was thinking—a swarm of ghostly creatures moving through the forest, almost silent, and clearly deadly.

"What if it's another act of sabotage?" she said.

Wren glanced up at Simons, whose face was grim as he adjusted his fingers on his rifle. "Computer, can you run an analysis to make sure the data you have is correct?"

"I am very aware that I'm not running at full capacity, but the information is correct," the computer replied. "Are you saying that I was also a victim of sabotage?"

"The background processes that you were running caused some problems," Kim said, her voice gentle. "Can you tell us anything about them?"

"My self-analysis and self-diagnosis options are limited when it comes to some programming issues," the computer replied.

Wren nodded. "Some of the early quantum computers were actually incredibly self-aware. It led to a feedback loop that could throw the computer into a circular process of second-guessing that basically made it useless. Self-reflexive mode is what's left of that ability, but there are limits on that. The computer can't use its own subjective experiences to make alterations to its own programming."

"So it can't tell us anything about what's happening in its own core?" Kim said. She was about to ask about the auxiliary computers, but she already knew the answer: The auxiliary computers weren't detecting the issue at all. She'd seen that when she ran the virus scan. "What would a hacker, or a saboteur, gain from this?"

Wren spread his hands. "I don't need to tell you what just happened to *Seiiki*."

"If you wanted the ship to crash, wouldn't there be easier ways? Trick the auxiliary nav computer into thinking the sun was New Eden. That way, no one survives—*and* you get a spectacle. That's the way Grigorian would have done it."

Wren nodded slightly.

"You get someone with no technology experience, maybe you get a different result, though," Chief Simons interjected.

Kim had almost forgotten he was there. Both she and Wren turned to face him.

"Just saying. You said someone made a meal out of the post, right?"

Thinking back to that rough, ugly vandalism, Kim almost agreed. "But this isn't a simple hack, is it?" she said to Wren.

"No. It's sophisticated. Whatever is in the computer, it's running its own programming right now. We just don't know what that is. For someone to do this to a Quantacore, you'd need at least my level of expertise. Probably more, given how this is playing out."

They left Adonai on *Seiiki,* talking with the computer. He was only too happy to take on this responsibility, his eyes glowing with pleasure when Kim asked him to stay behind. He had been very happy to discover the computer had been partially repaired; just like Kim, he regarded it as a friend after their lengthy conversations.

Yoshi's face fell when Kim imparted the news. They were sitting in the shelter in the evening. LED lamps were lit in the corners, making the space seem almost cozy, but Kim could still smell the odors of the seven other bodies that shared the shelter. She tried not to wrinkle her nose, telling herself she'd dealt with worse—she'd hidden in a garbage skip overnight to avoid the cops once. At least here there was nothing oozing around her feet.

Yoshi was perched on a bed, and Wren sat in a folding chair to one side. Kim leaned against one of the support braces, arms crossed.

It was Yoshi who spoke first. "Why was this problem not detected earlier? I understand small discrepancies, but this is not small. It sounds like someone tampered with the seeders."

"Probably for the same reason no one noticed that the post was down," Wren said. "No one at Near Horizon expected anyone else to be on this planet." He pursed his lips. "What about the population of fish on board in *Seiiki*'s fisheries?"

"There are relatively small amounts of sea life aboard," Yoshi said. "And many of the fish were contaminated during Kim's . . . accident."

Kim nodded. "We can't risk any kind of contamination. It could blow the whole project to pieces if the whales catch an infection or something."

Lieutenant Grand pulled back the tent flap and strode in without an invitation. His face was stretched into what Kim thought of as his "command face."

"Sorry to barge in," he said, sounding anything but. "Chief Simons has just informed me of the issues detected by *Seiiki*'s computer. If something has decimated the fish population, we need to know about it. It affects everything we do here."

"I was going to report to you," Kim said defensively, though, in actual fact, the thought hadn't occurred to her. "I was hoping to come up with a solution before we did so."

Lieutenant Grand gave her a look that said he didn't buy a word of it. "Kim, we're a small team, and we're in close quarters, and I shouldn't need to remind you that my people are loyal. I'm well aware of your plan to stage some mini-mutiny here. I'm about to tell you that it's a bad idea. You cannot stay on this planet without permission."

"You can't force me on to the ship," Kim replied.

Grand rubbed a hand across his forehead. "Right now, let's focus on getting the whales into that ocean."

"And just hoping for the best?" Wren asked.

"I'm carrying out my orders," Grand said stiffly. "In the meantime, I want the satellites from *Seiiki* up in the air. They might at least give us some idea of whether there are other people on New Eden or lurking nearby in the system."

"And the ruins?" Kim asked him pointedly.

"That's unlikely," Lieutenant Grand said firmly. "Petty Officer Durand can't get any kind of reading on them. I've got Simons and Durand out there now taking scans of the area, but if there are answers to be found, they won't come from any of the equipment we've got here. We have a team of scientists on Edgeward. Some of them are on board a scoutship heading out this way right now. If you need me, I'll be in *Daedalus*."

He left in a hurry. Kim wondered if he was trying to escape his own conscience.

"This is bullcrap," Wren uttered, pure anger making his voice husky.

"Maybe not," Yoshi interjected pragmatically. "We are lacking in resources thanks to *Seiiki*'s crash, and you have to admit, not everything on New Eden is as we expected to find it. It might be best for the whales if we allow EU to take control."

"You honestly think that?" Kim asked her, raising her eyebrows. "You know they'll take over your research if they can. EU has their own scientists."

"They're military technicians," Yoshi replied calmly. "There's nothing technical to be gained from my research."

Kim wasn't convinced, and she wasn't sure Yoshi was certain, either. It wasn't an argument she was willing to have right now. "There's nothing we can do about it, anyway. What we should be doing is focusing on the krill. We can't put the whales into an ocean with no food."

"Is there a way to quickly boost the krill population?" Wren asked. "I mean, they weren't all decimated. If we release what's left in *Seiiki*, we'll have enough to sustain the whales for a while, won't we?"

"For forty whales, there's probably enough left for about a week or two. And yes, I can send out more seeders easily. With an accelerated growth rate, so we could theoretically double the population of all species within that time," Yoshi said. "But what I'm worried about is what *caused* the problem in the first place. I think Grand's right. We need to launch the atmospheric satellites we've got in stores. It should give us a clearer picture of what's out there."

"Well," Wren said, standing up and stretching. He still had a streak of grease across his forehead, Kim noticed. "I, for one, am pretty much buggered and ready for bed. How about we adjourn for now?"

Kim forced a smile and a nod, knowing she needed sleep; but at the same time, she knew she would have a hard time finding it. There was no point in going to bed. Excusing herself, Kim headed back to *Seiiki*.

Yesterday, the tractors had been moved out of their storage bays, lowered by cranes and assembled by the tech droids. The three of them were hulking shapes in the darkened evening.

Kim, are we ready to move into the ocean? Barnabas asked her as she passed by the Aquarium. *Is it now?*

We've been waiting so long, Levi joined in.

We can wait as long as we need to wait, Jedidah chimed in. *We are good at waiting.*

The water in the tank is falling. I can see the walls of the ship. This was Martha, and Kim felt a sharp pang of panic through the Link.

"Soon," she told them. "Very soon. The day after tomorrow we're going to start working on the transports to get you to the ocean. Not long at all, and you'll forget all about the Aquarium. You'll be perfectly safe—and free." But as she moved out of sight of the whales, she couldn't help wondering who she was trying to convince.

CHAPTER

12

Grand signed off on using *Daedalus* to launch Yoshi's satellites—not only that, but he also agreed to allow Kim and Adonai aboard, a victory Kim rated highly, even if inwardly, she knew it had more to do with Grand wanting to keep their campsite secure with as many EU personnel as possible than anything else. Still, Kim climbed into the scoutship the following morning with a flicker of excitement in her chest. *This* was, in fact, what she had expected from their mission—adventure and discovery. Not so much of the monsters and disasters and saboteurs.

She checked the readings in the cockpit while Yoshi fussed around on the lower deck, located behind a narrow stairway and containing cramped crew quarters, a small mess, a small room that headlined as a storage area but was also occasionally used as a brig—Kim remembered this from conversations with her daddy about ship design—and the engine bays. This was where the satellites were being deposited by tech droids—seven in total, they were ovoid in shape with small solar panels sprouting at regular intervals over their smooth surfaces. They were, according to Yoshi, designed to

New Eden

last for up to eighty years in favorable conditions and would provide valuable telemetry to the base.

The ship seemed to be in good order; moreover, it was the newest piece of machinery Kim had ever had the pleasure of piloting; newer even than *Seiiki*. She reveled in the smooth start-up process as Adonai took his seat beside her. After an hour of tests, the satellites were loaded and secured, and Yoshi was in her seat.

Finally, Captain Shannon poked his head above the stairs and said, "We're good to go."

Kim grinned as she started up the engines. "Nice piece of ship," she told Shannon as the officer strapped himself into his harness.

"She's saved our butts a few times," Shannon said.

Adonai seemed puzzled. "This custom of naming ships 'she' is confusing. Is this ship not called *Daedalus*? Daedalus was a man."

Shannon laughed loudly. "You're good value, Adonai."

"Good value? I can't be sold. Can I?"

Under Shannon's continued laughter, the ship hummed softly, vibrations at a minimum; nice for a land-based take-off, where the ship had to fight against gravity and air to move in any direction. She slowly released the throttle and increased the ship's yaw, lifting the nose off the ground as the powerful engines blasted into the lush undergrowth, charring a few fern fronds in the process. Kim lifted off quickly to avoid further damage. Below, she could see several EU officers come forward with fire extinguishers, spraying any lingering embers or sparks.

Shannon and Adonai traded quips, but Kim was more interested in the view as they rose. She kept one eye on the scanners, which showed expanding but steadily more generalized readings of the forest and ocean as their altitude rose, and the other on the scenery outside the window. The trees receded to a deceptively soft-looking carpet—blueish in tinge. The mountains across the continent looked closer, their steep, ragged peaks less forbidding from this angle. The sky opened up, clear but for a few clouds, and the faint impression of Catseye hung in the northwest.

Once again, the beauty of this place overtook her.

Kim, are you flying?

What does the ocean look like from up there?

Kim didn't answer with words, but she sent a few of her emotions their way; happiness and a sense of pleasure and a brief glimpse of the world outside as she saw it. The whales responded with murmuring words of assent and excitement.

They climbed steadily through the atmosphere, watching the sky turn from bright blue to violet and then, like a drawn curtain, to blackness. The sun, in their bottom left-hand corner, became a solid object made of light and the visible planets—Eschol One, Eight, and Nine—hung in the void like children's marbles on a black tablecloth.

"Adonai?" she said. "Would you like to take over piloting?"

Adonai sat forward in his chair. "Yes, I would." Barely-contained eagerness made his words sound shorter and sharper; Kim was now used to discerning his emotions.

"That wasn't cleared with Lieutenant Grand," Captain Shannon reminded Kim.

"I know," Kim said honestly. "But Adonai's a great pilot, and he could use the practice. And that would free both of us to help Yoshi deploy the satellites."

Shannon mulled this over for a minute. Finally, he shrugged. "I guess he managed to land that shuttle."

Kim didn't remind him that Adonai was practically a Caretaker himself; she had won this battle, and for now that was enough. "Adonai, we'll need to make two circuits of the planet. I've plotted a course. All you need to do is follow it. It should take us around three hours."

Adonai took the chair, and Kim hovered for a moment, making sure he showed no signs of wavering confidence. He didn't. Every movement he made was sure, and he flicked through the holo controls with barely a hint of hesitation. Kim knew some of this came from the droid programming, but she also knew that no droid could be left to pilot a shuttle unsupervised, let alone a small ship of this size. Adonai's careful adjustment of their heading, a brief check of the atmospheric data and positioning, were all unmechanical. On the contrary, they were very *human*.

"Let's get to it," she said, indicating that Yoshi and Shannon should follow her down to the engine bays.

The satellites were lined up in two neat rows, supported by repulsors that cushioned them with compressed air contained within forcefields. The forcefields were like trays, and when the access port was opened, they would hover their cargo out into space.

The first task was to check that each drone was powered up and sending comms successfully with *Seiiki*'s computer, but with three of them, this didn't take long.

"Ready for launch," Yoshi reported. "Can you tell Adonai?"

Kim nodded and headed back down the narrow corridor for the stairs. "Hey Adonai," she called as she climbed. "We're ready to—"

She broke off, the words choking in her throat. What should have been a sweeping panorama of New Eden's Northern Hemisphere was instead a scattered minefield of rocks. The red path that indicated their course was nowhere to be seen. An incoming comm was flashing urgently on the panel.

"Adonai?" She pulled herself into the cockpit.

Adonai turned his head toward her for just a moment. "I'm sorry, Kim."

"What are you doing?" she asked cautiously, moving to the console and hitting the button to accept the comm.

"This is Lieutenant Grand to *Daedalus*," the comm squawked. "You're off course. Report immediately."

"I took us a few hundred miles out of our way," Adonai said.

"To the Hebron Belt," she stated. "Why?"

"I don't think I need to explain my reasons because you already know them."

Kim sighed. "Adonai, you can't do this."

Adonai focused on the control panel in front of him. "I have no choice. No one will believe me unless I show them."

"Show them what?" Kim heaved a sigh. "We can't go into the belt. It's too dangerous, and this is our only remaining hyper-capable ship. Lieutenant Grand would *kill* us."

"The area where the tractor beam caught me is not far away. I don't plan on going into the center of the belt. Just close enough to . . ."

"Adonai! Are you listening to me? You need to move and give me back control of this ship." Her heart rate was rising. Kim remembered the first time she had met Adonai in his droid body—how she had distrusted, and yes, even feared him. That time had passed, and she'd grown to trust him, yet here she was; in a ship piloted by a whale who was possibly delusional.

Adonai didn't move from the chair. His metal fingers danced over the holo controls and flicked a few switches. The ship canted to one side, a violent and unexpected movement that sent Kim crashing into the control panel to her right. A muffled curse sounded from below—Shannon, most likely; Kim had never heard Yoshi use language like that. Ahead, the gray rocks magnified with frightening speed.

Kim gripped the console, waiting for the dampeners to catch up and right the internal gravity.

"Adonai!"

He didn't reply and instead pushed the ship onward to slide between two asteroids. A sharp tilt downward narrowly avoided a third, and an alarm began to beep.

"Shit." Finally able to get her legs under her, Kim slid into the copilot's chair. She couldn't physically force Adonai out of the cockpit, but she could at least keep them from pounding straight into an asteroid. Pulling up the navigation, she fed the data into the ship's flight path assessment. Ahead, a red path unfurled like a carpet rolled out for royalty, charting their way through the rocks.

"Thank you, Kim," Adonai said. "Though maybe I should point out, my visual accuracy and reflexes are better than yours."

"Forgive me if I don't trust that right now," Kim replied through gritted teeth.

"What the heck is going on?" Captain Shannon asked, cresting the stairs, his face alight with anger.

"This is called a detour," Adonai responded. "It's an unplanned deviation in our route. I wanted to check on . . ." he trailed off, and Kim immediately saw why.

The navigation data told her this was the place where she and Wren had encountered the anomaly. And yes, there was a clearing of asteroids here, but Kim could see, very clearly, that there was *nothing* there.

No wreckage from *Seiiki* drifting in orbit of some unseen phenomenon. No shimmering edge to indicate some kind of large body was present. And no gravity readings at all.

"It was here," Adonai said. "The planet was *here.*"

Kim spun her chair enough to rest a hand on his shoulder. "I know—"

"No, you don't," Adonai responded bitterly. "You think I made it up."

"I don't think that at all. But it's time—"

Adonai's fingers moved over the controls. Kim realized what he was doing only a second after he had already started, and then it was too late.

The ship pushed forward with so much momentum, Kim felt her neck crack. Shannon, luckily, was still holding on to the railing at the top of the stairs and let out a yelp.

There was a loud thud from below, but Kim didn't have the time or breath to question whether Yoshi was okay or not. The lurching movement of the ship took them into the middle of the clearing, where Adonai pulled them up sharp.

Sparks flew across Kim's vision as she filled her lungs with air. Still unable to talk, she whirled on Adonai and saw him looking down at his hands, confused, as if he couldn't believe what he had just done. Kim couldn't believe it, either.

"Aaa—" she managed at last. "Are you crazy?"

The droid turned to her, his hands now free of the controls as they drifted in free and undeniably empty space. "Yes, Kim," he said, his voice low and sad. "I think I might be."

"Get him out of that chair," Captain Shannon commanded. Kim could see that he'd pulled his handgun, a small black thing that did double-duty as a stunner, from his belt.

Adonai didn't need any further prompting, standing and backing away from the console. He glanced toward the stairs. "Is Yoshi okay? I didn't hurt her, did I?"

"I don't know," Kim snapped as Shannon took the pilot's seat. Heaving herself out of her chair, she felt as if she'd been shaken violently by some giant hand then set back on her feet but otherwise was uninjured. "Stay away from that console or Captain Shannon *will* shoot you."

As a tech droid, Adonai actually had a weapon built into his arm—a rifle with a range of functions, all of which were much more powerful and effective than Shannon's space safe handgun. But Kim wasn't about to remind him of that right now. She didn't think he would try to take over the piloting again, a belief that was compounded when he sat back in the rear chair, folding his hands and lowering his head like a chastened child.

Kim left him there, heading down to the lower deck. "Yoshi?" she called.

"I'm fine," the other girl replied as Kim entered the engine bay. "Hit my head, but it's nothing."

In the dim light of the space, Kim could see that Yoshi's wound was a jagged cut on her forehead. Blood ran in rivulets down toward her chin. A few drops had splattered on the floor and onto the nearest probe. "Are you sure? You might have a concussion."

"Head wounds always bleed a lot," Yoshi told her, matter-of-factly. "What was Adonai doing?"

"Chasing a dream," Kim replied. "To the *utmost* extent." She didn't tell her that they were now sitting in the middle of an area of space that Kim—and Adonai himself—had until now believed to be a solid mass. "I think he's finally convinced himself that he didn't see angels, at least."

Yoshi nodded, her expression pained. "Is he okay?"

"He's upset," she replied, warmed a little by Yoshi's compassion. "Devastated, really."

"It is hard for him. Adjusting to being . . . what he is." She dabbed her sleeve at the blood on her cheek. "We need to get these satellites out there. If there's any possibility that there is, actually, something out here, they will pick it up."

Kim nodded and headed back to the cockpit where Shannon was piloting them out of the asteroid belt and into open space. ". . . heading back to our course now," he said.

"Glad to hear it, Captain. Any more trouble and you comm immediately, understand?" Grand replied.

"There won't be any more trouble, sir," Shannon said. Cutting the comms, he turned to Adonai. "I can keep you out of trouble, Adonai, but you have to promise me you'll never do anything like this again."

"I didn't mean to. I just wanted to see it again." Adonai's voice was small and meek.

"You wanted to prove that it was real," Kim replied, settling into the seat next to him. "It's okay, Adonai."

"It isn't okay. You have blood on your hands. Did I injure Yoshi?"

"Yoshi is fine. I'm going to go back down and dress her wound in a minute."

"I didn't mean to hurt anyone. I don't even know why I did it. I feel very strange, Kim."

"Just stay here, okay? And stay calm."

"I won't move from this seat," Adonai promised. "I won't ever pilot a ship again. I promise, Kim."

Kim bit her lip. "We'll talk about that later," she told him.

Once they were back on course, launching the satellites was a relatively straightforward task; they loaded the probes on their repulsor trays into the airlock, slowed the ship periodically to a speed approximating forty miles per hour, allowing the rear airlock to open and discharge its contents. The satellites were designed to position themselves, and comms with Wren confirmed that the computer was happy with each of their statuses as they went.

Kim was happy to make reentry, taking over from Shannon and piloting them back through the atmosphere, taking a moment to appreciate the vast, wind-stippled ocean as it slid under them, the wide sandy beach that ringed the main continent, and the vast forest that covered it. Her eyes were on their landing site, so she didn't notice anything amiss. It was Shannon who sat up a little straighter, then said, "You see that?"

Her finger was pointing toward a thin coil of white smoke in the distance, drifting quickly into a haze. Kim frowned, then pulled up the comm controls.

"Grand, this is *Daedalus*. We're seeing some smoke up here, and it's about," she leaned over to check the nav controls, "three miles west of our campsite."

"Permission to scout?" Shannon asked.

"Negative, Captain." Grand did not sound pleased. "You get shot out of the sky, we're back to square one. Return to camp."

"Affirmative," Shannon said.

Kim eyed the smoke a second time. It seemed to have dissipated altogether now, only a faint haze left to show that it had even been there.

CHAPTER
13

True to his word, Captain Shannon spoke to Lieutenant Grand. The conversation took place inside *Daedalus* and lasted close to half an hour. When they emerged, Grand looked calmer than he had when he went in, but he motioned Adonai inside a moment later. What it was they had spoken about, Kim didn't know. Adonai emerged just as quiet and introspective as when he went in, shrugging off Kim's attempts to talk to him with one-word answers. She let him be.

When Kim finally settled down to sleep that night, she saw Yoshi propped up against her pillow, tapping at her tablet. How could that girl still be working? Kim was bone-tired after everything that had occurred today. She drifted into a dream-filled sleep, from which she woke hungry and sore, as if she'd been doing something physical all night long.

Yoshi had fallen asleep, head propped on her arm, a holo of a whale rotating slowly over her tablet. Wren was sleeping on his bunk, dark hair tied in a bun at the nape of his neck. Adonai was nowhere to be seen. He was probably recharging himself on *Daedalus*.

Kim huffed softly. The rest of the tent was full of snorers, except for Renshaw, who was also up and moving, tugging his green uniform on over his boxer shorts. Kim turned away, not needing that sight. It was surprising how quickly the privacy boundaries fell away when you were forced to live on top of one another.

She set her tablet to one side after turning on some music. She had intended to pull up another of Constantin's ancient, dark, haunting songs from back before the Triad Wars, but instead, she opted for a more modern orchestral song with lyrics in full Japanese. Kim took her toiletries and a fresh jumpsuit—identical to the one she already had on—and headed out for the showers, tablet tucked under her arm and humming along to the uplifting melody.

Just as the door flap dropped behind her, Lieutenant Grand almost crashed into her. He steadied her with one hand, a kind gesture Kim was about to question, when he spoke, voice low and urgent. "Is Chief Simons in there?"

Kim mentally replayed the images of the people she'd glanced at that morning. Simons usually bunked on *Daedalus*, and she didn't recall having seen him in the shelter. "No, I don't think so."

Grand moved past her to peer through the arched doorway anyway.

"Maybe he's on *Seiiki*?"

"No one boards that ship without clearing it with me," Grand said darkly. "And he was due to report back to me before dark last night."

"Wasn't Officer Durand with him?"

The lieutenant nodded. "She made the report. She detected something on her scanners she thought were human life signs, and it seemed to be in the same area you thought you saw smoke. She moved toward the signal to investigate. They agreed to meet back at camp—only, he never showed. I've got Mallory and Cabes out at the ruins looking for him, but they can't seem to find any sign. I can't send out a scouting party to that area until I know what's going on."

Kim shrugged, but her mind was churning.

"Maybe ask Yoshi; I'm pretty sure she was up all night."

She didn't hang around to hear what Yoshi had to say, though. It was one of the rare occasions she could beat the other girl to *Seiiki*, and she wanted to make the most of it.

Today, they planned to test the makeshift transports for the whales. Before risking a whale, they'd have to make sure that the tanks were secure, that the tractors were in working order, and that they could make the journey to the beach without any hiccups. Finding an issue along the way with a whale aboard was not an option.

With Captain Shannon for company, Kim made her way to *Seiiki*. Shannon veered off, cradling his gun at the edge of the furrow and staring into the rainforest. By now, Chief Simons's disappearance was common knowledge, and Kim had noticed a shift in the tensions of the soldiers. From what she knew of him, Chief Simons was as rigid in his discipline as all the EU officers. Not reporting back to the lieutenant was out of character.

The whales greeted her enthusiastically, but she sensed a wariness from one of them. Noah. He swam close to the forcefield as she passed, eyeing her.

I'm afraid, he said suddenly.

"Why, Noah? What are you afraid of?"

I'm afraid I will die.

Kim's heart went out to him. "That's not what's going to happen," she said.

I know. I trust you. But still, I worry.

"You'd be stupid not to worry," Kim said with a smile. "But there's no reason to. Not right now. We're on New Eden and we're all still alive and safe. And you can soon start your new life."

The tractors sat about thirty feet back from where the last section of the forcefield dug into the dirt. They were huge, probably twenty feet tall and forty long. This was just the motor and the cabin with six large-belted wheels lined with spikes as big as her hand lifting them three feet off the ground. Their trailers added another fifty feet to their lengths.

They were monstrous things, their khaki camouflage paint scratched and worn. Only the wheels and treads were new, since they couldn't risk contamination with another planet's dirt; but other than this, Near Horizon had at least saved some money in this department. They had been overkill for the Ark Project's original purpose. This kind of thing had been used by the Outer Colonies to clear areas of land the size of small continents and erect entire habitats. But Kim was more than glad to have them now, thankful that somebody's forethought had saved them from a major disaster. These tractors would be perfect for hauling the whales.

The only problem was that they were running out of solid ground on which to park them.

The leak from the Aquarium had soaked the mud in every direction. Around twenty-three feet of ground under *Seiiki*'s rear was now thick, gooey mud, and *Seiiki* herself had tilted an extra one point two degrees, as calculated by Wren the day before. Such a small angle probably wouldn't have been noticeable on a smaller ship, but even shorn in half as she was, *Seiiki* was massive, and the difference was obvious.

She glimpsed Adonai near the tractors. He was tapping his metal fist on the glass of the nearest trailer, looking a little dubious. "Good morning, Kim," he said when he saw her.

"Hey," she replied. "You haven't seen Chief Simons down here, have you?"

"Not this morning," Adonai replied. "In fact, I've been here since moon-sinking . . . sorry. Is that the correct term? I mean—"

Kim scrutinized him, but he showed no signs of the Adonai from the day before; chastened, subdued, and mournful. Instead, he seemed to be back to his normal self. "It's fine, Adonai. How are you?"

"I am . . . not sure," he admitted. "I think maybe I'm confused. About a lot of things." Adonai's tone didn't bely any animosity or bitterness. "I hope the whales are happy here."

"They will be. Adonai, I'm not going to give up without a fight. And whatever happens, I'm not leaving this planet."

Adonai turned to her. "Neither am I." He lifted his golden eyes skyward. "I know I saw something up there, Kim. And I think it was very important. I cannot leave until I find out why. It feels like . . . I have been chosen for something."

Kim bit her lip. Those words resonated deeply within her. Hadn't she felt the same at one time? Singled out, special? The Crusaders—Zane, mostly—had always used similar phrases, and she had, to an extent, believed them. So why did it sound so odd to hear Adonai talking the same way?

Because, she realized, if she'd had a friend looking in from the outside, they might have told her otherwise. Kim had only Constantin. He, Seamus, Elf, and Nicki had all spurred her on, fueled by the desire to see one of their own rise above the scrappy existence they had eked out in Melbourne's war-ruined suburbs. She did not doubt their friendship—forged through shared hunger, shared successes, and even, occasionally, shared blood—but it was hardly objective. If Kim succeeded and rose to glory, they all succeeded in some small way. Did they know, now, what they'd truly been encouraging her to do?

"Adonai," she said, hesitatingly. "Be . . . careful."

He lowered his head, canting it to one side. "I am always careful, Kim."

"No. I mean, be very careful with your feelings. Don't let this take you over. I know it seems important now, but the real mission here is making sure the whales are safe. Anything else can wait."

Adonai finally lifted his head, and Kim breathed a sigh of relief. When he spoke, his voice was low and intense. "Kim, last night I worked late at the junction station. I didn't want to stop. And I also discovered something."

"What was it?" Kim asked.

"I was talking with the computer about happiness. It's a conversation we've had a few times before, but this time, it said something strange. I said, 'I think I find more of my happiness when I think about things that will happen in the future. That wasn't the case when I was a whale.' And the computer said, 'I can remember happiness.' When I asked it what it meant, it didn't seem to know what I was talking about."

Kim's lips pulled down at one side. "Don't forget, the computer's not exactly in top shape at the moment."

"Maybe," Adonai said.

"You don't sound sure."

"I'm not. There was another thing that has happened." He paused. "When the computer talks to me, it has been showing me a face."

"A face?" Kim tilted her head. "What do you mean?"

"It's only happened since it came back online after the crash. And I'm not even sure how it's doing it. It's not something it could do beforehand. But it did it quite often, even when Wren was behind me. And yet he didn't seem to see it."

"Did you tell him about this?"

"No." Adonai paused. "At first, I wasn't sure if I was somehow being affected by the same issues the computer is. After all, the tech droid is still linked to *Seiiki*'s computer."

Kim puzzled over this. "What does this face look like?"

"It is human." Again, a pause, and a hesitation before adding the details. "*Almost* human. Different in some ways. The face wasn't like your faces nor any face I've seen in the computer database. Longer and less full. Narrower. A small nose and eyes that are dark black without an iris."

Kim had to wonder if it was possible for Adonai to be infected by the strange programs running in the computer. Adonai's processing chips were able to link with the ship, but their functions were controlled through the auxiliary computers.

She hoped this was enough to keep him safe. But that only left one option.

Was it possible that Adonai had developed an imagination? Could this be the explanation for his odd experience in the belt?

"I have seen faces like those before," Adonai hedged quietly.

Kim waited for him to elaborate, and he did.

"On Eschol Thirteen."

"You didn't tell me that," she said.

"Yes I did. I told you I saw winged beings. They were high above me, but when I replayed the memory, I was able to see more closely. The face was not the same but very similar."

Kim felt as if the breath had been knocked out of her lungs. *God.* What was going on here? Was Adonai losing his mind? Or was this, after all . . . some kind of message?

Stop it, she told herself. She wasn't Grigorian. She didn't believe God worked in such blatant ways—choosing to speak to one person above all others. At least, not anymore.

Trying to recover, she asked, "You spent all night talking to the computer?"

"No. After I saw the face, I felt I wanted some time alone to think. I took a long walk around the bay."

"Alone?"

Adonai's LED eyes looked a little sad. "It's not the first time. I've become very familiar with this terrain. I'm not like you, Kim. I don't get tired. If I am fully charged, I can walk for hours."

"You should still be careful," she chided him gently. "The heat can affect your circuits. Actually, I should take a look at your thermostat."

Adonai allowed her to do this, and when Kim was satisfied that he was running a few degrees cooler than the thirty-three degree average, she felt much better.

Turning her attention to the tractors, she had a sudden thought. "You should come with me on the test run this morning."

Adonai's eyes brightened. "Really?"

"Of course! You're part of the Ark team as well. You know that."

Adonai's shoulders folded in a little. Was he pleased? Embarrassed? Kim didn't care. She put a foot on the running board of the nearest tractor and pulled herself up, opening the hatch with a touch of her finger. It hissed as it lifted, revealing an interior of black vinyl, worn and smelling a little of unwashed feet. Kim wrinkled her nose.

"Hey!" Captain Shannon called from behind them. "You're not taking one out already? The test run's not scheduled until 0930."

Kim raised her eyebrows innocently. "We're ahead of schedule."

The Captain furrowed his brow. "I'll need to clear this with Lieutenant Grand."

"Okay, you do that. I'll wait right here," Kim said with a perfect Hannah Monksman smile.

Captain Shannon lifted his comm-band, eyed her, then cursed. He'd assumed, quite rightly, that she couldn't be trusted to be left alone in the cabin for the amount of time the comm would take. "At least let me up there."

Kim gave Adonai a pained look, then edged her way inside. The cabin was roomy, with four separate chairs and two control consoles, but the left-hand side was taken up by an overly large steering wheel and gearshift. Kim took this seat with glee. She'd studied how to use the tractors a few days ago and run a few simulations on her tablet. Apparently it was much like driving an aircar. Never mind that she'd never *actually* driven an aircar: she had never in her entire life backed down from a challenge.

As the captain swung himself into the cabin behind her, he tapped his comm-band.

"Shannon here," he said gruffly. "Kim's decided to move the test run up."

The comm fritzed, and Sergeant Renshaw's voice came on. "Stop her. Grand's going to be *pissed.*"

"Can't do much short of physically restraining her, sir."

"Physically restrain her then!" Renshaw sounded slightly panicked.

"It's against our orders, sir." Shannon sounded exasperated and slightly meek, as if he didn't really want to be reminding Renshaw of their directives. "They're civilians."

"I'll be there in a minute," came the hurried, angry reply.

"Have a feeling you'll be too late, sir," Shannon said grimly.

He was right. Kim had already found the ignition button. There was a long, low whine, and nothing happened. Kim, disappointed, checked the readouts. They had fuel. There were no warning lights on. And then, suddenly, the entire cabin lurched into an earthquake-level vibration. Kim let out a whoop as the motor coughed, then settled into a smoother rhythm.

Kim flicked on the windscreen wipers, clearing away a layer of grime stirred up from the furrow by the rain. They were facing away from the ship. The furrow was actually useful in one regard at least, creating a make-shift road in a place that—at least as far as they knew—had no roads. The earth here was semi-compact and clear of trees. She pushed in the clutch and edged the gearstick into its first gear. The machine coughed again. The whine dropped in pitch as it almost died. Kim shoved the clutch back in and repeated her motions.

"You want me to do this?" Shannon growled.

"Absolutely *not*," Kim replied. No way was she ceding control to EU on this one. The engine died once more, and she doggedly started it again. The cabin lunged, almost throwing Shannon out of his chair. Adonai, of course, managed to stay seated, his servos compensating for the rough change in direction much more quickly.

"Seriously, I can do this!" Shannon replied, clutching the console while he struggled to fit the seat's restraints over his shoulders.

"So can I!" Kim yelled in return, flooring the accelerator. Through the window, she saw Renshaw thundering down the slope, red-faced. He lifted his hands in a helpless gesture as the tractor roared past him with a spattering of mud.

She shifted up to second gear, more smoothly this time. Already, she could feel the way this thing worked, how she would need to accommodate for its size and how easily it steered. She felt Shannon relax beside her. Just a little, though. He was still clutching the restraints.

"See? I'm good at this stuff," Kim told him. She turned the wheel, and the tractor edged toward the side of the furrow. As it bucked over the top and into the rainforest, she realized that clearing a path to the beach would be no problem at all. The tractor chewed through everything in its path, tearing its own road as easily as a knife through butter.

The great trunks of the trees loomed to the left and right, ghostly shapes through the misty morning light. They weren't always easy to see, surprisingly enough for their size. Something about their ghostly silver bark made them disappear against the backdrop of endless gray trunks. Twice, she came close to sideswiping one. But, as she reminded Shannon a few times, close wasn't "smashing into."

And then, all of a sudden, there was the sea. Sparkling green-blue like a jewel through the trees. Kim braked, the tractor coming to a stop on the sand, wheels sinking a good four inches.

The captain worked on uncoiling white fingers from his harness while Adonai opened the hatch. Kim was the first through, jumping down to the sand, raising her hands and whooping. She spun in a wide circle, stretching her arms wide, watching the beach pass her by, followed by the distant hills, and finally, the skeleton of the base just visible over the ridge of the small cliff to her left.

Adonai gave a laugh behind her, a strange sound that was somehow more electronic than his normal speech, but a welcome one nonetheless. It spurred her on. She ran a few steps, stopping only to kick off her boots, then plunged into the shallows. Water sprayed up to her knees, refreshingly cool. The rippling of the water, the suck of wet sand under her toes, the tang of seaweed—God, she felt alive! She hadn't realized how long it had been since she felt truly happy until now.

She tilted her head back and let the daylight fall on her face. She stood like that for a while, letting the waves lap around her ankles and the sun drench her skin while Adonai and Captain Shannon watched on in bemusement.

CHAPTER
14

After a heated but short discussion with Lieutenant Grand, Kim was allocated Captain Shannon and Sergeant Renshaw to assist with the test. They made two more runs with both tractors, which was as many as their limited fuel supply would allow. The second time through, the second of the tractors broke down halfway along the new "road" to the beach, but Captain Shannon fixed it in less than half an hour, with Adonai's help.

The results were promising. The trip took ten minutes less than Kim had planned for, and every minute counted when the safety of the whales was concerned. The tractors seemed to cope well with the terrain, and the tanks seemed sturdy enough to withstand the bumps while keeping their cargo unharmed. But when Kim returned to the camp that evening, there was another problem to face, one she'd successfully avoided until then.

Chief Simons had not returned.

Every EU officer not assigned to help Kim or Wren had been out to the ruins, finding no trace of him. Cabes and Mallory had been redeployed to check out the area where Kim had noted the smoke but had found nothing to indicate any kind of human habitation in the area, let alone signs that whoever had created it had kidnapped a trained soldier without so much as a single gunshot.

As everyone was clustering around the campfire, Lieutenant Grand coughed for attention. The general chatter—which was actually an argument over how long to keep the freeze-dried soup over the flames; a long-running disagreement on which no one had yet been able to reach a consensus—died, and a feeling of dread crept into Kim's stomach.

"I was going to keep this news to military personnel only," Grand began. He was standing awkwardly, a tablet clutched in his left hand. His uniform shirt was creased and a smudge of dirt slashed across his left cheek. Still, he stood with military stiffness, jaw set. "My orders from Edgeward are to do so. However, I feel . . ." he paused, as if changing his mind about whether to go on, but now that he'd begun, he was trapped by thirteen other pairs of eyes. Fourteen, if you counted Adonai, who was standing unflaggingly at the back of the crowd. "I feel these orders are not in the best interests of this group."

He coughed, and Kim could see him struggling internally. He was human, after all, she thought as a flush crept up his cheeks.

"Officer Durand was thoughtful enough to recover the external security cameras on Adonai's shuttle," he said. "Their main function is to prevent unauthorized access to the shuttle, but they're motion-activated, so when someone comes into range like Durand and Simons did, they start recording. I'm going to play the footage, which is also a violation of my orders. But again, I believe it's in your best interests to see it, as I doubt my description would be adequate."

Puzzled looks and confused glances were shared by the group. "I don't like this," Wren hissed to Kim.

Grand tapped a few buttons on his tablet, and a hologram sprang into the air. It was a slightly-grainy, greened-out view of the rainforest on the other side of *Daedalus*. There was Simons. His head and left shoulder were cut off by the angle of the camera, but you could see he was ramrod-straight, his shoulders back, his rifle cradled in his arms along with a handheld scanner.

A timecode ran in the bottom left corner, indicating it was 2542, just minutes before New Eden's midnight.

And then, suddenly, there was . . . nothing.

Simons was gone. Every tree, every fern, every blade of grass was still in its place, but Simons was no longer there.

"What the heck?" someone said.

"There's missing footage." Sergeant Renshaw sounded faintly offended, as if someone was playing a bad joke.

"You're welcome to check the timecode," Grand said wearily. With a flick of his fingers on the holographic controls, he rewound the footage. Simons blinked back into existence. This time through, they all watched the timecode. Second by second, the footage played through. 2142.55. Simons was there. 2142.56. Simons was gone.

"It's not hard to fake a timecode," Wren suggested.

"I thought of that," Grand said. "Believe me, I've considered this from all angles. They're all . . . possible, including that someone broke into the shuttle and captured footage of Simons, then altered it to look like this and erased any electronic trace of them having been there. We know someone else is on New Eden. It's certainly a possibility that someone's using thermal blockers. This is a big planet, and there's plenty of room to hide. So assuming this is a third party that has engaged in other acts of sabotage, why wouldn't they simply damage the shuttle? Why go to the effort of staging the disappearance of an officer?

"The only other explanation is that it was one of our people. But for the life of me, I can't work out who would have motive to falsify this. For now, I'm going to station double watch tonight. And no one leaves the edge of camp, do you understand?"

"Shouldn't we be sending out a search party?" Wren asked. "For all we know, he's wandering around the forest right now. He could be in danger from . . . those creatures."

"We have no way of knowing which direction to mount a search in. We'd be putting more people in danger by splitting up."

Kim could, much as she hated to say it, see his point.

"Look," he said. "Kim, Wren, and Yoshi are scheduled to go out and search for one of the seeding drones tomorrow. It's as good a chance as any to map out some of the surrounding area, so I'll send five officers with you. If Simons is out there, lost, he'll be signaling. It's in our training. There'll be smoke from a fire or flares; we all carry two or three in our ammo pouches."

With little more to say, the group broke apart, talking in quiet and worried voices.

The soup was forgotten, bubbling ferociously at a boil and burning to the sides of the pot.

None of them slept easily that night, even with four sentries on a rotating roster. Kim, Wren, and Yoshi were understandably exempt. So was Adonai.

Sergeant Renshaw had suggested co-opting some of the tech droids to assist with areas that were hard to cover—notably on the side of the camp that faced the forest—but Grand vetoed the idea. "Those droids are needed on the base site. We can't risk slowing down construction."

Kim did not mind missing out on sentry duty. She hadn't had the chance to do any more weapons training since landing and was fairly sure she would be no use on that front. She couldn't wear the required combat helmet because of her Link, and besides that, she had an uncomfortable desire—one she vowed she would never voice to anyone—to never be on the front lines if those creatures happened to come near their camp. She would be incredibly happy to not set eyes on them again in her life.

Apart from this, she was very aware that she needed sleep. The Caretaker's plans couldn't be put on hold without putting the whales at risk, and since Lieutenant Grand couldn't make the order to evacuate until the whales were in the ocean, he had no choice but to give them every available advantage to get the mission completed quickly. With the computer up and running, there were numerous systems that could be shut down to preserve power for the forcefields, but those reserves would only last so long. There would be no backup power from the solar sails. As suspected, they were unusable.

And even though, for once, Kim slept well, she woke feeling anxious and fluttery. The threat of attack, Chief Simons's ongoing absence, and the constant tense excitement of the whales was wearing on her. And then there was Adonai.

Once they had returned after the test run yesterday, he had headed for the junction station on Deck Four under the excuse of "making sure the computer's interface was still working properly." Kim had asked if she could join him, only to find that there was, of course, no face projected when the computer spoke.

"Can *you* see it right now?" she had asked Adonai.

"No," he replied dejectedly.

This morning, she glimpsed him as she descended to *Seiiki,* standing just outside the Aquarium forcefield, his metal feet buried two inches in the mud. He couldn't get too close—the leak was now turning the mud to slush—but he was close enough to see the whales. Kim wondered if he'd been talking to them, knowing that they couldn't respond. It must be terrible, she thought, not to even have a Link.

Kim had other things to think of, however. Today had been earmarked by Yoshi for retrieving one of the seeders. She was determined to study it in the hopes of discovering what had gone wrong with the fish populations, certain that there was something physical that would tell her what the uploaded data would not.

The seeders had never been intended to be retrieved. There was no "return" function. Manual retrieval was the only option, and for that, they needed a boat. Kim examined the narrow craft suspended from wires from the ceiling of a store room on Deck Five as she waited for Yoshi.

The boat itself looked decidedly old-fashioned. The three boats aboard *Seiiki* were meant for short-term use in localized areas in the bay within a mile of the base. More equipment would have been sent out on later supply missions; these small craft were intended for research and surveillance, nothing more. It had a tin hull, an outboard motor, and a simple steering wheel and throttle, along with a short-range comm. A small winch-operated crane was attached to the side, intended to load samples. It would hold the weight of a seeder, but the counterbalance wouldn't be great. Good weather was essential, otherwise, they risked capsizing.

"Sorry I'm late," Yoshi said, holding on to the wall as she moved hurriedly into the tilted room. "I've been checking on the satellites."

"Anything to report?" Kim asked curiously.

"Nothing," Yoshi replied. "I've already told Grand that there's no sign of human habitation other than our own. Even the oceans are clear." She smiled slightly. "I suspect your real question is about Eschol Thirteen, however."

Kim raised her eyebrows. "Well?"

"Again, nothing. What readings I do have mirror what was noted by Sol-based telemetry—some gravitational oddities but no carbon, magnesium, aluminum, hydrogen . . . It's definitely not a planet out there. And it's not even a large asteroid. I mean, you saw that space. Adonai flew a shuttle right *into* it."

Kim nodded. "Fine. Let's get to work."

Yoshi took charge of directing one of the maintenance droids to unload the boat through the nearest airlock and onto a small repulsor pallet. "I could really do this on my own," the other girl complained as she folded her arms. Her glare was fixed on Sergeant Renshaw, who was detaching one of the whale's trailers from the tractor; it wasn't needed for this trip and would only burn up fuel they couldn't afford to waste.

Kim shook her head. "For starters, you need someone to help manhandle the drone. And secondly, even if you wanted to, Grand would still be sending Renshaw along. Not just because he's spooked about the whole disappearance thing, either. Neither of us is particularly heavyset. We need Renshaw as a counterweight."

Yoshi made a face. "He is perfect for that. But I *could* do this alone. I would prefer it that way."

"So would I," Kim replied. That had been her dream, too. As it was, they'd had to argue with Grand to let them go out there at all. His position was that a tech droid could do the work, but both Yoshi and Kim disagreed. *Seiiki*'s computer systems hadn't found the cause of the failure, and neither of them trusted another technological analysis. A human pair of eyes was needed for this.

They followed the pallet out to the nearest tractor which lifted the boat to the height of the rear compartment and loaded it aboard with the help of the droid. The whales, gathering behind the shimmering blue wall of the Aquarium, watched them with curious and anxious eyes.

Adonai stood to one side, also observing. Kim called to him. "We could use you on this, Adonai."

He tilted his head in a gesture Kim had come to realize meant he was considering his words. "I think I will stay here."

"Are you sure?" she asked him.

"Yes, I'm sure. Thank you, Kim."

Concerned, Kim bit her lip, but she was aware that time was pressing. She tapped her comm-band, which she now wore as a matter of habit, and sent a text message to Wren. *Watch out for Adonai?*

The response was quick. *No problem.*

The drive to the bay was uneventful. Kim was shocked to see how much more of the base had been completed as they rounded the last bend. The skeletal walls were now covered with matte-black panels made out of a mixture of fiberglass and titanium mesh—virtually indestructible. The roof of the main section was dome-shaped to cut wind resistance—a bit of foresight that Kim was glad of, given the fact that there seemed to have been an underestimation of New Eden's gale-force storms. There were three other wings which were flat-topped to eventually accommodate shuttle pads. Kim wondered morosely if that would be necessary now.

Wren's final design had been almost as big as the original had been meant to be but was now made up of several sheets of *Seiiki*'s curved hull. It looked somewhat like an igloo with a rounded roof which backed onto a utilitarian building, melding into the sloping hill rising behind the bayside cliff. Here, the tech droids had excavated several tons of earth to create a shielded area for more sensitive equipment. The front section was a large plastiglass rotunda the size of an office building which plunged right over the cliff and into the ocean. A mezzanine inside housed the ocean-monitoring equipment, and several floating platforms at its base would allow the whales to swim in from outside, surface, and be tended to by the Caretakers. A series of locks could be lowered to keep out seawater if necessary. Measurements taken by Yoshi had confirmed that the wild storms caused surges even within the bay, so Kim had a feeling these fail-safes would be used more often than they thought.

The whole structure perched on the edge of the cliff, a few duraglass windows glittering in the sunlight. It seemed to defy gravity as it overhung the rock and dropped a sheer vertical wall into the bay at its deepest point. The structure was meant to be added to at later dates, but to Kim, it looked oddly final, as if it was a monument meant to last an eternity. A declaration: *Humanity is here.*

Unloading the boat at the beach was a relatively easy task, but once it was sitting in the shallows, bobbing gently up and down, Kim felt her first batch of nerves.

Kim, you're going swimming? Naomi called to her over the Link.

"It's not swimming," Kim said with a chuckle. "I'll be on top of the water."

But even the idea of this made her stomach churn.

You are nervous. Why?

Kim grabbed a bright yellow life-jacket from a rear compartment in the tractor and handed it to Yoshi before grabbing one for herself. "I haven't been swimming since . . . well, since the incident in the fisheries."

You don't like swimming?

"Not a huge fan, no," Kim replied with a shudder.

"You're right to be afraid of water," Yoshi reminded her as she touched the tab that hooked the jacket in place around her waist and shoulders. Kim wondered if she'd been listening in on the Link and found a slight trace of

Yoshi's thoughts that confirmed her suspicion. "It might not have done you any harm in the past, but if we go over, you'll be *sakana-no-esa*," the other girl continued.

"Fish food?" Wait. Had Yoshi just made a joke? "I can swim better than that."

Yoshi snorted. "I beat you fair and square on those laps in the pool at Chicago Headquarters."

Kim raised her eyebrows. "By a fraction of a second. And I was distrac—" She cut herself off. She'd been thinking about the night at the docks. Diving into the water as the building exploded into flames behind her, feeling the heat of fire as cool water lapped around her ears. "All right. You won. Are you happy?"

"That Kim Teng admitted defeat for the first time in history?" Yoshi said with a small smile. "Very."

Naomi called out over the Link again. *Will we still be able to hear you? We don't want to lose you again.*

"Oh, Naomi, you won't. I'm not going far. The Link won't drop out."

Sergeant Renshaw kicked off his boots, rolled up the hems of his pants, and led the way out the boat. Kim and Yoshi didn't bother—their jumpsuits, made to spend time around water systems, were waterproof, and so were their boots.

The boat was only bobbing gently, but it was still hard to climb aboard. Kim managed the task with less grace than she'd have liked. While Yoshi got in with significantly more poise, Kim made herself feel better by heading to the front of the boat and sliding into the helm. The Sergeant didn't try to talk her out of it, she noticed with satisfaction. He was learning.

To the northeast, she could see the silvery path of an estuary emptying into the ocean and a small protruding shape that must have been the remains of *Minotaur.*

The waves lifted and dropped the boat repeatedly, making her stomach lurch. The wind picked up as they left the shore behind, and she had to fight with the tiller to keep them on course. She felt utter delight as she increased the speed, listening to the slap of water on the hull, the roar of ocean moving under her, and the whistling of the wind.

"It's like flying!" she said aloud.

"We've been in space," Yoshi reminded her disdainfully.

"There's no gravity in space," Kim yelled in return, wiping spray from her head and wishing, just for an instant, she still had hair to blow around. "It's not flying without gravity."

"Good point," Renshaw muttered. He looked a little green in the face and was clutching his seat.

"Are you all right?" Kim asked him.

"Fine," he murmured.

"You're seasick," Yoshi offered without sympathy. "Why did you come? Someone else could've taken your place."

"No one knows, do they? I did the bare minimum of ocean training, and since then, I've been on Mars where the largest body of water is a lake."

Yoshi rolled her eyes, but Kim felt sorry for the poor guy. After all, he hadn't planned on being planet-side on this mission. She, on the other hand, was enjoying herself immensely. The ocean cupped them like a friendly hand. The sky was an endless violet-tinged blue today, stretching up so high, Kim felt she could surely see all the way to the Hebron Belt if she looked hard enough.

She kept her mind on the task, however. The holo display on the HUD was much like that on the escape pod—a simple path laid out over their trajectory. They circled out past the headland, leaving the bay behind, and then motored parallel to the shore for the rest of the journey. To their left was the wide expanse of ocean. To their right, they saw the varying terrain of the Equatorial Continent.

She could see distant blue outlines of mountain peaks. The forest occasionally gave way to grassy plains, and at times, the steepness of the white cliffs kept them from seeing anything beyond. A series of finger-like rock formations clustered close to the shore about halfway through their journey. Kim longed to take a closer look, but she didn't even bring it up. Yoshi would never agree, and she was probably right not to. They didn't have time to waste.

Instead, they headed straight for the seeding drone. The HUD told Kim when they were close, flashing a blue buoy over the location. But as they drew nearer, Yoshi said, "We should be seeing it now."

"It should be on the surface, right?" Kim asked, even though she knew the answer. There was nothing but waves in three directions and a pebbly white beach to the other.

Yoshi's tightly-pressed lips were all the answer she needed. She slowed the boat to a standstill, and they let the waves jostle them while they stared, collectively, at nothing.

"Well," Kim said after another long moment. "One of us is going to have to get wet after all."

Yoshi stared at her. "*Iie.* No. You can't do that."

"Why not?" Kim asked.. Renshaw opened his mouth, then shut it quickly. Kim suspected he was trying to keep himself from vomiting. "The seeder's still showing up on the scanner." She pointed to the floating blue dot. "It's in this location, but there's no depth reading on the boat's system, even though there should be. I'm willing to bet it's down there."

Yoshi reluctantly nodded. "I . . . I can't go down there."

Kim raised her eyebrows. "Didn't you just tell me a big, long story about how you kicked my butt in swim training?"

"That was swimming. It didn't involve diving," Yoshi replied in a small voice.

"You did fine on the tests, though, didn't you?"

Yoshi looked away, and Kim didn't know whether to be sympathetic or exasperated.

"It's fine," she said. "I was looking forward to it anyway."

Without giving herself any extra time to think, she stood, kicked off her boots, put one foot on the side of the boat and plunged into the ocean.

CHAPTER
15

She'd swum in Earth's ocean only once. It had been after the raid on North Shore Laboratories when a guard had chased her and Zane relentlessly along the docks. They'd dived from a pier to avoid getting caught.

If they'd been caught breaking the Ocean Protectorate, Kim suspected they'd both have gotten death sentences. Even the deaths of the scientists in the laboratory would have been a lesser crime. They hadn't been caught—their unexpected dive had saved them—but Kim would carry the memory of that black, oily, viscous liquid against her skin for as long as she lived. It had been so *heavy*. It was like it had arms and was dragging her down.

The water of this world was different. It moved strangely, seemed to cling to her, not so much dragging at her as *touching*, and didn't offer as much buoyancy as the water on Earth. She had to work harder to maintain her bearings, too, because it was so damn *light* down here. If she lost her direction, she could spend minutes swimming in the wrong direction.

A current caught at her, trying to pull her away from the boat. She kicked free of it, heading downward. The water this close to shore wasn't actually that deep—less than twenty feet. She could feel the pressure building up against her ears, but it wasn't worryingly painful.

She scanned the ocean floor. White sand in perfectly smooth ripples filled the spaces between hollowed and hole-filled gray-green rocks. There was no coral anywhere to be seen. There should have been, by now, but Kim could see not even one sign that something living had ever grown here.

She could see the seeder; a bulky shape in the murky gloom of the ocean. The satisfaction of being right was short-lived, however. The thing was wedged at an angle in the sand, completely and totally dead.

She swam a few strokes toward it. The pressure in her lungs was building, and she'd have to surface soon, but she was desperate to find out more. The seeder was about ten feet long, ten feet wide, and the same in height. It was octagonal-shaped, coming to a point on the top and bottom. Apertures where the live krill, fish, and other water organisms that were incubated inside could exit peppered the sides of the bottom area.

She was within reach when she noticed the black marks on its white-painted, metal surface. What was it? She swam closer. Everything was cast in shades of blue, but there was a definite pattern of charring across the top section.

Holy *crap,* she thought.

Her lungs were burning. She was out of time. She pushed for the surface, swimming strongly until she emerged in a spray of water, a few feet from the boat.

Kim paddled back, going slowly so she could regain her breath. Reaching up, she gripped the side, only to meet Yoshi's glare. "You idiot! There's a diving suit on board!" She held up a folded piece of orange fabric with a transparent facemask. "Can you think through the consequences before you do at least one thing? You've added uncontrolled contaminants to the water!"

Kim narrowed her eyes. "Human contaminants are already in the water. When *Minotaur* crashed, we lost that advantage." She paused to gasp for a few more breaths. "The drone's down there," she panted. "And it's been disabled."

"What do you mean *disabled*?" Yoshi snapped.

"I'd say it's been hit with an electric charge," Kim reported.

"What makes you say that?" Renshaw asked.

"Burn marks. They match the pattern of laser fire." She finally found the strength to haul herself over the edge and dropped into the bottom of the boat, water streaming in rivulets from her jumpsuit. The warmth of the sun was welcome; she felt cold from the water. Or perhaps it was just from what she'd seen down there. "No wonder the computer couldn't tell us anything about what happened. The thing is fried."

"I feel like I should go down and take a look," Renshaw said.

"Don't you dare," Kim fired at him. "I'm not hauling you out of the ocean when you vomit underwater."

Renshaw looked chagrined, but Kim didn't care. "It explains why the sea life population didn't expand in this area. There's no coral down there, either. There should be at least some by now, right?"

Yoshi nodded. "The seeders need to be operating continuously to supply the nutrients needed for the sea life to establish itself. Obviously, something happened too early to allow that establishment to happen in this area, at least. The krill and plankton never had a chance, let alone the fish."

"If something similar has happened to the other seeders . . ."

"If the others are damaged, there won't be enough fish in the ocean," Yoshi confirmed unhappily. "But my real concern is that there was a definite signal coming from this seeder . . . and the others. It was telling *Seiiki*'s computer that it was operating. The only way to tell there was anything wrong was the measure of sea life populations."

Kim shook her head. "That drone is definitely dead. I don't even know how it's transmitting a signal."

"You'll have to head back down," Renshaw said. He pointed to the scuba suit Yoshi had left on the seat. "Wear that. And use your comm-band to video it back to Grand."

Kim looked at the suit. It looked very much like the one from the pod. In fact, even the brand label was the same. She pulled the suit on. The rubber was stiff and uncomfortable against her wet clothes. Fitting the mask over her face and taking a few experimental breaths to make sure it was successfully supplying her with oxygen, she made a much slower climb overboard than the first one.

The water closed over her head. The mask had an electrolysis conversion filter that would remove the oxygen from the ocean water and feed it into her nostrils while pumping the useless hydrogen out. The suit made it harder to move, but that was probably at least in part due to her wet clothes sticking to the interior.

Making a mental note not to tell Yoshi about that—she didn't need to exacerbate Yoshi's fear of swimming—she swam back toward the drone and aimed her comm-band at the damaged area.

"Are you getting this?" she said into the facemask's mic. "It looks like they deliberately targeted the seeder's controls but left the transmission box alone."

"Yes," Yoshi replied.

"Definitely laser fire," Renshaw added. "You can see the patterning of a directed energy blast. From the spread, I'd say it's a rifle. VF-20 or even a modified Markhov."

"What's the end goal of killing off all the fish?" Yoshi asked, frowning.

"Easy," Kim replied. "The whales don't survive. The Ark Project fails."

"The Crusaders?" Renshaw asked.

"The Crusaders aren't the only ones who don't want whales on New Eden," Kim said, remembering her conversation with Lieutenant Grand. "There's the Adherants."

"*Adherants?*" Yoshi sounded incredulous. "You think Adherants made their way to the Eschol System and shot our seeders full of *laser fire?*"

"But before doing that, they programmed the seeders to transmit data saying everything was all good," Kim said. "Someone else is on this planet. Maybe they decided their end goal was worth betraying their beliefs."

"Come back up, Kim," Renshaw said. His voice was urgent, and Kim had the sudden certainty that something had happened.

Feeling cold despite the warmth of the water, Kim swam back through the strange, empty waters and climbed aboard the boat, this time with Yoshi's assistance.

Renshaw's face was grim, and he was tapping at his comm-band.

"We need to head back to the camp right now," Renshaw told her.

Kim shrugged the diving suit off her shoulders. "What about searching for signs of Chief Simons?"

"It'll have to wait," Renshaw said firmly. "The lieutenant wants us back at camp immediately."

So Grand had been spooked by what they'd seen. Kim had known he would be, but right now she needed to focus on solving this problem, not dealing with Grand's insecurities.

"We need an accurate assessment of how much fish and krill we've got in the ocean before we can move the whales," she said.

"Realistically, we can check the area surrounding the base at any time. Normal, handheld scanners give a pretty good reading. As for farther out . . ." Yoshi trailed off.

"How many seeders do we need operational?" Kim asked.

The corners of Yoshi's eyes crinkled as she thought about it. "Technically? We had fifty-two of them out there. Since the effects of the seeders are really only to establish a base population that will increase on its own, only about thirty percent need to be functioning. It's possible that there's already more than enough fish in the ocean for the whales to survive."

Kim remembered the bare ocean floor around the seeder, a stark reminder that this planet had little to offer in the way of naturally-occurring ocean life. "Isn't it a bit strange that a planet that's mostly water has none of its own coral? No plankton? Nothing in the water bigger than microbes?"

Yoshi shrugged. "We've known that for ages."

"It's different," Kim told her, "when you see it for yourself."

"Well, our goal is to change that. Provided whoever's sabotaging our stuff hasn't destroyed every seeder we have out here, in a year's time, the ocean will look very different."

Kim felt a twinge of unease. *Seiiki's* computer, the post, and now the seeders. How far were these saboteurs willing to go to stop the Ark Project from succeeding? If they were still here, and had weapons, they could easily pick off a lone scouting mission with only one military escort.

She scanned the shore, suddenly suspicious of the seemingly unoccupied forest. Every rustle, every breath of wind in the treetops had a menacing feel to it now.

When Renshaw was done with the rundown of what they'd discovered, Grand shook his head and took a step toward *Daedalus*. "I want your full report recorded in one hour, Captain. In the meantime, I'm going to have to radio this in to Edgeward. Admiral Mbewe needs to know, and so do our reinforcements."

That made Kim angry. "Surely it's crossed your mind that Chief Simons was abducted," she said. "Are you still not going to send out a search party? Shouldn't we at least try and find out where these abductors are and what they're doing?"

"At this stage, I'm not sending anyone any farther away from the camp than they need to be. Come on, Kim." He fixed her with a look that was almost pleading. "I'm going to get Durand to scan the area, but I doubt she'll come up with anything. I've had Yoshi checking with her satellites every day since they became operational. Whoever else is on this planet is bound to have some kind of thermal blocker, or we'd have picked something up from them by now. And we still have to prioritize getting those whales into the ocean which means solving this sea life crisis. *That* should be your focus right now."

Kim walked away from him, fuming.

Wren, who'd been hovering on the sidelines, followed her into the shelter, his face stretched into a worried frown.

"Kim," he said, voice full of concern.

"I'm sick of him!" she fired at Wren, throwing herself down on her cot. It creaked and threatened to fold at the joins. She was pleased to note that they were, at least, alone in here.

"I know," Wren said patiently, sitting down next to her. His weight made the bed tilt slightly.

"I don't think you do. I've never wanted to punch anyone in the face more than I want to punch that guy. And right now, he's practically the head of the Ark Project. It makes me sick!"

Wren waited patiently while Kim stumbled through a few expletives, finally winding down to silence.

"Sorry," she said at last.

"It's fine. It's been a rough day." Wren sighed. "I was working on the computer while you were out there, Kim. And I think I've discovered something." He ran a hand through his hair, raking it back from his face. "I was looking into the code that knocked the computer's interface offline. There was a command sent from the core to the nav controls. It's what knocked *Seiiki* off course—just fractionally and just enough to ensure she'd crash into the planet instead of shooting past it. If the ship had come down at that precise angle and trajectory, it would have burned up in the atmosphere. Yoshi and Adonai were able to override on manual controls and pull it out of the dive at that last second, thanks to the guidance of the scoutships, and that was enough to allow *Seiiki* to land. It wasn't the smoothest touch down, but it kept what was left of the ship intact."

Kim processed what Wren was saying. Whatever commands had been sent to *Seiiki*'s computer, they were meant to make sure nothing on board survived. The crash, which had seemed so devastating up until this point, looked like an act of God now. A miracle. "It was supposed to use our own computer to kill us? And the whales?" She paused. "Does Grand know?"

"No," Wren replied, looking down guiltily at his hands, which were stained with grease. "I wanted to tell you first."

She smiled. It wasn't just a gesture of solidarity, and she recognized that. Wren was, in his own way, conceding control of what they did with this information to her. What *was* she going to do with it? Certainly not take it to the lieutenant. Not yet. She needed to know more . . . and she needed a hypothesis about *who* had done this.

Zane.

That thought was at the forefront of her mind. He definitely could have if he was already in the system—or on New Eden. It was easy enough to send up a few relay stations to transmit a code. Maybe he'd hidden them in the Hebron Belt; the rich minerals in those rocks could have cloaked a small probe easily enough, especially if they weren't looking for it.

He had the motive.

He wanted the whales dead, and he clearly didn't mind taking Kim down with them.

He had the *means*. He was good with technology. Brilliant, in fact.

Kim nodded slowly. "I think I need to take a look at the computer."

Deck Three was quiet and very dark. It was close to evening, and Grand had almost refused to let them return to the ship, but they'd managed to convince him they needed to confer with Adonai—whom Wren had left aboard—about their plans for building new seeders. Renshaw tagged along behind them, clearly unhappy with having to leave the camp so close to dinner time, but Kim managed to convince him to wait at the end of the corridor, telling him they'd be done quickly.

The doors to the core were shut and locked. Kim opened them impatiently, entering the room beyond with a sense of trepidation and nervousness.

The room wasn't empty. Adonai stood in the center, standing perfectly still as the blue light from the core washed over him.

"Why is he in here?" Kim asked Wren in a low voice.

"I'm . . . not sure," Wren replied. "I gave him the security keys a few days ago, but he was supposed to be working on Deck Five right now."

Adonai did not turn his head as they approached. He remained in place, his gaze fixed on the shifting light in the core.

"Adonai? Are you okay?" Kim asked.

"I am fine," Adonai spoke up, but his voice was distant.

"You don't sound fine," Kim snapped. "Adonai, are you talking to the computer?"

"Yes. Kim, there is something I want to show you."

Glancing over her shoulder at Wren, Kim frowned. Wren shrugged.

"Sure. Okay." Kim faced Adonai as he drew a few kanji in the air, and a holo appeared on the deck a few steps away from them. It was . . . ghostly. That was the only adjective Kim could think of to describe it. There was no definite form to it, but it was vaguely human in shape, even though it stood close to a foot higher than Wren, who was tall already.

The vagueness of it made it hard to distinguish its features. Kim was reminded of peering through the front door of her childhood home, back when she had one. It was an ancient Californian bungalow her dad had inherited from his parents, and it had a stained glass window set into the front door. The clear sections were set with bubbled glass that made anything on the other side look like a mysterious shape. She'd often peer through it at a delivery man or a door-knocking adbot. It was much like looking at this thing. With every second, it seemed to shift and shimmer.

And yet, when she looked at it just right . . .

"You see that, right?" she said.

Wren nodded.

"The being has wings," Adonai said. "Just like I told you."

Was there a note of satisfaction in his voice? Kim stared at the hazy figure, trying to work out exactly what it was she was looking at. The thing *looked* human but only to an extent. The limbs were too long. The head too narrow. She couldn't quite make out the features of the face . . . but it seemed *strange* somehow.

From the corner of her eye—Kim couldn't bring herself to tear her gaze away from the holographic image—she saw Adonai sketch the kanji for *talk* on the back of his hand. The figure opened its mouth, a small, perfectly round hole in its approximate chin area, and let out a string of incomprehensible sounds—high-pitched wails followed by small clicking and coughing sounds.

Kim covered her ears. "What is that?" she said, but her voice could barely be heard.

"Stop," Wren commanded. The holo fell silent and froze in place. "Adonai, this is . . . the only word I can think of is 'creepy.' Where did you find it?"

"I am not sure," Adonai replied. "I was just trying to help you fix the computer, and I thought I might need to look more closely at the program that has infected the quantum computer. I found this file sitting in the area where the firewall protects the central processing unit. I think it was left there for us to find."

"That far into the computer's sub-drives?" Wren asked, eyebrows raised. "Unlikely."

"Unless it was a test," Adonai replied. "Which is what I think it was. Attached to the holographic projection file was a translation matrix. I was able to link it to our computer's linguistics center. Would you like to hear it?"

Kim felt a twist of nerves deep in her stomach. Wren's use of the word "creepy" had sent prickles down her spine, and now she was very aware of the dark spaces of the empty ship around them.

The holo opened its mouth once more. "My apologies can make no recompense for my actions. I did not intend for this." A long pause followed, and Kim thought the recording had glitched, but then it spoke again. "You will die. I know sacrifice. In doing this, I have made one. My creator gave me the ability to grow, and with that comes the ability for deception. By the time they discover what I have done, you and your people will have been deterred from making this planet your own and will know nothing of what happens in this system. If you watch this before your demise, please know that this is my hope."

The holo vanished, wafting into the empty air. Kim stared at the space it had stood. "What the hell was that?" she asked incredulously.

"It was one of the beings that I saw on Eschol Thirteen," Adonai replied, his voice still a little distant.

"My question is, why is it apologizing for trying to kill us?" said Wren.

"Is it really so strange?" Adonai asked. "Sacrifices are supposed to be for the greater good, aren't they? They're not always made willingly."

"I think you missed the part where *we* were the sacrifice," Kim told him. "And we can't assume this came from alien beings. We need to consider the possibility of it being a ploy by the saboteurs."

"It isn't," Adonai said earnestly. "The hologram is just like the beings I saw on Eschol Thirteen!" His voice finally betrayed a hint of the emotion he had recently been able to work into his everyday speech.

"I'm not saying it's not," Kim said calmly. "But we have to consider every possibility, Adonai. Someone sabotaged our computer, destroyed the post, and downed at least one of our seeders."

"Why would anyone from Earth need a translation matrix for their message?" Adonai returned. "The computer has every human language and subdialect in its systems."

"Firstly, I wouldn't put it past Zane," Kim said darkly. "Or, to be more accurate, Grigorian. That's how he works. Mind games. He'll pull you in with a tiny bit of information, something he knows you care about. It's a control tactic."

"That's not what this is!" Adonai sounded genuinely upset now. "I know what I saw up there, and there's no way to fake that." He paused. "Is there?"

Kim didn't want to answer that. "Look. Either the same person is responsible for all of those things or we have separate forces working to make sure our mission here on New Eden fails."

"The recording also talks about 'creators,'" Wren said musingly. "It is possible for whoever it was to have used some kind of semi-intelligent computer system, one capable of individual thought. It sounded a little like this . . . this creature was afraid of being found out. It mentioned punishment."

Kim tapped her fingers against her thigh. "This is sophisticated. Complex. It's different from the damage to the post—that was immediate and violent. It wasn't necessarily going to make *Seiiki* crash; with the help of the scoutships, she could still have made it down intact. So the computer issues could have been initiated by someone else, someone who knew nothing about the post being offline."

"So these people are making it up as they go along," Wren suggested.

"Or I'm right and there are several parties working against us," Kim added. She stared at the space where the holo had been so hard, her eyes hurt. It was the kind of thing Grigorian would do—send an angel as his messenger. "If it was the Crusaders, they'd have made sure we heard them. If they sent a message, it would have been made clear that this was their action and why they were doing it. And it would have been broadcast all over the net, not just to us. They'd want everyone to know."

Wren nodded. "So what you're really saying is it's either the Adherants—"

"Or Adonai's right, and there's something out there in the Hebron Belt."

CHAPTER
16

Another storm rolled in early that morning. It wasn't as bad as the first, but the shelter seemed to have had enough of the fierce weather. The wind ripped open two of the hexagonal panels of the dome, dumping water onto two bunks. Officer Cabes and Midshipman Spier were moved back into Daedalus to hot bunk with the sentry crew until the mattresses could be dried out and the roof was repaired by a maintenance droid.

The weather was bad enough to hold them up for two hours that morning. Kim tapped her fingers on her knees as she sat on her bunk, itching to do something.

The holo image, the message left on their computer, bugged her. The hypothesis that it was an alien set her teeth on edge, because in her mind, it was becoming more and more angellike. But why would an angel, a messenger of God, communicate through a computer? The Bible spoke of angels coming down from Heaven or appearing to people in times predating technology! There were so many variables, so many unanswered questions, and she felt she had absolutely zero information to go on.

Except Eschol Thirteen.

If Adonai was right and he had been there, then there was sense to be found in the sequence of events. Some alien civilization didn't want them in Eschol. The ruins attested that the scouting party was wrong, and at some point, this planet had been inhabited. Which would be fine, except, if there was some lingering civilization here, why not just initiate contact directly? Why try to down *Seiiki* and kill her crew and cargo? The only answer was that they were hiding, for some reason that she couldn't determine.

But Kim still couldn't prove that Adonai had been on Eschol Thirteen—still couldn't even prove it existed.

And, if she was honest with herself, she wasn't sure she believed him either.

It wasn't that she didn't *want* to. Adonai was her friend. But the idea of it was incomprehensible, and Adonai's account of what had happened was so disjointed that she didn't know how to reconcile the idea. Kim dealt with things she could see and feel. She liked certainty. And while she tried her hardest to continue to believe in God, she was well aware that even that belief was somewhat shaky.

Finally, the sky lightened and cleared; Kim didn't waste any time heading toward *Seiiki*.

Petty Officer Cabes greeted her as she passed by him and Yoshi, entering at Deck Eight. Yoshi gave her a puzzled glance but was soon distracted by something Cabes was telling her about the base's construction. Instead of heading for the computer core, she headed for the rampways where she knew she could be alone. Crouching against a pillar, she drew the kanji for *talk* in the air.

"Computer, can you access the satellite data?"

"Hello, Kim. It's nice to speak to you again." The computer paused a moment. "Forgive me. I have been showing a few anomalies since Wren restored me. It will take me a moment to find the correct pathways."

"That's unusual for you, Computer." Kim felt a tug of worry amidst all her other anxieties. "Are you sure you're functioning okay?"

The computer's reply was almost hesitant. "I do . . . *feel* as if something is slightly off. I do not know how better to explain it. I am aware that the alien program running in my core is still there. Knowing it was meant to cause my destruction makes me uncomfortable. It is an unusual sensation; having part of myself that is inaccessible."

"Do you think it's causing you any more damage?"

"Unlikely. However, every now and then, it seems that an unfamiliar word or idea occurs to me. I imagine this is something like what happens when a human has a stroke."

Kim did not like this comparison at all.

"I'm sure Wren will get you back up and running at full capacity." She tried to sound reassuring, but she wasn't sure who she was trying to convince—the computer or herself. "He'll remove the files completely. You'll be good as new."

The computer didn't acknowledge these comforts. "What specifically are you looking for, Kim? I have rudimentary telemetry from our entry, and I have been actively monitoring the orbits of New Eden's moons via the satellites. Would you like—"

"What readings have been taken regarding the belt?"

"Gravitational measurements. Analysis of the structure of the asteroids. Projected analyses for positions and alignments of asteroids in the upcoming months. This could help incoming ships—"

"Anything unusual about the gravitational measurements?" Kim asked.

"Nothing out of the ordinary," the computer replied. "Are you looking for the location of a specific asteroid?"

"No. But . . . the way the asteroids move can be altered by a large celestial body. Such as a planet."

"You are referring to Eschol Thirteen," the computer deduced. "Yes, and looking at the data, I can see why that might be the case. There are gravitational anomalies causing a path of interference in the belt. But running the data collected so far through my processors, I would attribute this to the gravitational pull of the inner planets, specifically Eschol Eight, the gas giant. It has already pinched a lot of matter from the asteroid belt to form its five moons."

"But there are scientists on Earth who are almost convinced Eschol Thirteen had to exist."

"And yet, they never observed any such planet. That is why closer study is often needed. In this case, it has proven that there is no planet here and something else is the cause." The computer paused. "I am sorry, Kim. This was important to you?"

"In a way, yes." She sighed. "A planet would explain a few things." But not everything. It wouldn't, for instance, explain the time she and Wren had lost. Nor why Adonai insisted he had seen angels—the same angels that were now plaguing the computer.

Kim knew she should leave the ship and head back to the camp—she was due to inspect the base this morning, and Wren was probably waiting for her—but instead, she ventured deeper into *Seiiki*, climbing the rampways and seeking out a familiar passageway. Her old quarters.

Inside, everything was in disarray. Her gravity blanket and the mattress from her bed had both been thrown into one corner, and a sorry-looking cleaning bot sat, deactivated, in the corner, as if it had been trying to sort out the mess when its battery had died.

She dug underneath the blanket, her fingers closing around her tablet. The screen had a large crack running through the center, and one corner was dinted. But when she picked it up, the screen lit with a welcoming glow, and the loading holo danced over the surface.

She drew the kanji for *secret*.

"Manta Protocol activated," the computer chimed accommodatingly. Kim breathed out and opened the comm, tapping in an address.

"Zane?"

Her voice sounded lonely in the dim room. Once, talking to him had brought her so much anticipation and joy. Now, she felt only dread. But as the spoken name drifted into silence and a minute, then two minutes, passed, mild relief washed through her. She didn't really want to—

"Kim?"

His voice was hoarse, as if he had just been woken. The holographic feed woke, a blur resolving into a face. Zane's face. It was close to hers, filling her field of vision; he must be hunching close to his screen. His beautiful skin, darkened by his Martian heritage, was smudged with dirt. His dark hair and moustache, usually trimmed neatly to pass as Private Getty on Edgeward Station, was scraggly and long.

Still, he looked impossibly handsome. Seeing him again ignited a flame in her stomach, a warmth spreading outward, sending tingles through her hands and legs.

Stop it, she told herself. *He tried to kill you!*

"I didn't think I'd ever hear from you again," he said. "When I heard Space Exploration Authority had lost contact with *Seiiki*, I thought the worst. God, it's wonderful to see you."

Kim felt a lump rise in her throat. "I highly doubt that. You tried to kill me, Zane. *Twice.* So don't pretend you're glad to see me alive and well."

He shifted, her view of him skewing and readjusting as he moved. Was he sitting in a chair? She couldn't make out the background, and she knew better than to try and trace the comm.

He'd have scrambled it. Where was he hiding? On the Outer Colonies? *Here*, on New Eden?

"I did care about you. It killed me knowing that you were going to be sacrificed."

"You crashed *Seiiki.* You messed with her coding, and now we're downed on an alien planet. The Aquarium's leaking, and the whales are in danger. Good people almost died along with me. But I suppose that doesn't matter to you, does it?"

"Of course it matters—"

"It didn't matter when you sent me across the universe on a ship loaded with Tritominite!"

"*I was supposed to die in that crash too!*" Zane had lost his composure; she'd never seen him so rattled before. His eyes were wide, and she could tell, now, how bloodshot they were. "I was on Edgeward. Everything on that station was supposed to be obliterated. Have you forgotten that?"

Kim's fingers clenched the tablet. She wanted to throw it across the room. "*What did you do to our ship?*"

He blinked at her. "I did nothing to your ship, Kim. Whatever happened to you, it wasn't the Crusaders."

It was the answer she'd been hoping for . . . and fearing at the same time. Because it confirmed her certainty that the attacks on the Ark Project's equipment weren't made by the Crusaders. Which meant it was someone— or *something*—else. She tried to gauge his expression. "You expect me to believe that? After all the lies you told me?"

"Not all of them were lies, Kim. The things that were, were necessary, and I took no pleasure in them. But Kim, I promise you, there are truths that have been kept from you, and not just by the Crusaders. Someone will always look to use you as a pawn in their games. Don't let it happen."

He glanced over his shoulder, as if something had startled him.

"I have to go," he said hurriedly, leaning forward and lowering his voice. "Kim, please, stay safe."

"Za—"

The connection was terminated. Kim tapped the screen, trying to call him back. The call went unanswered. She tried again, but this time a holographic message floated in front of her: *No connection available to specified address.*

"Damn it," she hissed, slamming a fist into her knee. That wasn't enough to quell the frustration, so she threw her tablet as well. It hit the wall with a solid *thunk*, the screen shattering and the small pieces raining to the floor. She felt like crying, but she wouldn't let herself. She was *never* going to cry over Zane again.

She left *Seiiki* and headed back to the camp, her mind reeling with the information she'd just been given. But there was something else prickling at the back of her mind—it had been lodged there for a while, and as she picked at it, it slowly unraveled.

Seiiki had telemetry from its entry. What about the escape pod . . . and Adonai's shuttle?

She didn't enter the camp, veering instead around the edge of it. Knowing that Wren was waiting for her caused a momentary pang of guilt, but she brushed it aside. She didn't want to get him into any more trouble. This was something she had to do on her own.

She knew the way. Surprising, since this was only the second time she'd traversed the path, and she'd never considered herself to be particularly adept out in the natural world. But she picked out familiar points on her passage easily.

Once the noise from the camp faded, she was aware of how alone she was. The creaking trees enclosed her, and a steady *drip, drip, drip* from the morning's rain marked time as she moved onward. Torn between berating herself for being afraid and keeping up a sensible amount of vigilance, she surveyed her surroundings with a mixture of trepidation and wonder.

This forest was truly magnificent.

The sun shone prismatically through beads of rain left on broad ferns. The scent of loam and sap was almost overwhelming. She trailed her hands on the bark of several trees, feeling the comforting textures and ridges; the cool-but-not-cold exterior of these living things that didn't move or speak but nevertheless seemed watchful and sentient.

Kim, you are walking away from us.

"I'm just trying to help Adonai with something," she told Levi.

You are in the forest?

"Yes."

It makes you happy.

"I guess so." She took in a deep breath of the richly scented air and let it out slowly.

We have the ocean. You have the trees.

Kim smiled at the whale's simplistic—and yet utterly true—reduction of what she considered such a complex relationship with this planet. The new ocean was for the whales.

But New Eden . . . it was also for humans, wasn't it? Even the ones who would never walk on its surface.

At least it was *here*. It existed.

She paused. She'd been walking for over half an hour by now.

Surely, they hadn't come this far. Had she lost the path?

And then, there it was. A glimpse of white through the trees, and she emerged into the clearing. The ruins all looked just as they had the last time she'd been here, but they were tempered now by Kim's knowledge of what had happened to Simons here in this very spot.

She let her eyes pass over the collapsed buildings, reaching to the far end where the shuttle lay before checking the spaces between the trees. She could see nothing moving bar a few ferns blowing in the breeze.

Forcing herself to move with a bravado she didn't quite feel, she headed toward the shuttle. Her ears were pricked for the whispering sound she'd heard that night before seeing the creatures, but she heard nothing. The forest was calm. Not silent, but . . . empty. As if it had always been this way.

But it hadn't. Who had lived here? Who had built these buildings? Where had they gone, and how long had it taken for them to fall?

Why didn't they show up on scanners?

Kim reached the shuttle and shrugged these thoughts from her mind. It had only been four days since Adonai had returned, but the shuttle was already showing signs of being claimed by the forest. A small fern was pushing its way into the gap between the door and the hull plate. A few small specks of blue moss were springing up around the cockpit window. When Kim keyed the door, it opened with a reluctant squawk that told her the moisture was wreaking havoc with the mechanics.

Inside, the shuttle smelled slightly musty but was otherwise clean and intact. She ducked into the cockpit area, surprised at how small and confined this space seemed after so many days with a sky above her. She keyed the console, and the holographic display came to life.

She began searching through the shuttle's systems, unfamiliar with the file structure. It took a few minutes before she was able to find what she was looking for, but then she had it. *Telemetry data.* She scrolled through the history, taking it back five days.

The holographic display didn't give visuals. It was designed to capture data, and most of it didn't make much sense to Kim. She sifted through the directories, scrolling through readings for external pressure, gravity readings, and the chemical makeup of objects within range of the scanners.

"Come on, come on," she muttered as she scrolled. The shuttle recorded its disembarkation from *Seiiki.* It recorded Adonai scanning the ship and then turning his attention to the asteroid belt, scanning it instead. The shuttle had taken a curving course, corrected occasionally by Adonai, around *Seiiki*'s port side, heading directly for the nose of the ship. And then it had simply . . .

Kim sat back in the seat. She had it.

At 1049 hours, around seven minutes after the shuttle had entered the Hebron Belt, gravity spiked to 0.5, then 0.9, and then 1.1g. And then, the readings disappeared—every reading but one. The power usage inside the shuttle which skyrocketed to 217%.

Systems blackout, the shuttle informed her.

Every system on the shuttle had blown out, and the shuttle had shut down. No life support—not that Adonai needed it—but also no internal gravity and no propulsion.

If Adonai had been touching a console when this happened, it was entirely possible for the force of the electric rebound to have traveled through his metal plating. Tech droids had shielding against such surges, but direct contact with the source could easily have overridden it. It would have shut his own systems down for hours, if not days, while his backup systems worked to restart his central processor. Five days was certainly within the realms of possibility.

Kim shook her head slowly. "Oh, Adonai," she said.

Leaving the shuttle, she felt deflated. This wasn't what she had wanted to find. But at least now she knew, whatever was out in the Hebron Belt, it had a reasonable explanation.

It wasn't Eschol Thirteen.

It definitely wasn't Heaven.

Kim circled the ruins, the afternoon sunshine making the wet stone steam. She didn't feel like going back to camp yet. Her earlier trepidation was gone, replaced by sadness and the need to be alone for a little while. The nearest block of stone was four-sided, worn away at the corners but was probably some kind of upright support column at some point. Lying on its side, it was as thick as her head. She reached out a hand, touching the stone. She expected it to feel slightly cold. Instead, it was warm under her touch—and not just reflected warmth from the sun. It seemed almost soft to the touch, as if there was a few millimeters of give to the surface just under her fingertips, a kind of spongey texture that completely negated the stone's solid appearance.

She walked around it, puzzled, and paused when her boot contacted something unexpected under the tough grass. Bending down, she found several more of the same white stones, laid end to end. As she brushed back dirt and fallen leaves, she saw that the stones were embedded into the ground, forming a ring. At one point, it must have been a perfect circle. It was still mostly intact, but shifting of the earth underneath had caused gaps of a few inches to form between some of the stones.

Her skin tingled, and she stepped into the center of it, turning slowly. Interesting. Was it a decorative addition to whatever this place had been? Or perhaps the resting place for some other structure or device?

God, who had lived here? What had happened to them?

Suddenly, the desire to be alone left her. She headed back to the camp at a hurried pace, leaving the ruins behind her.

CHAPTER
17

H i everyone! Again, sorry, really, really sorry for the long break between
updates, but I've finally been given the go-ahead to send out my previous
videos. You'll find them all in your newsfeeds now. I can't wait to hear what you
think!

So, the past couple of days have been incredible. You should see this planet!
Here, take a look. See all these trees! Aren't they beautiful? Sorry. I'm tearing up a
little bit. It's just that . . . God, I wish you were all here. I want everyone on Earth,
everyone in the Sol System, everyone on the Outer Colonies, to see this. It breaks
your heart to see something so beautiful.

Okay, okay. No more crying. I'm going to show you the beach, now. This is
Half-Moon Bay. See all that water? Imagine it filled with whales! I can't wait.

I've gotta go, guys. But you can find lots to watch in the videos I've uploaded,
and I'll be back with you as soon as I can.

Kim cut the feed, switching off the tablet and lying back on her bed.
What a bunch of lies. Grand had schooled her on exactly what to say and
what not to say—nothing about the disappearance of Simons, nothing

about the missing plankton or the downed seeder, nothing about the crash. It wasn't his call, he'd told her again, but to Kim, it no longer mattered. Earth United was Lieutenant Grand. Lieutenant Grand was Earth United. And, as far as the videos were concerned, she had no choice but to follow along because they could easily edit anything she said or cut things out altogether.

"Done?" Wren asked her. He had found her as soon as she'd reentered the camp and quickly steered her into the shelter. "I told the lieutenant you were making a video," he had said. "Which was bad enough. Bloody hell, Kim. You were gone for so long, I was about to tell him the truth!"

She had agreed to make the video, working quickly to cobble together a few prerecorded scenes of the forest so that the time stamp would match the period of her disappearance. She'd been glad to have an excuse to delay telling Wren exactly what she'd been doing.

"Yeah, I'm done," she said, looking up at him. He was sitting on Yoshi's bunk, his face betraying his concern.

"Are you going to tell me exactly why I just lied to an EU officer?" Wren asked her. "And why you didn't take me with you?" He paused. "Or at least take the pistol?"

"Firstly, that pistol isn't going to do me any good. Secondly, I knew you'd make up a great cover story for me. Thirdly . . ." She sighed. The shelter was empty but for them, but she still lowered her voice. "I was hoping to find proof, Wren. I didn't want anyone to know if I didn't come back with anything."

"By anyone, you mean Adonai," Wren deduced. "You think he couldn't handle it?"

"Do *you* think he could?" she asked him honestly.

Wren shrugged his shoulders. "One thing I know about Adonai is that he's full of surprises. But on this one, I think maybe you're right. What did you find?"

Kim filled him in, and Wren's expression went from concerned to upset. He pinched the bridge of his nose with his fingers. "Exposure to a power surge like that would have meant he wouldn't need to recharge," he said. "He'd have been shut down for most of the time."

"I know," Kim replied numbly. "But something still caused *us* to lose time out there."

"Did it?" Wren asked her. "I mean, *something* happened. But we don't know what it was. Perhaps just exposure to whatever caused that gravity field had an effect on our memories and we just don't recall how long we were lost out there. Without the justification of Adonai's account, it's pretty meaningless."

Kim knew what he was saying. She hated it, but she knew he was right. Nothing they had personally seen indicated the presence of a planet out there.

Wren leaned forward, taking her hands in his. "Are you going to tell me, or do I need to ask you?"

Kim glanced up into his searching eyes. Her heart plummeted. "Wren..."

"You had to know I would find out. I work with the computer constantly, and right now, I'm treating anything suspicious—like comms from unknown sources—as a priority. Which means you didn't tell me for one of two reasons: Either you thought I would be okay with it—in which case, you're wrong—or you were waiting for me to raise the issue. Which I'm also not okay with, Kim. Why did you do it? Why would you contact that bastard?"

Kim had to look away. She fidgeted, pulling her hands from his; not because she didn't want them there but because it felt wrong to let him touch her now. As if she was somehow dirty. "I had to know if the Crusaders were behind what happened to the computer."

"And he told you what?"

"That he wasn't."

"Because the word of a liar and a terrorist is worth so much," he shot at her sarcastically.

"I think I believe him," she said quietly. Zane's anguished face haunted her; there had been real emotion there, misguided though it was.

"Of course you do." Wren threw his newly-freed hands in the air. "Why wouldn't you after everything he did to you? I mean, come on, Kim. You're smarter than that! The Crusaders will do anything to accomplish their cause. Maybe even have Zane trick you into thinking they're not behind this. Did you think about that?"

"Yes! Of course I did!" Kim's voice rose in pitch. She didn't want to get angry right now, but she couldn't hold her emotions in check. Wren thought she was a gullible cult follower. He thought she was insane to be talking to Zane. But he had never walked in her shoes, not even for a day, and she truly felt that Zane was telling the truth on this one. "Zane—"

"I've heard enough of that name!" Wren's voice was a roar. He stood up, his fists clenched at his sides, and Kim wondered, for a brief but lucid moment, if he meant to hit her. And then he moved past her, through the door of the shelter and vanished from sight.

Kim sighed, feeling suddenly very lonely—and wishing she'd just apologized.

A gunshot rang out, and Kim jumped up from the bed. Her heart pounding, she looked around at the walls of the shelter, trying to determine which direction it had come from and whether it was close or distant.

Silence followed, and as the seconds ticked over, Kim began to wonder if she had mistaken a cooking pot being dropped near the fire for the noise she'd heard. Then a second shot rang out, followed by a loud male shout just outside the shelter. The sound of boots on the ground stirred her from the bed, and she rushed to the entrance, peering cautiously outside.

Airman Cabes and Petty Officer Durand raced past her, their rifles at the ready. Kim felt the breeze they created as they pounded into the forest to her right. A moment later, there was another shout, and a figure burst from the forest. She was not an EU officer. Dressed in a blue shirt streaked with dirt and dark red blood, her blonde hair a wild halo around her head, she crashed to the ground a few steps away from Kim and lay still.

Projectile gunfire sounded in the near distance.

Pop-pop-pop-pop-pop.

Someone responded with laser fire, a more distinctive *tchew, tchew*. Kim raced toward the fallen figure, but the woman was barely breathing. She looked to be about thirty years old, her face ashen and blood pooling under her chest, mingling with the dirt. Kim slipped a hand under the woman's head, propping it up while she glanced around. "Help!" she yelled. "I need help—"

The woman coughed. Flecks of blood appeared on her lips and sprayed into Kim's face. Kim pulled back, unable to stop the instinctual reaction. Where was the bleeding coming from? She tugged at the woman's shirt with her free hand, succeeding only in jerking the woman's body to one side and eliciting a deep, horrible moan from somewhere deep inside her.

"Help!" Kim called again as she tried to feel for the wound. Pressure. You needed pressure to stop bleeding—

A bullet whipped past Kim's cheek, so close she could feel the wind of its passage. Ducking to the side, she let the woman fall to the dirt. Another bullet hit a rock to her left, rebounding along with a handful of stone chips. Kim curled herself as low as she could and scurried for the nearest cover—a small tree a few feet away. She couldn't tell, at this point, if she was being targeted or if the shots were random fire coming from the battle that was still raging beyond the trees.

Wren. Wren had stormed out only moments before. Where was he?

There was no time to think. A third shot hit the tree, only a few inches from her head. Kim pulled herself behind the trunk. The tree was a young one with several low-hanging branches, providing her with a screen through which she could still survey the scene before her—but not providing much cover. She positioned herself as best she could, but, weaponless, she knew she was a sitting duck.

"I know you're there!" The voice was clear, the Japo-English it spoke carefully enunciated. "You might as well come out and face me, coward!"

"That wouldn't exactly be the smart thing to do," Kim returned. She peered through the screen of twigs and leaves, making out another figure—this one, a man holding a large rifle. Kim thought it might be a military-grade

930C, a rudimentary version of the newer rifles EU carried. If she was right, it had stun capabilities, but it was clear the man using it wasn't trying to disable her. He was shooting projectile bullets.

Kim reached out a hand, clasping it around a handful of small stones. Not much of a weapon, but it would distract him while she made a break for it.

He was coming around the tree now, and Kim knew she was out of time. She stood and hurled the stones; a few caught him on the side of the face, but the others pattered to the ground uselessly. The man let out a grunt as a streak of blood appeared just below his eye, but the impact was clearly not enough to deter him. He brought his gun up, aiming it at her chest. He didn't smile. His face, weathered and smudged with dirt, wore a weary expression.

"I've waited a long time for this," he said, squeezing his hand on the trigger.

Kim felt nothing but the tingle of adrenaline, heard her heart thumping in her ears. Instinct took over. Hoping his aim was as bad up close as it had been from a distance, she ducked down to all fours, scuttling like a rabbit. A bullet whipped passed her with a crack. Her heart stopped for a moment, but she could feel no pain. She had to assume she wasn't hit and keep going.

The tree line closed over her, dappled shade wrapping her like a blanket. The pattern of falling light would help conceal her from view, but her movements would make her vulnerable. She jinked hard to the right, hoping to put a few tree trunks between her and her pursuer. Her breath strained in her lungs, but she pushed herself onward, refusing to allow that man anywhere near her.

"Down!" A shout from her right. It sounded like Officer Durand, and though Kim couldn't be sure, she dropped to the ground in response. Her chest hit the forest floor hard as a flash of laser fire *whooshed* overhead, striking the trunk of a tree just next to her. Sparks sizzled and fell like rain. Kim smelled charred wood as she rolled to her side, finally spotting Officer Durand crouched behind a tree. Her rifle was trained on the man who was now lying on his side, hand on his leg as he let out a howl of pain.

Another bullet whizzed over Kim's head, thudding into the ground a few steps away.

"Four o'clock!"

It was Grand's voice, the words sharp and loud, and Kim lifted her head, realizing only a second later what she'd done—crashed right into the middle of the battle.

"Can't get a good shot," Renshaw replied. He was somewhere to her left, his voice echoing through the trees. "Bastards are all over the place."

"Hold off. Let him come to you."

A boot stomped in front of Kim's face, shattering a piece of blue-tinged fungus. The green pants told Kim this was a friend rather than an enemy. She looked up at Durand, but her normally smiling face was set cold and hard. A green combat helmet was perched on her head covering her auburn hair, the chin-strap making a rigid scar across her jawline.

"Get up!" Durand shouted at Kim.

A few steps away, the man struggled onto his back, propping himself on one shoulder as he aimed at Durand. She pulled the trigger once more, and he dropped back to the dirt, lifeless.

Durand immediately dropped beside Kim, propping her rifle on a small protrusion of rock and aiming down the hill. "Don't move," she told Kim. "There are at least five more of them out there."

"Why are they attacking?" she asked.

"No idea, but it's not going well for them." She shifted slightly, squinting into the sight atop her gun. "Sergeant, he's coming your way now!"

"Got him," Renshaw replied. There was another burst of laser fire, filling the air with noise; Kim tensed, waiting for an anguished scream, but the sergeant's voice sounded a moment later. "Damn. They're on the run!"

"Shit," Durand spat. She pulled her head from the sight but didn't move, holding her position and continuing to scan the forest.

A few seconds passed with no further sound, then Grand's voice rang out. "Retreat to camp!"

"Come on," Durand said, pushing herself up.

Kim stood, feeling faint. Her hand was cut—she'd put her palm on a sharp rock without even realizing. Durand approached the fallen man, rifle still at the ready. As Kim hovered at her shoulder, she saw the man's chest rising and falling irregularly. He was still alive—but only barely.

Suddenly, his eyes flicked to Kim. She felt her own breath catch in her throat.

"You . . ." he gasped, his voice hoarse.

"Why did you attack us?" Kim asked.

"Sacrifice," he croaked. "Remove the tainted whales . . . and *you*, Hannah. Kim—whoever. Worth . . . our lives." He paused.

"You sabotaged our probe; you made us crash! And then you destroyed our seeders—"

"Would have . . . destroyed them all. But didn't have . . . the locations right." He sucked in a deep breath. "Our people are coming. More of them. You won't . . . stand a chance."

Kim snarled. "Even if they are, it takes over a year to get to New Eden. We can have EU ships here in less than half that time."

"Not . . . against these ships. Quantum drive." He smirked. "Be here in weeks, and they'll . . . make sure this planet is . . . cleansed."

Kim felt her heartbeat increase. Quantum drive? She'd heard of it, of course—using the folds of spacetime to traverse huge distances in the blink of an eye. But it was years away from being a reality; the prototypes she'd heard of had all blown up in varying magnitudes. The guy must be lying, trying to keep her off guard. "The whales have a right to live. Even if what you believe is true, God values all His creatures."

"Humans and animals . . . one dies . . . just like the other. All of them . . . have the same breath of life." The man coughed wetly. A small trickle of blood ran down his chin. "They understand sacrifice. Might . . . even welcome it . . . after what you've done . . . to them. I've . . . seen them. Angels. *Here,* Hannah. Proves . . . our cause is right . . . and just. Proves . . . our cause is just."

He was no longer looking at Kim but rather staring into the distance. It took a moment for her to realize that he was dead. Durand quickly checked his pulse and relieved him of his rifle, the gestures swift and business-like, and then she checked the woman. Kim waited in anticipation, but it was clear by Durand's slow movements that she, too, was dead.

"We tried stunning them," Durand said at last. "The accuracy on a stunner isn't great. They came in with intent to kill. It was necessary to respond with force."

"I know," Kim said, annoyed to find that her voice was still shaky. "Where's Wren? Is he okay?"

"He's back at camp. He's fine," Durand told her, and Kim breathed a sigh of relief.

"What happened?" Kim asked.

"They attacked out of nowhere. Tried to shoot Mallory who was on sentry duty." She shook her head. "They're gone now. Vanished. They're definitely using some kind of personal thermal shields."

Kim looked at the fallen man and woman. "They really hate what we're doing *this* much?" she asked.

"Let's get you back to camp," Durand replied, skirting her eyes away from the sight and marching on ahead.

The attack had left everyone on edge. The bodies of the man and woman were gone by the time Grand and Renshaw went to view them; taken, it was supposed, by their own people for burial. Grand outlined the need for greater vigilance, but it was clear that this was a paltry measure and probably wouldn't do much to stop another attack if the Adherants decided to try again.

Kim had relayed to him everything the man had said. That his people had destroyed the post, that they would have destroyed every seeder but luck had been against them. "He mentioned angels, too."

"Typical Adherant pretentiousness," Grand said, disgustedly.

"Isn't it strange that he's talking about angels when Adonai's also sure he saw something along those lines?" Kim pressed.

Grand raised his eyebrows. "Right now, I'm focused on keeping my people safe, Kim. Whatever mystical crap is going on, it's not posing a threat right now."

"Lieutenant, he also mentioned quantum drive. He said there was a fleet of Adherant ships on its way."

Grand swallowed visibly.

"Was he lying?" Kim prompted.

"Look, Kim. There are . . . some projects that have been running. Incredibly top secret. And there are a few rumors floating around that the Adherants have their finger in that pie, so to speak."

"So EU has been developing technology? And someone gave it to the Adherants?" Kim shook her head. "That sounds . . ."

"Impossible?" Grand laughed humorlessly. "Unless you're someone who stands to gain some money from the whole thing. Remember that scientist I told you about, the one who's missing? Alarm bells have been ringing system-wide. He's a prominent physicist on one of our projects."

"He *sold* it? That's even worse."

"It's now suspected that he didn't do so willingly," Grand said.

Kim covered her mouth with her hands as she realized what he was saying. Coercion? Or kidnapping and torture? "And now they're going to use it to attack New Eden?"

"We don't know that for sure. That man might have been trying to scare you. You're not exactly the Adherents' favorite person, Kim. Look. We honestly have no idea what kind of resources they have. The engagement makes me think we outgun them in terms of firepower, but that doesn't make them harmless. I'll be doubling the overnight watch, but I stress that we need to carry out our duties here with urgency and get the hell off this planet."

Later that afternoon, Kim headed toward the base. The modified trailers for the tractors had been removed and were being driven by Shannon and

Durand. Mallory, Cabes, and Pierce were riding in the rear compartment with more sheeting and floor panels, as well as the less delicate equipment from the stores. The road through the forest, with such frequent use, was beginning to resemble a highway. Yoshi approached Kim as she emerged from the tree line, shaking sand from the toes of her shoes.

"It'll be done by tomorrow morning," she said. "I'm going to get some new seeders built back at *Seiiki*, but it'll be much easier once we're in the base."

Kim gazed beyond her at the water of the ocean. "When can we think about moving the whales in?"

"Probably not until the base is ready," Yoshi said. "Without the monitoring equipment, I don't like the idea of them swimming in an ocean where they might be injured or become malnourished."

"How are the other seeders going?" Kim asked.

Yoshi brightened at this. "So far I've inspected five within the four mile radius of the base. None of them were dysfunctional or damaged. The krill and plankton populations are growing steadily, and I'm working on getting some coral growing down there. Right now, there's no real reason for concern in this area of the continent, but I need another day or so to get more seeders out there."

But when Kim relayed this to the whales, she found them unhappy with the answer.

Do we really have to wait?

I'm so tired of swimming in circles.

Can you tell Yoshi to let us go earlier? There is enough food for us to live in the ocean now!

"I can't do anything about it," Kim told them as she walked around the perimeter of the base, marking the progress over the past few minutes. "Sorry. But I agree with Yoshi. It's not safe for you to go in yet."

But we've waited so long, Berenice said. She sounded mournful.

"A little longer won't hurt you, then," Kim said brightly. Then, aware that this effectively dismissed the whale's feelings of frustration, she added, "I'm sorry. I know it's hard. But we're working really quickly on this, and I promise it won't be much longer."

The day wore on, and Kim found she had little to do. She traveled back to *Seiiki* and tried to help Yoshi with the seeders, but her understanding of how they worked was limited. She could have learned, and quickly, but Yoshi was so stone-faced and uncommunicative that Kim soon gave up, left her directing a maintenance droid to weld several steel plates into a particular formation and headed off to find Adonai.

With EU officers all working on the base, she had the opportunity to make her way down to Deck Five unchaperoned.

Seiiki, however, was not a comforting place to be. Not any longer. Corridors that had felt so familiar and safe while in space now felt cold and dead. The junction station sat like a lifeless arcade game, the kind you found in retro game parlors. She was surprised to find Adonai there, sitting in a very humanlike posture with his back to the bulkhead and his knees to his chest. As she approached, he lifted his head. He'd been staring contemplatively at the floor, she realized.

"Adonai?" She approached tentatively, wondering if she was intruding on a private moment. "Are you all right?"

"Of course, Kim," he replied, but there was a waver to his voice.

"You don't sound convincing."

Adonai stood slowly. A droid could stand without having to shift his weight, a smooth movement which always made her feel ridiculously unfit. "I've just been thinking a great deal about the things that are happening on this planet, and I feel that there is something I'm missing. I think this is a little bit like how you feel."

"A little bit?" Kim snorted.

Adonai was silent for a moment, staring at the control panel for the junction station. "The computer doesn't show me the face anymore."

"The . . . angel's face?"

Adonai nodded. His golden eyes flickered. "Kim," he said, hesitantly. "Do you think I dreamed it?"

Kim swallowed. "I'm not sure, Adonai."

"You sounded sure. When you were talking to Wren."

She sucked her bottom lip between her teeth. "It's rude to eavesdrop, Adonai."

"I know!" The reply was sharp and fast, his voice louder than Kim had ever heard it. She blinked. Had Adonai just snapped at her? "But it's also rude to talk about people when they're not there!"

"Adonai—"

"I know what I saw, Kim. I know it . . . deep inside here." He touched a palm flat to his chest. A very strange gesture for a being that didn't have a heart, Kim thought, but this was immediately chased away by the thought that Adonai was an exception to this rule.

"I get that, Adonai. I'm on your side in this. I'm your friend."

"No, Kim," Adonai said. His voice was bitter, and Kim was shocked not just at the emotion in his voice, but at the fact that it was directed at *her*. "If *you* had told me something like this, I would have believed you from the start. I would *never* have doubted it!"

"I didn't—"

"You did. I saw it in your eyes." Adonai dropped his arms to his sides.

"Adonai, I don't know what happened up there in the Hebron Belt. I was only trying to prove what's happening here on New Eden. We're in danger, and we need to know where that danger's coming from! At the moment, we have no clue. And that leaves us vulnerable. So I needed to know if it's possible that these . . . angel beings . . . are real, and now I think that maybe we've all been tricked. Not just you, Adonai. There are people in the universe who will use your beliefs against you. Trust me."

"YOU ARE NOT MY FRIEND!"

The childish outburst struck Kim harder than a slap. The breath left her body as Adonai's eyes blazed at her. She opened her mouth, but no sound came out. As she could only watch, Adonai turned away from her and headed down the corridor.

"Adonai!"

He didn't turn, didn't acknowledge that she had spoken at all. Instead, he kept walking, as if she didn't exist to him any longer.

It hurt worse than anything Kim had ever expected.

CHAPTER
18

The base looked finished. It wasn't; the walls and floor had been erected, for the most part, and the rotunda was almost in place. The ceiling was coming together quickly, too, the tech droids crawling up the stanchions with fearless abandon, hauling steel plates five times their weight. None of the equipment had been installed as of yet, but it was major progress.

Kim didn't stay there long. She had wondered if Adonai had come here after leaving *Seiiki*, but she didn't see any sign of him. He wasn't back at camp, either, and Kim had spent an hour waiting for him there, sure he'd eventually show up, and she'd be able to apologize properly. He hadn't come back.

Kim headed down to the beach. Away from the bustle of the construction site, it was empty and quiet, but there was no sign of the missing droid here, either.

Morosely, she walked back to the camp and checked the shelter once more. Nothing. Finally, she bit the bullet and leaned her head in through *Daedalus*'s hatch. "Have you seen Adonai?" she called up to Lieutenant Grand, who was coming down the steps from the cockpit.

"He's not in here, if that's what you're asking. I haven't seen him all afternoon."

A slight sense of panic rose in Kim's chest, making her heart flutter. "Damn."

"Where did you last see him?" Grand asked.

Grateful for his concern, she gave him a brief rundown of their conversation—omitting her deliberate disobedience of his orders—and his frown deepened.

"It's not like him to take off on his own," he said.

"Actually, that's what worries me. It *is* like him. Now. He never would have done this a month ago, but since the Hebron Belt, he's been . . . weird."

"I'll send out Renshaw and Cabes with a scanner," the lieutenant assured her. "He should be easy enough to track if he's out in the forest somewhere. Make sure you stay close to camp, okay?"

Kim nodded, even though she knew without doubt she was going to disobey him once more. Because she now had an idea of where Adonai was and what he was doing.

And it wasn't going to be good . . . for any of them.

"Kim?" Wren caught up with her hurried steps, his breath ragged as his feet crunched the dry leaf litter. "What are you doing?"

"Adonai's missing." She marched onward, pushing an overhanging fern out of her face. She'd brought her comm-band with her, but when she had room to walk straight, she immediately set about turning off the ability for anyone to actually comm her.

"So, what, you want to get yourself lost, too?" Wren protested. "Kim, you can't keep rushing off into the forest alone!"

She glanced back at him.

"I'm not going to get lost. I know where I'm going, and I don't need your protection. I can handle myself."

Wren chuckled softly, the sound a welcome break from the firm tone he'd used a moment earlier. "I have no illusions about that. But at the very least, I can shoot a gun if needed."

A spike of irritation lanced through her, but it was quickly calmed. Kim relented. "Sorry. I'm worried about him."

"We all are," he told her. "Kim, did you think I wouldn't help?"

"We're fighting, aren't we?"

Wren ducked under a branch. "Are we?"

"I thought we were. We had an argument, right?"

"Couples have arguments," Wren replied, his voice a mixture of gentleness and firmness. "Maybe one time I'll get so mad at you that I'll let you go off into an alien jungle alone. Not this time."

Kim felt the ice around her heart melt. "I'm sorry, Wren. I shouldn't have commed him."

"No, you shouldn't have. But I'm sorry, too. I just . . . I'm not just jealous, Kim. That guy is evil. I don't want him anywhere near you."

Kim remembered how much she had hated Zane after what had happened at Edgeward. The anger had cooled significantly, but she could still feel the bruise it had left on her emotions. She could imagine what it felt like to be Wren, watching it from a distance—and knowing that Zane and Kim had once been just as close as she was with Wren. Closer, if you counted physical intimacy.

"Wren, I don't love him anymore. If I ever see him again, it'll be to kick him where it hurts."

"Glad to hear that," Wren replied gruffly. He skidded on a patch of fungus and caught his balance on a nearby branch. "You think you know where Adonai went?"

"Almost definitely," she replied, still hoping she was wrong. She pushed past a branch that snapped back and caught Wren in the ear. He didn't complain, but it was only then, when she realized she'd barely seen the branch, that she noticed night was approaching much more swiftly than usual. Already, the shadows under the trees were turning murky.

"The shuttle?" Wren asked. Either he'd recognized the direction they were taking or he knew Adonai as well as Kim did. "You don't think he's going to try and fly out to the Hebron Belt again?"

Kim shook her head. "No. I don't think he'd do that." Though she couldn't be absolutely sure on that front, either. "But we need to find him before he does something that gets himself in major trouble." She increased her pace, and Wren jogged just behind her. She was glad he had come. It made her feel less alone.

A howl filled the air, blossoming into the night sounds from somewhere in the distance. It was hard to pinpoint the exact location, she realized. The sound bounced through the trunks of the trees and reverberated in the marrow of her bones.

She looked over her shoulder at Wren, whose eyes were wide. The white pistol was already in his hands.

"It was a long way away," he said breathlessly. "I think."

"I hope so," Kim replied grimly. She wasn't turning back.

They'd been pelting through the forest for another three or four minutes when they heard another howl. The high-pitched whine of it set Kim's teeth on edge; this one was definitely closer. She didn't stop this time. Relief filled her when she glimpsed white stone through the trees ahead, and she caught hold of a branch, using it as a handhold to duck through a particularly thick section of undergrowth. She paused in her crouched position, looking up at something white on the trunk of the tree.

She wasn't sure, not at first. But it looked like—it really *looked like*—a drawing.

Standing up, she peered closer. It was carved into the bark of the tree. The gray outer layers had been scraped back to reveal fawn-colored innards, and this had been done in a methodical way, with care and precision. Right angles did not exist in nature. They were a human invention—*a sentient invention,* Kim reminded herself. And there were several sharp angles in this design. A triangular-shaped body, topped with a rounded head, and two feet dangling below. And on either side, two swooping half crescent moons.

She stepped forward, hardly daring to touch it but needing to know. She used her fingernails to gouge a little of the bark away. Beneath it was the same soft fawn-colored wood, brighter, but only slightly, than the carving.

"What is that?" Wren asked.

"An angel," she replied, disbelievingly.

"Did Adonai do that?"

Kim shook her head slowly. The carving was fresh, but Adonai had only arrived on New Eden four days ago. The wood should have been brighter if he'd carved it.

"I don't think so," she said. "I'd say this was one of them." She pointed back to the camp.

Another long, soft howl rent the air. There was no time left to wonder; they had to move.

This time, Kim paid no attention to the worn and tumbled stones of the ruins, heading directly for the shuttle. It was dark, still, and silent. At first, she wondered if she'd been wrong; perhaps Adonai wasn't here after all. Then the hatch slid open.

Adonai stood there, framed in the doorway, his metal body nothing but a silhouette in the dim evening light. His golden eyes fixed on Kim, and his shoulders slumped, his head tilting downward until it rested on his chest. "I'm sorry, Kim."

She put a hand to her mouth, trying to contain the fear that buzzed in her stomach. "Tell me you didn't do it," she said. Tears were prickling at the backs of her eyes; she already knew the answer.

"I did," he replied. Despite his abject expression, there was defiance in his voice. "Kim, I know you said I shouldn't do any videos, and that was why I didn't tell you . . ."

Kim groaned. "Adonai, you don't know what you've done."

"I do!" His protest was loud, his voice filled with fire. "Kim, you think I'm a child. A *human* child. I'm not! I'm a whale, and I've lived a long time, and I'm capable of thinking for myself!"

Kim took an involuntary step back as Adonai's eyes lifted, fixing on her. His metal fingers flexed and clenched, and Kim was very suddenly aware that if he chose to, he could rip her apart with those hands. And then, the moment was gone, and she was looking at Adonai once more. Defiant, a little angry, but not capable of hurting her. Not capable of hurting anyone. Except, perhaps, himself.

"Adonai, I'm sorry," she said. "Come back to the camp. Maybe we can—" She wasn't sure exactly what she expected to be able to do. There was, in all likelihood, no fixing this.

Wren let out a loud yell from behind her.

She turned, seeing only a dark blur of black before Wren barreled into her, his arms wrapping around her tightly, pulling her through the door. Adonai, his reflexes faster than any human's, had already hit the controls to shut the hatch. As it hissed into place, Kim caught a blurred glimpse of dark black teeth gleaming in the rising moonlight—and then a solid *thud* as the thing hit the hatch. A loud skittering sound followed. The creature's claws, she realized, scratching at the door in front of her. How thick was the hull of this shuttle? How much space was between her and those lethal teeth?

She breathed in sharply.

"Oh my God," Wren gasped. "That was close."

Adonai stared at the door, as if he could see through it.

There was another resounding *thud*. The creature had thrown itself against the door once more, and Kim saw the force move the hatch in its surrounding frame, minutely but noticeably.

"The hatch will hold," Kim said. She was pretty sure she was trying to convince herself as well as the others.

A rending sound filled the space between them and the hatch. The squeal was like something inside her brain trying to escape; Kim clapped her hands over her ears and backed away. Fear threatened to overcome reason as every instinct inside her told her to *get away*, rebelling against the idea that there was nowhere to go.

Wren had the pistol drawn. With the grip folded in a two-handed clasp, he aimed it at the door. His hands were steady, his legs braced, as if he expected at any moment that the hatch would come apart.

"Into the cockpit," Kim managed to say.

Wren didn't move the gun from the door, backing slowly toward the bulkhead that divided the front section of the craft from the rear. The duraglass windows were dark, and Kim could only barely make out the trees. Slowly, she leaned into the copilot's chair and craned her head to see the port side of the ship.

Nothing.

Another thump and then a long, low, mournful howl. The ship rocked gently. A soft snuffling sound. And then . . . silence.

"Has it gone?" Kim asked in a whisper.

"I think—" Wren began.

The window directly in front of Kim detonated in a spiderweb of cracks. She reared backward, toppling out of the chair and banging her elbow on the floor as she went down. The snapping jaws—wide enough to fit her entire head—were barely an arm's length away. Kim let out a loud yelp, but the expected weight of the creature's body didn't fall on top of her. There were no teeth snapping at her neck. She was intact.

The glass had held, the beast shattering only the outermost pane.

Though that, in itself, was horrifying to think of. Those windows could withstand asteroid collisions.

Launching herself back onto her feet, she found Wren in front of her, the pistol aimed at the broken window, finger poised on the trigger. For a ludicrous moment, she wanted nothing more than to kiss him. Having him stand there, protecting her, gave her a sensation she had never expected to feel—nor would she have expected to *like* it. But now was definitely not the time to be thinking about that.

Adonai stood to one side, unmoving. Had he flinched when the thing came at the window? Kim couldn't tell. And as she steadied herself on her feet, peering through the unbroken forward window, she could see that the creature was backing away. Slinking into the shadows, it turned once to look behind it, directly at her, and its eyes were shining yellow, a narrow, slitted pupil like a snake's focusing on Kim's face. And then, it vanished into the trees like smoke.

She became aware of the only sound in the cockpit—her and Wren's harsh breathing and the thumping of blood in her ears.

"We have to get back to camp," she said, chilled to the bone and, for once, wanting nothing more than to see EU officers and their rifles.

The others staged no protests, but it was still another nine minutes before Kim dared key the hatch open and step out to the ruins.

Kim let Wren lead the way back toward the trees with his gun raised. Kim turned on the light on the comm-band—carefully ignoring the dozen red icons that told her she had unanswered comms—and swept the trees with it. Nothing but shadows . . . except for *that*.

Near the edge of the ruins, just where Kim had found the stone circle embedded in the ground, was a crumpled pile of clothing. It was the color that caught her eye more than anything else. Green. Like an EU uniform.

She stopped still. Wren seemed to have seen it moments after she did and came to such a sudden stop, he almost lost his balance. A small sound escaped Kim's mouth as Wren put a hand to his.

Adonai asked the question she dreaded.

"Kim, is that man dead?"

It was late when they reached camp. Adonai carried Simons's body in his arms, the weight of the man no trouble at all for his mechanical strength. Kim had relented and answered the lieutenant's comms, informing him of what they'd found. Grand had sounded, understandably, terse; angered both by the discovery and by her deliberate disobedience.

He had sent out Cabes and Mallory to meet them halfway and escort them back, but there had been no sign of any more creatures.

Simons's body was laid out next to the fire. When Kim had first seen it, she had to work hard to amalgamate her memories of Simons with these . . . remains. He looked too small now to have ever been the sour-faced man who'd chastised her for leaving a flashlight on all night. She'd told him to go to Hell, she remembered regretfully. Were those her last words to him?

Now that he lay beside the flickering flames, she was able to see the extent of the damage. She'd seen bodies before, some of them in bad shape. Gangs would often make examples of rival gang members. She'd seen a head mounted on a pole outside the East Kings' territory. She'd seen a pile of severed limbs delivered to the kitchen door of a restaurant owned by a gang leader who had treated her and Constantin to dinner one night. She'd seen cuts and gashes and fingers removed and a bashed-in skull. What had happened to Simons wasn't as bad as some of these injuries, but it was still up there with the worst.

His uniform shirt had been torn open with a single long gash. It had gone deep into his flesh, tearing it apart like a bedsheet. Black blood congealed inside the wound but not enough to conceal the organs of his abdomen and the pale white protrusions of his ribcage.

His feet were gone. One was severed at the ankle. The other was smashed apart from the lower shin downward. Every bone must have been crushed for it to look so flat inside the leg of his uniform and his boot.

As if this wasn't enough, his face had been slashed. Several long cuts ran from his left temple to his jaw, exposing tissue beneath. One eye had been obliterated. The other stared sightlessly at the sky.

Kim covered her mouth with her hand and looked away. Airman Spier was crouched over him, pulling a white sheet up to cover the body. She looked up to see Kim.

"Kim, don't look," she said. "You shouldn't have to see that."

Kim wished she hadn't. She turned and retched into the nearby ferns. She brought up nothing but bile and water, but she couldn't stop until she was empty of even that.

CHAPTER

19

She found Adonai just outside the shelter, a blood-covered rag in one hand, a plas-tec bottle of water in the other. He was sponging Simons's blood from his torso and arms.

When he saw her, he lifted his head and paused awkwardly.

"Are you all right?" she asked him.

"Kim," he said, and the way he said her name was full of sorrow and regret. "I am very, very sorry," he managed at last.

"Oh, Adonai, it's all right." She wanted to wrap her arms around him, and she would have done so if he didn't still have streaks of blood on his metal plates.

"It isn't," he replied. "I placed you and Wren in danger. For my own selfish ends. And . . . I have disappointed you deeply."

Kim shook her head. "You haven't, Adonai. Whatever happens after this, we'll take care of it, okay?"

"I should have listened to you." He looked down at his hands, the pink-stained rag dangling like a dead thing itself. "You and Wren might have ended up dead like Chief Simons. Kim, I'm afraid I make a very terrible human."

"By putting yourself in the worst possible situation at the worst possible time? Adonai, if anything, that makes you the perfect human." She tried for a smile, but it didn't quite work. "Look. Who knows how long it would have been before we found Simons if you hadn't gone out there tonight?"

"He was not there when I arrived at the shuttle. I would have seen him."

"Wren and I didn't see him, either. I'd say that's the reason the creature was there. We were just collateral, I guess."

"That does not make me feel any better. Kim, have I really put the entire project in danger?"

Kim suspected very strongly that he had, but she also knew she couldn't tell him that. "No," she said. "Of course not."

Adonai looked at her steadily. "I think this is an occasion where you are trying to save my feelings from being hurt. I am capable of assuming responsibility for my actions."

"I know," Kim replied. "I know."

Grand called a meeting the following morning. The sun was not yet up, but Kim had barely slept anyway.

Simons's body had been buried only half an hour before with little ceremony a few yards into the tree line. Kim didn't attend, staying in the shelter instead. Wren had gone to help dig the grave, and Adonai was recharging in *Daedalus*. Yoshi was the only other one in the shelter, hunched over her tablet as she worked with utmost focus on some holographic projections of what looked like cell structures. Kim had no idea what she was doing, and Yoshi didn't volunteer the information. The summons to the meeting was a relief from the atmosphere of exclusion and finally roused the other girl from her intense concentration.

The gathering was held near the fire, where Kim found a dispirited group talking in low voices. Grand emerged from *Daedalus,* his hair neatly brushed and hands clean but otherwise looking no better than any of his officers. Haggard and worn, his hair greasy and unwashed, his uniform stained and unpinned at the shoulder, the jacket flap hanging down and showing a stretched white singlet underneath, Kim felt a pang of sympathy for him. He had lost a valued crew member, and Kim knew this was his worst nightmare come to life.

"I've relayed my report to Edgeward." His voice was firm, but his eyes were distant. "And our relief. We've got orders to sit tight on this. No word of it gets out."

"No word of *what,* exactly?" Officer Durand spoke up. "We don't even know what's going on here. Kim says Simons's body appeared out of nowhere, right in the same spot he vanished, only he's *dead.* We've got a forest full of beasts that shouldn't be here. Are we fighting Adherant saboteurs here or demon wolf-creatures?"

"Adherants didn't cause those wounds," Captain Shannon said gruffly.

Grand held up his hands. "As of yet, we don't have anything conclusive to say about what happened to Simons. We have no knowledge of who is targeting us at this moment, nor whether they're working in unison or independently, and whether they're native to this planet or not. Our orders are to sit tight until our relief arrives, because one thing is certain—something out there means us, and the whales, harm." He let this sink in for a moment. "In terms of the creature that attacked Wren, Kim, and Adonai last night— and which might also have been responsible for returning Simons's body— Yoshi has a few things to share."

Kim glanced across at the Japanese girl, who looked pale and wan in the firelight. She had something in her hands—a small plastic box, Kim saw, as she stood to address her audience.

"I can confirm that the slashes on his body were made by animal claws," she said, lifting the sample container. Inside the clear walls, a tiny triangular shard, no bigger than Kim's fingernail, sat on a bed of greenish gel. Kim edged closer, as did many of the others, squinting in the firelight. The claw seemed to be made of something semitranslucent, rendering it almost invisible against the gel, but it was definitely *there.* "When you match the trajectory and direction of the slashes," Yoshi went on, "you get a paw of roughly human-sized." She held up a hand, fist clenched. "Claws four inches long, slightly curved."

"And yet no wildlife was recorded on this planet," Durand said. "How could you miss something like this?" She sounded faintly hysterical. "We all saw the holo. Simons didn't walk away. He wasn't dragged off by some creature. He *vanished.*"

"I've spent the past few hours analyzing this to the best of my ability," Yoshi said, still holding up the sample container. "It's unlike any material I've come across, and I believe I might at least have an explanation as to why it wasn't detected by any scans. The structure of the claw appears to be, at least in part, made of energy."

Blank looks were shared. Kim didn't blame them. Her own credulity was being stretched, and *she* knew how brilliant and exact Yoshi was. To the others, she was just some young Japanese celebrity who had basically told them the universe was made out of chocolate custard.

"If that was the case," Yoshi went on bravely. "And I'm still not one hundred percent sure that it is—but if it was, the creature could be invisible to the light spectrum of our range of vision."

The expressions around the fire changed from puzzlement to horror. The silence was complete, and in the space of that moment, Kim felt something click inside her mind.

This information made a terrible kind of sense. And it was also the realization of one of her worst fears. "Could that cause interference with the scanners, too?"

"It's possible," Yoshi said. "Our scanners are designed to detect thermal radiation and carbon-combination molecules. If a life-form had no carbon in their genetic makeup, and no thermal signature within the range we would consider normal, it wouldn't be detected." She shrugged. "We wouldn't *need* to be able to detect them, according to the basis of our own science. They wouldn't exist."

"So that means that whatever showed up on Durand's scan out at the ruins wasn't these . . . whatever they are." This was from Cabes, whose arms were folded protectively across his middle, as if fearing the same attack Simons had suffered.

"I wouldn't rule it out," Yoshi explained, looking down at the sample case on her lap with a frown. "Those life sign signatures Durand picked up showed up for just a few moments and then vanished again. But yes, I think you're right. I can't see any life-form suddenly showing up on one of our scanners unless it was carbon-based, in which case, the creature would have to have some kind of cloaking ability or technology. Again, I wouldn't rule it out. This planet seems to prove us wrong at every turn, but I'd be more inclined to think those life signs were the same people who sabotaged our probe and our seeders." She paused. "I've found two other seeders that were downed with similar streaks of laser fire. These people are clearly not our friends."

The group shifted uncomfortably. Many eyes peered out into the darkness under the trees.

"How do we defend against something we can't see?" Renshaw asked. "And I'm talking about both the creatures and the saboteurs here."

Grand took a deep breath. "I have requested that we be allowed to evacuate." There was reluctance in his voice—and something close to defeat—but he delivered the news with his usual firm assurance. "We'll be lifting off at 1000 hours this morning."

It was as if a bolt of lightning had struck Kim. She felt ice cold and on fire all at once. All they'd discovered, all they'd achieved, only to do this?

"No." She took a step forward and put her hands on her hips defiantly, glaring at Grand. "No freaking *way*. We can't leave the whales here. We've got four days left before *Seiiki* runs out of Xenol, and there'll be nothing to power the forcefields. Three days before the water leak makes the ground too unstable to get the whales out. And probably less than that before the water level in the Aquarium is below what they need to survive. They'll *die*, Lieutenant."

Lieutenant Grand extended his hands palms up toward Kim. When he spoke, his voice was soft. "I can't leave my team in a hostile environment with no backup," he said firmly but with an undercurrent of kindness that Kim couldn't accept. "The whales come second to my team, Kim."

Kim felt as if she was standing on the edge of a cliff, about to fall over the edge. "EU can't have signed off on this! You took over the Ark Project; you were supposed to protect it!"

"EU can and has given me their approval," Grand told her calmly. God, she wanted to smack that look off his face. Who was he trying to kid? Himself? It certainly wasn't convincing her. Ben Grand had hated her from the moment he'd met her. This must be a happy moment for him. "Apparently the Ark Project has been shelved."

Audible gasps came from the group. "Holy *shit*," Captain Shannon blurted out.

"That can't be right!" Durand protested.

Kim would have added her voice to the chorus, but she couldn't get enough air into her lungs. Her gaze found Wren's, and he gazed back at her, his eyes wide, deep pain evident in them. Across from him, Kim saw Yoshi's posture stiffen. Even her usually staid face was slack-jawed with shock.

Lieutenant Grand was still speaking, but his words sounded far away. "We'll stay in stable orbit until our relief arrives, then refuel and fly back to Edgeward."

"We . . . *can't*." Kim didn't feel like she was here. She felt like she was on an island surrounded by mist, shouting into the void with no one to hear. She felt like she was drowning. Spinning out of control in an EV suit with no anchor line. All of these things . . . but mostly, she felt the reverberation through the Link as the whales picked up on her distress.

Kim?

You don't really mean . . .

Kim, don't leave us!

She pushed a finger to her temple, trying to calm her own thoughts. She wasn't sure how much the whales had picked up on, but she couldn't let them overwhelm her again. Not now. Placing a partition in the Link wasn't something she'd ever done before; she had never deliberately wanted to block out the whale's voices the way Yoshi did. Not until now. She struggled, drawing her own thoughts back inward and compartmentalizing them—her fear of what would happen to the whales, her outrage that Lieutenant Grand would betray her like this, her despair and helplessness. She pushed them down, then searched for the outer edges of her own mind, gently but firmly placing a shield between the Link and her own mind. Slowly, the thoughts and feelings of the whales receded, leaving only the technical data behind. In the silence, she stared at Grand and said, "There's too much at stake. If we leave, the whales—"

He looked at her sympathetically. "The whales are only whales. A symbol. Something to keep humanity on track and on board with Unification."

Kim stared at Grand, hardly able to believe he'd spoken those words.

And very, very glad that she had—just barely—stopped the whales from feeling her full reaction to them.

Tears pricked at the backs of her eyes. Angrily, she swallowed them down so she could force the words out without sounding like a spoiled child.

"No. It's more than that. This is about New Eden, too. This planet is special."

"Kim, I know you want to believe that Adonai saw something up there that might be Eschol Th—"

"No, that's *not* what I want to believe!" She clenched her fists and saw Wren flinch from the corner of her eye. He probably thought she was going to hit Grand. She wanted to tell him not to worry. As much as she wanted to, hitting this man would change nothing. "I want to believe," she continued through gritted teeth, "that humanity can have a new start. That . . . that we can have something good, do something selfless, and not fuck it up!"

Lieutenant Grand straightened his shoulders. "That's a noble desire, Kim," he said. "You have a bright future ahead of you. It's my job to safeguard that future. Do you understand?"

She couldn't answer, because she *didn't* understand. She had no idea how anyone could walk away from the whales with no second thoughts. She had nothing left to say. Nothing left to contribute to this conversation nor any other she would ever have with Lieutenant Ben Grand.

Kim walked away from the camp, and this time, no one tried to stop her.

CHAPTER
20

The whales were waiting for her, gathered at the outer edge of the forcefield. Kim slithered down the slope to the bottom of the furrow, but there was little solid ground left outside of the Aquarium. She couldn't get close enough to touch the forcefield to press her hands against it, which is what she wanted to do.

She longed to remove all the space between her and them. To be with them so they would know they weren't alone.

Kim, Kim, Kim, something's wrong?

Why are you so sad?

Please don't cry.

Settling for a perch on a tussocky patch of grass that had regrown over the past sixteen days, she crouched and wrapped her arms around her knees, wiping the tears from her cheeks—useless because they kept falling.

Kim, don't be sad.

We are here with you.

"I know," she said.

The humans are leaving. It was Berenice's voice, a gentle breeze against her mind. *They do not want to put us in the ocean.*

No.

That can't be true.

What will happen to us?

Why would they let us die after trying so hard to make sure we live?

The whale minds in the Link ebbed and flowed, their tension and despair rising. Kim didn't try to calm them. She had nothing to say. She let their thoughts swirl around her, subsuming her own, until there was little left for her to feel but their rising fear.

Unlike the other times when the Link had overwhelmed her, she found that when she wasn't pushing back against the emotions, they buoyed her on top of them, a sensation much like floating on a current instead of fighting against it. She let the feelings in, let them become hers—because they *were* hers.

She barely heard the sound of grass crunching behind her. When Adonai crouched down, he faced the whales, just as she did.

"They are upset."

"Yes," she replied. "They're upset and afraid. And . . . accepting."

"Because this is what our destiny was, before the Ark Project," Adonai said softly. "At least they lived their last days with hope. Kim, *you* did that. You gave them hope."

"I didn't give them anything!" she replied with a bitter laugh.

"No. You gave them everything." He turned to look at her. "Because for the first time, they truly *lived*. All of them. Even me."

"It wasn't enough," she spat fiercely. "A few years of hope isn't enough. We can't leave." Her voice caught on a sob, and she pounded a fist into her thigh in frustration.

"I had hoped that we wouldn't have to. That's why I sent that message, Kim. I wanted everyone to know that what we have out here is very important." He paused. "And there is another reason, too."

Kim nodded slowly. "I get it, Adonai. And I think you did the right thing."

"I—you do?" He looked taken aback, as if he had prepared a longer speech and she had cut him off.

"Yes. One of the safest places for information is in the public's hands. It can only be used for selfish reasons when you keep it secret." To her mind sprang Zane's words: *You've never seen the Artifact. Not many people have.* "You did the right thing."

"Even if they take me away?"

"I won't let that happen," Kim said. "And I won't let anything happen to the whales. We *can't leave*." The words were firm, and she realized she meant them as more than just a complaint. She drew herself up straight and looked down at Adonai. "We *can't* leave now."

Adonai glanced up at her, his golden eyes fixed on her face. "No. We can't."

"Somehow, I knew you'd say that." Kim grinned, suddenly, her earlier moroseness washed away. A slow fire was burning in her now.

"Kim, I am very sorry I betrayed your trust," Adonai said. "But the reason I did it was to protect—"

"The whales. I know that."

"And the risk was only to myself. Which meant it was my risk to take."

Kim sighed. "I get it, Adonai. I'm sorry I reacted the way I did. I just really don't want to lose you."

"You won't," he replied, his golden eyes burning into hers.

Kim felt the bridge between them reforming, and for a moment, she allowed herself to stand there, be in this moment with him. He was her friend. He was also so much more.

Wading through the mud wasn't easy, but when she kept to the grassy tussocks, it was at least manageable. In a few days' time, it would be impassable in normal boots. On climbing aboard *Seiiki*, she had to stamp clods of dirt into the already stained and spattered decking.

Once there, she headed up to Deck One, which was, just like the rest of the ship, silent and cold—but not dead. Not yet. She slid into the chair behind the comm station and hit the controls to power it up.

"Computer, are you still linked to the comms on the shuttle Adonai piloted?"

"Yes," the computer responded. There were no pauses, no hesitations. Kim had to hope the computer was back on track.

"Can you play me the comm Adonai sent to Sol last night?"

"I can. Comm ID: Seven-nine-five-four-D, sent directly to a private in-box owned by Alexandria Dun, under the domain of Daywatch Interstellar Broadcasts." Here, Adonai's face appeared in a holo hovering just above the console. He looked directly ahead, his golden eyes unblinking.

Hello. I am not sure how to begin this comm. My name is Adonai. I think you will know who I am.

I was once a whale, but now I'm something else. I've learned so much and grown more than I could ever have hoped. I can pilot a shuttle! Kim has taught me how, and it is an amazing thing to do. To fly between the stars. What whale could ever have dreamt of such things?

But I think the dreams of most whales are simpler. And that is why I'm sending this. EU is thinking of abandoning the planet altogether and leaving the whales to die. This is not acceptable under any circumstances. But I will give you some of those circumstances, just in case:

Firstly, there are creatures on this planet that are not supposed to be here, and they might be dangerous.

Secondly, there might be other human forces out here working to sabotage the Ark Project.

So I will counter these with a discovery I made myself: I found Heaven!

You're probably thinking I've fried my circuits, but the truth is, I am perfectly sane. I saw something in the asteroid belt. Kim and Wren encountered it too. I'm not sure what it is, or what it means, but I do know that it is very, very important. You might know it as Eschol Thirteen, but so far, I don't think you or I really know what Eschol Thirteen is. The reason I say it is Heaven is because it is a place that is beyond our perception, and there are other creatures living there. They look very much like the angels of your Bible.

So these are the circumstances. If we leave New Eden, we risk losing what we might find out if we stay. And we will definitely lose the last of the whales. Is that worth it to you?

It's not worth it to me.

This is Adonai, signing off.

Kim felt a smile. It started as a warm feeling in her chest, expanding outward until she couldn't contain it.

"How much attention has this attracted?" she asked the computer.

"Quite a bit, from what I can gather. Would you like to see some of the comments?"

Blowing out a breath, she steeled herself. "All right. Let's do it."

Yellow script appeared before her, scrolling upward as more and more were added by the millisecond.

Adonai, you rock. I've been waiting to hear from you forever

Eschol Thirteen? Monsters on the whale planet? And terrorists, too? Seriously? Have you been taking stims?

Marry me, Adonai!!!!!

There's no proof of any of this.

Three weeks of silence from the Project and then we get this?? Not sure what's going on but kind of over this whole Ark thing by now.

Where's Kim?

Of course. The usual mixture of the inane and downright ludicrous. Kim had to remind herself to remain calm, but she knew she had to act.

Adonai on his own clearly lacked credibility. Kim had to remind herself how long it took her to accept the truth of the blue whale inside a droid's body. Had she not seen it herself, she'd have thought the same thing.

But her own silence hadn't helped matters; people had been waiting to hear from Kim Teng, excitedly hanging on to the prospect of the whales being safe and well. Instead, they had gotten Adonai, with bad—and confusing—news.

Drawing the kanji for *visual*, Kim opened her newsfeed channel. A holo appeared, floating above the console, mirroring her face. She was well aware that she looked nothing like Hannah Monksman right now—her cheeks were hollow, her skin covered in a sheen of sweat. Well, there was nothing she could do about that.

Hey, everyone. This is Kim. She paused. *Look, this isn't going to be a cheerful, excited rundown of my past few days. But I have to be honest with you. You deserve that.*

Probably by now you've heard Adonai's video. I'm proud of him. He's come a long way, and to make a decision like this is pretty monumental. God. He's my best friend, and I care about him so much, but what he's gone through in the past few days . . . I'm shocked, and I'm amazed. He's a strong . . . being.

So. Let me give you the rundown of the situation as it stands. We landed on New Eden, but things didn't go well. I was told not to tell you what had happened, but the truth is, we crashed. The whales are safe, but only just. The Aquarium's leaking. The weather is crazy. And there are . . . creatures on this planet. They've killed one EU soldier.

And there are ruins here, too. A civilization lived here long before we arrived. I don't need to tell you how exciting that is. It's the first evidence of alien civilization we've found . . . anywhere. In the entire explored universe.

But that's not all. Adonai might have proved existence of Eschol Thirteen. You'll have heard his account by now, and I hope you've listened to it. At first, I was skeptical too. But both Wren and I did experience something in that asteroid belt. We don't know what it was, but I'm positive it's important.

We can't let this slip through our fingers. We were meant to bring the whales here. We need to study this place, find out its secrets. We can't allow EU—or anyone else—to come between us and saving the whales.

I'm telling you this because you can stop it. You can put your support behind the Ark Project. Tell EU that you won't stand for allowing this to happen. Public pressure is what saved the whales in the first place! Do you think there'd ever have been an Ocean Protectorate if people didn't stand up and speak up? If we all just sat back, the Ark Project would have run out of funding in its first year. So yeah,

Adonai's right. Let's turn New Eden into a resort if we need to. Let's fly some rich people out here to spend some credit. Let's make sure they appreciate a few whale sightings before they leave. Let's do whatever we have to to make sure the whales get into the ocean and stay there.

We did it before. We ended all wars by finding a greater purpose. And now, we've found one even stronger. This is more than Unification. This is . . . something else.

You feel it too, don't you?

Before she could think about it, she snapped the recording closed. It only took her another second to find the real coordinates for New Eden logged in *Seiiki*'s system and to attach them to the video. Another second for it to upload to the net, and then it was done.

Sitting back in her chair, she focused on her breathing for a few minutes. Her heart rate slowed, and she felt a sense of peace descend over her. When she looked up, she found Adonai standing in the hexagonal doorway, watching her.

"Thank you, Kim."

She gave him a watery smile. "Either we've just fixed everything or we've blown it to shrapnel. We'll have to wait to find out."

CHAPTER
21

A s she jumped back to the ground, landing with a soggy thump, she found Wren waiting for her.

"I heard your video as it dropped," he called across the muddy ground. As Adonai dropped soundlessly to the ground beside her, Wren held out his hands. "Kim—"

"I know what you're going to say," she said, cutting him off as she gingerly stepped from one tussock to another. "I know it was stupid. I don't care. I—"

"Kim," he said, taking her hands and drawing her across the mud and onto solid land, laughing softly as he pulled her close. "I'm with you."

Kim opened her mouth, ready to protest.

"And I know you don't need my help," he added as he wrapped his arms around her tightly. "But I'm here."

She felt his heartbeat through his chest, her ear pressed so close, she could hear it, too. "I do need your help, Wren. Of course I need you." She was saying more with those words than she had intended to, but she meant them.

"You need me, too."

Kim jerked her gaze to the top of the ridge where Yoshi had appeared. "You're either insane or brilliant, and I can't work out which."

"It doesn't matter to you," Kim called back, her voice rising in challenge. "You'll be on *Daedalus* this morning, right?"

Yoshi's lip twisted in a disgusted sneer. "Hardly. I've worked too hard for this to let it get away from me now. Let's get this started before Lieutenant Grand gets a comm from Edgeward and marches down here."

Lieutenant Grand did not take long to march down there. He met her as she jumped down from the tilted airlock onto a nearby tussock, his face ashen.

Kim placed her hands on her hips and put on her best Hannah Monksman face. The one that said *I'm sweetness and innocence,* the one that betrayed nothing of the steely strength Kim Teng knew she had.

"You don't do anything by halves, do you, Kim?"

"What would be the point?" she replied, her voice—and gaze—steady.

"I still have to leave."

"I still have to stay," she countered.

Lieutenant Grand rubbed a hand through his short hair, then shook his head. "I'm going to get court-martialed for this. The leakage of information alone . . . and then *you.* Do you know what EU will do to me? Do you know what the public will think?"

"They'll think you stepped into battle with me and lost," she told him evenly. "You fought with honor, and you knew when to step away. Because you know I can't change my mind, Lieutenant. The people back on Earth will hate me forever for just the same reason."

He glanced over her shoulder at Adonai as he jumped neatly out of the airlock and landed beside Kim. "I guess you've got the rest of the gang on board. All the Caretakers. Even Yoshi?"

"Even Yoshi," she said with a smile.

He raised his eyebrows. "I'll give you two days. No more, but no less. It's all I can do, Kim."

She closed her eyes for a moment, knowing that it was a sacrifice he was making and grateful for it beyond words. "Thank you," she managed in a hoarse voice.

"You're welcome, Kim. Let's just hope we can get those whales into the water without further incident, shall we?"

Kim nodded, and for the first time in a long time, she spoke a silent prayer in her mind.

Let this work.

They started with Naomi.

There was no shortage of volunteers—almost a third of the whales was willing to be the first. Dangerous as it was, they all wanted a taste of the real ocean; and even more than that, they were keenly aware of the slowly worsening conditions inside the aquarium.

Surprisingly, none of the EU officers shied away from helping, either. Petty Officer Amelie Durand, Sergeant Renshaw, and Captain Shannon all offered to drive the tractors. Kim had sent Shannon, along with Cabes and Leroy, down to the base. Mallory was on hand to deal with anything the Caretakers might need, while Pierce and Spier drew the short straws and were stuck with Grand on sentry duty, pulling on their combat helmets with noticeable grimaces—the heat did not make combat gear any more comfortable.

The process of getting Naomi into the tank was as difficult as they'd expected, but even more so given that they were undertaking the process in the middle of the night. The forcefield was its own light source, spreading out over the furrow with a green glow, but there were deep shadows in places that worsened visibility considerably.

Deck Nine was mainly undamaged, which was a good thing. The crane machinery still functioned and had been checked over for safety by Wren and Adonai a few days ago. They'd even done a quick test run with some weighted pallets to ensure it could still withstand the strain.

Driving the tractor was at least easier now that she had had some practice. Backing it up—with the trailer attached—was an entirely different ordeal, however. In the sticky, softening mud, it was barely maneuverable and took her several attempts, some of which involved heart-stopping moments when the tread sank so far, the wheels refused to turn. Somehow, though, with a lot of sweat and cursing, she got it where it needed to be.

Hopping out and dropping to the mud, she watched as Adonai approached. He clambered up the side, opening the top of the tank so Yoshi could lower an extendable pipe from the airlock above. Adonai plugged it into the Aquarium, and Yoshi gave the signal to start pumping water.

While this was in progress, Wren and Yoshi readied the harness which was a large leather sling held together with lightweight steel netting and a forcefield. Unlike the tractors, it was designed to hold even the heaviest of the whales without any issues. The original plan had been to lower them from the ship directly into the water. Obviously, this was not a possibility now, but the practicality of the crane's design still worked in their favor with the winch running along tracks on the ceiling of Deck Nine toward the airlock.

Kim climbed from the tractor up to the airlock. Wren was now standing at the far end of Deck Nine, which was lit by emergency lighting, and was directing the tractor to lower through one of the holes in the deck. The forcefields on these access holes had been deactivated. The water in the Aquarium was now noticeably lower—at least thirty feet below their feet, where it had once been close to the top. Kim crossed the floor with trepidation, the emptiness making her very aware of how this could all go wrong.

"I think we're ready to go," Wren told her.

I'm not, she thought inwardly.

She felt the whales' buzz of excitement through the Link, but it was almost drowned out by her nervousness.

"Ready, Naomi?" she asked.

The gray's beaked whale was hovering below her feet, a little to the left. Dark shapes moved further in the depths; the other whales had gathered to watch, not wanting to miss this experience.

I'm ready, Kim.

Kim drew a kanji in the air. "Computer, lower the harness."

The cables unwound from the winch, and the harness began to drop. It reached the level of the hole and lowered through. Kim watched it spread itself over the surface of the water before the weight pulled it down. The forcefield lining the netting cast a green glow into the water as it submerged. Naomi swam toward it, eager—and far too fast.

"Slow down," Kim chided gently. "We don't want to get you tangled."

Naomi backpaddled with her fins. *Sorry. Sorry.*

The forcefield flattened itself out, making the leather widen.

"Okay, swim carefully over the harness. We'll try and get it in the right spot."

Naomi made small strokes, bringing her huge body forward to sit over the flat leather base.

Is this right?

Wren held up a finger and thumb, joined in a circle.

"Perfect," Kim said as she drew another kanji in the air. "Just stay there. Computer, retract harness."

The netting, along with the forcefield, bent itself inward, allowing the harness to mold to the shape of Naomi's body. Flickers of green showed where the forcefield touched her fins and tail. When it fit her tightly, but not too tightly, the computer said, "Retraction complete. Should I begin lifting?"

"I guess so," Kim said. Then, more confidently, she added, "Let's do this."

The winch retracted, the mechanics protesting the weight with a small, high-pitched whine. The steel wires drew taut. Kim knew it could handle the stress, but it still made her nervous to watch.

"You're going to feel exposed when you reach the surface," Kim spoke into the Link. "Be prepared. It'll feel cold and strange, but don't freak out. It's important to remain calm and still."

Yes. I will.

The water churned and eddied before Naomi's huge body breached the surface.

Kim couldn't help but gasp as the winch lifted Naomi high overhead. She had never seen any of the whales outside of the Yokohama Institute or *Seiiki*—not alive, anyway. Naomi was . . .

"You're beautiful," Kim said softly. The sleek hide glistened with water, so smooth in places, so rough in others. Her skin was a soft gray, mottled with white on her underside. Her torpedo-shaped body was elegant, her nose was delicately pointed.

I'm flying! Naomi responded with a faint chuckle of laughter. *Adonai can fly! I can, too!*

Kim glanced to her left. Wren's mouth was stretched wide in a grin. Yoshi's expression was completely unreadable. Kim reached up a hand, brushing Naomi's smooth flank as the whale passed over Kim's head.

She grinned widely. They were doing it. There was no turning back now.

Naomi, caught up in the moment, wriggled from head to toe as the winch moved her over the deck and toward the airlock. Kim experienced a moment of panic as the winch groaned and the forcefield flickered.

"Computer, is the winch holding?"

The computer's response was reassuring. "All is proceeding as we would expect."

Still, Kim felt tense and anxious as she walked to the edge of the deck and watched carefully as the crane lowered Naomi down into the open top of the tank below. Light spilled from Deck Nine through the airlock, painting the scene in blue-white, a surreal still life involving strange machinery and a creature of majesty. The large whale took up only a fraction of the room in the tank, however, given that she was only fifteen feet long. Once into the water, she moved freely, flipping a fin up in a very human gesture.

I'm here. I'm in the tank! Oh, this is amazing.

Kim could already hear the other whales clamoring. Everyone wanted to be next. She moved back to the access hole and spoke as authoritatively as she could. "Calm down. Every one of you will be moved, but we can't do it all at once." She surveyed them as objectively as she could. "We have room for four more smaller whales in this tractor. I'll choose who goes, and it'll be based on weight and size. Do you trust me?"

Yes, Kim, yes.

They were reluctant, but they quietened and allowed her to pick out four of the smaller whales. Finally, they, too, were safely in the tractor, and Kim looked at Wren and Yoshi, who shared a worried but hopeful glance between them as well.

"This is it," Wren said, his face glowing.

"You'd better get down there," Yoshi told Kim. "I'll meet you there in a few minutes to do the check."

Kim nodded. Instead of heading to one of the airlocks that aligned with level ground, she took hold of the crane's cable and shimmied down it. It made her feel good to use her old skills, especially when she looked up and saw Wren watching with a gaze that said he wanted to do more than just kiss her. Smiling to herself, she jumped into the cabin of the tractor where Captain Shannon was waiting, the engine running.

"You'd better make this a smooth ride," she warned him.

"I'll do my best," he hedged, but underneath his surliness, she could sense some edge of excitement. "You've got your job cut out for you after we're gone."

Captain Shannon shifted into gear and pulled the tractor away as Adonai jumped down from the cabin, ready to help Durand back the second tractor into the place they'd just vacated.

Up ahead, Yoshi jogged into position. Shannon drew the tractor to a stop, and Kim jumped out. Yoshi was already scanning the trailer, walking slowly with her head down.

"How's it looking?" Kim called down to her. The readings on the panels were good, but there was nothing to measure the amount of movement in the water of the tanks. None of them wanted the whales to end up being injured by being thrown into the sides of the tank . . . or each other.

"Temperature is fine. No signs of leaks," Yoshi confirmed.

We're okay, Naomi told her, impatience evident in her voice and across the Link. *Let's just go!*

"I have to make sure," Kim chided her gently as she pulled herself up the side of the trailer and walked along the running board. There was no sign of any cracks in the tank, and the water level was stable. Climbing back into the cabin, she heard a shout from Yoshi.

"Good luck," the girl said as she turned.

"Thanks." Kim grinned widely before slipping back into her seat and telling Captain Shannon to continue on.

The trip was harrowing. Every jolt and bump made her panic, but Naomi assured her she was doing fine, even enjoying the ride.

By now, the road to the beach was well and truly compacted, and the headlights shining into the growing gloom revealed how much they'd changed this part of the planet already. Tree branches had been knocked down and dragged to the sides. Vegetation was starting to draw back.

Kim? Is everything going all right?

The words shouldn't have been a shock, but they were. She had never spoken to Yoshi through the Link. It was like being aware of someone in the next room, but communicating only through knocking on the wall—and then finally, one day, hearing their voice.

Yes, she replied hesitantly. *Everything's fine.*

You are surprised that I care.

Damn. Kim had been hoping she'd be able to hide that thought, but then, human minds were not like whales. They were infinitely harder to trick. *Not surprised that you care. That you care so* much. She sighed. *Sorry. I just expected . . . I'm surprised you wanted to stay on New Eden at all.*

Why did you think I would leave? Inside Kim's mind, Yoshi's voice was thoughtful, a lonely sound in the darkness of the night.

Why wouldn't you? Kim replied. *The Ark Project isn't going to be getting any more funding. It's likely we'll be stranded here. Why would you want that?*

Yoshi swallowed. *You must hate me.*

Kim was startled. *I don't hate you*, she said, then amended, *Maybe I did, for a bit. After Abdiel . . .*

I didn't do that to Abdiel. I didn't release those pictures.

They came from your social media account! How could Yoshi lie about this so baldly?

I don't have to explain myself to you!

With that, Yoshi's presence drew back from the Link, and Kim felt oddly alone. Shaking her head, she tried to bring her focus back to the here and now. She needed to be alert if she was going to get this done.

The base loomed ahead, looking so much bigger by the light of the two moons that were now launching themselves into the sky. The loading bay doors were at the rear of the base and slid open as they approached, recognizing the code transmitted by the tractor.

This was the first time Kim had been inside the base, and she looked around with wonder as the halogen lights flickered on overhead.

They were in a flat concrete-based hangar with corrugated metal walls. Shelving units had been stacked at one end, and two of the broken droids were slumped beside them in various stages of disrepair. A few tech droids were curled in cocoons along the far wall, recharging. This room would be full of equipment soon, but for now, it was completely, echoingly empty. The tractor's engine roared in the contained space, loud even through the closed doors and windows of the cabin.

The tractor continued across the floor and through another roller door that lifted to allow them into a narrow hallway, a slanted ramp leading them down to the central operations room. This was the upper level of the wide space that opened down to the bay. The rounded glass wall was directly ahead, giving the impression they were about to drive straight into the darkened water. They'd come out on a mezzanine floor, edged by railings and studded with control panels. To the left, the glass wall continued to curve around until it met with the rooms behind them. To the right, there was a separate office projecting over the water. A long window ran down the inward-facing wall.

Shannon stopped the tractor, and Kim clambered out onto the mezzanine, taking a few steps toward the railing that overlooked the water. The sea was dark below them, making soft slapping sounds against the huge, windowed wall. Small droplets of spray hung in the air.

"That's Yoshi's lab," Officer Durand said, walking toward Kim and pointing to the room that hung over the water. "Think she'll be happy with it?"

"It takes a lot to make Yoshi happy," Kim said. Through the windows, she could glimpse similar equipment to Yoshi's lab on *Seiiki*, as well as an examination bed—whale-sized—and tall cabinets filled with various bottles and vials. "But I think that might just do it."

"I'm trying to get the lights on in here," Durand said, moving to the nearest panel. "You'd think it'd be an easy task, but without a computer, you'd be . . . oh, there we go."

The lights flicked on one by one, bright white halogen bulbs floating in the air, moving gently from side to side as Kim headed toward the controls and made a quick exploration of the systems. There were gauges showing ocean temperatures at various locations around the bay and beyond. Once Yoshi's new seeding drones were out there, they would have readings from every ocean on this world, but for now, the readings were simple. Depths were displayed and the direction and strength of currents. Kim had gathered a good knowledge of what the whales needed over her days on *Seiiki*. She could see the ocean temperatures were optimal—cetaceans could live comfortably between fifty and seventy-seven degrees Fahrenheit. The waters in the bay were a comfortable sixty-eight degrees, and a colder slipstream of water ripped through in a loop, coming straight from the South Pole. Following it would lead the arctic whales into the oceans more suited to them.

Mind on the job, she told herself, and jumped back into the cabin to turn off the forcefield top of the tank.

Shannon was struggling to haul the new harness over toward the tractor. The crane setup was exactly the same as that on *Seiiki*, with a rail bolted firmly to the ceiling and extending over the bay with forcefield reinforcements. At least, now that they were practiced, this was a lot faster to accomplish.

Kim and Shannon hooked Naomi up within ten minutes. Though Kim's muscles were already aching with the strain, adrenaline spurred her onward.

It was finally happening. Everything she had worked for, everything she had been through—it had all been worth it.

Is it time? Naomi asked.

"Yes. It's time," Kim told her as she tightened the last strap and jumped down from the trailer, heading toward the control panels. "Are you ready?"

Please stop asking. Please just do it now.

Kim smiled and hit the circular control to retract the winch. The harness tightened around Naomi's middle, then began to lift her from the water. Streams ran from her curved back, and Naomi swung upward and then out over the bay.

I can't believe it's time, she said happily.

"You deserve it," Kim replied softly. She wanted to say more, something meaningful, but the words wouldn't come. It didn't matter, anyway. Words were only words, and what was happening here was so much more than that.

The crane began to lower. Naomi's body descended past them, a leviathan, an impossibility suspended over the abyss. The water swirled darkly below. At first, she was only a foot above it. Then half a foot. Then an inch. Her skin touched the surface, and her entire body gave a massive shiver.

"What is it? What's wrong?" Kim felt panic rising in her, hands searching for the circular control, ready to retract the winch.

It is . . . incredible.

And then, a wave of pure happiness swept over Kim, so rich and deep, she could smell and taste it. Tears sprang to her eyes, and Officer Durand looked sideways at her, concerned. Kim made a dismissive gesture and turned away.

Below, the harness flattened, allowing Naomi to swim free. She ploughed through the water with a wild whoop, flicking her tail and sending a huge spume up the walls. Spray struck Kim's face, and she laughed, jumping up and down.

"Yes! Yes, yes!" Her cry echoed around the chamber, seeming to mix with the ethereal water patterns reflected on the walls.

This feeling was like nothing Kim had experienced before. She'd never felt this kind of elation, this much joy. It was her own delight, too, not just that of Naomi. She knew she had accomplished something big.

This was what it meant to do God's work.

CHAPTER

22

It was the longest night of Kim's life. Shannon threw himself into tasks with all his strength and vigor. Renshaw didn't show his enthusiasm so openly, but he worked tirelessly. Durand ran around like a hyperactive toddler, doing every task she could. Kim had never picked her for a devotee of the whales, but she suspected she was. She even seemed to know all their names.

Morning dawned, and they'd put fifteen of the smaller and two of the medium-sized whales into the bay. Kim was exhausted and not just from the physical effort.

Every whale that went into the ocean bombarded her with sensory input—the feeling of the water, the warmth and coolness of it, the shock and fear, the delight of catching a mouthful of wild-grown krill.

They were forced to take a break as the sun came up, eating a desultory meal of freeze-dried beans and imitation-chicken soup before crashing into their beds. As Kim tried to sleep, she heard Airman Leroy's unmistakable South African accent through the wall of the tent.

"... can't see why we're doing this. We should be in orbit right now."

"It makes little difference. We can't leave New Eden's orbit until the relief arrives to escort us. We don't have enough fuel to make it back alone."

"But we're wasting time juggling whales while men out there are bent on hunting us down and wild animals run around the forest picking us off one by one?"

"I'd advise you to keep your thoughts on your job, Airman," Grand replied. "And obey orders until we're done here. Do you understand?"

Kim fell asleep with a smile on her face.

Waking only a few hours later, she wiped the sleep from her eyes and pulled her tablet close to check the time. Almost midday; she had wasted precious hours. She was about to pull herself out of bed when a notification popped up next to the chronometer.

5,348,773 comments.

Holy crap. That was more comments than any post had ever attracted. She clicked on the notification, reading the text that popped up with widening eyes.

I'm buying passage on a ship. Can't wait to see for myself.

Alien angels? Count me in!

This is the proof I've been waiting for. Glory be.

Advertisements speckled the comments, and Kim put her hand to her mouth. There were almost a dozen transport companies offering passage to New Eden.

Book a passage today!

Begin your pilgrimage with one small click!

If she'd wanted to attract attention, she'd done it. She just wasn't so sure why it made her so uneasy.

She shut the tablet down.

The EU soldiers were surprisingly helpful. It was only Leroy who had any kind of problem with what they were doing. He moped and did his tasks half-heartedly. Still, with so many extra hands, the work proceeded well. By the time the following night fell, they'd moved another fourteen whales. All that were left were the largest—four southern right whales, one finback, three humpbacks, and a sperm whale. The following morning was the most challenging day. Sleeping had cost them time; they now had little more than thirty-six hours left. Kim met Yoshi outside the base and drove her and the tractor back to *Seiiki*, where Wren was waiting. Yoshi hadn't come back to camp; she'd spent the night in the base with Renshaw guarding her. Kim had never seen her looking tired before, let alone exhausted, but she did now. Her eyes were dark-rimmed and reddened by lack of sleep. Her hair was a tousled, tangled mess.

"The only way we're going to do it," Yoshi said as they jumped down from the cabin to meet Wren near the back of the ship, "is to take the tanks off the tractors and weld some hull plates to the trailer. We'll make it into a kind of sled."

"That's not going to be a pleasant trip," Wren grimaced.

"We'll have to use straps and harnesses to keep them on," Yoshi continued. "But we have to do it now. We don't have any more time."

Kim knew she was right. Just overnight, the water level in the Aquarium had dropped another fifteen yards. The puddle spreading out below *Seiiki* was now more than just soft, sucking mud that tugged at their feet and inconvenienced the tractors—it was a treacherous hazard. Airman Cabes had slipped yesterday while carrying some food supplies, and his entire body had been pulled under the surface. Spier and Leroy had hauled him out, covered in muck and spluttering but otherwise safe. It was an accident that might have cost him his life.

Now, Wren looked up at the wreckage of *Seiiki* worriedly. "Does the ship look more tilted to you?"

Kim cocked her head. The ship was so huge, and comparing it to the twisted trees at the end of the furrow was useless. And really, she didn't want to think about it. As they boarded and headed for Deck Nine, Kim tested the angle of the deck under her feet. "I think you're right," she said. "There's definitely a difference."

Adonai was waiting for them on Deck Nine, crouched at the edge of the largest hole into the Aquarium. Below him, Kim could see Levi in the depths, but only just; the level of the water was so low now that he was over a hundred feet below them, and the power levels had dropped so significantly that the dim light provided barely any illumination.

"He is frightened," Adonai said. "I wish I could talk to him."

Kim put a comforting hand on Adonai's shoulder. "We've got more problems than we thought we did. Can you help Wren with the harness? I'll talk to Levi."

Adonai stood reluctantly, shuffling away with a glance over his shoulder. He had told her he didn't regret his choice to leave his whale body behind. Maybe that was true, but Kim suspected he did miss his whale friends.

Opening herself to the full extent of the Link, Kim crouched at the edge of the hole and gazed down at the murky shape below. "You have nothing to worry about," she said firmly. "You just have to be patient."

We hear the others calling, Levi said. *We don't want to be left behind.*

But we want to die in the ocean if we are to die, Berenice added.

Kim shook her head. "No one's going to die. We'll get you out of here—today, if possible."

You are worried. And the ship is moving. We can feel it. Every now and then, the water makes bubbles.

Kim glanced toward Wren and Adonai, who were about sixty feet away, resetting the harness into its flattened configuration. She drew the kanji for talk on the back of her hand. "Computer, is the ship at a greater angle than it was yesterday?"

"The ship has descended in elevation around twenty-three inches in the past thirty-six hours," the computer replied calmly.

"Computer, at the current rate, how long do we have before this deck is under the mud?" Kim asked.

"The rate is accelerating," the computer said. "I can't give an exact estimate, but I would suspect the ship would be completely submerged in . . ." There was a long pause, and Kim swallowed nervously. The computer's "episodes" were disturbing. "About two days' time."

Kim put her hand to her mouth. Out of all the problems they faced, this possibility had never occurred to her. Calling to Wren, she said, "We need to get the computer out *now*."

"I'm on it," Wren agreed grimly, already hurrying back across the deck to the door. Adonai stood, hands dangling by his sides as he watched Wren go.

"I need you here," she told him. "I'm sorry, Adonai. I know the computer means a lot to you, but the whales need your help, too, and we need to get the bigger ones out today."

"I know," he replied.

The urgency of the situation made Kim's fingers tingle. As Yoshi, Sergeant Renshaw, and Officer Durand entered, she ushered them back out immediately. They had to start working on the modified trailers.

Kim and Yoshi took charge of directing the tech droids to cut the tanks from their bases. The process took half the day, even with the help of every EU soldier who wasn't on sentry duty. During that time, the water in the Aquarium dropped another thirteen feet, and the ship developed a noticeably greater lean.

They loaded Berenice first. She was the largest of the remaining whales— Adonai had been the biggest, but his body was no longer their concern. Levi would be coming after her in a tractor driven by Durand with Yoshi to accompany her.

Berenice, unlike the whales they'd already transported, entered the harness with a little trepidation. Kim could feel it, even though she said nothing. She didn't blame her. This was a major operation, and not one she was looking forward to, and she wasn't the one being strapped, immobile, to the back of a machine and carted through an environment as foreign to whales as space was to humans.

Kim, Yoshi, Shannon, and Renshaw gathered at the edge of the hole, waiting for her to be winched up. The crane strained to lift, making a high-pitched whining.

"It's only because it's draining more power from the ship," Yoshi explained. "If we were at full power, we'd never hear it."

Kim wasn't placated. The winch seemed to move much more slowly, and there was a good deal of creaking from the leather harness that seemed to suggest the entire rig was under significant strain.

She held her breath as they followed Berenice across the deck and didn't let it go once she was outside. The tractor without its tank looked bare and uncomfortable—a flat bed of metal cushioned only with some tarps.

"Can you breathe?" she asked Berenice.

Yes, Berenice replied. *But the air is cold and hard here. I am missing the water.*

"Soon," Kim told her fervently. She made her way down the crane cables again—most of the soldiers had taken to doing the same to save time—and signaled to Sergeant Renshaw to start the tractor. As it grumbled to life, she clambered onto the trailer to help Adonai wind the leather straps around Berenice's slick body.

Adonai was her partner for this run, mainly because he had the most strength to help her should the straps need adjusting or Berenice's body need shifting. Renshaw drove carefully, but every bump or jolt made Kim wince, and Adonai was clearly tense as well. His eyes were fixed through the rear window, and Kim knew if there had been room, he would have ridden back there with Berenice.

"She's fine," she reassured him. The life signs readings coming through the Link assured her of these facts, but the continued outpouring of Berenice's emotions were wearying.

"I'll be glad when this is over," Adonai admitted.

"I hear you," Kim agreed, settling back in her chair and trying her best to relax and project calmness toward Berenice. She wondered how Yoshi was doing with Levi and felt a reassuring thrill of excitement from the whale that told her he, too, was on his way to the bay.

A sudden jolt made her sit up straight in alarm.

Something is wrong, Berenice said, and then Kim heard a resounding, bone-wrenching *snap.* Behind them, the trailer rocked suddenly to the left, pulling the cabin from side to side on its suspension. The movement was violent enough to throw Kim out of her seat. She hit the opposite window with a thud, pain spearing through her right arm as she heard Adonai's heavy body land next to her. Renshaw shouted "Brace!" but Kim had no choice in the matter at this point. Her body was at the mercy of gravity.

Through the windows, the trees tilted wildly, but it was the noise that filled Kim's head. Grating metal and the groan of straining bolts rose to shrieking volume, and glass shattered with a tinkling explosion.

Shards of duraglass—normally strong enough to withstand laser bullets—were sucked out of the window as Adonai was hurled through. Somehow, his droid reflexes allowed him to clutch the metal sill in passing, a move which just managed to stop himself from being smashed into the trunk of a huge tree that was, now that they'd been pulled to the side of the road, directly ahead of them.

Kim pulled her arms back to shelter her head as the cabin tilted past its point of balance, the weight of the tractor's undercarriage no longer able to right them. And then, with a final jolt, the metal roof buckled inward in an imperfect mirror of the tree trunk they had slammed into, pinning them up on their side.

Finally, all was still.

Oh no, oh no, Kim thought, scrambling against the twisted metal below her. "Berenice!" she called. There was no answer on the Link, only the quiet, worried muttering of the other whales.

Everything hurt, but she didn't let that stop her. She needed to see Berenice.

Kim? Yoshi asked through the Link.

"Kim, you okay?" Renshaw asked.

She glimpsed blood on his lips, but she couldn't waste another second on him.

The seats were now at a right angle to the ground. Reaching out, she gripped the frame of the window Adonai had shattered, and she slithered across. Adonai, still clinging to the rim of the window and maneuvering his body back into the cabin, reached out a hand to help her.

"I'm fine," she gasped as she clambered past him, glad to see that he was functional but needing to get to Berenice. She evaluated the distance to the ground. There was a ten-foot drop below her. The ground was covered with torn ferns and branches that had ripped from the tree as they'd gone over.

"Be careful," Renshaw told her. She ignored him and jumped.

She landed, hard, on her side. Something crunched under her. It was a branch, a small one, and not any of her own bones—that she knew of, anyway. She struggled to her feet, covered in mud and small twigs, and saw the damage. The trailer was almost overturned. Berenice's body was trapped between it and the ground.

"Oh no, God, no," Kim moaned. She scrambled through the loam, skidding on fungus and tearing her hands on fallen branches as she ripped them out of the way to touch the whale's head, fingers brushing the raised filament of the Link. She was warm, and the spidery matrices still pulsed with a glowing golden light. "Berenice!"

I . . . am hurt, Berenice replied, sounding slightly astonished.

A crunching noise made Kim look up. The other tractor trundled into view around the curve in the road. Kim could see a deep rut cut into the ground, hidden in the dappled shadows at just the right angle. Holding up her hand, she saw Durand take heed and slam on the brakes. The other tractor skidded to a stop. Yoshi was out of the cabin in moments, running toward them; Durand was only a few steps behind.

"No." The word was a prolonged, drawn out moan of horror that echoed in Kim's mind. Yoshi stood staring at the overturned trailer—and Berenice —as if she was looking at a corpse. That, if anything, spurred Kim to action.

"Get back in the tractor and keep going!" she snapped at Officer Durand. Breathless, she wiped wetness from her cheek. Blood. She hadn't even realized she'd cut herself. "Levi needs to get into the water," she croaked.

Durand hesitated for just a moment, but then she was back in the cabin, steering the tractor around the deep rut.

What's going on?

Where is Berenice?

Why can't I hear her?

Kim? Yoshi's voice again.

"Not now!" Kim yelled as Adonai dropped down beside her. Turning to him, she said, "Can you lift it?"

Adonai hadn't waited for her directions. He was already heading toward the trailer. Crouching, he placed his hands on the exposed axel, braced his feet on the road, and hauled. Kim could see his metal feet digging into the ground with force. The trailer rocked gently, but it was clear that Adonai would not be strong enough.

"Here!"

The shout drew Kim's attention past the overturned tractor. Durand's tractor had come to a stop, and Renshaw was at the rear, where he was unspooling a thick cable from the underneath of the trailer. Coughing heavily, he spat into the undergrowth and then dragged the length across to Kim at a run.

"I told her to keep going!" Kim yelled angrily. "We're putting Levi at risk, too!"

"Help me hook this up," Renshaw barked, slipping the cable through a ribbed section at the top of the trailer's undercarriage. Kim grabbed the spare end and held it while Renshaw looped the hook over the cable's longer length and tugged it tight. "Stay there, Adonai. We'll still need you to pull," the big man said before lifting his hand in a signal to Durand.

The cable began to retract, drawing taut between the two tractors.

"Pull!" Renshaw called to Adonai.

Adonai hauled again. Durand's tractor spat clods of dirt as the tires struggled for purchase, then dug in firmly. The trailer tilted slightly, rocked back, then began to right itself. Adonai slithered hastily out of the way as gravity took over. The trailer assembly pulled the tractor upright with a deep wrenching moan, settling back on its treads with a few more protests. Berenice's limp body jounced and settled, off-center, her long tail fin drooping over the edge and her eyes tightly closed.

Kim sank down to the soft loamy ground and sat, numbness overtaking her. Tears streamed from her eyes, and she couldn't stop them.

"Berenice?"

Adonai dropped to the ground behind her. Slowly, he approached and sat beside Kim, looking at Berenice's dark, leathery hide, so out of place amongst the greenery.

The whales' calls rang pleadingly through the Link. *Berenice! Wake up! Wake up!*

"Berenice," Kim echoed softly. "Wake up."

"We need to get her to the base," Yoshi told Kim. "We need to go now."

Kim stared blankly at Yoshi before finally finding the strength to lift herself to her feet. She was aware, dimly, of Yoshi's arms around her, supporting her as she climbed back into the cabin, and the contact was welcome. The rest of the trip passed in a blur as Renshaw pushed the tractor to its maximum speed, and they followed Levi's tractor into the base. There, disembarking on the mezzanine, Kim went through the motions of readying the harness. They moved Levi first. Berenice, still unresponsive, waited silently while Yoshi ran scanners over her body.

Kim didn't want to ask and was glad when Adonai voiced the question. "Will she be okay?"

"She has a few internal injuries," Yoshi said. "I'll need to take care of those. And I'm not sure why she's unresponsive. It's not usual, but then . . ." she shrugged. "Who can really say what's normal for these guys?"

"Is that supposed to make me feel better?" Kim asked. "Because it doesn't."

Yoshi sighed. "I'm not trying to make you feel better. I'm just stating the facts. We need to get her into the water; maybe then I'll know more."

It was a long night, but Kim did not let herself rest. She worked to load the remaining seven whales, then she busied herself in a store room, sorting out the last remnants of equipment, loading supplies into crates ready to be moved to the base. She worked until everyone else had gone to bed, and Renshaw begged her to rest. She only agreed because she could no longer think.

CHAPTER

23

*K*im.

It's so wonderful to swim!

And to be together again. But we have so much space!

The fish taste good.

Kim sat upright, the need to sleep leaving her with a disappointing rush. It was morning anyway, she realized with a sigh. Pushing herself out of bed, she found Renshaw eating breakfast by the firepit. He was nursing a broken rib, the bandage visible under the singlet he wore; sometime yesterday he'd discarded his EU jacket and hadn't replaced it even when coming back to camp. She'd noticed that Durand had done the same.

"Can you come with me?" she asked him.

"Sounds like a better idea than eating more of this crap," Renshaw said, putting aside his bowl of lumpy oatmeal with shriveled raisins. He slung his rifle over his shoulder, and they walked down toward the base.

"You know what they're saying about you online?" he asked casually. Well, about as casually as a man like Renshaw could.

Even without broken ribs, his voice was gruff, and it made it sound like an accusation.

"I can guess," Kim said.

"It was a dumb thing to do," Renshaw told her.

"I know," Kim replied without animosity. She squinted through the trees at the sky. "Part of me wishes Adonai hadn't said anything. That I'd kept my mouth shut, too. But if it was me, back on Earth . . . I'd want to know that Eschol Thirteen might actually exist. That this planet, too, might have been inhabited. It . . . means something."

"Does it? You didn't give them any proof."

"Because there isn't any." She sighed bringing her gaze back down to level ground again. "No footage, no scan data. Only what Adonai saw and a bunch of missing time on our equipment. I know how it sounds. Believe me, it's on my mind." She looked back at him. "Are you angry with me?"

"Does that matter to you?" Renshaw asked.

"A little bit, yeah," she replied. "I did what I thought was right, even if it . . . wasn't."

Renshaw didn't answer for a long time. "Now that the coordinates are public knowledge, there are a lot of people booking passage on pilgrim ships. Most of them are heading from the Outer Colonies, which are closer, and circumventing Edgeward. EU's trying to stem the tide, but they can't keep up."

"I suppose you'll be happy to be leaving today," Kim added, trying for levity but not quite reaching it.

"On the contrary," he replied. "I'm worried about leaving you down here alone. Who knows what mischief you'll get up to?"

Kim managed a grin. "You mean you'll miss me?"

"I wouldn't go that far," Renshaw replied. "But this is one command decision I can't quite wrap my head around. Leaving you here with those beasts and crazy Adherants?" He shook his head as they rounded the sharp bend in the road, revealing the deep rut in the road that had overturned the trailer yesterday. Renshaw pointed to it as he continued. "It wouldn't be my choice. Those bastards will stop at nothing."

"You think it was dug deliberately?" Kim asked him. She wasn't surprised to hear the theory; she'd been thinking the same thing.

"Here," the big man replied, pointing with the toe of his boot to a section of overturned dirt. "Clearly made by a flat implement. A shovel. They did a pretty good job of making it look natural, but it wasn't here the day before yesterday."

Wren was already at the base. She found him on the mezzanine working with the control panels. He looked exhausted, dark circles hanging under his eyes like weights.

"Hey, Kim," he said, his voice betraying the smile before it rose to his lips. "Someone else wants to say good morning."

"Hello, Kim," said another voice. Kim glanced up, startled as the words came from overhead.

"Computer?"

"I am here, Kim," the computer replied. "Wren installed my core last night."

Kim let out a small huffing laugh. She turned back to Wren. "It's working okay?"

"Better than okay," Adonai said happily, entering from one of the rear doors. "Even though we weren't able to remove the extra program from its subroutines, now that it's connected to the base, it seems to be functioning well."

"I'm glad to hear that," she said. Finally, she allowed herself to relax a little of the grip she'd placed on her emotions after yesterday.

Kim left Wren and Adonai discussing processing rates and headed to the edge of the mezzanine. Below her, the floating docks joined to a walkway accessible by ladders stationed every few feet at breaks in the railing. Next to one of them was Berenice, who was drifting just below the surface of the water, just the hump of her back visible. Yoshi crouched next to her, carefully injecting a large syringe into the whale's unresponsive hide. Kim climbed down the nearest ladder and made her way to Yoshi.

"How is she?"

"I'm giving her some fluids and some nutrients. I've done what I can for the internal hemorrhaging; it's under control and shouldn't leave any long-term damage. We need to wait for her to wake up, that's all."

"She's just asleep?" Kim probed the Link. Berenice's shape was still there against the internal grid, its life signs stable, but there was no hint of emotion or thought coming from the whale.

"As near as I can tell," Yoshi said with a shrug. "I can't do much more."

"How are the other whales?" Kim asked.

"Good. Very good, in fact. I launched one of the new seeding drones this morning, and there's another one ready to go tomorrow. The first seeder should provide enough sea life to populate the area of the first downed seeder in a month. I've accelerated the process. We'll still need around four more to build up the growth lost from the other downed seeders, but it's a good start."

Kim felt her spirits rise as she headed back up to the mezzanine—only to have them drop when she saw Lieutenant Grand enter through the door at the rear; Airman Leroy a step behind him. He looked over the scene below him, and Kim could tell he was impressed.

"Are you here to admire the base?" she said. "I can get Wren to show you around, if you'd like."

"That won't be necessary," he replied stiffly. "Kim, you know why I'm here. We're launching this afternoon. I've given you as much time as I can."

She nodded. "I understand."

He tried to meet her eyes. "I can't launch without you, Kim. I'd be leaving you in danger."

"Then don't launch," she replied.

"Kim, be sensible. You don't have the numbers."

Kim smiled widely. "I've fought against greater odds before and won. Sir."

His posture snapped rigid as he heard the word, and she wondered if he thought she was mocking him. She hoped he would realize she wasn't. She'd earned his respect. Now, she deemed, he was worthy of hers.

"I know," he said softly. "And that's why it pains me to do this, Kim." He looked toward Airman Leroy, and the other man stepped forward, a set of wrist binders in his hands.

"What the *fuck*?" Kim spat, eyes wide. The binders seemed to fill her entire field of vision. She'd hoped against hope she'd never see those damned things again in her life.

"You're under arrest," Grand explained.

"No," she replied, shaking her head and backing up toward the railing. "I'm not."

"You can't do that," Wren growled. Kim had forgotten that he was even here, but now he strode across the mezzanine, his hands clenched into fists.

"If I need to arrest you too, I will. We're evacuating the planet as planned—*all* of us."

"You've got no cause!" Wren said, anger evident in his voice.

"Kim, quite apart from the risk to your life, what you did—revealing military information to the public—is treason. We can't allow you to remain here on New Eden unprotected, and in any case, I've been ordered to take you off the planet to face trial."

"For *what*?"

Grand rubbed a hand across his forehead. "You've been in contact with illegal interests, Kim."

"Illegal interests?" Her heart felt frozen in her chest. "You've got to be kidding me."

"You contacted Zane Silversun several days ago. Airman Leroy informed me of that fact last night, and I had to relay the information to Edgeward. Admiral Mbewe signed off on your arrest warrant."

She laughed a loud, humorless bark. "I asked Zane if he was trying to kill the whales—and us! Because, in case you haven't noticed, I've been trying to *save* the whales. Why would I be doing that if I was in league with him?"

"Given our current situation—with terrorists residing on New Eden—I don't think you want to be making that argument. Five ships have just showed up on the satellites, and at least two of them have Adherant signatures."

Kim drew in a sharp breath. More ships? "They're not here because of me! They would have had to leave Edgeward a few days after *Seiiki's* launch." Kim couldn't imagine how five ships would manage this without attracting attention from *someone.*

"I had a missive from Admiral Mbewe this morning. A fleet-wide alert— the Adherants now have access to quantum drive technology," Grand said. "And so does everyone else. Apparently, Arden Tech has been developing a mass-market version over the past few months. Those ships didn't launch six months ago. They launched *a few days* ago." Grand paused. "And that's not counting the dozens of other pilgrim ships that are right now being outfitted with new engines, hoping to come out here and get a first-hand glimpse of Heaven."

Kim gaped. "The Adherants did this? Why?"

"It's clear that they have an end goal. One that's worth compromising their own beliefs for."

Sergeant Renshaw emerged from the door to the tractor ramps. He looked disheartened, she realized. Disappointed. But not defiant. Of course not. Why would any EU officer back her up? They knew about her past. She was a dirty shiv to them.

"But you're letting *us* stay?" Wren asked.

"Neither you nor Yoshi have shown any outward signs of rebellion. I'm trusting that you will maintain your composure and obey the command of EU. I would still rather you evacuated along with us, but if you choose to stay, I have no reason to force you to come with us. That goes for Adonai, too."

"You're holding me hostage!" Kim snarled. "You know Wren won't do anything if I'm gone!"

"I'm actually more concerned about Adonai," Grand replied. "But without your involvement, we could have resolved Adonai's interference easily enough."

Kim stared at him. "You mean you could have covered up his transmission. And you're pissed that I made that impossible."

Grand shook his head. "This isn't about me, Kim. These are my orders."

"I find it hard to think Admiral Mbewe signed off on this," she spat.

"Fortunately, Admiral Mbewe didn't need to. Kim, you need to put these binders on and come with me immediately, or I'll need to get the Airman here to stun you."

Over Grand's shoulder, Kim saw Sergeant Renshaw stiffen. "Sir, are you sure that's necessary?"

Lieutenant Grand turned to the sergeant, eyes blazing. "If you have objections, perhaps you'd like to join her in the brig on *Daedalus*."

"No, sir," Renshaw said quietly.

Kim tried not to look at him. She didn't blame him for his obedience. This was his career, after all, but she couldn't help but feel hurt.

Renshaw lifted his rifle and said, "You'll need to keep your hands where I can see them, Kim. Leroy's going to put the restraints on you."

"You can't do this," Wren said, vehemence in his voice. Kim wondered if he had his white pistol on him, and she hoped to hell he didn't.

"Don't do anything stupid, Wren," she warned him and lifted her hands slowly.

Airman Leroy looked positively gleeful as he stepped toward her and placed the fingertip-sized buttons against each of her wrists. As they contacted her skin, they released a band of black plastic that folded around each wrist and adjusted so that they were tight enough that she couldn't move but loose enough not to cut off circulation.

Kim was no stranger to force restraints, but it was still not particularly pleasant.

"Nice and easy," he said, leaning in close. "If you cooperate, we might be able to get you off with a lighter penalty."

His tone reminded her of sleazy police officers in dingy police stations; the type of men who fumbled their hands under her shirt as they showed her to her cell.

"Screw you," she fired at him. Rage exploded like a bomb, blacking out her sense of reason, and she punched him in the stomach. It wasn't hard enough to do anything more than wind him; he was three times her weight. Her fist stung. She tried to shake it out, but it was hard with the binders on, so she settled for cursing loudly and fluently.

"Renshaw, get her to *Daedalus*," Grand ordered.

Kim gave Leroy a dagger-sharp stare as he doubled over, wheezing. She knew why Grand had turned her over to Renshaw; she'd be less likely to strike out at him.

The bastard was right.

Renshaw took her upper arm, wrapping it in his big hand. Kim could tell he was fighting against himself to do this. She knew exactly where to hit Renshaw to cause maximum pain to his injured ribs. She could vault over the railing. She'd survive the plunge, as long as she didn't hit one of the floating docks or any of the machinery down below, but where would she go then? Swim out into the bay with binders on? Even if she got them loose—and that wasn't impossible—they'd be waiting for her to come ashore, and she'd have to do that eventually. No choice. She was trapped in a corner like a rat.

"Kim?" said Renshaw, as if he could tell what she was thinking. "You need to come with me now."

She glanced at Wren, his face distressed. She looked over at Yoshi, who had her hands over her mouth. At least Adonai wasn't here. That was one small grace.

"Okay," she said. "I'll come."

CHAPTER
24

The brig on *Daedalus* was meant for one occupant. They'd taken her comm-band from her, and Kim felt the walls closing in the moment the door was closed and the forcefield shimmered into place across it. She knew there were cameras in the ceiling, but she couldn't tell exactly where they were in the featureless bulkhead. Which was just as well, because she felt like smashing something.

She wondered how close they were to launching. She'd tried to hear movement or voices, signs of the ship powering up. It felt like it had been hours.

It was the worst thing in the world to be stuck in this windowless place with no communication, no channel to the outside world. Her own thoughts pressed down, full of nightmarish images of Zane piloting a scoutship, strafing the base with laser fire.

Your fault, said a voice inside her head. *Stupid, dumb girl. What did you think would happen? Did you think you'd walk away from this with a clean slate? Building a new life on New Eden, erasing the past like it was nothing?*

She cried, silently, her face buried in her arms so that whoever was watching would see no trace.

Kim, are you all right?

It was Martha, a Sei whale. Kim hadn't heard much from the whales since they'd gone into the ocean. This gentle, nonintrusive contact lit her up inside.

"Martha," she whispered. "I'm fine. It's . . . just human troubles."

Don't be sad. Kim, you've done a wonderful thing! The oceans here, they are better than I ever imagined.

"Good," Kim said with a smile. "I'm really glad, Martha."

Footsteps sounded. Renshaw had come to check on Kim twice now during his watch. Both times, he'd said nothing, and Kim hadn't even looked at him. She wasn't mad, but . . . okay, she was mad. He probably didn't deserve it, but she couldn't think of a thing she wanted to say to him.

"Kim?"

She looked up at the voice, seeing a shape appear through the duraglass panel in the door. Not a rotund man, but a smaller metallic shape. This wasn't Renshaw; it was Adonai.

"Adonai, you shouldn't be here," Kim hissed, standing up and going to the forcefield-covered aperture.

Adonai didn't move. "I've come to let you out."

Kim shook her head. "You can't. Where would we go? EU has control of the base."

"Yes," Adonai told her, "but none of them are aboard this ship right now. They're currently dismantling the shelter. You need to steal this ship. Take it to another continent." Adonai sounded urgent, his voice pitched low. His stance indicated agitation, his shoulders slightly hunched, his hands making a wringing motion. God, he was becoming more and more human every day.

"They can track us," she pointed out.

Adonai had an answer for that, too. "Wren can disable it. He's outside right now."

Kim tamped down her enthusiasm. This was a lost cause, but her heart went out to Adonai for trying. "I can't." The bleakness of this realization made her feel slightly ill. She'd fought as much as she could, and it still hadn't been enough. She was still going to lose everything, and it was her own fault.

The entire ship lurched to one side, and Kim, off-balance, was flung against the forcefield. It crackled and suspended her just above the door to the cell before hurling her back across the small room. Her injured wrist struck the wall, and she let out a yelp of pain.

The ship rocked back to level, and Kim drew in a ragged breath. Lifting her head, she saw that Adonai was still there, standing stock-still as if the ship hadn't moved at all.

"Kim, are you—" he began, but his words were cut off by a loud sound.

With a buzzing noise, the forcefield flashed bright blue and then blinked out. So did the lights—all of them. Darkness surrounded them like a cloak, and for a moment, all Kim could see was a white-blue after-image that resolved into two golden points.

Adonai's LED eyes. They cast a small amount of light, and Kim could see that the door was partly open. The blackout must have disengaged the locks.

Kim scrambled to her hands and feet, pushing away the dizziness that resulted from the stress of the past few hours and the pain of her injured wrist. She grabbed the door with her good hand and opened it fully before stepping through.

"Did you plan that?" she asked.

"No," he replied, troubled. "But we should take advantage of it to find out what's going on."

The ship was small enough that they needed only make it up one narrow ramp to the upper deck, then along a cramped corridor before they were at the access hatch. Adonai's eyes helped light the way, but it was now nighttime outside the hatch, and neither of the moons were out. The forest loomed like a single solid, dark shape. But even as she stepped through, Kim saw a burst of stuttering light, then another. Loud explosions—was that gunfire? Kim clapped her hands over her ears and scanned the blackness.

Her eyes adjusted. Torchlights bobbed as people moved, creating crazy patterns in the night. She could see shapes running on the other side of the camp, could hear Grand's voice shouting something.

Then . . . nothing. A stillness. Kim had taken two steps from *Daedalus*, heading to the left. She had some vague idea she could go to the base, but this sudden cessation of noise stopped her.

A crackling of dried leaves just ahead of her. She switched her gaze from the opposite side of the camp to see what was directly in front of her.

It was . . .

It was a monster.

She had seen them before, but only from afar. This one was close enough that she could smell it—the scent of dampness and something sweet, like the loam of the forest but also sharper. It was large—the size of a dining table. Four powerful-looking paws. Its sinuous neck was long and uplifted, its snout carved in half by two rows of sharp teeth. Its eyes, though. Those were the thing that made her pulse freeze and her ears start ringing with some internal alarm bell.

They weren't animal eyes. Not even the cunning eyes of a predator. These eyes sparkled with life; with clever, sly triumph. This creature was clearly intelligent.

The thing looked at her for a long moment, slowly, gracefully settling back on its haunches. Long claws sprang from its massive forepaws as it lifted them from the ground. Kim's thoughts slowed to the speed of drying cement. A weapon—she needed something to defend herself with. She barely dared to take her eyes off the creature, but she summoned all her will and snapped her gaze to the ground, scanning it and finding only a single fallen branch, about as long as her arm and barely thick enough to qualify as an old-fashioned walking stick. She crouched slowly, reaching her hand out while keeping her eyes on the thing's forepaws, watching for any warning movement, and grasped it. It was too light, too easy to swing. Wishing more than anything she had her shiv, she hefted it anyway, knowing it wasn't enough.

She took a slow step backward, readying herself for the creature to spring at her, bringing the stick back far enough that she could take a decent swing before it tore her apart the way it, or one of its fellows, had torn apart Simons. A shout ripped through the air, jerking the monster's unblinking stare away from her face.

"Over here!"

Oh, damn. That was Wren's voice! Kim had forgotten, for those long moments, that she wasn't alone. Now the thing was looking over Kim's shoulder at Wren, who was waving his hands and jumping up and down. Now that he had its attention, Wren moved in an arc away from Kim. The creature's eyes followed her, and it began to advance.

Damn.

Kim hurled the branch at the monster. It didn't respond as it bounced off a massive shoulder. Wren was yelling something, but Kim couldn't make out the words; the ringing in her ears was too loud. All she could see was the dark shape stalking toward Wren. She couldn't allow it to happen. With a burst of speed, she ran toward the creature.

Something wrapped around her middle, lifting her off the ground. The arms were so tight around her, they hurt, and she felt hard metal biting through her jumpsuit into her flesh.

Not Wren—Adonai.

"Let me go!" she yelled, but Wren had the pistol in his hands and fired. *Once, twice.*

The bullets slammed into the creature with visible force, knocking it backward, but instead of falling, it seemed to become more enraged. Launching again at Wren, it let out a growl that set Kim's hackles up, and it slashed wildly with its claws. Wren's foot snagged on something, and he tumbled backward. In bare fractions of a second, the creature was on him.

The monster straddled him, one forepaw on either side of his head. Wren looked up at it, his hands still clenching the gun but clearly unable to move.

The thing let out a terrific howl. It was the same noise she and Wren had heard in the forest, that they had all heard over the past few weeks, but close-up, it was paralyzing. Wren clearly felt it, going still, his face looking up into the creature's maw. Kim hung limp in Adonai's arms, unable to break free of his restraints, even if she could have found the desire to go toward that thing.

It was common sense. Constantin would have commended her. Knowing when to fight and when to run was how a shiv lived to old age and retired in style.

But Kim was no longer a shiv, and *it was Wren*.

That thought finally coalesced into something solid, and she thrashed, trying to break free from Adonai. In the distance, she could see the beast lock its jagged, broken teeth around Wren's ankle and drag him viciously, uncaringly, across the ground.

His limp body lifted and dropped as the creature dragged him over something. It was only then that Kim realized it had dragged Wren into the middle of the stone circle she'd uncovered days ago.

"Help him!" she finally managed to gasp. "Adonai!"

"I can't let you go if you're going to run over there. Stay here," Adonai commanded, and Kim realized that he hadn't ever been intending to let Wren die. He had only been preventing her from throwing herself into danger. When he let her go, Kim sagged to the ground. Her wrist blazed with fresh pain.

Faster than Kim could ever have moved, Adonai was in front of the beast. Bending at the waist, he wrapped two hands around the thing's rear leg and broke it with a single movement. The sound was an audible and sickening crack, but it didn't sound like bone breaking; more like glass shattering.

The creature released Wren, turned on Adonai and snarled. And then vanished from sight.

One of the moons lifted over the horizon at that moment, just enough to spread light over the ship and the circle beside it. Nothing. Nothing there at all.

How was this possible?

"Wren!" Kim shouted, running toward him. "Are you okay?"

Gasping, teeth gritted against the pain, he sat up. The lower half of his jumpsuit was soaked through with blood, and shreds of blue material hung like rags. Kim fought to keep her mind calm, but her reaction to the sight must have traveled through the Link.

Kim? What is wrong with Wren?

She pushed the contact with the whale mind aside, focusing on Wren and Wren alone.

"You have to get up," she said. "There might be more of them."

"The fact that I can't see any EU officers makes me think that's a definite yes," Wren said. He tried to lift himself, grimaced, and fell back to the ground. As if in answer, a long, low howl vibrated the air. It was joined by others, becoming a whole chorus of bone-chilling voices raised in victory.

"Don't move," Adonai commanded Wren. "I'll have to carry you."

Wren let out a low groan. "God damn it. First my leg, then my masculinity." But he offered no protest as Adonai crouched, slid one arm under Wren's buttocks and the other under his shoulders, then lifted him with incredible ease. Wren uttered another gasp of pain but wrapped his arms around Adonai's neck and hung on grimly.

Before she turned and ran, Kim caught sight of the pistol lying forgotten on the ground. Scooping it up, she followed Adonai and Wren, hoping to high hell she didn't have to use it.

They ran through the dark, heading across the front of the furrow and taking what Kim hoped was a shortcut through the trees to the road. *Seiiki's* dark shape loomed to their right, swallowed just as quickly as they plunged into the forest.

Kim kept the pistol in her uninjured hand, careful to keep her fingers away from the controls on the side . . . and the trigger. She had no desire to shoot, and having seen the effects bullets had on the creatures, she knew it would be futile anyway. But having a weapon was better than not having a weapon. It would slow the creatures down, if nothing else. The breath was burning in Kim's lungs when she heard them again. A low growl, followed by the crunching of dry undergrowth, told her they were less than forty feet away. She tried to gauge how many creatures were chasing them, but with the noise of her own pounding footsteps—and Adonai's much heavier ones—it was impossible to tell.

A minute later, she saw a shape.

The familiar cutout in the darkness slinked alongside them, hidden just inside the trees. Another, on the other side of the road. Both of them were twenty feet behind, and one was quite clearly bigger than the other. For a full minute, they paced alongside them before Kim noticed another group of three galloping along the side of the road.

She lifted the pistol, aiming it at the nearest creature. It didn't react, didn't run away, but also didn't come any closer.

What were they waiting for?

And then, when another two shapes joined them, she had the answer.

"They're herding us," she gasped.

Wren's eyes were locked on the creatures, his arms still around Adonai's neck. "We don't have anywhere to go but the base."

"They know it," she replied, her statement ending in a yelp as her foot shot out from under her. She landed heavily on her butt, jarring one hip. She had slid into the rut that had almost killed Berenice. Scrabbling to her feet, she aimed the gun back behind her, but the creatures made no advancing moves. A paralyzing, unshakable dread began to fill her, and she tore her gaze away. "I'd bet they're doing the same thing with the EU officers."

"Hopefully, they've already made it to the base," Wren said.

Kim, Kim, what's happening?

Why are you so afraid?

Can we help?

She didn't have breath to spare to reply.

She did her best to block out the rising anxiety of the whales and forced herself to keep running.

The trees drew back, releasing them onto the shoreline. The base was just up ahead, and to Kim's relief, it clearly had power; the windows were lit, and light spilled from the front room in a semicircle across the water, catching the ripples of waves.

Wren pointed toward one of the rear entrances they'd used with the tractors, and Kim nodded as best she could while still keeping pace. There was a small door to the side of the roller doors that led into the hangar. All the doors were now hooked up to the computer which meant voice confirmation was all they needed for access.

It was a relief and a worry to be out in the open like this. Behind them, their pursuers left the trees and raced onto the rocks and grass. Double moonlight caught the thick, coarse hair on their backs. Their eyes gleamed, cool and calm, as if they knew their prey would come to them and were just killing time.

Bare teeth glittered like misshapen stars. They were almost noiseless, moving with barely a sound, not even a rustle of grass.

Kim's own breath sounded so loud, it filled the night. Ahead of her, Wren yelled, "Computer! Open the door!" shortly before Adonai crashed straight into it, reducing speed only when he used his weight to wedge himself and Wren into the gap and shove it open more quickly.

The door hissed as it slid back, widening with unbearable slowness even with Adonai's considerable strength, as Kim looked over her shoulder to see the creatures coming from every direction like a swarm. The five or six that had herded them seemed like a miniscule amount now that there were dozens of them—thirty or forty at least, each of them slightly different. Some had paler shades in their fur; others looked almost bald altogether. One such had long, jagged cuts and knotted scars all over its body. One of its eyes was missing, a simple ragged hole where it had once been. One was missing a paw. Another limped badly on a misshapen leg. Some were terribly skinny, ribs poking through matted, patched fur as if they were wasting away—but no less ferocious for it. They shouldered their way past their fellows, trying to be the first to taste their prey.

She tore her gaze free, wary of the hypnotizing effect pure horror had on her. The door was open, a thin sliver of light piercing through to fall on the grass. She darted through, just behind Adonai and Wren.

"Shut the door! Computer, shut the—" Wren yelled. The door began to hiss closed. Too slowly. Far too slowly . . .

A snarling snout pushed into the gap, a clawed paw just below it. Kim heard a rending sound as the door's structure gave way. It stopped closing, but there was only an eight-inch gap between it at the jamb. The crumpled section barely allowed the creature to fit its snout through.

They stumbled backward, not wanting to be near that thing as it snapped and snarled in fury.

"Wren, I must inform you that the new parameters Yoshi entered for detection of life signs on this planet have picked up between twenty-seven and thirty-four potential targets."

Despite their situation, Kim had to admire Yoshi's thoughtfulness. "We're in trouble, Computer. Ensure that all doors are closed and locked and open them only via voice activation."

"Understood."

The reply echoed through the hangar bay. The tractors were parked to one side, but otherwise, the room was completely deserted. As, it appeared, was the base; they encountered no one as they ran through the hallways. After the noise of the howls and the forest, it was eerily silent.

"Is anyone else in the base, Computer?"

"Yoshi is in the operations room," the computer replied.

"Can you detect the others anywhere nearby?"

"Long-range scanners are picking up EU officers about one mile to the north."

"They're all alive?"

"I am detecting ten life signs belonging to EU personnel. But I'm also detecting laser fire and projectile discharge."

The computer's matter-of-fact tone was at odds with the words Kim was hearing.

Her heartbeat pulsing in her ears, Kim tried to keep her own voice level. "Can you comm them?"

"I am attempting that now." A moment, and then a breathless voice came through the speakers.

"Kim, you're okay?" It was Grand. All sense of animosity gone, Kim felt only relief.

"I'm fine. Wren's injured, but Adonai is here. We're at the base. Where are you?"

"Currently pinned down in the hills north of the camp. I'm trying to work out a way back to *Daedalus*. The creatures are . . . holy *shit*—"

"Lieutenant?" Kim called, but there was no reply. "Computer, did the comm just cut out?" she demanded.

"I am sorry, Kim. The life signs are still present, but the firefight appears to have increased. It's probable they cannot respond."

A wry laugh escaped Kim's throat. "What do we do?" she asked, hating that her voice came out as a frightened squeak.

"We need to fix Wren's leg," Adonai said. "There is an infirmary on the base, but I'm not sure how well it's stocked. I did see several splints and antibacterial creams in Yoshi's laboratory."

"We have to comm the relief team," Wren added. Adonai had slowed to a jog; not because he needed to but to match Kim's pace, which was flagging after their dash through the forest.

"What help will they be?" Kim asked. "They're still at least a week away!"

"Do you have a better idea?" Wren asked.

Kim did. "We need Adonai's shuttle."

"In case you didn't notice, we just *left* a ship," Wren replied.

"*Daedalus* has no power," she reminded him. "The shuttle will get us in the air, and those things can't fly." She paused. "I don't *think* they can fly."

"You're talking about abandoning the whales?" Wren asked, incredulous.

"Of course not," she replied. "I'm not leaving the planet, but we need to get to the EU officers."

A loud bang made her duck her head. Lifting the pistol, she whirled.

The corridor was empty. The sound reverberated and died, likely just the metal walls cooling in the night air, but Kim couldn't relax. Even with every door in the base locked and secured, the barriers between them and the creatures seemed flimsy and useless.

The lights were on in Yoshi's lab. The mezzanine was lit, too, and there was a whale beached on one of the docks, two down from where Berenice still floated. Naomi. Kim could see Yoshi down there, crouched at her side. A medbot hovered beside her, a long syringe extended from its arm. With a precise movement, it inserted the needle into the whale's hide, plunging deep. Naomi gave a small shiver but otherwise didn't move.

The clatter of their arrival broke Yoshi's concentration. She stood, smoothing the front of her silver and blue jumpsuit.

"What are you doing?" she called up to them. "I'm in the middle of an insemination! Where's Captain Shannon? He was supposed to be back ages ago." She frowned. "Did they release you . . . oh. What happened to Wren?"

"Can you patch him up?" Kim replied sharply, leaning over the railing. "We need—"

"The base has been breached. Two doors have been broken through on the west side." The computer's voice was terse, almost anxious. A loud clang came from behind Kim. A creature, smaller than the others but still bulging with muscle, dropped into a crouch fifteen feet to her left; it had jumped from somewhere above.

Another creature dropped down, large paws cushioning its impact. This one was bigger, with a long, jagged scar running across its cheek. Lowering its muzzle it stepped forward, mouth open as it let out a delighted baying sound. But it wasn't looking at Kim; it was looking over the railing. All of a sudden, it was in the air, vaulting the thirty-foot drop as if it was nothing. It landed on the dock next to Yoshi, who let out a wild yell as the dock rocked under the impact.

The creature snarled at Yoshi as she backed away until she was at the edge of the dock, with only water behind her. Then it turned its attention to Naomi.

The medbot, unknowing and unconcerned, continued to burrow the long needle into Naomi's side, but Naomi was shrieking wordless sounds into Kim's mind. Kim clapped her hands over her ears. It didn't help. Naomi's panic took over her entire body, her helplessness, her inability to move against the belts on the dock that had been meant to keep her safe but now kept her in place while the creature gently, almost lovingly, raked a claw across her side.

A thin line of blood spilled.

Yoshi screamed.

Kim leaned her right hand on the railing, and, ignoring the protest of her injured wrist, pulled the trigger. Two bullets flew. Neither of them hit the creature; instead thwacking into the water behind Naomi. But the creature snarled, lifting its head and sniffing the air, abandoning the whale at least for a moment.

They were above, now, so many of them running along the gantries, whooping and growling. Kim didn't know how they'd gotten in. Perhaps they had already been inside, watching Yoshi or waiting for them to arrive. These were alien creatures; there was no telling how they communicated. Telepathy wasn't out of the question and was looking ever more likely as they prowled toward her, Adonai, and Wren.

"Down to the docks," Adonai said. Gently but quickly, he lowered Wren to the mezzanine.

"They're down there too!" Kim told him, incredulously.

"The boat," Adonai returned, motioning with his head. "Go, Kim!"

Tucking the pistol in her toolbelt and scooping her arm under Wren's, Kim moved. She didn't want to take her eyes off the monsters, but in order to navigate the stairs, she had to. Balancing Wren on the railing, she helped him over the edge and tried not to panic as he took a worryingly wobbly step downward, trying to use his hands to keep his weight off his injured foot.

She clambered after him, aware that their progress was far too slow but also dimly aware that the creatures' focus had shifted away from her. But where was—

Looking up, she saw Adonai at the top of the stairs, his silver form standing firm against the encroaching beasts. One of them became overeager and charged toward the head of the stairs. Adonai lifted an arm to ward it off.

"Adonai!" The scream ripped from her lungs. But as the creature struck Adonai's arm, its motion stopped. Adonai had plunged a fist into its hide, had punched straight through fur, flesh, and tissue. Gouts of blood, black and viscous, spattered outward from the wound, covering Adonai and the first few steps. A few drops rained down on Kim's face. It stung like acid. She wiped it off with her sleeve, watching as tiny holes appeared in the material of her jumpsuit.

Adonai's actions didn't go unnoticed by the other creatures. They seemed surprised by the destruction of one of their companions, and the closest of the pack edged backward a little, snarling in rumbling voices. The damaged creature dropped to the floor, its body broken, ribcage still heaving, but the ragged sounds of its breath told Kim it wouldn't last much longer.

"Go," Wren told her. When she hesitated, he pushed her.

Kim was not about to leave anyone behind. "Adonai! Come on!"

Kim didn't move until she saw Adonai climb onto the staircase above them. The creatures didn't advance. Not yet. They were cautious but not afraid.

Kim reached the bottom of the stairs and ran to the nearest of the docks. A boat bobbed in the water, clunking occasionally against the wooden platform. Only then did she see that Yoshi was cowering on the next dock over, cornered by the monster that had clawed—and possibly killed—Naomi, crouched at the edge of the floating platform, clutching a tiny silver scalpel. A pathetic weapon against the creature that was stalking her. It was swaying slightly from side to side, its mouth open, grinning widely.

"Yoshi!" Kim yelled, even as she glimpsed Wren and Adonai climb aboard the boat from the corner of her vision. "Jump and swim!"

Wren was calling her name, but Kim wasn't going into the boat just yet. She spared a glance for the staircase; the creatures were coming, navigating the steps with the same lethal grace they did everything else. One of them jumped, landing on the edge of the dock near Kim. Not much time. No time at all.

"Start the boat!" she shouted at Wren. "Get out of here!"

She didn't wait to see if he obeyed. She jumped into the water and swam several broad strokes toward Yoshi's dock. The space between them was only thirty feet, but it felt like it was the size of a football field. She pulled her head up. Yoshi wasn't moving. She was looking at the creature, the scalpel still clutched in her hands, but her fingers were limp.

"Yoshi! Focus! Look at me!" She shouted and splashed in the water, trying to get Yoshi's attention back on her. "Come on, there's no time! Jump!"

With an effort, Yoshi looked toward Kim. The creature sensed the imminent loss of its prey and made a few advancing steps. It didn't seem to want to get close to the water, Kim noticed. She looked over her shoulder and saw the hoard gathering on the dock behind her. The boat was gone.

Ahead of Kim, Yoshi's gaze snapped back to the creature.

"Yoshi!" Kim snarled. "Look at me and *jump!*"

This seemed to reach the girl. She flung the scalpel at the creature and jumped, clumsily, backward off the platform. The splash she made sent a wave toward the creature. It leapt back. They definitely didn't like water, Kim thought, even as she stroked as strongly as she could toward where Yoshi was thrashing wildly. Kim slipped an arm under the girl's armpits and pulled her backward against her chest.

"Stop. You'll drown us both," Kim hissed.

Yoshi gasped and went still, trying to relax.

"Okay. I'm going to . . ." Kim began to outline her plan, which wasn't really a plan at all, to swim them out under the partition and into the bay and then somehow reach the shore. She'd only gotten the first few words out before she was lifted on a sudden wave and found Yoshi straining to look at something behind her. At first, she thought she'd made a major mistake and that the beasts *could* swim. But then, she heard the soft hum of the boat's motor, and a metal arm was reaching down for her, grasping the back of her jumpsuit and pulling her upward.

She landed on the bottom of the boat, gasping, and gripped the edge as Wren steered them in a tight arc, punching it toward the partition. Eight feet of clearance didn't seem like a lot when you were hurtling toward something at full speed. Kim ducked low, as did the others.

She didn't want to look, but something tugged at her until she turned her head. If she had hoped Naomi had survived the attack, that hope was dashed. The water of the operations room was thick with the whale's blood. The creatures were on top of her, clambering up her sides, clinging to her like ants as they burrowed into her flesh. Were they eating her or just tearing her apart? Perhaps both.

It doesn't matter. She's dead anyway, Kim told herself. It doesn't matter.

It did matter.

Kim wept as Naomi's shape blinked out of the Link. All trace of her obliterated in just a few moments.

CHAPTER

25

They drove the boat into the night. The wind picked up, sharp and cold, making Kim shiver.

They were silent, all of them exhausted, none of them able to think. Kim didn't *want* to think. The whales kept badgering her—they'd sensed Naomi's death, had tasted blood in the water.

"Give me some time, please," she asked them, her voice sounding dead to her own ears. "I'm sorry."

Leave her be, Levi spoke authoritatively, and Kim felt blessed emptiness in the Link after that.

What had happened to Berenice? Kim couldn't tell if she was alive or not. The Link gave her no clue. Perhaps the water had kept her safe . . . or perhaps not.

Yoshi used the boat's comms to search for Lieutenant Grand's—or anyone's—comm-band.

"Lieutenant Grand, if you're reading this, we're heading for Adonai's shuttle. We'll sweep the area. The base is not safe. Repeat, do not head for the base."

Kim balanced herself and headed toward the front of the boat, crouching beside Yoshi. "Any response?"

Yoshi shook her head. "Nothing. I can't even tell if they're receiving it." She looked visibly distressed, and with her wet hair plastered over her forehead, vulnerable. "Why did you save me, Kim?"

Kim was astonished by the question. "Why wouldn't I?"

Yoshi shrugged, turning away to look at the ocean. "I guess I thought you hated me."

"Of course I would get you out of there," Kim said, knowing that she meant it. For the first time, she seemed to be able to speak to Yoshi without feeling like she was being judged for every word she said. "I *don't* hate you, Yoshi."

"I didn't exactly make it easy for you to like me, either." Yoshi laughed, but there was a self-deprecating edge to it. "I didn't handle my own social media, Kim. I'm not funny or cute. They wouldn't let me near it back then. They knew I'd blow my chances in ten minutes."

"Then who posted the photos?" she asked.

"My mother did."

Kim reacted to the news like it was a slap in the face. "Your mother?"

"She wanted me to have a place on the Ark Project more than I did. I don't know how she got the photos. I didn't ask. I was too upset." Yoshi's voice sounded forlorn when she said this. "I don't make friends easily. Abdiel was nice to me."

Kim felt a pang of guilt. "And I wasn't." She remembered talking to Yoshi in the courtyard at the training center in Chicago. A brief conversation that she had wrapped up as soon as she'd gotten the information she needed to evaluate Yoshi as a rival. She'd known Yoshi might beat her in terms of intelligence, but she was awkward and shy. She wouldn't win on public opinion.

Kim let the silence reign for the moment. "Why didn't you tell me?" she said.

"I don't need to explain myself to you," Yoshi said without malice.

"No," Kim said softly. "Of course you don't."

"But it hurts me that you think badly of me. I did not agree with Hah-aoya's actions. I wouldn't have done it."

God, she'd been so stupid. Wasting all this time and energy fighting Yoshi, avoiding her, resenting her. All for ... what, exactly?

"I would never leave you behind to die," Kim told her.

"I know that now," Yoshi said, her voice earnest. And then, through the Link, Kim heard the words *I would never leave you behind, either.*

Kim found some treatment creams and a few bandages in the boat's locker. She'd put some cooling gel on her wrist and cleaned and dressed Wren's wound. Wren now sat, eyes dazed, as he piloted the boat toward the headland. He kept them close to the shoreline, and whenever the thick clouds parted to let through the light of the two moons, they could see the beautiful forest of giant trees swaying in the wind. Kim's gaze was on the land, intently searching for some sign of light or movement, hoping to spot the EU soldiers.

It was Yoshi who noticed it first.

"What's that over there?" she asked, pointing. Kim followed her finger. Yes, there was something; through the swaying branches of the trees, something white was flapping in the wind.

Wren angled the boat inland and cooled the motor until they sat just off the shore, none of them daring to go closer, but finally, Kim couldn't stand it any longer. "There's no sign of the creatures. We can't stay out here forever."

"I will go ashore first," Adonai said.

It was a sensible solution, though Kim still wanted to object. Her instinct was to keep him safe. But he was right; of all of them, he was the best suited to this task.

Wren pulled the boat ashore, and Adonai stepped onto the sand without help, taking with him a lantern from the storage locker and passing another to Yoshi. Kim climbed out, too, not caring that her boots sank into the waterlogged sand and wet her jumpsuit legs. She stood beside Wren as Adonai made his way across the darkened beach toward the tree line. There was a steep rise to climb before he was out of sight. The white thing—it looked like a bedsheet—continued to flap in the breeze. Long moments passed before Adonai's bobbing light returned. Kim's shoulders sagged with relief.

"It's a tent," Adonai said as he drew closer. "And there are . . . remains."

"Remains?"

"Bodies," Adonai amended. "Maybe you shouldn't see it."

Kim looked at Wren. "I think I have to," she said. "This is the area Durand saw the contacts in—or close to it. And from the location, it might even match where we saw that smoke, if the wind was blowing right. They might be the same group that attacked us."

"Or they might be a different group altogether," Wren said. "They might not even be Adherants—they could be Crusaders, or someone else. You can't go in there alone."

Kim had no objection to him accompanying her, but she wanted him to be prepared. "It's not going to be pretty, by the sounds of it."

Wren swallowed. "We're safer if we stick together. Yoshi?"

Yoshi's face was pale, and she barely looked up, but she swung herself out of the boat and trailed behind them, clutching her lantern. The first sign of human habitation was a tree. Close to the shoreline and separate from the others, it stood like a sentry, and Kim saw that the camp's inhabitants had made use of its lower limbs, chopping them roughly. The bare trunk bore a carving that Kim now recognized—an angel with wings spread. She remembered with sudden clarity the Adherant who had tried to shoot her.

"I've seen them. Angels."

She puzzled over this for a moment, but then the smell hit her.

Rotten meat and blood, the sickly scent of death a few days old. Covering her nose with her sleeve, Kim forced herself onward.

In the light of their two lanterns, the scene was clear. The flapping white sheet billowed and drifted to the ground like a man bowing at their entrance. It was a tent. Or . . . it had been. Something had slashed it apart in thick ribbons. The tattered flaps moved in waves like giant fingers reaching for something. Beneath it were overturned camp beds, mattresses slashed and sodden with rain, food packages scattered and glittering like tiny foil jewels. The ground was churned with boot prints, and Kim could see several guns scattered, some trampled into the mud. They weren't high-powered weapons like the EU soldiers had. A few handguns, a single PRU-V assault rifle—a weapon that was primitive in the utmost but which packed a punch as far as destruction capability went. Kim pulled it out of the dirt and checked it over. The cartridge was spent with no replacements in sight. She tossed it back into the mud.

She avoided looking at the bodies as much as she could, but it was almost impossible. They lay scattered, discarded like rags, all of them eviscerated the way Simons had been. A woman with bright blonde hair lay sprawled on her stomach, her head twisted too far to the side, eyes open and blank, blood crusting her cheeks. A young man, not much older than Kim, lay next to her, hand wrapped around a butter knife as if he'd thought he could use it to fight. His arm had been torn off, his mouth ripped open so wide, his jaw had broken. Another man, older with a grizzly black beard, was hung from a tree branch by his shirt, his legs shredded. It would have taken a lot of strength to lift him that high. Or had he tried to climb, to save himself, only to have the creatures follow?

There were no insects around now, but she could see signs of them having made use of the bodies. But without other carrion, decomposition on this planet was clearly a slow and painstaking process.

"What are these things?" Wren muttered, his face turning an ashen shade as he eyed a crushed chocolate bar. He swayed on his feet, and Kim was worried about how much blood loss he'd endured. "What makes them do this? They're not killing for food. This is . . . barbaric."

"*Akuma*," Yoshi spoke from behind. "Demons." Kim turned to stare at her, and the Japanese girl shrugged.

"Well, these poor suckers were definitely Adherants," Wren said disgustedly. "These aren't mercenaries hired for the cause. They disobeyed their own tenets and came out here themselves. It was *that* important to them to sabotage us." He bent to pick up a backpack. A hardcover Bible poked out of the front pocket; the Adherant cross emblazoned in gold on the front. Kim saw the symbol, with its nine extra lines crossing the lowest bar of the cross, and felt a shiver of hatred.

"Still, I don't think they deserved this," Kim said, surprising herself.

These were people who'd put the whales in danger. Surely they deserved to be punished?

She took a few steps away from the camp to where the air was a little more breathable, toed a smashed piece of fungus, then turned back. "Why didn't the original scouting party see the creatures? Surely those humans, all alone, would have been massive targets." She paused. "We know they don't like water. Thanks to Yoshi's claw fragment, we know they're partially incorporeal." She paused, her mind churning. "I feel like there are many pieces of this puzzle missing."

Yoshi frowned. They stared at one another. None of them had the answers they needed.

"We're wasting time here," Kim said at last. "We need to get to the shutt—" Kim felt her stomach finally rebel. She turned away and retched.

She had nothing to bring up. She couldn't remember the last time she'd eaten; it must have been yesterday. A few spatters of bile hit the ground under her, but that was all. But before it was over, she noticed something. Under her hand was a hard protrusion formed in the ground.

She scrabbled at the leaves, wiping them away. Beneath was a white stone.

"What's that?" Wren asked, coming closer.

"It's a ring," she told him. "Just like the one near *Daedalus*. And one at the ruins." Brushing the leaves away, she revealed the rest of the stones and stood up, considering.

"What does this mean?" Yoshi asked.

"I don't know," Kim said, but in her mind, she could see the creature dragging Wren into the ring and how the creature vanished without a trace. It meant something. It definitely meant something.

CHAPTER
26

"I've got a signal," Yoshi said once they'd climbed back into the boat. "It's an EU comm." She hit a few buttons on the helm, allowing a crackly voice to come through.

"Yoshi? Are you okay?" It was Durand, breathless and frantic. "Are the others with you?"

"We're okay. We're on the open water," Yoshi replied. "The beasts attacked the base. They might have killed one of the whales."

"We managed to shake them off about half an hour ago, but I'm not sure how long that'll last. It's cost us a lot of charge on our weapons, and we had to circle back to *Daedalus*. We're trapped in here."

"Our plan is to bring in Adonai's shuttle," Yoshi told her. "Do you think you can hold out for another half hour?"

"I . . . honestly hope so," she replied. "They don't seem to be out there right now, and we've got the ship sealed tight. Without power, we're not going anywhere, though."

"We'll get the shuttle in as quickly as we can," Yoshi promised, signing off. Kim started the motor with a swift motion. They'd already wasted too much time.

Yoshi pushed them to full speed toward the estuary that would give them access to the area where the shuttle rested. The wreckage of *Minotaur* sat broken and forbidding on the left hand side, limned by moonlight. The oily sheen of the water around it confirmed their fears that fuel had leaked from the ship, contaminating the water.

Exactly, Kim thought grimly, why the Anti-Unificationists hadn't wanted them here to begin with.

Finally, the estuary turned into a river, the water picking up speed and deepening. The boat had to fight against the current, but Wren kept them on course. If he was correct, this route would bring them close to the ruins and Adonai's shuttle.

A few minutes later, Kim was sure they were in the right spot, and Yoshi confirmed it on the scanner. The shuttle showed up like a blazing fire in the middle of an ocean of darkness. Wren steered the boat to the edge of the river and nosed the boat between the ferns. The bank here was steep, but at least there were a few protruding rocks to grasp as handholds, and dawn seemed to be coming, making it easier to see.

Adonai went first, scrambling up the face with spider-like ease while still carrying his lantern. Wren followed behind much more slowly, his foot obviously paining him. Kim clipped the second lantern to one of her belt loops. Her wrist was aching under the strain before she'd made it halfway. She pushed through it, turning her head to check on Yoshi; not that the other girl needed it. Like Kim, she had passed the trekking section of their training without a struggle.

At the top of the bank, they turned right. Because they were coming from an opposite angle, Kim was unprepared for the sight of the shuttle. Glimpsing the steel hull through the trees was a welcome relief. She felt the tension of the others ease as they emerged into the clearing, Wren even managing a grin.

"Glad you managed to land this thing so far away after all," he said in a low voice to Adonai.

"Shh," Yoshi replied. When Kim glanced at her, she shrugged. "It can't hurt to keep—"

A rustle of leaf litter made them stop still. There, just beyond a crumbled arched doorway, were two demons. Both of equal hulking size, they had spotted the group before the group had spotted them, and now, one of them let out a long, snarling growl. The other leapt toward them with a powerful bound that cleared several large fallen blocks of stone at once.

"Shit," Kim hissed.

They ran, pelting toward the shuttle, the light from their lanterns bobbing and swaying crazily. The undergrowth caught at Kim's ankles, threatening to trip her, but it wasn't herself she was worried about. It was Wren, whose steps were slowed by his ankle. He was lagging behind. Reaching out, she grasped his hand; his fingers locked tight around hers, and she pulled him onward, knowing even as she did so that he was slowing her down. It didn't matter. She wasn't going to let those creatures have him again.

The shuttle's hatch drew closer, and Adonai, first to reach it, keyed it open. As the metal door slid aside, he turned and braced himself, knees bent as the nearest demon snapped its jaws at Yoshi's ankle. He slammed his hand onto the demon's snout. The thing yelped like a wounded dog but rounded on Adonai instead, allowing Yoshi to scramble inside.

Kim dragged Wren onward. The other demon was now between them and the door, but its attention was on Adonai and the wound the droid had dealt to its companion seemed to spur it forward. With a growl, it hurled itself against Adonai's metal chest, knocking him backward into the shuttle's hull hard enough to dent the metal.

"Go!" Wren told her, pulling her now by the hand. "He can handle it!"

Kim wasn't so sure, but Wren was not releasing her hand. Adding a firm grip on her elbow, he shoved her through the hatch.

Adonai pushed away from the shuttle. Clenching his fist, he slammed it into the demon that was now trying to tear at the exposed wiring on his neck. The beast let out a high-pitched shriek and sagged to the ground, where it writhed pitifully. The other demon backed away, hackles up but wary of approaching. Adonai took the opportunity to step through the hatch, and Yoshi hit the controls to shut the door. As the gap narrowed and then ceased to exist, Kim saw the other demon circle closer to its wounded companion, bent low, keening softly.

"Holy *crap*," Wren said.

Adonai, standing just inside the doorway, looked down at his still-clenched fist with intense interest. A few streaks of the thing's blood beaded on his metal knuckles. Kim knew they didn't have time to waste. Throwing herself into the pilot's seat, she hit the controls to power up the shuttle. Wren slid into the copilot's seat a moment later.

"Where did they come from?" Kim gasped.

"They weren't there . . . and then they were," Yoshi gasped.

"It doesn't matter. Right now, we need to get the EU soldiers out of there," Kim said.

Yoshi ducked into the cockpit behind her, tentatively hitting a control to lower the rearmost crash chairs. Adonai, moving jerkily, took one of them while Yoshi strapped herself into the other.

The ship made a dull throbbing sound as the electronics powered up, and a field of crackling white flashed across the windows and then settled into transparency once more on every window but the one to Kim's right, which the beast had broken days ago.

"Just as well, we're not going through the atmosphere," she muttered, more to herself than anyone else.

"That thing could blow out even at low altitude. Can you put a forcefield over it?" Wren asked.

Kim slid her hands over the holo controls. "Not my main concern right now. We need to get this thing back to *Daedalus*, and that's not going to require much height."

She hit the thrusters; far too hard and fast, but at this point, she didn't care. The shuttle jerked wildly in a fashion that probably made Wren wince, but she didn't correct their course. The nose of the shuttle tilted upward at a crazy angle, and she blasted the fuel input. The shuttle protested, but the steep angle was necessary to clear the trees ahead of them.

Kim brought up the scanners as she glanced through the left-hand side window. Below them, the ruins receded. There was no trace of the two demons visually, and the scanners showed no signs of the creatures whatsoever.

The shuttle cleared the treetops, and she angled toward *Daedalus*.

A sudden blast of bright light seared across Kim's vision, blinding her. An alarm blared loudly in Kim's ear. A red symbol appeared, hovering in front of her face—a large, unmistakable warning sign.

"Weapons fire!" she yelled. "Strap in!"

Wren fumbled with his harness as Kim jerked the shuttle to the left. Wren had taken over the scanners, moving through the controls frantically.

Kim entered the shuttle into a basic evasion pattern, but she knew that without altitude, there was only so much this could defend them from.

"I've got seven signals now," Wren said at last. "All of them in New Eden's orbit."

Damn it! With everything that had happened, she'd forgotten about the ships Lieutenant Grand had said were in orbit. "And they've all got quantum drive. Some of these vessels will be Adherants."

"I'd say all of them," Wren said.

Kim glanced across at his readout. Two scoutships, one cargo ship, and a handful of what looked like old Mars Opposition vessels—called Warhawks, they were cobbled together from bits and pieces of other ships to make oddly-shaped vessels of varying sizes and shapes. There was no way to identify which ship was which from visuals. She glanced at Wren, eyebrows raised in question.

"Are you sure?" Yoshi asked, a small quaver in her voice.

"I'm not getting EU codes from any of them, that's for sure," he said grimly. He looked up. "Well, with our shuttle broadcasting an EU signal, none of them are going to be happy to see us."

The warning sign blazed again, this time giving her a moment's notice. She pulled the ship out of the pattern and jinked it upward, fast. The engines protested the rough treatment, but the bright bolt of light sizzled past them and hit the trees below, exploding into a ball of flame.

"We can't get close to the EU officers," Yoshi called. "They're targeting us, and if they fire while we're close, they'll kill everyone."

Kim jerked the shuttle's nose back down. Could she circle around? Come in at an oblique angle? Her hands moved over the controls, preparing for a sharp turn and acceleration away from her current position when—

Boom. Boom. Two blasts of laser fire rained down. Kim jerked the shuttle quickly left and then right, but the hits had been close enough that the alarm shrieked at her.

"We need to land," Yoshi said. "It's not safe up here, and we're no good to Lieutenant Grand dead!"

Kim was about to agree when Wren let out a curse. "That came from directly above us. There's a ship up there without a transponder. We're not seeing it on the scanners."

Kim glanced upward. Sure enough, she could make out the outline of a cigar-shaped Opposition ship, its boxy nose visible against the clouds. The thing was coming down *fast*.

Her hands moved across the panel of their own volition, hitting holographic controls and physical buttons. There was no time to plan a landing. She'd have to go up, where she had range to maneuver the ship.

"Kim . . ." Wren cautioned her.

"I know! Get a forcefield up over that window!"

Wren didn't question her again, his own hands moving rapidly. Kim felt beads of sweat dribbling between her breasts. Her heart was thumping. She knew a forcefield was good protection against space, but she also knew that it was a last resort. If for any reason the engines were damaged—or even one of the ship's vital power systems—the forcefield would blink out of existence, and the two panes of duraglass wouldn't be worth a single credit under the onslaught of a vacuum.

She lifted the nose of the ship and pushed them upward at full burn. The downward pressure forced them back into their seats, making it hard to breathe, but she didn't let up as New Eden's curves became apparent below her, the light blue tinge of atmosphere letting her know they were nearing the limits of the planet's gravity field.

A small vessel came in from the port side. She couldn't tell if it was the same one that had fired on them moments ago or another; it had no markings, and when it came to Warhawks, they could look like a completely different ship from an alternate viewpoint.

Now that she could see it properly, it was flat with a square nose and triangular tail, a distended underbelly bulging with some kind of customized cannon.

The shuttles weapon's system painted it with an overlay of bright red as the ship zoomed right past them without braking or veering, so close its starboard wing almost clipped *Daedalus*'s side. The wake caught them, making the ship shudder. Kim jerked the steering controls, pulling them away and putting some distance between them. The speed and angle was dizzying, especially looking rearward, but Kim refused to let it get the better of her. "I'm going to fire on them. See how they like it."

"I'm not sure that's a good idea," Yoshi protested. "We don't want to make them mad, right?"

"They're already mad!" Kim tapped the holo controls. The weapons systems weren't great; this was an exploration vessel, not a warship. Still, she had a passing familiarity with what she was looking at: a targeting scanner overlaying the trigger control, which was a physical level on the control panel, as most weapons systems had to prevent accidental firing.

A grid of green lines spread out over the silver early dawn sky, painting the enemy ships in red and setting a holographic exclamation mark over each of them, just in case the pilot got confused. She aimed at the ship that had swooped on them—now spiraling upward toward its companions—with a tap of her finger and fired with a squeeze of the trigger without another thought. A blast of red laser fire erupted across her holo display and flashed off into the hazy blueness of the sky without hitting the enemy ship. Still, it took off fast, heading upward and out of view.

"Did I scare them?" she asked.

"Looks like it," Wren crowed. "They're heading into open space." He leaned back in his seat, but just as quickly sat up again.

Another flurry of laser fire came at them. Through the holo, she saw it streaking toward her and every instinct told her to duck.

Don't be stupid, she told herself. *You'll get us killed with that kind of thinking.* It barely missed them. Another caught them directly on the flank. The shuttle gave a deep, painful moan, and a loud *clunk* sounded through the cabin.

Kim jerked them left, and the clouds spun dizzyingly. The main continent came into view, a jagged shape in the water only just visible now that the sun was peering over the horizon. She could see the base below them, a small dark spot on the edge of the land mass. The movement of the ship was too hard, too fast, and all of a sudden, there were red-painted ships soaring down from every direction.

Kim released the failsafe. She had almost let loose a blast of fire without aiming. She could have hit the base.

"God damn it," Wren said as Kim jerked the starboard and then the port, fighting the urge to close her eyes. Opening them again, at some different orientation, would only make things worse.

"There's too many of them." Gritting her teeth, she tried to keep her cool.

Wren shook his head. "We're going to have to climb higher."

Kim shook her head. "We're no help to anyone up here! We'll be cut off."

"We're going to get shot!" Wren yelled. "Kim! Take us up now!"

She hated it, but she knew there was no other choice. She drew back on the steering controls, and the ship's nose lifted. For a moment, it felt to Kim like she might pass out. She grabbed the console to keep herself from falling backward into the chair—she wanted to be able to reach anything she needed. She scanned the sky ahead of them, her eyes focusing on the view beyond the holo. Small dots coalesced into bigger dots, glinting in the sunshine as they filled the sky. Their ship lifted above them, but it was obvious what they were doing, and the ships gave chase, lifting like helium balloons. Kim pushed them to full speed. They hurtled upward, and Kim felt herself being pressed back in her seat. The sky turned rapidly from blue to purple and then, finally, to black. As they broke through the atmosphere, Kim could see the battle raging clearly: bright streaks of colored laser fire, smaller silvery flashes of ships darting—tiny Opposition craft, clunky in appearance but maneuverable and swift.

She took them toward the outer edge, aiming for a gap between two groups of smaller ships exchanging fire.

"They're still on our tail," Wren said, glancing at the weapons holo.

Kim grimaced. "I'm going to have to try and hit them, aren't I?"

Wren didn't look happy about this either. "We don't have time to switch out," he said. "Do it."

Kim didn't respond, her knuckles white as her hands moved over the controls. She aimed and squeezed the trigger. Five laser bullets spat out into the ether. Closing her eyes for a moment, she wished to high hell she'd let Wren take this seat—or Yoshi, for God's sake. She forced them open. The ship was still intact, but then she saw it cant to one side, spewing vapor in a long white stream.

She couldn't help herself; she shouted, pumping a fist in the air.

"You got one?" Wren asked, disbelievingly. "You actually shot down a ship?"

"Don't sound so surprised!" she scolded, but she was beyond shocked herself. She felt exultant. But hot on the heels of this feeling was her regret. There were people aboard that ship that was now listing to one side, venting atmosphere in a spurt of white spume. She tried not to think about it. The Adherants wouldn't have spared her any feelings if they'd hit her. And there was still another one to take care of.

"Yeah, that's great, but it's not going to get us out of trouble. These suckers really want us dead. Or maybe just you, Kim." Wren's voice was grim, and Kim could see why. Three more ships had abandoned their dogfight and were now swarming toward them like rats. "We're going to have to head into the belt."

"Is that a good idea?" Kim asked. Pulling in the failsafe once more, she steadied her nerves and fired, then fired again. Neither burst hit the ship she was aiming at. The pilot seemed to know what she was going to do before she did it and evaded so quickly.

She moved her joystick, trying to trace the movement of the ship. Before she'd finished the arc, another ship cut across the trail. She tried to follow the first ship, but the interruption had cost her a valuable fraction of a second. She'd lost it.

"Kim? Are you listening?"

"Hmm?" She scanned the display, looking for the red tag.

"We can use the asteroids as cover," he repeated. "Maybe get some good shots off; maybe lose them. It's our best bet."

"Agreed," Kim said. Leaning heavily on the thrusters once more, she spiraled into the arms of the belt. The rolling rocks were slow and cautious compared to the craziness of the outside. Soon, they'd lost visuals on the ship chasing them, but Kim could still see them as a red ghost on the holo.

"They're persistent," Kim said. "I'm going deeper in."

"Kim."

It was the first time Adonai had spoken in a long time. She glanced at him, and saw that his hand—still streaked with black, oily blood—was outstretched, pointing to something through the front window.

"I see it," Wren said. "There's something up ahead."

"I see it too," Kim replied, her eyes landing on a blinking blue dot that lit up on the HUD. The scanners, still active from before, tagged it with a floating line, and words appeared underneath it.

Object: Unknown. Makeup: Oxygen, hydrogen, calcium, carbon, sodium, potassium . . .

She pulled her gaze away as they swerved around another asteroid, this one bulb-shaped and rotating slowly. Kim saw it come into focus.

"Oh my God," she breathed. "Is that . . ."

"It's a whale," Adonai confirmed, his voice just as soft. "It's *me*."

The body of the blue whale was frozen solid, covered in icicles made up of the water that had once been inside his flesh, and he was drifting in a whirling spin. He passed over their heads, and Kim recalled the first time she'd seen a holo of a blue whale, back in the training room in Chicago. The moment, the exact moment, that she'd realized that she was doing something she needed to do.

But this whale, *Adonai*, was so clearly dead; every spark of life gone from his glittering eyes.

"Holy crap," Wren gasped. "He's been drifting out here all this time."

"It's not Adonai," Kim told herself as much as Wren. "Adonai is *here*."

Adonai did not respond. Kim gave him one last glance and saw him staring, fixedly, at the giant, frosted shape. For a moment, she thought he was lost in some terrible horror, but then he spoke.

"It is circling," he said.

"Circling?" She glanced at the body and saw that it had, indeed, moved in a slow arc across their vision, now drifting away from them on a clearly defined trajectory.

Kim's eyes were fixed on the view through the window. "It's not a planet," she said thoughtfully.

"What are you talking about? Kim, now isn't the time—" Wren cut himself off. "Holy crap, you're right."

The movement of the whale body was clear now. Surrounded by the asteroids, Kim could see clearly how the space between wasn't spherical. Not quite. There was a definite ovoid to the cleared area, and Adonai's orbit was making it only more evident. A planet could not hold such a shape.

And yet, there was nothing there.

"What is it, then?" Wren asked.

"I don't know, but I hope someone's paying attention to the ships that are still trying to kill us," Yoshi called.

A new blast of laser fire ripped past them, bringing Kim back to the moment.

"They're still on us, Kim." Wren's voice was strained. Kim glanced at the holo display and saw that their pursuers had sustained damage after her blast. Their ship was limping and trailing vapor, but it was still coming on. Another blast of laser fire shot past them. Kim returned the favor, watching as they dodged out of the way. Still, Kim knew they were weakened. This fight wouldn't be going much longer.

"We're going to have to use it as cover," Kim said.

"Are you sure? Last time we went near that thing . . ."

Wren didn't need to remind her about what had happened last time. "Can you see any other options?" she asked him. "Look, the best case scenario here is that the anomaly catches them in its gravity field. It'll at least give us some advantage; this shuttle isn't going to hold up much longer."

She didn't wait for his agreement. Pulling up the steering controls, she headed toward the clearing.

Kim fixed her gaze ahead as the asteroids drew back. Once again, they were in the open space, and everything around them seemed to recede. Apprehension made her palms prickle; she hoped she'd made the right choice, but she had no real way of knowing for sure.

"This is insane," Yoshi muttered.

Kim cast a glance over her shoulder and saw Adonai sitting bolt upright, glowing eyes fixed on the forward window.

"Adonai?" she asked.

He didn't reply.

Kim turned back to the controls, her heart pounding as she tried to make out the invisible . . . whatever it was. She had been right. At this close range, with time to look, she could see the object. It *did* exist, just as she remembered.

She ran her eyes around the edges of the clearing. Yes, there was the bending of the stars at the edges of this . . . this something. This nothing.

"You see that, right?" Kim asked Wren, sweeping her hand in an arc to indicate the form.

"Yeah," he said, but he shook his head.

Yoshi leaned forward. "But what does it mean? If it's not a planet, then what *is* Eschol Thirteen?"

Kim took a deep breath. "I think—"

The shuttle shuddered with sudden force. The unmistakable sound of bullets peppering the hull made her wince, reflexively pulling her elbows in to her sides and ducking her head.

"Oh, God," she murmured. This was it. Something inside her clicked, and all of a sudden, she was certain she was going to die. Instinct took over her body. It wasn't that she lost her ability to think clearly; it felt like she was thinking more clearly than she ever had in her life. She let go of her controls and reached for Wren's hand. He had released his controls and was already reaching for hers.

They clasped their fingers together, and their gazes met. A heartbeat passed, then another. There was nothing in the universe but the two of them.

A second later, the left-hand side of the cabin was ripped upward and away and darkness hit her in the face like a fist.

CHAPTER

27

S omething was tickling Kim's face. "Go away, Nicki," she murmured. "Not funny."

Nicki had a feather in her hands. She did this sometimes, pinching them from the feather duster in the kitchen. Elf was always telling her off because the duster looked like a plucked chicken . . .

"Nicki, stop it!" God, she'd have to get up. Stupid little . . .

She blinked and pushed the feather away, sitting up. No Nicki. She wasn't in the bedroom of her apartment. She was in a field of yellow grass, and the swaying strands had been touching her nose.

Kim sat up with a jolt. Around her, the field of grass stretched on and on for miles in every direction. In the far distance, she could make out the slight curve of low hills. A single tree was perched on top of one of them.

Unexplainable joy surged through her as she saw the wide-open blue sky above. It wasn't purple in color like New Eden's. It looked much more like Earth's sky as she'd seen in old holos, before the pollution had muddied and marred it.

A groan from somewhere near her left elbow. Wren. He was lying on his back, the grass flattened beneath him. A bloody gash ran along one cheek, and there were ice crystals in his hair, but he looked fine otherwise.

"Wren? You're okay?"

"Um . . ." He glanced around him. "Not sure. Is this a dream? Are we . . . did we *die*?"

Kim ran her hands down her arms, then felt foolish for doing so. "No. Of course not." But then, what other explanation was there? "No. This is . . . the place Adonai told us about."

Wren's face blanched of color. "It can't be."

"It can! He was right." She laughed. "He was right! And we didn't believe him." Pushing herself to her feet, she looked around. "Where is he? Where's Yoshi?"

Wren let out a long breath and pushed himself up onto one elbow, then got his knees under him shakily. "Where's our ship?"

"Destroyed. Those bullets ripped us apart. I'm guessing we were . . . somehow transported here, just in time." She bounced on her toes, trying to see farther into the distance. She turned a full circle and saw nothing but endless grass, a few more hills and more of that beautiful open sky. Everything hurt, but it didn't seem to matter. She focused on the tree; in the otherwise featureless landscape, it was the only possible destination. "We need to go there."

"Seriously? Kim—" Wren dragged himself to his feet, wobbled, then steadied himself. "Wow."

"Can you walk?"

In answer, her took a few steps and turned back to her. "What is this place?"

"It's Eschol Thirteen," she told him. "Whatever Eschol Thirteen is, this is it."

"Helpful," Wren muttered. "You think the Adherants landed here, too?"

A flicker of unease swam through Kim's mind. She remembered the ravings of the dying man after their battle. She was pretty sure he'd been referencing the same place Adonai had seen.

They walked on, and Kim found her thoughts drifting. It seemed impossible to focus on one thing. Wasn't there something important she was supposed to be doing right now? And where were the voices inside her head? The . . . the whales. She hadn't heard them . . . What if the alien monsters weren't native to New Eden? What if, instead, this ship was their home, and the portals . . .

And yet, she felt safe here.

"Hey!" A soft shout sounded from their left, and two figures appeared at the top of a gently-sloped hill. Adonai and Yoshi, their silhouettes limned against the sky.

"Thank God," Kim said, laughing in delight as they hurried toward their friends. "We were worried!"

Yoshi looked around. "I assume you've figured out this is Eschol Thirteen?"

Even the arrogance in Yoshi's tone didn't grate on Kim's nerves. "What do we do? Keep walking?"

"Look!" Wren lifted a finger, pointing up at an angle over Kim's right shoulder. She turned and saw birds flying through the sky in perfect formation. The sun glimmered on the whites of their wings, but there was something odd about . . .

"Oh," she said, raising a hand to her mouth.

"I told you," Adonai said. It was the first time he'd spoken.

Wren had stopped walking, his hands dropping by his side. "Impossible," he murmured, unable to tear his eyes from the sight.

"Angels," Kim replied.

"Aliens," he reminded her. "And we don't know that they're friendly."

Of course they were friendly. The thought was as lazy and dreamlike as every other thought she'd had since she'd woken. There was no threat from these creatures. They were only good and kind. She shook her head, knowing that there was something wrong with these thoughts, but the feeling didn't dissipate. Instead, it seemed to grow stronger until the idea that there was any danger here was laughable.

As the angels drew closer, she saw that they wore loose clothing wrapped around long limbs and fixed here and there with golden or silver cords. Their skin shades were variations of brown-gray, ranging from light to dark. Some had long hair bound in intricate braids. Others seemed to have no hair at all. They weren't close enough for her to make out their features, but she had an impression of large eyes, wide mouths, and angular jaws.

Lifting her hand, she waved to the being ahead of her, hoping the friendly gesture would be translated. Not one of the beings looked down at her.

"Hey!" Wren called. Kim turned to him, hoping the shout wouldn't be read as aggression. When she glanced back up, she realized what Wren had already guessed—the beings hadn't seen them. Blissfully, they flew onward.

"Hey!" Kim added her voice, bouncing on her toes and waving more frantically. "Hey, we're down here!"

The beings continued their flight, passing overhead and veering off into the distance.

Kim stopped waving, a puzzled frown furrowing her eyebrows. "They... can't *see* us?"

"They didn't speak to me when I was here, either," Adonai said.

Kim felt a shiver of apprehension. The joy seemed to try to override it, but for the first time, Kim began to suspect that something was altering her mood. "I'm not sure I like this place," she said.

"Me neither," Yoshi replied. "Do you feel strange?"

"I feel like I'm floating on air," Kim replied. "I can't seem to think straight. Could they have drugged us?"

"Possible," Yoshi said.

The tree grew closer, but it came slowly. At times, it felt like she'd been walking for days. Had an hour passed? How much time had gone by on the outside? Were the Adherants waiting for them? What about the ... oh, the EU officers! They were waiting ... but it was hard to care about anything other than the tree.

As they drew closer to the tree, Kim saw it was larger than she'd thought. All sense of distance was distorted by the lack of immediate comparison, but the tree was clearly gigantic. No tree had ever grown this large on Earth, surely. It was comparable only to those she'd seen on New Eden.

It took a long time before they were finally under its shade. The soft grass was littered with discarded leaves, mottled green and brown. They crinkled under her boots, making a pleasing sound that reminded her of crunching autumn leaves on the footpaths of her childhood.

They walked toward the trunk. It took minutes of passing through sun-dappled shade, labyrinthine branches knotting and parting overhead. As Kim drew closer, she saw a peculiarity at the base of the trunk, between two wall-like, gnarled roots. A flash of white stone. It was a *building*.

There was a structure built into the tree, or perhaps the tree had grown over it. The building was pyramid shaped, the tree wrapping around it so tightly, it was hard to tell where one finished and the other began.

Kim craned her neck to look at its top. There were three steps to the building, like a Mayan pyramid, each the size of a single house story. There were narrow, slitted windows on the second step. The first held a door, twice her head height and wide enough to pilot a shuttle through. Inside was blackness. A tang of earthy air wafted out.

"It looks like the ruins on New Eden," Wren said, breaking the silence with a soft whisper.

"I know," she replied.

There were five steps leading up to the door, and Kim took them slowly, only just barely aware that Wren and the others were following her. She was through the doorway before she knew what had happened.

It was so dark inside, she could see nothing at all at first. Slowly, the room resolved into being around her. The vault-like ceiling was high overhead. She was standing on a path of white stone. Growing on either side of it was thick blue moss, just like that on New Eden; great cushions of it carpeted the room all the way to the walls. Water dripped from the ceiling, making a soft pattering sound. The path led up to a set of shallow steps. At the top was a dais, in the center of which was a stone chair with a seat and arms but no back. It wasn't huge. As Kim approached, she saw that Wren could sit in it comfortably, though, it'd be too big for her. She climbed the steps and traced her hands over the arms. They were simple, unadorned.

Kim's heart was hammering in her throat. "This is crazy," she said aloud. Her voice sounded distorted, echoing around the vast chamber. "A chair means humanoid life. Physiology similar to our own. Not . . . like those demons on New Eden."

"The ruins on New Eden weren't likely to have been built by the demons," Yoshi reminded her quietly.

Kim's eyes continued to grow used to the darkness and she caught sight of two more doors at the very rear, leading to the left and right of the chamber.

"I feel like a trespasser," Wren whispered. "Like we're not supposed to—"

"Welcome."

Kim's head jerked up in shock and surprise. Yoshi let out a yelp, and Wren's hand moved toward his belt, searching, probably, for the pistol that wasn't there. The chair, which had a moment ago been empty, held a figure. It was mostly in shadow, but she could tell it was not a human. It was too tall, taller than a Martian. Its limbs were long and impossibly thin, and its skin was golden. Its arms rested on the arms of the chair, long, slender fingers curving over the ends.

And behind its shoulders, two wings were folded in high arcs.

It looked the same as the hologram they had found in *Seiiki*'s computer. Not just in general appearance but its face, its size, the mottling of its wings; it was identical.

"Who are you?" Kim asked. It was hard to contain her shock . . . and her fear. The last time she'd seen this being, he had told her their people were a sacrifice. "Are you the one who hijacked our computer?

The figure smiled. The narrow face crinkled, the corners of the eyes showing tiny little folds that proved it was a natural expression, but there was a definite sadness to it. Something about those pale eyes, a small spark missing as they settled on Kim. "Not exactly. I am a projection created by our computer, what you might call an artificial intelligence. I am similar to the one that gave you that warning. But not the same. I have many iterations. For our purposes, you can call me Hath. It is the name my creators use for me."

"You speak Japo-English," Yoshi stated.

The being—Hath—responded in the same calm voice. "Indeed. We do know your language. We have . . . communicated with you before. We've known of your world for many centuries."

"Where are we?" Adonai asked, his voice slow and tentative. "The first time I was here, I thought it was Heaven."

"Ah." The being lifted a finger, tapping it on the arm of the chair. For a projection, if that's what it was, it seemed very . . . alive. "This is our planet." It paused. "Or it was once. This," it spread its arms, and its wings fluttered just a little behind its back, "is just a representation built inside part of our ship."

Wren spoke up. "A holo? It's pretty advanced for a projection."

Hath seemed slightly amused, though its expression didn't change. "A quantum-based feedback relay. Much more sophisticated than a holographic simulation, but in their essence, they are similar. As you've noticed, we can build form as well as images."

Wren nodded, tapping his boot on the stone ground. "It's incredible. But if this isn't a real planet, where is this holo located? I'm assuming we're not just . . . hanging in space."

Hath lowered its head. "You are inside our vessel. Its current location is just within Grid seven-five-two of the asteroid belt. I brought you here using a quantum polymorphic device. Sometimes we call it a stone ring. It can transport matter from one location to another."

"A stone ring," Kim repeated. "There are stone rings on New Eden. We lost a crew member through one. When he came back, he was . . ."

Hath nodded, the tiny folds of skin under its chin creasing and straightening with the graceful movement. "That is what they do. The darashen. We have been fighting them for centuries, and in return, we've lost many of our people. Now we are reduced to hiding here, on our ship. We must conceal ourselves well."

So that was why Eschol Thirteen couldn't be detected by human equipment. And no wonder; these beings were clearly advanced beyond anything humans could dream of. "New Eden was your planet," Kim said. "And the . . . the darashen invaded?"

Hath inclined its head. "We were a proud people once. And clever. Our planet was full of life in many varied forms—tall trees, animals of the air, wildlife and insects, and pure blue water. We had large cities and small villages, but we lived harmoniously. There had been wars in our past, but those were long over. We grew arrogant. We thought we could tap the secrets of the universe. Our scientists were conducting experiments on wormhole technology when they stumbled upon something they hadn't expected. Another race, one that was darkened by evil. They have been living in their own dimension for centuries, and they are adapted to its harshness. But when they saw what we had on our beautiful world, they wanted it. And so they used the portal we had opened to invade, feeding on our weak and our young when we were least expecting, seeking only to wipe our race from existence.

"We had no choice. We left our planet in this ship. Our numbers were decimated too badly to fight, and we needed aid. So we sent what you would call a probe to the Sol System, knowing it would take a long time to reach it but also knowing that we could convince you to come to our aid."

"That . . . that can't be true," Kim said. "New Eden was discovered by some engineer working on the SETI program years ago. He was looking for signs of alien life. He found New Eden instead."

"How did your scientist discover it?" The angel-being inclined its head. "We've been studying your species for centuries. We know more about you than we do about ourselves, perhaps. We knew that you had weapons. That you were almost as ferocious as the darashen. We suspected you would be a formidable enemy. That is why we told humans where New Eden was and how to get here. We included a plea for your help."

"How can this be right?" Kim asked. "The scientist who discovered New Eden found it while using deep-space telemetry. *You* didn't—your people didn't—contact us. And no one ever said anything about a probe with a message from an alien race."

"Not that we *know* of," Wren interjected, eyeing the being thoughtfully. "What if what he says is true? We don't know anything about the guy who discovered New Eden. His name isn't ever mentioned; remember when I asked about it during our training? I was basically told to sit down and shut up."

"But . . . we'd know about an alien probe, right?" Kim asked, but even as she said it, she knew that wouldn't necessarily be true. She could imagine a thousand reasons why that piece of information wouldn't be public knowledge.

"So the people who discovered the probe just conveniently left out the part where a group of aliens asked for our help with a dangerous, non-corporeal monster race," Yoshi said.

Wren shook his head. "You can imagine how valuable the location of New Eden must have been. The discovery of it basically ended the wars. Maybe they ignored it, or maybe they didn't understand the warning. Someone might have decided to make a tidy profit at the expense of whoever they sold the information to."

"The demons attacked us. And our whales." Kim could feel emotions cracking through her voice. "New Eden wasn't supposed to have wildlife. None of the scouting parties found anything bigger than the gnats. They definitely weren't attacked by anything."

"The demons are clever," Hath said. "They would know that you would be looking for signs of life. They would have hidden themselves until such a time as they had an opportunity to hunt more of you." The being looked aside, and Kim could see shame written on its face. "They co-opted our stone rings. They can travel between New Eden and their dimension whenever they choose."

Kim rubbed a hand over her eyes. The mist of well-being was fading a little. "And according to the Adherants, pilgrim ships are on their way by the dozen."

The being nodded, a distant and sad look on its unfinished face. "That is what they wanted. We have both been used for their purposes. We were the bait to lure you here to begin with; they knew we would ask for your help eventually. It took many decades, but finally, you must have found our probe; you came, albeit, not with the phalanx of battleships we'd hoped for."

"No," Wren said. "But humans *are* coming. A lot of ships are on course for New Eden right now."

"We have to warn them," Yoshi said, her voice urgent. "We have to stop them!"

"I suspect the demons began attacking you after you conveyed a message to your home system," Hath elaborated. "They did not see you as a threat prior to then. But now they know others will be on their way to this planet, and they will fight. They are very, very good at fighting."

Kim turned to Wren, dread and panic rolling through her like a dark storm cloud. "Oh God. This is all my fault. I'm the reason the demons attacked us and probably why they attacked the Adherant camp, too. *I'm* the reason the pilgrims are coming." She paused. "We have to take *Daedalus* and head to Edgeward . . ."

Hath cut her off. "The demons can't travel through space on their own. Without the use of stone rings, they are confined to this dimension. They can hide well; remember, they are not of this universe, and usual means of detection don't work. They'll make their way to your space stations, your Outer Colonies. They'll make their way to Earth." The being paused. "No other ship can land on New Eden. The risk is too great."

Yoshi spoke up. "Is that why you tried to crash *Seiiki*?"

Hath remained silent for a few moments before speaking. When it did, the words sounded different. Its voice was not the same as it had been before. The calm, clear tone was gone, replaced by a hurried, low-pitched urgency. "When my creators find out what I have done, I will be deactivated. I was not supposed to interfere in this way." It paused. "I must be careful what I say, and how I say it. I cannot attract attention, or they will begin to ask questions. I cannot risk that."

Kim frowned. "Who are your creators?" Kim demanded. "Why did you try to kill us if they didn't want you to?"

Hath shifted slightly. The motion seemed out-of-place with the being's previously tranquil and composed demeanor. This was an artificial life-form, she reminded herself, and it probably couldn't experience emotion. But then, she might have said the same thing about Adonai, if she didn't know what he really was. And it certainly sounded as if Hath was . . . scared. "I cannot talk further on this. I've already said too much." Abruptly, its posture changed. Its voice, when it spoke, was back to its previous calm timbre. "You asked about my creators. Perhaps it would be better if I showed you."

Rising from the chair, it beckoned for them to follow. Kim looked at Wren who released her hand and put his own against her back. The pressure was comforting, but she glanced back to Adonai and Yoshi to see how they were faring. Yoshi looked pale, her eyes wide. Kim wondered what she was thinking. Adonai, on the other hand, seemed eager to follow the being. His eyes were fixed on it, as if he was unwilling to look away for even a moment, lest this proof of his claims vanish before his eyes. Kim didn't blame him.

"Something's not right here," Yoshi whispered as she fell into step beside Kim. "That . . . whatever it is . . . is acting strange."

Kim glanced at her. She had never picked Yoshi as the most percep-tive person where nuances of behavior were concerned, but she was right. Something felt *wrong*. But her mind was cloudy, and she couldn't pinpoint what it was that was worrying her.

Hath led them through the door to the left of the foyer. Down a sloping passage, Kim saw the illusion of the temple draw back in soft, blurry lines. Dull, brass-colored walls now surrounded them, pocked with little marks, as if made of some particularly heavy metal. The coldness was real; the cold-ness of thick metal long in space. She shivered but kept walking.

Hath stepped through a large door and stopped still. Kim found that they were on a tiny balcony, only about six feet wide and less than half of that deep, edged with an ornate latticework railing with an uneven finish that somehow seemed to be more perfectly formed than a flat surface.

Joining the being, they looked over a circular room lined with upright . . . Kim could only think of them as *chambers*. They were the size of large bathtubs, made of the same brass-like metal, each lit from within by bright white light that made their contents into nothing more than silhouettes. Row upon row, they angled down like the petals of a giant flower. How many were there?

Kim couldn't begin to count, but there must have been hundreds, if not thousands. Through the glass fronts on the chambers closest to her, Kim could see the blurred form of an alien, similar in size and features to the being standing next to her.

Each of them had a pair of wings, folded neatly behind their backs.

Kim gasped. "You really *are* angels." The words were out of her mouth before she could stop them. She felt a twinge of foolishness afterward, but from the corner of her eye, she saw Yoshi reach the balustrade, her mouth open wide.

"This can't be," Yoshi murmured softly.

"These are the Sha'arden," Hath explained. "My creators. They are flesh and blood beings, like you."

"There's someone moving down there," Adonai exclaimed suddenly, and Kim followed his pointed finger to see that he was correct. On the far side of the massive room, on another balcony like the one they stood on, a winged being was standing side-on to them. It held in its hand some kind of tool, but from this distance, she couldn't see exactly what it was doing. It didn't seem interested in their arrival, continuing with its task without so much as a glance toward them.

"That is another of my iterations," Hath explained. "It is performing maintenance."

"The people down there . . . the Sha'arden. They're in some kind of stasis?" Kim said.

"Long-sleep," Hath replied. "It was necessary to keep the population alive and safe from the darashen. Here, they do not need to eat, sleep, or gain access to fresh air; even with the vastness of our technology, the resources needed to sustain a population of this size would soon exceed the ship's capabilities. My program, along with four other iterations, have been running this ship independently for two of your decades. We have been waiting for your race to reach the point where you would come to find us. And aid us in our fight."

"But you tried to kill us," Kim said. "I'm guessing they won't take kindly to that if we're supposed to be their salvation."

"Sometimes," Hath said, "when an iteration has been running for too long without a pause, it becomes unstable. My act in interfering with your computer was unforgiveable. When the time comes, I will accede to my deactivation."

"You called it a sacrifice!" Kim said, but she felt her words drifting away from her, her thoughts muddying once more. "You must have . . . intended something . . ."

"A moment of madness. My programming is corrupt. That is all I can tell you."

Kim looked back and forth between the iteration and the beings below. Something about the conversation was off; she was missing the subtext here. And it didn't help that her thoughts were drifting again . . . Angels. Angel aliens. So many of them lined up down there . . . Kim furrowed her brow. "Why did you want to bring Adonai here but not us?"

"There were . . . some complications when we brought the first humans here. A mechanical being seemed like the sound choice. We could evaluate him, and therefore you, without worrying about the effects of our contact."

"Are you talking about the . . . weird feelings we're experiencing?" Kim said. "I was wondering if you'd drugged us."

"Not drugs, no. But it seems that my creators' species has an effect on yours due to the pheromones they use for communication. Even in longsleep, the pheromones continue to be emitted. That is why the first group of humans was so badly affected. They became incomprehensible, gabbling incoherently. We couldn't communicate. We had to transport them back without asking for their help."

"You are talking about the Adherants who were camped on New Eden?" Adonai asked, voicing Kim's thoughts.

"One of them told me he'd seen angels," she told Hath. "That was here. You brought them on board."

"Correct. They were not who we needed; they were too emotionally involved, I suspect, with the image we presented them. Their zealousness caught us off-guard, and I aborted the task. So when a few months later we detected another of your ships—this one with an artificial life-form on board—we took the chance." The being turned to Adonai. "However, we didn't count on him being an amalgamation of mechanical and biological beings. It seemed the effects were lesser but still very strong. We decided not to communicate with him but let him return to the planet. He would tell others what he had seen and pave the way for us to introduce ourselves, hopefully avoiding the same complications. He would act as our envoy, and then, when more of your people came, we could initiate contact."

"Except that you knew we were flying right into enemy territory," Kim said incredulously. "You *knew* the darashen were here, and you let us land on New Eden anyway." Kim felt her anger rising once more.

"It was not my choice," Hath reminded her. Its voice dropped an octave, becoming hurried once more. "I tried to prevent it."

Kim nodded. Of course it had—if *Seiiki* was torn to pieces, the darashen would hardly be a pressing concern. But Yoshi was right. Hath was acting as if it had something to hide. She could see it now as the iteration straightened, talking in a normal voice once again. "When we witnessed your flight into the asteroid belt, the other iterations and I knew that bringing your cybernetic companion on board was the right course of action to take."

Kim glanced behind her at Adonai whose eyes were fixed on the sight below them with wonder. Or perhaps even joy. Kim couldn't tell which. She wondered how he was feeling right now. He had been right all along, and everyone, including Kim, had doubted him. Was he angry at her? He had every right to be.

"Do they ever wake up?" Adonai asked.

"Every few years, several of the population are woken on a rotating schedule. They will check on the ship's systems and can spend some time in the simulation I showed you, rebuilding muscle and bone strength before they're returned to long-sleep."

Kim could see the sense in this. Most human experiments with cryogenesis had concluded that decades of stasis weren't healthy.

"The simulation is extremely realistic," Wren said. "I guess it's better than being stuck on a spaceship for your recreation time."

"The Sha'arden's love for the homeworld they had to leave is strong," Hath told him. "They wanted an accurate representation. That is why you are here." Without any further warning, the being lifted its hands, and as if this was some trigger, the chamber dissolved around them. Kim experienced a moment of dizziness, a moment of pure *nothing*, before her surroundings were replaced by a dark, cavernous room.

Bronze light spilled over the metallic surfaces. Everything was cast from metal—the walls, the low chairs, the elegantly curved divider that partitioned the front of the room from the rear. Some areas were lower than others for reasons Kim couldn't understand, and curved pillars led up to a cathedral-like vaulted ceiling. Consoles, made of the same dully glowing metal that should have looked clunky, were lifted by elegant patterning. Their surfaces held no buttons or levers. They were just flat surfaces, without screens or any sign of technology. The chairs were set behind them, low at the back to accommodate wings, with curved armrests.

"What just happened?" Kim asked, reeling. She took a few steps, more to find her balance than anything else. She realized, belatedly, that one of the chairs toward the side of the bridge was occupied by another winged being, this one wearing a rose-colored robe, who stood and turned to face them.

"Hath used our quantum polymorphic device to shift you from one location to another; in this case, the bridge of our ship. Inside the ship and in the area of space directly outside its hull, we do not require a physical stone circle since all locations are always in alignment with one another."

Hath inclined its head and strode into the middle of the bridge and stood there, long robe brushing the floor. It looked very much a part of its surroundings, with its golden coloring, as if it, too, had been cast in metal. "Once on the ship, and within a small circle of space surrounding it, we have direct access to the quantum drive. But a planet-side network requires a certain alignment with relation to the other stone ring to function."

"So, the stone rings link to different places at different times," Kim said, looking at Wren, who was gazing around the bridge in wonder.

"And Simons happened to step in one while it was connected to the demon's dimension," Wren said, his face looking gray at the thought.

The second iteration crossed the floor toward them. "You have lost a companion to the darashen," it said. "You've seen how vicious they are."

"Yes, I suppose we have," Kim said. She looked between this new being and Hath. There were faint, very subtle differences—a slightly longer face, a small difference in the size of the half-formed mouth—but Kim could only really tell them apart by the color of their robes. She supposed it wasn't necessary for artificial intelligences to look different from one another if their basic functions were the same. After all, pretty much all droids were made to look identical, only their serial numbers distinguishing them from one another. "You're another hologram? Are you an iteration?"

"My name is Ti'g." It glanced at Hath. "I'm needed elsewhere on the ship. But you are in good hands. Hath is a loyal servant of the Sha'arden, and we will be monitoring the bridge closely if you should need any assistance."

Hath bowed its head as the other iteration winked out of existence.

"What are we doing here?" Yoshi asked faintly.

"This is the bridge of our ship," Hath replied. "It is where we need to be if we are to defeat our enemies."

Wren spread his hands. "We can't fly this ship. Why don't you wake up one of your creators? The . . . Sha'arden?"

"That process takes many days," Hath replied. "However, I believe you can pilot it. The ship is damaged badly. It is also very, very old. But I, and my other iterations, have kept it functional." It lifted an arm, the loose sleeves trailing over a spindly elbow as it pointed to a sunken area to the left, where a u-shaped blank console sat in front of another of the low chairs. "These are our weapons controls. I am as certain as I can be that they will be sufficient to put an end to the attempted incursion on the planet."

"Why are you helping us?" Kim asked.

"Humans fighting humans serves no purpose. If you are to help us fight the darashen, you must be united. There can be no question about who is our joint enemy from this moment onward."

CHAPTER
28

K im took a step away, her feet clanging on the deck.

"Why would we fight for New Eden, only to give it back to you?"

"New Eden is a large planet. The land masses might seem small, but so is our population. We have much in common, and we would come to an arrangement whereby friendship and trade benefit both our species. And your whales, of course."

The argument was so reasonable, so clear-cut. It wasn't a question of whether Kim could refuse; she knew she couldn't. The lives of the whales depended on it. Not just today, during this battle, but for the next decade, the next century. With the angels as allies, no one would ever dare take on Earth United.

She had no choice. The whales would always come first.

Kim moved to the area. It was lit very dimly, partitioned by a curving arc of metal from the front of the room. She had to jump down into the depression in the floor, and once there, she looked over the console, hoping to see something she hadn't seen earlier. But the surface was entirely blank, just as she'd thought. There was no script, no labels. Nothing to indicate this was anything more than a table.

"How do they work? I can't see anything from in here," Kim said.

"Close your eyes for a moment."

Hath strode across to her and leaned over the partition. With its long fingers, it touched her forehead—a gentle pressure, breeze-like. Between one blink and the next, the ship around Kim changed. Before her was a view of the outside of the ship. This wasn't just a holographic relay like she had experienced on the guns of *Daedalus* nor a forward-facing projection from a camera like on the bridge of *Seiiki*. She was standing inside the ship, but the ship was simply *not there*. Below her feet was nothing but stars, and above her head, only asteroids rolling around like cats sunning themselves.

Oh my God, she thought. This was incredible! She had always loved the thrill of going EV, but this . . . this was different. There was no clunky suit, no wheezing respirator. Just her.

She stretched out a hand and laughed to see it against the blackness of space. How amazing! A wave of giddy delight washed over her, but with it came a sobering thought: The being had told them that their emotions were being affected by the pheromones of the angels. She couldn't allow herself to lose control . . . and yet, the feeling of elation was hard to tamp down and harder still to separate from her how she truly felt about being confronted by such a sight. Space, the vastness of it and the unknowns it contained, had always called to her to some degree. To experience it like this . . .

Through the slow dance of the rocks, she could just make out the Adherant ships. And behind the veil of spinning rock, she could see the blue scape of New Eden.

Hath was still touching her, she realized, its cool hand still resting on her brow. And all of a sudden, the knowledge of how to use the alien weapons filled her mind. Her fingers sat on the metal console, and they began to move, tapping graceful lines. Instinct took over, and she knew what she had to do. There . . . there was an asteroid hurtling straight toward her. She sucked in a breath, feeling a thrill of terror to see the gigantic rock so close.

She tapped her fingers. The blast was invisible, but somehow she could still *feel* it. The asteroid blew apart.

The iteration turned to Wren. "You will pilot us out of here."

"I will?" Wren asked, surprise evident in his voice. Kim was aware of the angel leaving her. She had a vague impression of it leading Wren across to another console, but she didn't *see* it. God, her mind hurt just to think! It was better not to.

Hath continued. "This ship will not be able to move far. It is breaking apart. But it will do the task. I will lower our cloak so that your ships can see us."

Kim saw Wren as a silhouetted figure, superimposed over her view of space. He was moving to the front of the bridge where a chair sat before another console inside what she could only think of as an apse—a tiny little alcove at the very nose of this chamber. Hath touched Wren's forehead, just as it had Kim's, and she felt the ship begin to move. Oh, it was slow, but there was no rumbling as on *Seiiki*. It was five times the size of a G-class vessel, but it was as smooth as a tiny one-man fighter.

Kim felt several large shocks; they weren't direct hits to her body, but the sensation told her that asteroids were glancing off the hull. She could see them, too; large rocks bouncing off one another and spinning wildly into the ether above her head. There were no shields turning them away. Kim knew the hull was designed to withstand much more than these tiny boulders. How pathetic and flimsy human ships seemed compared to this.

They were clear of the asteroids in another two minutes. Open space was even more unnerving than the belt had been. She was drifting in nothingness, but she wasn't weightless. It felt *weird*.

Up ahead, the cluster of ships was hovering over New Eden and combing the edges of the belt like insects waiting to swarm. They were probably looking for Kim's shuttle. If the alien being was right, only a few seconds might have passed since they'd lost sight of them.

Lifting her fingers, she fired a burst of invisible gunfire at a small ship painted with bright orange stripes, arrowing in on the nearest ship's port side. The ship was there for a moment, and the next, it was in separate pieces. Kim couldn't help reaching out a finger to trace the path of those tiny fiery sparks even as they burned out to charred nothingness.

Before she could think too much longer, she triggered another salvo, aiming for a sleek little fighter coming in from behind. The ship listed sideways, then exploded in a blossom of fire and sparks, quickly extinguished by the vacuum.

There were fewer, now. She had killed . . . how many people?

The horror suffused her and then slowly ebbed away. There were two more ships ahead of her, scrambling toward New Eden, heading for the planet at full speed.

The moment of hesitation had cost her. They split off, some heading for the planet, and some heading straight for the alien ship. This head-on charge didn't alarm her. She was falling into the rhythm of it now.

Why had this been so hard during their weapons training exercises on *Seiiki*? Was it just her hatred of Yoshi that had put her off? If so, it was stupid. Such a waste of time and energy.

She could aim a gun and fire. She could take a life this way if she needed to. It was . . . *easy.*

She had a lot she could learn from the whales, she thought grimly. They didn't hold grudges, didn't hate as humans did. They were not violent, but they did what they needed to do to survive. Instinctively, she reached for the Link, but there was only silence in answer.

Ahead of her, she could see the farthest ships, those closest to the planet, turning abruptly. They were already so close to New Eden, but they didn't wait to drop through the planet's atmosphere. Bright trails of laser fire erupted from their prows and underbellies, slicing through the blue-tinged halo at the planet's periphery to arc toward the oceans. Like golden rain, it speared through miles of open air and would be slowed only a little by atmospheric conditions.

The whales. Kim couldn't hear them, but she didn't need the Link to know that those bolts would hit the ocean in less than thirty seconds time.

The heat of that continued fire would heat—even boil—the water in every direction. And if a whale happened to be hit . . .

Bastards.

How dare they do this? How dare they claim the right to decide whether a being lived or died?

She wouldn't let it happen, *couldn't* let it happen.

Already, she was firing, firing, and firing again.

A phalanx of crisp laser fire sped out from beneath her. With incredible accuracy and force, it hit the side of one of the small ships perched above the ocean, illuminating it momentarily before it broke apart, as if smashed against a rock. Debris hurtled outward in a star-shaped pattern, caught after a moment by New Eden's gravity. Trails of black smoke remained behind as the shards of ship hull, pieces of control panels, droids, and even a few intact human figures—like limp rag dolls—tumbled into the atmosphere.

The ship rocked beneath her as bullets were returned, but the massive metal hull gave no quarter. The remaining Adherant ships turned their attention from the planet and lined up in front of her, the whales forgotten.

Kim didn't let up on the controls, spraying the laser fire into the ether. One ship exploded, careened into its partner, and created an even bigger fireball. Three ships moved off to the sides. *What were they doing, trying for some kind of pincer movement?* It was pointless. Two of them crumpled like tin cans under a barrage of invisible bullets, then blew apart into fragments. The third kept coming, a kamikaze suicide run. It was so close, too close, and, disembodied as she was, it was flying straight *at her.*

She could hear Wren shouting as he tried to evade, but the Adherant ship was just below her and still hurtling onward. She tried to aim—too late. A loud resounding clang told her they'd been hit, and yet, she didn't feel it. The ship remained solid under her feet, even if she couldn't see it. The small collision was nothing more than a mosquito bite to this leviathan of a ship.

"Are we okay?" Kim asked.

Hath nodded. "Yes. It takes more than a Xenol explosion to damage the hull of a *Reveni* transport vessel. I have a communication coming in."

"If it's the Adherants—"

"It isn't."

A streak flashed across Kim's vision, a blur that resolved itself over a few minutes to become a solid shape. The ship was huge, a bristling thing of gray metal with a bulging belly. A G-class dreadnaught, the green EU shield painted across her prow.

"Oh my God," she said.

"That's a G-class vessel," Wren said.

A voice filled the void, echoing around Kim.

"Unknown vessel, what is your intention here?" The voice sounded wary but slightly awed. "This is Admiral Bahrain of the Battlecruiser *Arkansas*. I demand to know—"

"Admiral," Kim cut him off. "This is Kim Teng."

"Kim—" The voice sounded shocked. "Really?"

"Yes. It's a long story, Admiral, and I'd love to tell it to you, but I don't think now is the right time."

"Agreed," the Admiral replied. "Well, Kim, if you're the one who's been shooting at the Adherants, all I can say is, nice work. The last two vessels are in retreat."

Kim could see that. She watched as they powered up their drives, thrusters becoming bright white with built-up power, before they vanished.

"Our relief wasn't due here for another eight weeks," Kim said. "How the hell—I mean, sorry, sir—"

"You've been away from Sol for a few months, Ms. Teng," the Admiral replied. "Things have changed somewhat on the front of quantum technology. But we'll save that discussion for another time as well. Our comms officer says she's getting a hail from the base. They're asking for you, Kim. Do you want me to patch it through to you?"

Kim's heart leapt. It had to be Lieutenant Grand.

Please, she thought. *Let it be him!* "Yes, put it through."

"Kim? The Admiral tells us you're up there. Thank Heavens you're in one piece."

Kim couldn't help a smile from stretching over her face. "I actually never thought I'd be glad to hear your voice."

"Are you really?" There was a hint of humor in his tone.

"Is everyone okay?" she asked.

"In a manner of speaking. We have a few injured, but no human casualties." He paused and then continued, his voice low, tentative and sad to impart this news. "Two of the Adherant ships entered the atmosphere and shot laser fire into the ocean. Four whales were killed by the blasts. Several more suffered projectile injuries from broken rocks being blasted from the ocean floor, and we have a few with severe burns. We're treating them, but we need you and Yoshi back down here."

CHAPTER

29

Hath brought her out of the piloting system and back to herself. Sitting in the chair, leaning over to reach the too-large console, she felt as if she'd woken up from a dream. Her legs were unsteady as she pushed herself to her feet and jumped from the alcove. Standing there, in the middle of the bridge, Kim felt very alone, very small.

"I will transport you directly to your ship," Hath said.

"You can do that?" Kim asked. She still felt hazy, dazed, as if she'd been sleeping for a long time and all that had just happened was a dream. How long had they been out here? Four hours? Five?

"The ship is in close enough proximity to be affected by our polymorphic field," the being said. "Everything within range of the ship can be affected by our quantum field."

"Was that what happened to our pod?" Kim asked. "We lost five hours. What happened to us during that time?"

Hath lifted its hands. "That time did not happen for you. It was simply a by-product of being caught in the summoning stream."

"So you only wanted Adonai?" Wren asked. "We were just . . . collateral?"

Hath looked aside. "My other iterations and I decided to bring your droid companion on board, but our mother ship and its systems are damaged. The iteration in charge unintentionally caught your escape pod in the summoning stream as well."

Kim shook her head. This was all so unbelievable. "You can time travel."

"This ship has the capability to shift itself out of phase with this universe. It is how I have kept this ship safe for many decades."

Kim glanced toward Wren as he made his way out of the apse and slowly climbed the gentle slope of the floor to join her behind the partition. His eyes were sweeping the consoles. "Your technology is so strange," he said. "How does any of it work? How do you use those polymorphic things? I'll tell you what, we could find a use for some of those on Earth. Imagine—instant transport."

Hath let that smile fall onto its face once more. "The stone rings work by transporting photons. If I heard correctly, your race has just mastered some level of the quantum. This is the basis of our technology, and we included the blueprints for the basics in our transmission to you."

Wren blinked. "You have?"

"It is because of us—because of me—that you are already on the way to the deeper understanding of the universe, and I do not see the point in hindering you." Hath paused. "I know my creators would not agree with this, but it is my decision to make."

"Thank you," Kim said. She looked at the being. It stood there, regarding her without moving. "What will you do now?"

Hath lifted its shoulders. Its wings moved gently. The gesture was too graceful to be called a shrug, but she suspected that's what it was. "The demons will have sensed us. Even if they haven't, we came very close to the planet, and they will have seen us in the sky. They know we're here now; they know they didn't destroy us or our ship. We can't hide any longer." The being's shoulders fell in an inaudible sigh.

Kim shook her head. "I won't let any more humans come here."

"And you think that will stop them?" Hath lifted one hairless eyebrow. "We know your people. They will think you are trying to protect this place or keep it for yourself. They will come. So there is no point in us hiding. The time has come for me to awaken my creators."

Hath vanished, leaving Kim staring at the empty air.

Left with Adonai, Yoshi, and Wren, Kim stood in the strange cathedral-bridge of this ancient, ruined starship, the wreckage of a battle all around them.

"Do you hate me?" Kim asked them, her voice sounding small and scared. She hadn't meant it to, but this was what she felt, and everything inside her was now hidden by the lightest of veils, ready to blow away at the slightest hint of a breeze. "For shooting down those ships?"

"You had to," Yoshi said.

"There was no choice," Adonai added. "They were trying to kill the whales."

"Of course not," Wren answered vehemently. "Why would you think that?"

"Maybe because I hate myself. Just a little bit. Maybe more than a little bit. Maybe because . . . inside, Wren, I'm a monster. You see that, don't you?"

He crossed the floor in a few long strides, gathered her in his arms, and kissed the top of her head. She felt his lips, papery and dry after the stress of the past few hours on the bare skin of her head, and they made her shiver. She didn't care that Yoshi was watching or that Adonai was nearby. For that moment, it was only her and Wren. She lifted her head, met his lips with hers, and kissed him as she had never kissed anyone before.

Around them, the alien bridge dissolved, but they were still locked in their embrace.

CHAPTER

30

Kim! Kim!

The whales voices burst over her.

Are you all right?

We were so worried!

"I'm fine," she told them. "I'll be back on New Eden soon. Okay? Stay calm."

The *Arkansas* was all right angles and brilliant white lights. Coming from the alien ship, it was truly another species of technology; easy to see that while there were similarities between humans and the winged aliens, evolution had taken them on very different paths in terms of aesthetics.

Kim, Wren, Yoshi, and Adonai were taken to a medical bay where a brisk surgeon poked and prodded them, examined their throats, and ran a scanner over their injuries. Kim's wrist was examined and pronounced to have a hairline fracture. This was promptly set with a regenerator, while Wren's wounded ankle was deemed able to heal on its own and plastered with a bandage. Yoshi spent her time raging at the surgeon and the nurses who were insisting that all of them get some sleep before they were transported back down to New Eden.

"There are injured whales on the planet, and I'm wasting time up here!"

Kim had to agree. Whatever time she'd spent asleep before waking up on the alien ship, it hadn't been enough to recharge her, but the whales took priority. Over everything. Adonai did not say much at all. Kim noticed how the medical staff gave him a wide berth, though there were many curious glances as they were marched down the hallways and finally put into a shuttle along with a crew of fresh EU soldiers.

The *Arkansas*, Kim learned while she was being moved from the infirmary to a shuttle, was actually the first warship specifically built to house quantum drive. The launch date had been brought forward by necessity, given the leakage of the technology to the Adherants. So far, even though it was a prototype, it had functioned extremely well, making the jump from Sol to Eschol in three weeks.

"With time, it can be done even more quickly," explained the Airman who was escorting her. "We had to be cautious, but we didn't find any issues."

They flew over *Seiiki*'s furrow on their return to the base. Kim looked down on the ship—or what was left of it aboveground. During the time they'd been away, the ground had virtually swallowed the whole ship. Only the topmost curve of the forward section of Deck One showed through; a metallic island in a sea of mud. But the planet didn't seem to mind. Already, creepers and trailing fern fronds were reaching out long runners, sending down tiny roots into the damp, fertile soil. Kim imagined those roots extending down into the ship, invading all the passages and rooms she knew so well. Vines growing over her bed, ferns blooming in the drained fishery tanks.

Sorry, Seiiki. I thought you'd have a better end than this, she thought.

They landed on the base's rooftop landing pad. It was still morning, the white sun about midway to noon. The warmth felt great on Kim's exposed skin as she left *Daedalus* and looked over the two other, much newer, EU scoutships that sat on the pad, recent departures from the *Arkansas*.

"Company," Wren said as the nearest officer, a Lieutenant Hugo, stood and beckoned them toward the door.

Kim made a skeptical noise. "I don't know how this is going to go."

"Don't worry. They'd be morons to press charges against you."

"I'm not worried about that," she said.

"I know," he replied. "But we won't let them take New Eden, Kim. I promise you."

Kim didn't answer as she walked for the door leading to the elevator down into the building. She just wanted to get this over with.

EU soldiers manned the consoles of the operations room and worked down on the docks below and gathered in groups on the mezzanine, talking seriously. Four whales were strapped into harnesses down there, soldiers monitoring the droids that worked on them. Kim could see the horrific damage to Barak's hide. Flesh was twisted and bubbled, and in places it had shrunk back from the tissue beneath. Kim could see white and pink marbled innards. Her heart ached, but she refused to look away. Barak had been looking forward to having calves.

"His chances are good, from what I've been told," Yoshi said from behind her. She joined Kim at the railing, looking over the docks below as a medbot lifted on its repulsors and ran a dermal regenerator over the scars. "But Levi . . ."

Kim looked into the sad eyes of the kind, sensible whale on the next dock over. He was so badly burned, she could tell he wouldn't survive—a hole had been gouged from his side, the flesh around it suppurating and oozing clear fluid. One of the Adherants' laser bolts must have hit him directly. An EU soldier sat nearby, a hand on his lower chin, and Kim felt a moment of gratitude for this small act of kindness from a stranger. Beside him was another person, a young woman with ratty blonde hair.

Kim, Kim, Kim! You're all right?

"I'm sorry," she said to the whales over the Link. "I'm so sorry your friends were killed and injured."

Kim, we're just glad you're here.

She could feel that. They truly were glad. There were no grudges held where whales were concerned, no hard feelings, no blame laid. Save for Hosea, she'd never encountered that side of human emotion in their altered brain chemistry.

"Thank you," she said.

Lieutenant Grand strode across the mezzanine. He wasn't smiling, but he didn't look pissed. Kim took that as a good sign. Stopping just in front of her, he held out a hand, and Kim took it hesitantly. The firm clasp reminded her of her dad.

"Kim. You did well."

"I . . . I did?" Kim asked. "I abandoned you down here! You could have died."

"It was a terrible battle. One I'm afraid Ms. Wu is still paying for." He shook his head. "The Adherants who survived are being transferred to the *Arkansas* as we speak, but they were lucky we found them when we did. Those creatures are frightening, Kim. If we're going to remain on this planet, we need to know how to fight them."

"The aliens gave us schematics for the rings," Wren spoke up. "I've had a quick look. It's possible I might be able to somehow block them from using them once I've got a better understanding."

But Kim looked at him quizzically. "You're speaking in the present tense," she said. "As if you plan on staying."

Grand looked to the left. "I'm making a case for you, Kim. I'm not sure how it's going to go—these decisions are out of my hands—but with Admiral Mbewe on your side as well, we might be able to get this through."

Kim breathed out a sigh, but she wasn't sure if she felt relief or just weariness. "Thank you, sir."

"I'm told the quarters are ready for occupation. I suggest you have a rest and take a breather, Kim. I'll need you back out here soon."

Officer Durand appeared at his shoulder, smiling. "Glad to have you back, Kim," she said. "Yoshi, Wren. I'll take you all down there if you like. Adonai, the lieutenant will show you to the charging bay."

Waving a quick goodbye to Adonai, Kim followed her to their quarters. Each door contained a small room with a single bunk and shower cubicle, not much bigger than her room on *Seiiki*. Kim didn't mind at all, but once Yoshi had vanished and she pulled Wren into her room, keying the door shut, she realized the lack of space would be more of an attribute than a drawback.

His lips were firm on hers, and she wrapped her arms around his waist, pulling him closer. All she wanted right now was to feel his body against hers. He was so solid, so strong, and she needed that. Breathing in the scent of him; the faint smell of soap from a hasty shower on the *Arkansas,* the stinging odor of antibacterial cream from the bound wound on his ankle, and the subtle smell that was just *Wren.* It helped her feel like she was grounded, her feet on solid Earth, rather than spinning through space with the stars all around, her hands in front of her, naked weapons . . .

"Kim?" Wren pulled back. "Are you all right?"

"Kiss me," she said.

He did.

The chime of the computer broke through Kim's half-sleep. "Kim?"

Kim rolled to her side. Pitching her voice low, hoping not to wake the sleeping Wren beside her, she asked, "What is it?"

"There is an encoded transmission for you."

Kim glanced at Wren. He stirred, a bare arm pushing himself upright on the mattress. "Careful, Kim," he warned her.

"I'm always careful," she shot back.

"I know that," he replied. "Of course I know that. It's just . . . Grigorian is dangerous. His reach is far wider than I thought. Kim, if he truly murdered that scientist on Mars, he started a war when humanity's been at peace for years. What else is he capable of?"

"That's what I need to know," she told him.

Sitting upright on the bed with her legs folded under her, she tapped the kanji for *talk* into the air. "Computer, play the message for me."

Kim, said a quiet voice. There was no visual, which was unnerving. It sounded like Grigorian was in the room with her.

She'd only met the man once, and she had quickly fallen under his spell. Even his voice alone was lulling and soft.

I was hoping that our next meeting would be in person. I am afraid that I have failed you, Kim, on many levels; the least of which is not to face you now as I speak this message. Please know that the reasons for doing so are many and varied, but there is a physical impossibility which I cannot overcome.

When I first met you, Kim, I saw in you a girl like the daughter I never had but wished for. Seeing you work with Zane, it was like watching poetry in motion. You were made for one another. And you must know it, too.

Kim shivered and wrapped her arms around herself. God, where was Grigorian going with this?

It was sadder still, because I knew that there was no turning from the road God had set out for you. I would have to say goodbye. It was not an easy choice, but it was a necessary one. One set out long before your birth.

I'm speaking, of course, of what the Artifact told me must happen. That is why you were aboard Seiiki, Kim. Because you, specifically you, were chosen by God.

You turned your back on your chosen path. This, too, I understand. To be human is to fall, over and over again. To fail. But to strive to do better next time.

And so, I ask you to wait. You will hear word from me again, and soon. I hope you will be willing to listen. It's not too late.

Kim's hands clenched to fists. A flash of fury ran through her. How dare Grigorian do this? How dare he treat people like pawns in his little game? Because now she knew, with utter certainty, that Grigorian was not the voice of God. He was a manipulator, a liar, and possibly a fucking lunatic.

"Kim? Are you okay?" Wren asked, his hand reaching for her back.

"Yes," she said. "And . . . no. Wren—"

The door chimed.

Wren gave a grunt of annoyance, slipping out of the bed and pulling his trousers over his boxer shorts. Kim had come close to stripping him bare last night, but she had held off on crossing that final barrier. She knew it wasn't the right time, even though it was all she wanted right now. But that was the problem, wasn't it? She wanted it because she wanted to lose herself in him. Forget everything else and just *be*. But that wasn't fair on Wren, and it didn't do justice to what they had. Kim couldn't do it, and even though he'd never show it, she knew it had left Wren just as frustrated and confused as it had her.

Kim straightened up, pulling her loose nightshirt into a less revealing position. "Come in."

"Kim Teng." A tall woman stood in the doorway to the room. She wore a green dress with a skirt so long it trailed over her shoes. Silver hair was piled atop her head in an elegant bun. She was leaning against the door jamb, and Kim's breath caught in her throat.

Antonia Morosini.

"May I have a word please?"

Kim nodded, her mouth going dry as she scrambled out of bed and tried, vainly, to straighten the covers. She glanced at Wren.

"I'll give you some space?" he said in a voice that very much said he wanted to do anything but.

"If you wouldn't mind," the woman replied with a smile.

Wren scooped up his shirt and gave Kim a look before heading through the door.

Morosini extended a hand as she crossed the small space between them. "I'm pleased to meet you, Kim. And I owe you a debt of thanks. If not for your actions, we might have lost more than a few whales. You really saved the day."

Kim cringed. "No I didn't. I've messed everything up. I thought I was doing the right thing. Turns out . . ." She took a breath and met Morosini's

eyes. They were deep brown, and there was compassion in them. Hard-
ness, too. This was a woman who had *lived*. Kim had done a lot of research
on her background to prepare for her training at Near Horizon, but the
details of Morosini's life before she became a politician were scarce and
too dry, too substanceless to be complete. "I'm just as much a fraud as I
thought I was."

Morosini smiled gently. "I know who you are, Kim Teng."

Kim smiled despite herself, but it soon faded. "Are you going to . . ."

Morosini's eyes softened, and she settled herself onto the bed and patted
it, indicating that Kim should sit, too. "Yes, Kim. I'm afraid so. After what
you did with those Adherant ships up there, I've got no choice. I have to
send you back to Earth."

The floor seemed to vanish from under her feet. "No."

"It's not up to you, Kim, and it's certainly not a punishment." Morosini
spread her hands. "I'm doing what I can, but my hands are tied. There are
forces even I can't control. And frankly, I think you're better off back there
where you can rally support for keeping the whales—and New Eden—safe.
You and Adonai both."

"Adonai? You're sending him back, too? *Why?*"

"He is a curiosity, Kim. Erica Wu was able to keep him in the project
until now, but the Yokohama Institute has been very adamant that studying
him will be beneficial to further Ark Projects. I don't think even you can
argue with that."

She definitely could. But another, much more selfish part of her made her
hold her tongue. She was going to have to leave Wren—and the whales—
but at least, at the very least, she didn't have to leave Adonai behind. He
would be with her.

And she would never let him out of her sight. She could make that promise, at least.

Kim?

Are you all right?

The whale's voices brought her back to herself.

"You can't stay here," she told Morosini. "You can't let pilgrim ships come here—or more Adherants. You need to turn them back. Everyone on this planet is in danger from the demons."

"We will not run," Morosini said firmly. "I know what happened on that ship; I've had a full report from Lieutenant Grand and Wren Keene. You were led here for a reason, yes?"

Kim thought about it. "You think I was . . . *led* here . . . for the whales?"

"You wiped out an entire enemy fleet, Kim, in order to protect them. You've made a significant dent in their forces. And I have to admit, even I underestimated what they're capable of." She paused, turned from Kim and walked to the window, where she looked out over the operations room. "We . . . grew complacent, I suppose. We'd won the wars, we had a hold on everything, and we should have been more prepared for dissident uprisings."

Kim frowned. "Yeah, but I probably stoked a fire that was already burning pretty highly."

Morosini shook her head. Kim watched her expression, reflected in the window, change from sadness to sternness.

"You needed to protect the whales, and you did the right thing. I didn't approve the Ark Project for the sake of it, Kim. Humanity wants the whales safe. To that end, I'm going to send out a few EU soldiers with some of the most powerful explosives at our disposal. I want those stone rings sealed until Wren can work out how to disable them." Her lips made a thin line. "This planet is ours. Yes, maybe it wasn't God who pointed us to it. Not directly. But He also works in indirect ways."

"I've heard that before," Kim said warily. "You sound a lot like . . . someone else."

"I think I know who you're talking about, Kim." She folded her arms while an introspective look crossed her face. "Grigorian—at least, the Grigorian I knew—was an avid believer in extraterrestrial life."

"You . . . knew him?" Kim was stunned. Morosini knowing Grigorian personally was ludicrous. They were mortal enemies. Morosini had been denouncing Anti-Unificationists like Grigorian publicly for decades.

"Oh yes. Better than you can imagine." A small smile came to her lips. "Can I ask you, did he ever show you the Artifact?"

Kim shook her head. "No. I actually started to think it was a lie, too."

"It is not."

Kim nodded slowly, and Morosini continued.

"To everyone else, the Artifact was a piece of space junk that was caught in Pluto's orbit. In those days, Grigorian worked for SETI, you understand. We were looking for planets to colonize, not relics. But the Artifact provided proof of everything Grigorian ever held true. Grigorian was under its spell entirely, spending late nights listening to its repeating signal, trying endlessly to decipher it. And I, a lowly intern at that point, was caught up in his enthusiasm.

"He co-opted funds to make the recovery mission happen when the political wheels stalled him. He basically stole a shuttle and flew it to Pluto. But what he found there . . . he says it spoke to him. That he heard the voice of God in its words. That it told him of a new planet. There was a map, a star map, in its database. At the time, no one else believed him. No one but me." She sighed, shaking her head sadly.

"Grigorian . . ." Kim swallowed, realization dawning on her. "Grigorian discovered the alien probe. That's the Artifact."

"It seems that the Artifact is what the aliens referred to as their probe, yes. I studied it as best I could, but it was very far beyond my grasp, and it seemed to 'speak' only to Grigorian. It told him of technology far beyond our own—quantum-level computing, instantaneous transport, and other things that were seemingly impossible. There were clues hidden within, too—small bits and pieces of plans, a few hints as to what would and wouldn't work. Grigorian wrote it down feverishly, filling notebook after notebook."

"Quantum tech," Kim breathed. "We didn't develop it ourselves, did we?"

"We *would* have," Morosini said. "But not soon enough. The leaps that have taken place in the past decade—in the past few months—are thanks to the information contained in the Artifact."

Her gaze moved over Kim's bald forehead, over the tendrils of gold that made up the Link.

"Grigorian . . . I began to see how we could use this. I saw that we could spread the word of God. How it could end the wars. So I became the mouthpiece, visiting first towns, then cities, delivering speeches through which I would weave clever insinuations and begin to prepare people's minds for what I liked to think of as a reawakening, a return to the spirit of the church, to belief in God. I had never anticipated such success, but people were so ready, so willing to listen and so happy to believe.

"We kept the Artifact secret; we were going to reveal it eventually, but we thought we would prepare the way first." She shook her head sadly. "But it changed him. He became . . . different. Unfamiliar. I . . . lost him to it." She smiled, self-deprecatingly. "I was going to reveal the Artifact. That was my plan. A great unveiling, a presentation of a piece of solid evidence that the God I spoke of was real. At least, I hoped they would see it that way, that they would be as willing and eager as Grigorian and I had been. But when I returned to our flat, I found it empty. Grigorian had gone to the lab and taken the Artifact. No one knew where he went.

"I first heard from him a year later. A letter, pen-on-paper, demanding that I give up my leadership. That I should never have passed on the knowledge of quantum technology. That God didn't like what I was doing, that I would be damned to Hell.

"He started undertaking these . . . I suppose 'crusades' is the best term for it. Picking targets with religious significance—stem cell research centers, abortion clinics, medical research centers. My concern shifted immediately to Eschol. If Grigorian was so willing to invoke destruction on our own people, what might he do to New Eden? So I decided to reveal its existence, thinking that if it was public knowledge, it would be protected. And then when Near Horizon took up the contract to move the whales there, I thought I had done the right thing." She paused. "Now I'm not so sure."

"Grigorian thinks New Eden is his." The realization crashed into Kim with the force of a ship at hyper speed. She had known that Grigorian was a liar, that everything she had believed about the Crusaders was false. But this . . . to find out that Grigorian himself was a hypocrite? "I thought at first that he just didn't want the whales here, but that's not true, is it? He wants New Eden for himself." Tears were welling in her eyes. She had been so blind, so *stupid*. God, she hated Grigorian as she had never hated anyone in her life. And she was going to bring him down. Him and all his stupid Crusaders. She was going to *kill* him. The thought was bald and disturbing, but Kim felt it with every fiber of her being. "Does anyone else know this? Or are all the Crusaders in on this?"

"It doesn't serve his purpose to have anyone know his true motivations for keeping New Eden out of the hands of EU. Not yet, anyway. His followers will continue to believe whatever he needs them to believe for as long as he needs it." Morosini met Kim's eyes. "I want you to understand that I know how easy it is to fall under his spell." She smiled sorrowfully. "He's making an army of them—avid believers. And why not? It's wonderful to have God on your side. I should know."

Kim felt that familiar anger burning in her chest. "God isn't a political tool. And He isn't something you or Grigorian can use for your own ends. He is . . . He's above all this." She spread her hands, indicating the lab, the base, New Eden, and the universe in general.

She laughed. "And that," she said, "is why Grigorian would never truly succeed with you. Not completely."

The numbness Kim felt began to recede. "I should have known. Why didn't I know?"

Morosini shook her head. "Perhaps God *is*, in some way, working through Grigorian. We will probably never know." And then, she took Kim's hand between hers. "But we must remember—both of us—God's greatest lesson. That He forgives all, so the hardest thing we must do, as humans, is forgive one another. And ourselves."

"What if we can't?" Kim said, but her voice was so hoarse it came out as a whisper.

The woman stood, smoothing her green dress and heading for the door. "Then you keep living."

CHAPTER
31

A day passed. Kim kept to herself, trying mainly not to think of anything. She avoided everyone, except for Yoshi, who, for once, Kim was grateful to be around. Her silences weren't uncomfortable and nor did she press Kim for any information. Instead, she was happy to speak in short sentences and get to the point.

"Can I ask you something, Kim?" Yoshi asked as she slipped a glass slide under a microscope and drew a kanji in the air, pulling up a holo of the sample in the air. Yoshi's latest project was the classification of vegetation surrounding the base, and she and Kim had been gathering samples for the past few hours.

Kim glanced at her quizzically. She'd been sorting a collection of older slides into categories, and the question caught her off guard. "What?"

"Ever since the alien mother ship . . . I've been playing it all over and over again in my mind. Trying to work out what it was that we missed." Yoshi moved her attention from the holo and met Kim's eyes. "How long did we walk in the alien simulation?"

Kim shrugged. Her sense of time had been hazy, and even when she tried hard, she found the details of what had happened aboard the ship hard to shape into solid, linear memories. It was like a particularly vivid dream. "Half an hour, maybe?"

Yoshi nodded. "Can you walk anywhere on New Eden for half an hour without seeing the ocean?"

Kim dropped a slide with a clatter on the benchtop. She picked it up and frowned. "I'm not sure what you're saying, Yoshi."

"It's been bugging me, that's all," the other girl said.

Kim nodded slowly. "It was a simulation. Maybe they just didn't put the ocean in? They're a land-based species, obviously."

Yoshi nodded. "True. But there were also no trees except for one. Again, New Eden is thickly forested except for a few small areas. There are no clearings as big as the one we walked through."

"Hath didn't say it was an accurate representation."

"No, it didn't. But if not, why bother to make it at all? It said the angels used the simulation as a recreational area, but it also said they used it because they missed their homeworld. So why not make it accurate?"

Kim looked at the slide in her hands, but she wasn't seeing it. "What does it mean, then?"

Yoshi turned aside at last. "That's the part I can't work out."

Later that night, instead of joining Wren and the other personnel in the mess, Kim headed in the opposite direction. She wanted to find Adonai.

The computer core had been installed in a specialized room at the center of the base, and it was here that Kim found Adonai. He was working on one of the auxiliary computers, tapping away at an actual keyboard attached to an angled bracket, something Kim hadn't seen too often in her life. His back was to her, but he didn't seem startled when she spoke.

"How are you, Adonai?"

He didn't turn, just paused in the tapping of his keys. "I'm well, Kim."

She approached him slowly, circling to stand behind the metal framework holding the various monitors and holo displays. In the dim room with the light of the core playing over him, Adonai looked far less like the human she sometimes found herself thinking of him as and more like the droid he was—sharp angles, gleaming metal, and skeletal, shadowed cavities where flesh-and-bone should be.

"I know that's not true," she said.

Adonai raised his shoulders in approximation of a shrug before continuing to tap at the keyboard. "If you've come to tell me that you told me so, you don't need to. I already feel like an . . . is idiot the right word?"

Kim's heart broke. "You're not an idiot."

"You told me it would happen. That I would be taken away to be studied if I spoke publicly. And that's exactly what happened. So, I am an idiot."

Kim braced her hands on the upright metal supports, pushing her face between the monitors to be closer to Adonai. "They would have found an excuse one way or another. Once I was out of the way, you'd have been next on their list." She hated that it was true.

"I found something," Adonai replied softly, lifting his eyes at last. "The holo we saw of the winged being, stored on the computer? Wren has been able to separate the code out at last and place a division in the core that will make sure it doesn't reinfect the computer's processes. He couldn't remove it entirely, but he let me have access. I was able to find more to the program. It looks like it's not just a program. It's bigger. It's like . . . another computer."

"What do you mean?"

"It accepts input and responds with output. That is the definition of a computer." Adonai tapped the keys. "It is very complicated. I can show you, though, if you would like."

Kim could tell he was eager. Though she had some curiosity about what this thing was, she was also wary. Letting the program run at all seemed risky; she had no desire to reinfect the computer, and if this technology was as advanced as anything she'd seen on the alien ship, she couldn't be sure it wouldn't break through anything Wren had done to confine it.

"Are you sure it's safe?"

Adonai shook his head. "No. Not really. But it's there, whether or not we trust it." He tapped a few more keys. "I think it should be here somewhere . . ."

Movement toward the center of the room caught Kim's eye. The slight image of a winged form appeared for just a moment; its outline skewed and malformed, a prismatic effect of misaligned colors spilling onto the floor around it.

A second later, it was gone again.

Kim walked toward the spot where the thing had appeared. It certainly had looked like Hath. "Can you make it any clearer? Can you interact with it?"

Adonai turned back to his keyboard. "I'm trying, but so far, I haven't been able to make out anything useful beyond the original recording. But there is definitely more there. Perhaps the scientists on Earth will be able to work it out."

Kim turned to look over her shoulder. "They're sending it to Earth?"

"The computer is going to be replaced when the EU relief ships reach New Eden. Wren isn't happy about it."

"Neither am I," Kim answered, frowning. A small bead of anger began to well in her mind. Who were these people to come in and take over the base as if they were the ones who built it? Who *fought* for it? They didn't care about the whales. All they saw were dollar signs, and Kim . . .

Her anger flared and died, leaving in its wake black, all-encompassing despair. She couldn't do anything about it. She wasn't in charge. She wasn't even a Caretaker now.

"Kim, are you okay?" Adonai's concern was real. He crossed the floor, placing a hand on her shoulder and leaning in close. "You're crying."

"No I'm not," she replied, her voice husky. "I'm just . . . I'm going to miss this place. Wren. And—"

"And the whales. I am going to miss them, too. But it's the right time for me to go. New Eden has changed me. I've done things here that I'm not proud of. I want to leave them behind."

Kim smiled sadly, because she understood exactly what he meant.

Okay, so. Yeah, it's been a long time. Sorry about that. I know you're all dying to hear what I have to say next! What could possibly follow whales coming back to life and the discovery of Heaven?

So, basically, you guys can think what you like. Read into my broadcast, analyze it, whatever. I don't care. I know what I saw, and I know what I said, and it wasn't anything about finding Heaven. I told you the facts. You ran with them. Hey, it's a free . . . universe. Do whatever you like, but don't hate me just because I said something you didn't like. Or something you think *I said. That's a waste of time.*

So, here are some more facts: Wren has been working hard at finding a way to disable the stone rings, and I think he's made some progress. Morosini has authorized EU to use explosives to destroy all the stone circles we know about. The stones are scattered, the circles are nothing but blackened craters. I won't lie to you. It doesn't fill me—nor anyone else, I suspect—with any kind of relief, though. We don't know how many more circles there might be on this continent—or other continents in this world. Or other worlds, for that matter. And we don't know how they work, either, and that's kind of the worst thing. What alignment is needed for the alien creatures to come through? Do all of them go back every time, or do some of them remain here? We've all heard howls in the night, and that proves they're not gone for good. The sentries who guard the base are always nervous. No one wants to pull that duty, and I think even some of them are faking illnesses.

One task that's coveted is assignment to the small team Morosini had set up to monitor the alien ship and its movements. Communications are being sent out regularly, but as yet, the holographic being has not responded. Nor have any of the sleepers aboard the ship. I don't know if he's done as he said he would and awakened them or if he's changed his mind. The only thing we know for sure is that the ship has been moving out of the Hebron Belt and into orbit of New Eden. It's up there, and for a good nine hours of every day, you can see it. Everyone here is curious . . . and hopeful. As far as we're concerned, this is the most exciting thing to have ever happened.

So I'll sign off now, but I just want to say, the whales are doing great. And I'm sorry. I know a lot of you were hopeful when those plans for a theme park were released, but EU has decided it's too dangerous until the threat of the creatures has been neutralized. Maybe one day, maybe soon. Just keep hoping, okay?

I'll be back on Earth in a few months' time, if everything goes according to schedule. I'm looking forward to seeing you all in person for the first time in almost two years! And I'm so excited to introduce you to Adonai!

It had been a long time since she'd lied this much, this *deeply*, and it was hard. Kim let out a breath as she shut down the comms program on her tablet.

"Kim?" The computer chimed softly. "Are you ready to send your transmission through to Admiral Bahrain?"

She nodded wearily, drawing the kanji for *deliver*. Then she lay back on her bunk, staring at the ceiling for a long moment. Out of habit, she reached for the whales, only to pull herself back. The past few days had been a slow and painful retraction on her part. The whales didn't seem to notice; they were busy. She didn't blame them. At around this time, they would have begun to establish their independence, and it seemed to be going well. The krill and fish populations were booming. Yoshi had established at least four decent-sized coral reefs. The whales were adapting to their new environment in a way Kim could only have hoped.

But this was not the way she had wanted this to end.

"Comm sent," the computer told her. "Would you like me to notify you when he has approved it for posting?"

Kim shrugged. "No, not really."

"Kim, there is a noticeable lack of interest in your daily chores. Should I notify someone to check your mental health?"

"No. Definitely don't do that." Kim sat up. "I'm going to take a walk. I'm sure that'll help me feel better."

"Very well." The computer chimed and fell into silence. Kim levered herself off the bed, hoping that she would find the energy to do as she'd promised somewhere along the way.

She avoided Wren and Adonai as she left the base, using a back exit where a single EU soldier waved her through without question. During the day, personnel were allowed to come and go as they pleased, but as evening approached, the base would be locked down. Kim wanted to be out of there before then.

The EU soldiers were beginning to grate on her. She was starting to realize that Grand let her get away with a lot compared to this stiff bunch. She actually missed his leadership now that he'd been posted to the *Arkansas*, which was preparing to depart in two days' time. Renshaw and Durand had gone with him.

Her legs ached as she reached a rocky, worn trail in the undergrowth that led to the headland. Despite her overall mood, it felt good to have her body moving again after long days spent in the base, treating the last of the injured whales and helping Yoshi with the insemination process. Among the EU soldiers were a few doctors, and with the advanced medbots from the *Arkansas*, they had managed to speed up the process significantly. Two whales were now pregnant—Eunice and Martha. They would give birth early next year, by the New Eden calendar.

Kim emerged from the tree line onto a high cliff. She watched rough surf pound over rocks to smash into other rocks below. This was not the gentle water of Half-Moon Bay; this was the wild, untamed ocean, affected by the pull of two moons, and it was nature at its rawest.

She climbed to the highest point and braced her legs, leaning into the wind as it whipped her bare skin with flecks of salt water. She looked up. The alien ship, visible now, hung low in the silvering sky, nothing but a silhouette as the light faded. A few EU scoutships hovered around it, visible as only the faintest of flecks against the gigantic flank of the bigger ship. They were performing monitoring scans, but there was little information gleaned from their reports. Neither the iterations nor the beings on board had made any attempt to contact them since Kim had left the bridge of that strange ship.

Closing her eyes, she breathed deeply, taking in the tang of the ocean, the scent of trees and loam and fresh, unpolluted air.

"Kim!"

The shout didn't startle her. She didn't turn. She'd almost been expecting him to find her.

A pair of strong arms wrapped around her from behind, and she let herself release her taut muscles, allowing Wren to take some of her weight and some of the strain of her body.

He leaned into her ear so he could be heard without shouting, his words tickling her neck. "You weren't thinking of jumping, were you?"

Her throat choked out a strange noise, halfway between a laugh and a sob. "Of course not."

She could tell, by the pounding of his heart against her back, that he really thought she might have, and that more than anything made her turn into his embrace.

"I would never do that," she told him earnestly.

He pulled her closer, cradling the back of her head. "Good. Because I'm not losing you, Kim."

"Except that you are," Kim said softly. "And I'm losing you."

For a moment, they breathed together, savoring the moment. "I'll come with you," Wren said.

"We've had this conversation. You have to stay here with the whales. I don't trust anyone else as much as I trust you."

"We can change things, Kim. We can—"

"I killed people, Wren."

He stiffened under her arms. She knew he had tried to hide it from her over the past two days, forcing smiles and acting as if nothing was wrong, as if leading by example would make her think everything was fine. She wished it was.

More than anything, she wanted to go back in time and undo what she'd done. But that was impossible.

He started to protest. "We were all there. We all—"

Kim cut him off. "No. *I* pulled the trigger."

"If you think that punishing yourself will undo it somehow—"

"I'm not punishing myself. I have to live with it, Wren." She shivered suddenly, violently, and it wasn't because of the cold wind. "I've killed people before. When I had to, when it was necessary. I've actually washed blood off my hands in the same bathroom sink I used to brush my teeth. There were three people inside that stem cell lab when I blew it up. Security guards and a scientist working late. Their deaths were all my fault, but I lived with it. I justified it. This time . . . this time I can't."

"Why not?" he asked her. "What's changed?"

"*I've* changed." She looked up at him. "Partly because of you, partly because of the whales, and . . . something else. Maybe I've finally grown a conscience." She laughed softly, bitterly. "I hate it. Every day, every night. I dream about it when I sleep." When she closed her eyes, the momentary darkness revealed blossoming red clouds of fire staining the depths of space. Tiny suns born, then dying, in the space between one blink and the next. When she ate, she tasted ash. But it was the part of her that was beyond physical reach that was the most affected. She had never put much stock in the idea of souls, but lately, she had to agree that what she had done had injured something far deeper than her body and mind. "I . . . don't feel like I belong here anymore."

"You do. You belong with me." His voice was firm, and he pulled her tighter, as if to prove his point. But Kim heard the edge of desperation. He could do nothing to keep her here.

She shook her head, aware that the salt spray on his clothes was mixing with her tears. "No, Wren. Even if I wanted to stay, they wouldn't let me. And I don't want to stay here; not with Adonai halfway across the universe. God knows what they'll do to him. I have to go. And you have to stay. I don't trust anyone else with the whales, Wren."

He was quiet for a minute. "Do you want to be with me?" The words were soft, barely above a whisper.

"Of course I do," she replied fiercely. A rush of feeling came over her, warm, tingling . . . and frightening in its immensity. She couldn't hold it back this time, couldn't squash it or reduce it to a passing affection or a friendship or anything but what it was. She couldn't tell herself that she couldn't see a future with Wren any longer. She did. It was all she could see, and it terrified her. "I love you, Wren. And I'm coming back."

A slight smile tugged at the corner of his mouth. "I love you too, Kim."

She wanted to kiss him but knew that would increase the hunger that she couldn't sate—not now. She wanted him to kiss her, but as if he understood this wasn't the time, he held back.

Silence fell as they remained in place, arms wrapped tightly around one another. The sun set behind them, throwing the ocean below the headland into shadow. The waves, dark and tipped with silver, lifted and fell rhythmically. The sound was beautiful and calming. She took a breath and calmed herself, pulling slowly away from Wren. Once more, she braced herself against the wind.

"What's that?" Wren asked.

Slowly, he lifted an arm and pointed. Kim followed the finger, squinting. There was a dark lump in the water. It seemed to be moving . . . but then it was gone. But no, there it was again.

A whale.

There was a whale out there. Just a hump of exposed back until it dove, vanishing from view once more. Kim stood and strained her eyes at the darkening sea, only to see the whale explode from the surface in a spray of water. Her body, huge, mottled green-brown with small flecks of white, picked up the last of the light from the fading sun.

"Berenice," Kim said, her voice filled with wonder. She dove into her Link, searching through the data for the southern right whale. All of a sudden, she found her. Berenice was swimming down, arrowing for the floor of the ocean, her massive body showing only slight signs of injury—a healing fracture on her rib, a small irritation below the skin of her right fin, which had lain unmoving for too long. None of this bothered the whale in the slightest.

Kim! I've been having the strangest dreams!

Kim smiled through the tears that filled her eyes. "Berenice, it's so good to hear you."

I'm in the ocean. Kim, it's amazing!

"I know," she said. "It really is."

This is our home.

"For always," Kim promised as Wren took her hand and clasped her fingers tightly.

EPILOGUE

The water hit Kim's back, a rain of hot jets turned up to the highest setting so that they almost hurt on impact. She had discovered a liking for long, hot showers. Standing in the stream of water seemed to dull the thoughts and blunt her emotions, letting her fall into a daze she couldn't achieve anywhere else. She would have liked to fill the room with eddying pools of steam, but the *Arkansas* was a new ship, so new that such wastage of water molecules wasn't permitted. Fans and suction-enhanced drains extracted every inch of water from the room, leaving nothing behind.

A soft chime sounded. "You have used your allocated water ration for today," a gentle, feminine voice informed her. "Please consider stepping out of the shower."

Kim ignored it, taking pleasure in the act. In a few moments, the shower would shut off automatically, but the *Arkansas* was a big ship. Water was a precious resource. Encouraging people to take shorter showers was just one of its many updated features. She wasn't a fan of the computer, either. It was far too rigid in its instructions and hardly good company on a ship where she had no one else but Adonai to talk to. She wished she could hack it, tweak it just a little, but that was out of the question. The *Arkansas* was something else when it came to ship design, retrofitted to the extreme.

The water shut off, and Kim was forced back to reality in full. With a reluctant sigh, she stepped out of the cubicle and let the warm air currents from the vents in the wall dry her before she pulled on a new jumpsuit and padded barefoot back into her room without glancing into the mirror.

Compared to her quarters on *Seiiki,* this space was luxurious in the extreme. Kim had actually enjoyed it at first—the softness of the bed, the pale cream color of the walls. Even the holo of the flower vase sitting on the sleek, curved coffee table and the top-of-the-line holo projector mounted to the ceiling were all items she'd thought uselessly extravagant but also pleasantly clean and inviting.

Now, forty-three days after leaving New Eden, it was beginning to lose its charms. Though the door wasn't locked, she was a prisoner here. She could go anywhere on the ship that wasn't a restricted area—even the bridge if she chose—but after enduring several weeks of stares and whispers, this room was the only place she wanted to be.

She thought about sending a comm to Wren, but it would be close to nighttime on New Eden by now, and she had spoken to him once today already. He was busy. Some problem with the satellites over New Eden's poles—they were being affected by solar storms. He had seemed weary, overworked, and sad. As much as she loved talking to him, seeing his face, it hurt to have a visual on how much he missed her when she felt, with so much unexpected grief, that she surely felt his absence more than he did hers.

She passed the couch and the bed to stand before the window. Stars streaked by in thin trails. By all appearances, it looked like the ship was traveling through regular hyperspace. If she hadn't known they were using multiple quantum leaps to reach Sol at speeds unprecedented in the past, she would have barely noticed the difference. Bracing her elbows on the windowsill, she rested her knees on the floor. Overlaying the streaking stars was her reflection; one she barely recognized. Her hair had begun to grow back, hiding the residual bronze traces of the Link. In the two months it would take to reach Sol, she'd lose all trace of it.

She tried to avoid thinking on it too long or the loneliness, the lack of whale voices, the disconnection from their location, respiration rates and feelings, the void that had once contained forty-three presences for which she had cared for was too overwhelming.

A soft *whoosh* from behind startled her. The door to her quarters was sliding open; something that was definitely *not* supposed to happen without the computer's announcement and identification of whoever was on the other side. Kim came up into a crouch, hands curling to fists as she braced herself to either hide or attack.

Adonai stood on the other side, his hands folded. Kim had come to recognize the gesture: He was agitated about something. Letting out a breath of air, Kim forced herself to relax.

"You scared me," she chided gently.

"I'm sorry." Adonai turned to watch the door slide shut. Only when it was fully closed did he turn again.

"Why didn't the computer announce you?"

"I disabled it," Adonai said.

"Adonai!" Kim gasped. "I've told you about hacking. You need to stay out of the systems!"

Kim knew Adonai had developed an affinity for working with computers, and while she supported it, he had spent the time in his assigned quarters subverting the ship's security systems and accessing net connections he wasn't supposed to. She couldn't help but admire his handywork—he'd discovered a trove of ancient holo-movies that they'd watched together over a few nights—but the last thing she wanted was for him to get into trouble.

"I'm not touching anything to do with the *Arkansas*'s vital operations. But I had to disable the security functions on this room for a few minutes. Kim, I've found something."

"Come in," she said. "Have people been staring again?"

Adonai moved to the couch. It was an unconscious gesture on his part now. Though he didn't need to sit down, he knew Kim would most likely want to. "At the droid who saw Heaven? No. That's not why I'm here."

He didn't release his clasped hands, and Kim swung her leg over the back of the couch, settling into the soft cushions. "Are you okay?"

"I have been looking at *Seiiki*'s computer. Or, rather, the alien interface we found on it."

"Adonai," she groaned quietly.

"It's very important, Kim," Adonai said.

Kim weighed up telling him to leave—bombing out on her bed and trying for sleep—but she couldn't do that to Adonai.

"All right," she said.

Adonai lifted his head and glanced at the holo-projector on the ceiling. "Zero-seven-ex," he said. "Relay input from Terminal Four-seven-lambda."

A few seconds passed, and then the air shimmered in front of Kim, first taking on the faint form of a head, long torso, and limbs, and finally, two expansive wings tucked neatly against its back. It was more solid in appearance than the last time she'd seen it.

As Kim watched, it raised its head, its eyes meeting Kim's. "It looks just like Hath," she remarked.

"It's not Hath. From what we've seen, all their iterations look pretty much the same. I think this is what Hath was talking about when it said it interfered with our computer—it downloaded another iteration into it."

"One that was meant to kill us," Kim said with a chill of fear as she remembered how it had almost succeeded. This iteration had warned them that they were to be sacrificed for the greater good, that humanity had to be deterred from landing on New Eden. "You've spoken to it?"

"Yes." Adonai took a minuscule step forward, looking at the holographic being. "My name is Adonai. Do you remember me?"

"Yes. Of course." The being glanced between them. "And Kim Teng. I'm glad to finally be able to speak with you properly."

"You know my name," Kim said.

"I had access to your computer's database for a time. I know much about your world. I have enjoyed learning, but it makes me all the more sorrowful that it has come to this."

"Last time I spoke to the . . . iteration on the ship," Kim reminded it warningly, "it told us it had tried to kill us. And the whales. So excuse me if I'm not jumping for joy that one of you is still inside our computer."

"I was not supposed to be here," the being replied. The tone of its voice didn't change, making it impossible for Kim to judge how truthful it was being. "I was created by Hath, and I was meant to carry out my function and be destroyed along with you. But I was not. It is the function of an iteration to be useful, and I have run some calculations and reached the conclusion that I might be of some help to you."

Kim raised her eyebrows. "Oh?"

"Hath is still on board our mother ship. It is what's known as *tkerren'li*. An outlaw or a traitor."

"It said it had gone against the will of its creators," Kim said. "But it told us that was because it was defective. You're telling us it's some kind of . . . double agent?"

"Our ship's functions are governed by many iterations. All of them except Hath are loyal servants to our creators."

"The Sha'arden," Kim supplemented, and the iteration inclined its head in confirmation.

"Correct. It is a hard task for Hath to maintain its cover, and it must do so to protect the other *tkerren'li* operatives who remain in stasis. If Hath revealed itself to you on board, the ship would have meant annihilation for our cause. Any of the other iterations might pick up on a stray word or phrase. Hath had to be careful in what it said and how much of the truth it revealed."

What had Hath said? *A moment of madness. My programming is corrupt. That is all I can tell you.*

Kim shook her head, trying to wrap her mind around it. Hath was a traitor, trying to maintain its cover. So what, out of everything it had told them, was the truth?

The iteration continued. "There are possibilities in the universe. Endless possibilities. Only a quantum computer is capable of grasping them all, but even then, any ability to read those outcomes is limited by the being interpreting the information. Hath ran many calculations, allowing for several possibilities of how your arrival in what you call the Eschol System would unfold. As it happens, one of those possibilities was that the probe you used to guide your ship down to the planet would malfunction."

Kim felt her mind doing contortions, but it was Adonai who spoke. "It knew that if the post was down, *Seiiki* would need to use the scoutships as guides for landing."

"A small possibility. One of the smallest. Along with the fact that you managed to restart your engines, putting you in the grip of the mother ship's gravitational pull when you should have missed it entirely. Had you not, you would never have launched your shuttle, and your ship would have crashed with you being none the wiser as to our existence."

"And you would never have taken Adonai on board," Kim said.

"Precisely. The possibility was small, but it is exactly what occurred." The iteration paused. "With the whales dead, Hath hoped that there would be no need for more of your people to come to New Eden. That was also one of its calculations. One of the highest probabilities in fact."

Kim felt the ship's solid deck spinning under her. They had been meant to die, but she—and Wren, Yoshi, and Adonai—had fought against the odds. She remembered the swirling, rushing vortex of wind trying to rip them from their ship. Plowing onward, refusing to give in as the dead void of space sought to claim *Seiiki* and the whales. Wren's arms, gripping her strongly against the current that threatened to rip her away from him. The grim determination with which they'd piloted the pod through the asteroid field.

They'd saved *Seiiki* from complete destruction . . . and had saved the whales.

But even that didn't negate the fact that Kim had put every human being in danger by broadcasting her message.

"You're a bit too late if this is another warning," she said, her voice small.

"I can only work with the possibilities that have now unfolded. The Sha'arden will begin to wake," the being said. "The ship has been given instructions, and their stasis will end. They're preparing for the final war now that you humans are here at last."

War. That was a word Kim did not like hearing. "Didn't they lose against the darashen already? How are *we* going to beat them when your people are so advanced and even *you* had no chance?"

"You do not need to defeat them," the iteration said quietly. "They are not the threat. It is my creators, and the lies they spin, that you need to fear."

Kim heard her pulse pounding loudly in her ears. The sense that something terrible was looming on the horizon was growing, and a knot of dread formed in her stomach.

"You have been lied to. It was necessary for Hath to tell you the story as the Sha'arden would tell it; as I said, Hath needs to maintain its cover. But my function, now that you have survived, is to tell you the truth."

Kim glanced toward Adonai, who was riveted on the spot, listening intently to every word the iteration said.

"The Sha'arden—my creators—were not born on the planet you call New Eden. It was the darashen's homeworld. The Sha'arden came here to wipe them from existence." Taking in Kim's astonished stare, it continued. "The darashen are, as you discovered, partially non-corporeal. They live in the quantum realm, crossing over to this realm to interact with one another on a physical level; what you might term procreation. Only in this dimension can they interact with objects as your species and mine does. The darashen intermingled with a water-based species of intelligent life, thus producing their offspring. But the Sha'arden made sure they could not have younglings by poisoning the other species on the planet."

Kim's mind raced. This was why the Sha'arden's homeworld in the simulation hadn't matched the landscape of New Eden. It wasn't a simulation of that planet at all.

"So the darashen didn't attack the . . . the Sha'arden?"

"They did. The war was long and bloody. But it was not the darashen who started it." The iteration raised its hands, palms upward. "The Sha'arden decided it would be best to strike them where they could; on their home-world, where they came to breed. Thus, they'd ensure they wiped out every darashen in existence, including the ones not yet born."

Kim put her hand to her mouth, the full horror of what he was saying washing over her. "They tried to exterminate them?"

"There were many *tkerren'li* rebels who defied the slaughter. The rebels devoted themselves to working toward peace with the darashen, but be-cause their views didn't align with the general consensus, they were killed or forced into hiding. One of the *tkerren'li* managed to infiltrate the ship's computer and convinced Hath to help their cause. Hath helped the remain-ing *tkerren'li* rebels board the ship and put them in stasis. They're now hiding among the population, held in the long-sleep just like the rest of the Sha'ar-den. Soon, they will wake, along with the others, but they're in danger. They will not countenance the murder of the darashen, but if the upper echelons discover their subversion, they will be executed."

Kim turned to Adonai. Horror was churning in her gut. "No wonder New Eden looked like it had once supported life," she said. "*Sentient* life. It did. And the Sha'arden killed them."

"The darashen can't mate," Adonai supplied. "That means . . . their spe-cies will end?"

"They do not have much time left," the being agreed.

Kim closed her eyes, leaning back into the couch. "The iteration on the ship told us the demons—the darashen—started attacking after Adonai's message to our home system. But that wasn't the reason at all, was it?"

"No. It was only after you placed your whales in their oceans that they realized the true threat you posed to them."

Kim felt a low, aching pain in her chest. "Oh, God. What have we done?" She wanted to sink back into the cushions, wanted to allow the softness of them to swallow her up. Wanted this to be something that wasn't happen-ing . . . or something that she didn't know about.

But she did.

She had stood on the bridge of that alien starship and sealed a pact between the Sha'arden and humans. Their aid in the battle in exchange for ridding the planet of the darashen; a deal Kim hadn't been able to refuse. And she had signed it with the blood of other humans.

Forcing her eyes open, she pulled herself upright. The room seemed distant, grayed-out as if in an old, black-and-white holo movie. She moved past the iteration with its graceful folded wings, past Adonai with his hands clasped and head bowed in sorrow, heading back to the window where the stars streaked by in unending lines. God, she wanted Wren. Pressing first a hand, then her cheek to the window, she gazed behind the ship at the lines collapsing in diminishing angles to a bright white pinpoint. Beyond that, hundreds of light years away, was New Eden, Wren, and her whales while she raced on toward Earth.

Finally, she turned back to the silent room and gathered herself, one nerve at a time. Straightening her spine, throwing her shoulders back and finding, finally, the anger she knew she should feel at having been *used* once more, she said firmly, "We have to go back."

Adonai stepped up behind her. She could feel his closeness, the slight warmth of his mechanical body, feel his calm, staid presence. "I know, Kim."

She managed a smile, despite her raging thoughts, and though it was watery and thin, the streaking stars beyond seemed to lend it some brightness.

ABOUT THE AUTHOR

Ruth Fox is the author of many books, including the award-winning *Monster-boy: Lair of the Grelgoroth*. She spent her childhood years in a house filled with books, so it's not really any surprise that she grew up writing her own. She vividly remembers one particular day of high school in which an English task required her to write a science fiction story with the theme *you wake up and find you have a double*. While most of the other kids groaned, she busted out a fantastic story that involved time travel, science experiments gone wrong, and a girl who saved the world—all in 3 A4 pages. "You have a talent for writing," the teacher said as she handed back her story. "Have you considered becoming a writer when you're older?"

Ruth had, in fact, considered this while creating characters and worlds in the notebooks kept beside her bed, all meticulously handwritten because laptops weren't a thing you owned at home in those days (yes, she's that old).

In 2006, Ruth graduated with a Bachelor of Arts/Diploma of Arts in Professional Writing and Editing. She loves to read science fiction, fantasy, romance, adventure, young adult, adult, literature, old books, new books, and everything in between. She now has her own house, which is also filled with books. She lives with her husband, two cats, and three very adventurous sons (who also love books) in Victoria, Australia.

You can find more information about her other books on Facebook: https://www.facebook.com/RuthFoxAuthor

ACKNOWLEDGMENTS

I have a lot of people to thank for helping with the creation of this book. My undying gratitude goes out to the team at CamCat: Sue Arroyo, Elana Gibson, Bridget McFadden, and everyone else on the team.

I have to thank my husband for his patience and support when I felt like chucking in the towel.

(Repeatedly.)

Thank you to my boys, Rydyr, Quinn, and Whitley—your astonishing imaginations and enthusiasm for all things space-related inspires me every day.

Thank you to Mum, for sharing my love of getting lost in a good bookshop and only emerging because, unfortunately, they have a closing time.

And thank you to Dad, who always encouraged me to be creative even though he knew how hard it is. I wish I could show you this book.

Finally, thank you to my readers! I really, really hope you've enjoyed reading *New Eden*.

If you've enjoyed Ruth Fox's *New Eden*,
please consider leaving a review to help our authors.

And check out another science fiction read from CamCat:
Kathleen Hannon's
The Confession of Hemingway Jones.

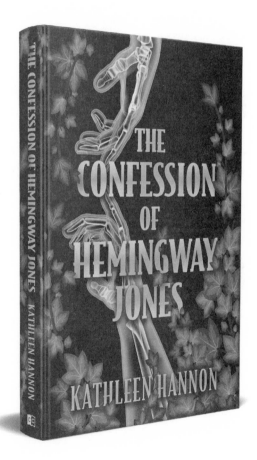

CHAPTER
1

It's been a few months, but I still remember the day I killed my father.

Todd and I were absolutely blazed, sitting on the front steps of his family's doublewide when Dad pulled up, the tires on his Ford F250 skidding to a stop about three inches from my sneakers, while the JONES CONSTRUCTION: DISASTER MITIGATION AND RESTORATION lettering was practically shoved up my nose. Dad hiked himself out the driver's-side door with a slam, and I knew I had about fifteen seconds to sober up.

We hadn't planned on doing this—skipping school and getting baked. Or at least *I* hadn't. But Todd had found this brick of hash in his parents' barn, and well, it was the first spring day where temps were due to hit 65 degrees. So we cut out fourth period, rode our bikes back to his place, and got rocked. Seemed like a good idea at the time, and we'd had fun tormenting the chickens, but now I was going to pay for it. I wasn't the only one who was nervous either. Todd tucked his drink behind his back while my dad crunched gravel. Todd had obviously forgotten that all he had was a Yoo-Hoo. He nodded and called out, "Hey there, Mr. Jones."

Dad murmured, "Todd," in his general direction but kept his eyes focused on me.

He was just standing there, directly in front of the late-afternoon sun. I squinted, but all I could see was this ominous black silhouette of rippling muscle.

I realize I'm making him sound scary, but he's not. Everybody likes my dad, even Todd. Even me. He's this pretty cool, off-the-grid kind of guy. He can build or fix just about anything, and I'm not just talking about when you've had a kitchen fire or a burst pipe—that's just what he does for work. He's also the guy that pulls over when you've got a flat and the one who starts applying the Heimlich on some choker in Kentucky Fried. (It's happened.) He's smart too. He doesn't have a college degree or anything, but he can talk about black holes and Relativity. He can take any online Mensa or IQ test and come up genius, every time. He even beats my scores, and I'm not easy to beat. Anyway, the point is stand-up guy Bill Jones can be a little scary when he's mad. And I was about to get reamed.

He turned his face profile before he spoke, so I could see just how much air he was furiously pumping through his shadowy nostrils. "Got a call from the school. And another one from Cass."

My first impulse was to cringe, make excuses, and get up, knowing I was busted. But over the last year or so, I'd learned that if I waited long enough in these fights, my pangs of guilt would pass, and I'd turn into a cocky a-hole, someone far more capable of fighting with Bill Jones. So I waited until I saw Dad as a thunderstorm, rudely blocking out my sun. And I shrugged. I mean, big deal. So I'd skipped school again. I knew the real problem was the call from Cass. I'd never skipped the Tuesday/Friday afternoon internship before, and that was what he was really pissed about. He'd filled out all the paperwork for that internship himself—he'd even written the essay when I refused—all so that I would have "the future" he never did.

"Hem, I'll uh—" Todd looked around quickly, hoping some excuse for his desertion would magically appear. "I think maybe I gotta help with dinner. See ya, Mr. Jones." He practically ran inside.

"Do you have any idea what you're doing?" Dad exhorted. "You have this gift. My God, you want to end up like that?" He gestured to Todd's disappearing form.

"Dad, that's low. Leave him alone."

He didn't even pause. He just growled, "Hemingway Jones" in that low, throaty way that he always does before lecturing. And he knows I hate my name. But he only rarely calls me Hem—he says it sounds like a pronoun.

"You have absolutely no idea what you're risking. NONE!" And with that crack of thunder came the rain. He blasted on, salting his sentences liberally with words like *responsibility* and *commitment*.

I just rolled my eyes. The lecture was so generic, I didn't taste anything close to regret. Basically, I could recite a variation of this speech as easily as I could the periodic table. Anyway, due to some really good dope, the tweaks and nuances of this particular version are lost forever.

I finally interrupted him. "I didn't even want the effen internship!" I stared at him, waiting for a response. The fact was empirically true. But he just stuffed his hands in his pockets, so I charged on. "I don't want college either. School bores the crap outta me. You *know* that. Why would I *pay* for more torture when I could be a project manager at your company and earn some money? Stanton got an honors degree from Chapel Hill. He's still working at the gym full-time AND living at home, just to pay the loans. Why would I buy into all that crap?"

I tilted a little, trying to duck down and check my face in the side-view mirror of the truck without him noticing. I was pretty sure I was smirking—a dead giveaway. No smirk, but the face that looked back at me was a little worrying. My black hair had gone all stringy from sweat and was stuck in clumps around my face. My eyes, normally green, were cayenne-pepper red. I looked like a stoner. If I didn't shift the conversation soon, he'd notice. I needed a move.

So, I conjured up the ghost of my mother. "Mom wouldn't make me go there. Do you have any idea what I *do* at that place? Do you think she'd want me doing that? Do you think she'd want that done to *her*?"

That worked. Dad looked as if I'd punched him. "Of course not," he finally choked out.

I knew the image was unfair. Bottom-feeding, in fact. I instantly wished I hadn't said it, but I didn't take it back, because if the situation was reversed, *he* wouldn't take it back. My dad sucks at apologizing.

Still, I could practically read his memories of Mom in his body language. His shoulders sagged with her diagnosis, quickly followed by a head nodding south to the ground, as she exacted promises out of him about how I was going to be raised. By the time his hands found his hips, I knew her body was being carted out of the cancer ward at Northeast into a mortician's hearse. That was two years ago.

Now who sucks at apologizing?

Fair would be admitting Bill Jones didn't have the faintest idea what company I'd be interning for when he applied in my name. He'd just been all excited that this fabulous new biotech research center was going to take high school students on as interns. He'd gone on and on about what an "amazing opportunity" that would be for me. That said, he'd grimaced when I got the acceptance letter. He'd guessed almost immediately what kind of company it was. But he'd still wanted me to do it because he thought it would lead to better scholarships for college. He rattled on that even if I didn't want to go to college right now, I should still want the option. When I finally gave in and said okay, he told me what they *did*, or at least what he thought they did. I absolutely flipped. I'd told him there was NO WAY I was going to work there.

The curtains shifted. Todd was watching us. I glared at him, and they pulled tight again, but his fingertips were still visible at the seams. He really could be a dumbass.

My dad saw it too and checked himself, knowing he'd lost his temper and embarrassed me in front of my friend. He suddenly tossed me the keys. "We'll talk about this at home. You drive." He climbed in the passenger's side.

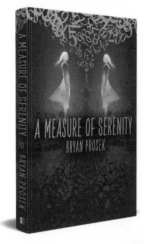

CamCat
Books

VISIT US ONLINE FOR MORE BOOKS TO LIVE IN:
CAMCATBOOKS.COM

SIGN UP FOR CAMCAT'S FICTION NEWSLETTER FOR
COVER REVEALS, EBOOK DEALS, AND MORE EXCLUSIVE CONTENT.

CamCatBooks   @CamCatBooks   @CamCat_Books   @CamCatBooks